THE DREAM MADE REAL

Oh, he was a good kisser. A really good kisser.

She wanted to put her arms around him, to participate more fully, but he denied her efforts with a masculine growl. Harriet didn't like being dictated to and she balked, wrapping her arms around his wide shoulders. "Steve," she protested.

In a heartbeat, her wrists were imprisoned above her head, pinned to the mattress by their interlaced fingers. Holding her eyes, he used his knees to spread her legs wide. With slow, slow insinuation, he let his body weight settle over hers.

"I am not Steve Morgan. I am Etienne Baptiste."

"Oh." She hadn't realized she'd spoken Steve's name.

"Say it."

"Etienne," she breathed.

"This is not a dream," he gritted out.

"I know," she whispered. This was so much more.

Sweeter Savage Love

SANDRA HILL

LOVE SPELL NEW YORK CITY

LOVE SPELL®

August 2006

Published by

Dorchester Publishing Co., Inc.
200 Madison Avenue
New York, NY 10016

ISBN 0-505-52212-8

Visit us on the web at www.dorchesterpub.com.

To my longtime friend, Julie Daley,
who has been so wonderfully enthusiastic
about my writing and is one of my
most avid fans.

And to her outrageous husband, Tom,
who has "sold" innumerable copies of
my books on golf courses across the country.
Without a doubt, Tom will take great
pleasure in unabashedly claiming
that he posed for this cover.

When a rogue kisses you, count your teeth
—Hebrew Proverb

Prologue

Chicago, 1997

It was the most politically incorrect sexual fantasy in the world.

With surprising gentleness, he forced both hands above her shoulders . . .

Dr. Harriet Ginoza should have been outraged.

. . . and circled her wrists with his strong fingers, pinning them to the mattress.

Instead, Harriet was loving every minute of her recurring erotic dream . . . a dream that had been plaguing her for the past two weeks, ever since her new book hit the stands. *No, not an erotic dream,* she amended. More like a forbidden nightmare, challenging all her cherished beliefs.

And the leading role was played by Steve Morgan—the quintessential male chauvinist.

He lowered his face—his dark, sexy, outlaw face, stubbled with a week-old beard. He was primitive, dangerous, barely civilized.

9

Sandra Hill

She tried to look away. She couldn't.

Deep blue, fathomless eyes flashed arrogantly as they held hers captive, demanding her surrender.

"Stop," she protested. "I don't want this."

He laughed—a cynical, disbelieving contradiction to her all-too-obvious arousal. "Liar," he murmured, his breath hot against her lips—lips already parting, involuntarily, with invitation.

At first, she tried to examine the unfolding event with the clinical detachment of her PhD training ... as if she weren't truly involved. It didn't work.

She was naked. Steve was fully clothed, right down to the spurs that jangled softly as he adjusted his body with blunt aggression against the vee of her thighs.

Guilt. She felt so guilty.

And he knew. Coolly amused at her struggles, he withheld the kiss she dreaded ... and anticipated.

With her personal integrity, not to mention her professional reputation, at stake, Harriet strove for one last vestige of sanity. Finally—*thank God!*—logic came to the rescue, rearing its head like a stumbling beast. Thus fortified, she fought wildly now against Steve's restraining hands. She bit his shoulder. She kicked. She bucked upward. All to no avail.

"I want you, Ginny," he said quietly against her ear. "Yield to me, my love."

She groaned, and tried to tell him she wasn't his legendary Ginny. The words wouldn't come.

His mouth came down hard on hers, bruising the soft flesh. Scorching and brutal, he kissed and kissed and kissed her till she opened for him. A willing victim.

"Yes," she gasped out finally.

He lifted his head to study her for one long moment, then smiled in satisfaction. A dazzling display of white teeth against dark skin. Ruthless. Feral. Possessive.

She didn't care.

"Tell me," he insisted.

With her hands still pressed to the bed and her lower body immobilized by his hips, she raised her head to meet his lips, murmuring, "I want you, too."

The forceful seduction was complete.

Once again.

And her nighttime lover took her with sweet savage love.

Chapter One

"Women of the nineties are still in the Stone Age when it comes to sexual fantasies."

Harriet spoke directly to the TV camera as she tossed out her deliberately provocative assertion, trying to ignore the guilt nagging her conscience. *Yeah, I know all about the Stone Age. Just call me Wilma Flintstone. What a hypocrite I am!*

She crossed her black silk–clad legs, tugging down the short skirt of her scarlet Dior suit—a delaying tactic, one she'd perfected for dramatic effect over the years during innumerable interviews. *I'd better practice a few other things, too—like what I preach.*

Reflexively, Harriet swung one black patent-leather Ferragamo pump with a mesmerizing rhythm to give the appearance of casual confidence. *Confidence? Hah! Many more of those erotic dreams and I'm going to sign myself into a padded cell.*

During the brief seconds these thoughts flitted through her mind, Harriet waited out the murmuring that rippled through the mostly female, Chicago TV audience. The ''Stone Age sex'' remark was always a great ice-breaker to generate discussion.

Oprah, who stood at the edge of the stage preparing to hand the microphone over to questioners, put her hands on her hips and tilted her head in question. ''Oh? Women have out-of-date fantasies, huh? Really?''

''Really. Today's women are liberated. They've gained the vote. They're breaking through the glass ceilings in corporate America. Achieving the 'Big O' is a given,'' Harriet explained. ''But you'd be surprised at how unimaginative we all are, and no different from women through the ages. When it comes to sexual fantasies, modern women still dream of the number-one no-no, forceful seduction.'' *Yep! Count me at the front of that line. Darn it!* ''In many ways, we're no different from prehistoric cave women. We swoon at the prospect of some Neanderthal version of Mel Gibson in an animal pelt dragging us by the hair to his cave to have his way with us.'' *Forget Mel Gibson. I'm picturing another dark-skinned rogue.*

''Well, now, it would depend on what Mel had on under that fur thingee,'' Oprah quipped. A lot of other women concurred, as evidenced by their mirthful howls and embarrassed giggles.

''I don't have any sexual fantasies at all,'' one young lady yelled out. ''I'm too tired from chasin' my three kids to have naughty thoughts.''

Everybody laughed, including Oprah, who immediately picked up the cue. ''That brings up an interesting point, Dr. Ginoza. Do all women have sexual fantasies?''

''Absolutely.'' Harriet smiled, the implication clear that even Oprah Winfrey was included in that statement, not to mention the overtired mother, as well as the entire audience.

A contemplative expression crossed Oprah's face. ''And you think some of those fantasies are objectionable?''

''No, no, no,'' Harriet corrected quickly. ''I would never

presume to judge another person's private thoughts or sexual life." *Now, that's a lie. I know these dreams are wrong for me. Wrong, wrong, wrong!* "I'm merely suggesting that modern women fought tooth and nail for equal rights, but when it comes to their secret erotic yearnings, it's the same old same old." *And it feels sooo good.*

"Same old same old? Hah!" Oprah snapped back saucily as she sank into a wing-back chair next to Harriet. "You haven't been inside my head, girl." She arched her eyebrows meaningfully.

"You're the exception then," Harriet countered, not about to accuse the number-one talk-show hostess in the country of being less than honest. "Based on more than ten years of research, I can tell you unequivocally, Oprah, that most women give lip service to sweet and sensitive—what I call S & S in my book—as a male ideal. But what they dream about is D & D—dark and dangerous. When no one's looking, women think with their glands, not their brains . . . just like men." *And my traitorous glands have been in overdrive lately.*

"I beg your pardon," Oprah sputtered with mock indignation.

"And what's so bad about dark and dangerous?" a well-dressed, thirtyish woman asked, stepping up to a microphone in the aisle.

Harriet beamed, recognizing a perfect opening. Holding up her latest *New York Times* best-seller, *Female Fantasies Never Die*, she answered, "If you'd read my book"—and the audience twittered with appreciation at her blatant plug—"you'd know that forceful seduction is still the number-one female fantasy. And the darker and more dangerous the man, the better."

As the audience leaned forward with interest, Oprah pursed her lips pensively. "Forceful seduction, huh? I don't know about that."

The next audience member at the microphone, a young man of college age, asked with a nervous ducking of his head, "What exactly is forceful seduction?"

"I'm so glad you asked," Harriet said with a teasing flutter of her eyelashes. "Forceful seduction is the use of everything from sweet words to physical pressure to convince a woman to make love, against her will. Or, at least, against her will in the beginning. The key word is *convince*; otherwise, it would be rape. As you can imagine, feminists are appalled that women still have such politically incorrect fantasies." *I know I am.*

"I find it impossible to believe that any woman would find force enjoyable," Oprah opined with a shiver of disgust.

"You've got to understand, Oprah. A woman doesn't dream about some overweight thug with bad breath and zits attacking her in an alley. It's more like Brad Pitt or Kevin Costner, so overcome with passion for her that he holds her down to have his way with her." *Or Steve.*

Oh, God, where did that thought come from?

Even Oprah had to smile at that picture and added, "Or Denzel Washington."

"There you go!"

"I think it's a generational thing," an elegant, elderly lady in a business suit and chic gray chignon said. "My generation was taught to equate sex with sin. But if we enjoyed ourselves against our will, so to speak, that would be okay."

"Exactly!" Harriet agreed.

Oprah threw her hands up in the air. "So what's the problem?"

"The problem is women." Harriet displayed her book again. "For decades now, women have been told that forceful seduction is wrong. Outwardly, they agree, but behind closed doors, many of them admit to this closet fantasy."

She put her book down and picked up another. *Sweet Savage Love.* "This book was written twenty-three years ago by Rosemary Rogers. It launched a revolution in romance publishing and has been read by millions—yes, I said millions—of women across the world. The story portrays a classic case of forceful seduction . . . some might even say 'love at first rape.' No question that the hero in this novel, Steve Morgan, takes forceful seduction too far. He was a total brute . . . a sexy, gorgeous, enticing man . . . but a brute all the same.''

Whoa! Who are you calling a brute? Harriet could swear she heard a voice inside her head. She really was going off the deep end, hearing conversations outside her dreams now. Maybe she needed a psychiatrist, she thought with self-deprecating humor.

''Your point?'' Oprah inquired.

''My point is that, despite all their education, despite the enlightenment of women about sex, despite the power of the feminist cause, despite all logic . . . women still dream—in their fantasies—of a strong, domineering man seducing them into mindless surrender. They might want Tom Hanks for a husband, but in their fantasies, it's the bad boy Johnny Depp. Or Daniel Day-Lewis with an attitude. Dark and dangerous. Single-minded in pursuit of his passions. Hot, hot, hot!''

''Wow!'' Oprah said, fanning herself with her hand mike. ''Sort of like taming the magnificent wild beast, huh?''

''Right! To many women, the greater the risk, the more intense the thrill. But only in their fantasies, remember.''

''We had to read *Sweet Savage Love* in my Modern Cultures class at college, and my professor said it was a thorn in the women's movement,'' a young girl commented. ''Have you actually read *Sweet Savage Love,* Dr. Ginoza?''

''Of course.''

''Did you like it?'' the girl persisted.

''Not particularly.'' *Well, actually . . .*

Liar! the husky male voice in her head accused.

Shut up, she thought back.

''What I'd really like is to meet Steve Morgan face-to-face and show him how modern women react to male chauvinist pigs,'' Harriet added. "He's become a symbol in some psychological circles for a particular type of male personality.''

"A jerk?" Oprah asked dryly.

Harriet smiled. "Actually, Steve and Ginny, the hero and heroine, have become legendary lovers to many romance novel fans; so the book is certainly worthy of study," Harriet continued. "I'm not sure I'd assess its detrimental effect on feminism in quite the same way as that professor, though. After all, men's adventure novels use the same principle, in reverse, with no criticism. Really, how many mystery novels have you read where the detective is aggressively seduced by some villainous female? Big deal!''

After further discussion on feminism, fantasies and their relationship to romance novels, Oprah switched gears. "Dr. Ginoza, this is your fourth book to hit the *New York Times* best-seller list in the past seven years. Your others have dealt with phobias, body language and hypnotherapy. With respect to this latest book . . . if you aren't making judgments about women's fantasies, how do you see your role as an author?''

"A reporter . . . pure and simple. I dig up the facts, ma'am,'' she replied in a gruff Sergeant Friday–"Dragnet" style.

"Aren't we supposed to learn some lesson from the books we read? Shouldn't the author help us draw conclusions?" Oprah's forehead creased with puzzlement.

"Oh, I want to give a message, all right. I hope women . . . especially young women . . . will understand the potential pitfalls of such sexual behavior and handle their personal lives accordingly. Know the boundaries of what is acceptable to them. Draw all the proper lines. And, most of all, be able to separate fantasy from reality.''

"One last question before the break," Oprah announced. "Tell me, Dr. Ginoza, do you, personally, ever fantasize about forceful seduction?"

To her chagrin, Harriet felt her face grow hot, and an

image of her nighttime dream lover clouded her vision. She could swear he winked. *The rascal!*

Harriet considered lying, but her innate honesty kicked in. "Sometimes," she admitted, adding with a rueful grin, "but I'm working on it." *I'm a control freak, no doubt about it. And the ultimate loss of control is surrender to a forcefully seductive man. But I can't admit that before a nationwide TV audience. Nope, the answer is to work on my "weakness."*

A look of astonishment passed over Oprah's expressive face, which Harriet understood perfectly. Harriet's cool, professional demeanor hid her sensual nature.

"Working on it? Lordy, Lordy! Are you also saying we can change our sexual fantasies?" Oprah chuckled with disbelief.

"Hey, if they can reprogram a computer, a woman ought to be able to upgrade her libido." Harriet's lips twitched with amusement as she shrugged. "Sort of like sweeping the cobwebs from the erotic imagination."

Oprah's theme song prompted them into a commercial break as the audience laughed.

A deep, male voice laughed in her head. *Are you calling me a spider, sweetheart? Hmmm. Welcome to my web.*

Unfortunately, Harriet knew too well that he wasn't talking about the Internet.

Clackety-clack, clackety-clack, clackety-clack . . .

Later that evening on the late-night Amtrak Superliner to New Orleans, Harriet lay bleary eyed and exhausted, fighting sleep. She tried to ignore the entrancing cadence of the train wheels clicking on steel rails—metronomic sounds that lured her to succumb. To sleep. And to the blasted, unwanted dreams.

Clackety-clack, clackety-clack, clackety-clack . . .

You have to get some sleep.

No, I can't fall asleep. Harriet grimaced as the two sides of her brain waged a silent battle.

Clackety-clack, clackety-clack, clackety-clack . . .

Maybe the dream won't come tonight.

Maybe it will.

After all, I've only had the dreams for a few weeks. No doubt they'll stop as abruptly as they commenced.

Dream on, girl.

Harriet rolled over for about the fiftieth time on her narrow mattress. The deluxe bedroom accommodation had an upper berth, which she'd chosen not to fold down from the wall, and a long bench seat that pulled out into a bed.

Clackety-clack, clackety-clack, clackety-clack . . .

It's only a dream.

Huh! She hitched down the hem of her leopard-print silk nightie, which she'd donned because of the stifling atmosphere in her compartment, unrelieved by the low-humming air conditioner. Perhaps she should get up and take an aspirin. Or read. Her silver pill box and paperwork were in her briefcase on the opposite seat. She could even take a shower in the minuscule bathroom. But her limbs felt heavy, weighing her down.

Clackety-clack, clackety-clack, clackety-clack . . .

You can't avoid the dream forever.

I can try.

Clackety-clack, clackety-clack, clackety-clack . . .

You're behaving worse than one of your phobic clients.

I know.

You need a therapist.

I am a therapist.

Physician, heal thyself.

This "physician" is going bonkers.

Clackety-clack, clackety-clack, clackety-clack . . .

What's so wrong with the dream anyhow? You told Oprah that forceful seduction fantasies are all right.

For other women. Not me.

Oh, so you're smarter than the average woman? Stronger?

I should be.

19

Sandra Hill

Clackety-clack, clackety-clack, clackety-clack . . .

Lighten up, girl. And live a little.

No! I'm thirty-four years old. I've worked too hard for my professional reputation and success. If I give in to this . . . weakness, I might give in to others. It could undermine all my goals.

You're still obsessing over your mother.

Of course I obsess over my mother. I learned my lesson good and well from Mama. Five husbands. Codependency. Her financial and emotional well-being always tied to the latest man in residence. My sisters and I never knowing from one day to the next if we'd be playing tennis at the country club, or begging for food stamps. Whether Mom would be elated when we got home from school, or in a deep depression. Never, never, never will I let the need for a man control my life that way.

Well, golly, I didn't ask for a lecture.

Go away!

Clackety-clack, clackety-clack, clackety-clack . . .

Come on, close your eyes. You feel so sleepy.

Stop tempting me. I should have taken a plane. Damn that air-traffic controllers' strike. I'm going to look like a bloodshot rag doll for my speech at the Louisiana Women's Convention tomorrow night. And it's all his fault.

Hey, don't blame me, sweetheart, a familiar, masculine voice intruded in her thoughts. *Forceful seduction is your dream, not mine.*

"Oh, no!" Harriet groaned.

Oh, yes! he said with a silky growl of promise.

He was back.

Flipping his black, flat-crowned, cowboy-style hat off his head and to the left, where it landed on her briefcase, Steve eased himself down beside her on the narrow railway bed with bold aggression. His spurs jingled in counterpoint to the clicking rails.

And with a sigh, Harriet surrendered once again. To slumber, and her nighttime lover.

* * *

Harriet awakened abruptly, hours later, to a loud screeching noise and a violent lurch of the railway car, which caused her to fall to the floor. She was alone.

Of course I'm alone. It's not as if my dream tormentor is a real person.

As she scrambled to her feet in the darkness, she heard the squeal of air brakes, and tried to keep her balance despite the bumpy ride of the train.

Within minutes, the raucous noises and teeth-rattling shimmy of the train faded as it came to a full stop. A strange hush pervaded the air, soon followed by the babble of frightened voices in the corridor.

"Everything's okay, folks," she heard a man—presumably the conductor—call out. "The train derailed just as we entered Cairo—a slight mishap, not an accident. We should be back on track in less than an hour. Nothin' to fret about. Just you go back to sleep and we'll be on our way again in no time."

Harriet fumbled her way back to bed, and despite the lack of electricity was able to put the delay to good use, silently practicing her speech, which was tailored specifically to her Southern audience: "Looking For Rhett in All the Wrong Places." Then she mentally checked over her two-week book-tour schedule and even dictated some notes into her new mini–tape recorder, which she managed to blindly locate in her briefcase.

The palm-size box was a spiffy, high-tech, solar-powered device her mother's latest boyfriend, Riff Castanza, had given her last week to celebrate making the *New York Times* list once again. Riff worked for one of those Sharper Image–type companies. She'd been afraid he would give her the remote-control vibrator his company was selling this month on QVC.

It was more like two hours before the train restarted. There was still plenty of time for Harriet to make her evening speaking engagement. Finally, Harriet yielded to sleep.

Maybe the trick was to stop fighting. To go with the flow. Face her demon head-on.

Demon? Lady, your insults are pushing my limits. Be careful, or you might find out what I can do with a fallen angel.

Tennessee, 1870

"I'm not going back to prison ... ever," Etienne declared vehemently to his two companions in the cramped railway car. "So no slipups. We follow the plan exactly. Is that clear?"

"Yassuh, master," Cain replied with an exaggerated subservient whine, nudging his twin brother, who slouched on the seat next to him. "Stop that damn humming, Abel. Master Baptiste is gonna regale us with his war stories. Praise be!"

Abel mumbled something unintelligible and went back to scribbling on a piece of paper, humming, then trying a few notes on his faithful trumpet. The man could tune out all his surroundings when in the midst of composing. He was oblivious to their conversation as he sang softly and wrote down the words:

> *"If you were a bird, my friend,*
> *And I a gun, my friend,*
> *I would kill you, my friend,*
> *Because I love you so ..."*

"Does you want me to git you a mint julep, suh?" Cain persisted, ignoring his brother's preoccupation. From the time he was a small boy, Abel was always off in his own world, where he claimed to hear music in his head.

"Oh, shut up, you fool," Etienne grumbled at Cain. The man held a medical degree from a Paris college, could speak four languages and only used a Negro dialect to annoy him. "Don't start your sorry games, Cain. I'm not in the mood for—"

Cain ripped out a foul expletive. "Dammit, Etienne, you're never in the mood anymore . . . for anything. In fact, I reckon you lost your sense of humor back in Andersonville."

"I lost a hell of a lot more in that Reb prison than my sense of humor, as you well know," Etienne lashed out.

Cain stiffened, then relaxed with a visible effort. "Yes, I know," he said softly, leaning forward to pat Etienne's arm.

> *"If you were a bayou, my friend*
> *And I a fish, my friend,*
> *I would swim in you, my friend,*
> *Because I love you so . . ."*

He and Cain both looked at Abel and shook their heads.

But Cain wasn't getting off the hook so easily. "Don't patronize me," Etienne warned. "Our situation is too dangerous for you to treat it so lightly. And I'm damned tired of you two sticking on my back like swamp suckers, watching my every move. *Sacrebleu!* I told you to stay at Bayou Noir this time."

"And let you take all the glory with President Grant? No sirree. I wants to get me a new medal, too. The womenfolk do like them shiny medals."

Etienne clenched his fists, counting silently to ten. Cain knew he detested that blasted Medal of Honor. He'd much rather have the back pay Congress owed him for all the war years, but refused to pay because he had no proof of service. Proof? Hell, he'd worked as a double agent for President Lincoln without paper credentials, as trusting as a bare-assed babe. Unfortunately, good ol' Abe was no longer alive to support his claim.

But President Grant had promised to lend his support in getting his rightful pay released, *if* he would complete this one last commission. Recover the gold shipment that some corrupt government employees had stolen from the U.S. Mint in Philadelphia, and Etienne would be home free. His own man again. No obligations to anyone, North or South. Finally, he would be able to go home. Until then, it was serious, dangerous business.

And Cain insisted on treating it as a lark.

"Why don't you go purge yourself, sawbones?" Etienne suggested. "Give yourself a thrill and stop entertaining yourself at my expense."

Cain just grinned at him, knowing full well that his needling was drawing blood.

> *"If you were mud, my friend*
> *And I a pig, my friend,*
> *I would wallow in you, my friend,*
> *Because I love you so . . ."*

"Holy thunderation, Abel. Where did you get those ridiculous lyrics?" Cain exclaimed.

"Mud-wallowing and love?" Etienne added.

Abel finally peered up at them and blinked, as if seeing them for the first time. "Oh, these aren't my words. I heard some cotton workers in Alabama chanting them one day. I'm just trying to fit the words to my music."

"At least he's not singing the filthy lyrics he was last week," Etienne pointed out to Cain. " 'All the whores like the way I ride.' "

"Etienne is right, Abel; you are developing a nasty tongue, hanging with all those Nawleans street musicians. 'Playing the dozens . . . ' isn't that what you call that dirty-insults routine?"

How did they get from President Grant and their assignment to cotton workers and low-down music? Etienne wondered.

"Don't try changing the subject on me, Cain. I don't

24

appreciate your implication that I enjoy talking about Andersonville Prison."

"Oh, hell, Etienne," Cain sighed, no longer amused. "Can't you take a little ribbing anymore? I know you suffered during the war. We all did. But it's time to get over it and move on. If we can't laugh at our pain, we might as well be dead."

"*Merde!* You might want to laugh yourself to death, but I'm not quite ready to meet my maker. This mission is very important to me, Cain. All the pieces of the puzzle are finally coming together. Soon it should all be over, *Grâce à Dieu.*"

"Have you ever noticed that you slip into French whenever you get tense? Must be your high-strung, Creole heritage. Now . . . now, don't get all in a dither. I'll shut up now. Even if you say something really dumb, I won't blink an eye."

Meanwhile, Cain crossed his long legs at the ankles and propped them on the upholstered seat opposite him, close to Etienne's thigh.

Etienne pressed the bridge of his nose with a thumb and forefinger. It was a reflexive action when the dull throbbing began behind his eyes.

"Do you need one of my headache powders?" Cain asked, immediately solicitous.

Etienne shook his head. The debilitating headaches he'd suffered ever since prison occurred rarely now, and the pain was only mild tonight.

Seeing that he was all right, Cain relaxed. Then his dark eyes twinkled with mischief as he nudged Etienne's upper thigh slightly with the heel of one scruffy boot, just to irritate him. So much for his promise to behave.

"Move those damn spurs."

"What? You skeered I'm gonna harm your precious rooster?" Cain teased, slipping back into his slave patois as he used their childhood name for their private parts.

"You skeered the lady hens won't cluck all over you no more?"

"Hah! This rooster hasn't seen any clucking in ages. He's probably forgotten how to cock-a-doodle," he said, palming his crotch. "Besides, you and Abel are the ones doing all the crowing these days. Good Lord! I can't believe I caught the two of you in bed—together—with those whores last night at Clarice's . . . rather, Madame Dubois's Opera House. That is what she calls her place now, isn't it?"

"How was I to know there was no singing at that opera house?" Abel spoke up, setting aside his trumpet and papers. "Here I was expectin' an aria or two. At least a libretto." He grinned companionably at them.

"You wouldn't know an aria from a barroom ditty. The low-down music you play on that trumpet of yours is a far cry from hoity-toity opera," Cain shot back.

Cain was bluffing. Everyone, most of all Cain, was proud of Abel's genius with his horn.

"And you're the one who talked me into that double pleasurin' thing," Cain rambled on. "I'm just a poor country doctor. I ain't never heard of such goin's on."

The brothers smiled guilelessly at each other.

"If Simone ever caught you with another woman, she'd turn that black hide of yours red," Cain advised.

"If Simone and I could marry, I wouldn't be waving my black snake at every whore from here to Atchafalaya," Abel answered.

"God, you two are perverted," Etienne said, shaking his head hopelessly.

"Yes," Cain and Abel said at the same time, smiling. Their ebony skin gleamed in the dim light of a lantern, showing off their handsome faces and muscled bodies, which attracted women of all colors and ages and classes, no matter where they went.

Etienne's heart expanded with warmth when he regarded the two brothers. He knew these good friends—his only friends, actually—were making a concerted effort to lift his dark mood with their banter. Hell, they told him often enough that he had to get over the past, start living again. Easier said than done, of course. But he was touched, nonetheless, by their concern.

"Back to business," Etienne reminded them in a voice choked with emotion. "Once we get the shipment off this train tomorrow in Memphis, the rest of the trip should run smoothly. Anything could go wrong, though. Pope's network of grubby cohorts stretches across the country. We've got to be extremely careful."

Both men nodded.

"Let's get a few hours of shut-eye." Etienne stood with a groan, his knees creaking in protest after sitting so long.

"I know a sweet girl in Chattanooga who could get the kinks out of your tired old bones," Abel suggested reflectively.

"Old?" Etienne exclaimed. "I'm no older than you." In fact, all three men were thirty-one years old, having been born the same year on the same Louisiana bayou sugar plantation.

Abel ignored Etienne's interruption and went on, with relish, "This girl has a trick where she slathers warm buttermilk all over a man from head to toe. When he's naked, of course."

"Of course," Etienne and Cain chimed in sarcastically, knowing there was no stopping Abel once he got rolling with one of his risqué tales.

"Then she has the man hang by his feet from the low limb of a hickory tree in her courtyard while she proceeds to lick him clean. Somehow, all the kinks just disappear. Must have somethin' to do with all that blood rushin' to his head. What's your medical opinion on that, brother?" Abel paused, waiting for Cain to bite. When he didn't, he carried on, "Did I mention she has a tongue like a cat, sort of rough and abrasive? Whoo-ee!"

Etienne and Cain gaped at Abel in absolute awe. Then they both asked simultaneously, "Really?"

"God, you two are dumber'n gator spit," Abel hooted, slapping his knee appreciatively. "You'll believe anything."

Etienne and Cain glanced at each other with mutual self-disgust. Abel had a particular talent for fooling them, and they fell for his bait every time. In truth, this camaraderie and the ability to find comedy in their own foibles was the only thing that had kept them sane during an insane war, not to mention the insanity that had dogged them since then, too.

The engine jerked into motion suddenly and began to chug along. They all squinted out the train windows into the moonlit night, seeing nothing. There had been a problem with one of the tracks a short time ago, but apparently it had been corrected.

"Well, I'll see you two in the morning," Etienne said, heading toward the door and his own compartment. "We should arrive in Memphis about ten." He stared at each of them in turn. "Abel, you'll get the wagon and have it ready at the far end of the station, and Cain, make sure you meet me in the freight car before the train stops."

Both men rolled their eyes, having heard these instructions a dozen times already tonight.

Etienne yawned widely, then added over his shoulder, "Lord, I hope the coffins are still there."

Chapter Two

Harriet had been asleep only a short time, or so it seemed, when she heard a jingle of spurs. She winced inwardly but wasn't unduly anxious. As she'd told Oprah, it was the same old same old. And it was about time she handled this problem with maturity, instead of letting the problem handle her.

Opening her eyes, she watched, by the light of a full moon, as her personal rogue closed the compartment door and locked it carefully, double-checking the knob to make sure it was secure. Harriet recognized the exact moment he sensed her presence. With a hiss of indrawn breath and a curse of "Hellfire!" Steve froze in place and immediately whipped a revolver from the holster at his side.

Golly gee, a gunslinger, too. Will my fantasies never cease to amaze me?

"Well, well, well, darlin'," he remarked in a lazy drawl, after lighting a kerosene lantern affixed to one wall. A yellowish, muted light filled the room. "Aren't you a sweet little surprise?" The teasing words were delivered in an icy tone which held no welcome. Stepping closer, he aimed the pistol in the vicinity of her heart and loomed over her. "What are you doin' in my bed?"

"Well, I'm not one of the three bears, and you're sure as shootin' not Goldilocks," she wisecracked. "And it's my bed, cowboy, not yours."

"Golden luck?" he asked, then jabbed her rudely on one breast with the tip of his gun barrel. "Listen, honey, you look downright delectable in that little wisp of a garment—and my favorite animal, too . . . the leopard—but I'm not interested tonight. I've got the beginnings of a blinding headache. I'm sure you understand."

Not interested? Now, this is a new twist on the forceful seduction theme.

"I don't know where you've come from, but—"

"Chicago." Still unafraid—why should she be afraid of a dream gunslinger?—she shoved aside the gun, which was pressed into the soft flesh of her breast, and leaned back on her elbows.

His jaw dropped open at her brazen posture and what he must consider a foolhardy action on her part in deflecting his weapon, but he immediately schooled his features into a cool mask. Then, with a whoosh of exhaled exasperation, he straightened, the gun dangling from his fingertips, and shifted impatiently from one booted foot to the other. The whole time, he studied her intently. "You boarded the train at Chicago?"

"Yep. I'm going to New Orleans."

"I didn't see you on the steamboat," he said, still surveying her suspiciously.

If this weren't a dream, she would have been embarrassed to be displaying herself so openly, like a nubile, airbrushed *Playboy* centerfold. The only thing missing was the staples.

"Well? Were you on the steamboat?"

"What steamboat?" she asked, disconcerted to realize she hadn't been paying attention.

"At Cairo," he explained crankily, putting his free hand to his forehead.

She had several patients who underwent hypnotherapy as a migraine treatment. If she wasn't mistaken, his pale skin and bloodshot eyes were indicators of a stage-two migraine. His head probably throbbed like a jackhammer. "Cairo?"

"*Oui.*"

"What's this *oui* business? Steve Morgan isn't French. He's half-Mexican."

He blinked at her as if she spoke a foreign language, then tried again. "You must know, if you got on the Illinois Central in Chicago, that it only goes to Cairo. Then we had to take the steamboat across the river before boarding another train." All that talking apparently made his head throb and he let out a painful exhalation of breath.

"Huh?" She shook her head to clear it, beginning to feel foolish as she maintained her provocative pose. Especially since Steve, after his initial shock, didn't appear to appreciate the view. "You're mistaken. I got the Amtrak Superliner in Chicago, and I'm going directly through to New Orleans."

He scowled at her incredulously, then seemed to think of something else. "Why did the conductor let you into my compartment?" Harriet couldn't see a speck of the usual lust in his glittering eyes.

Gee, he really isn't interested tonight. Maybe he does have a migraine. But that can't be so. Dream lovers don't get headaches. Do they? She giggled, even when Steve continued to glower. *Criminey! Why bother having erotic dreams if there's no sex? Another of Steve's mind games, no doubt. He's probably waiting to pounce when I let down my guard. Well, I'll put an end to it right now.* "Did the conductor let me into your compartment? No, silly. I already told you, this is *my* compartment."

"That's where you're mistaken, *silly*. I left my *locked* compartment hours ago. So why don't you just skedaddle on out of here? I want to get catch a few winks." He advanced on her as if he planned to throw her bodily from the chamber.

She shimmied back against the wall, holding up a halting hand. "Oh, no! If anyone's skedaddling, it's you, buster." Harriet was beginning to take affront at his easy dismissal of her near nakedness, not to mention the threat of violence in his tightly clenched jaw. She folded her arms over her chest with belated modesty. Even if it was only a dream, she should be the one who brushed him off. "You don't look as good as usual," she commented, hoping to set him off balance. Actually, he looked a lot better, although there was a hardness about his features that normally would have frightened her.

"As usual?" he retorted testily, raising the gun again. "When in blazes have you seen me before?"

"Every darn night for the past two weeks."

"What? In Washington?"

"No, not Washington. I was in Chicago on the Oprah show, and—"

"Oh, so that's it. The opera." He lowered his gun with a snicker. "You're with Madame Dubois's Opera House. Why didn't you tell me that Cain and Abel hired you from Clarice at the opera show?"

"No, you misunderstood—"

But Steve just talked over her. "Those two are great ones for pranks, but, damnation, even they should know the timing is wrong tonight."

"I don't understand." Who were Cain and Abel? And what did he mean about an opera house? "Why are you acting like this, Steve?"

"Steve? My name is Etienne."

Harriet frowned, then immediately brightened. "Isn't Etienne the French word for Steven?"

"Well, yes, but—"

"See," she said, tossing her hands in the air in a "So there!" fashion.

"Whether my name is Etienne, or Steve, or Jefferson

Davis is not the issue," he said stonily, then rubbed a hand over his whiskery jaw in frustration.

"That's where I beg to differ. You're Steve, of course, and you're acting like I'm the intruder here, not you. Why are you trying to muddy the waters?"

"Muddy . . . muddy? *You* are the intruder." Taking a deep breath, he tried a different approach. "I'd be obliged, ma'am, if you'd tote your delectable ass to someone else's bed. Some fellow more randy than me. Is that clear enough for your *muddy waters*, darlin'?"

"Well, you sweet-talker, you!" she countered, not budging an inch. "And where'd you pick up the Southern drawl?"

Harriet had always loved the soft, melodious tones of a Dixie accent. Especially when spoken in the slow, lazy cadence of a self-assured man. But Steve probably knew that and had added it to his arsenal of sexual ammunition to use against her.

"I was born in Loo-zee-anna," he replied, exaggerating his drawl.

"No, you weren't," she started to say. Steve Morgan was born in Baja California. But it wasn't worth arguing about such a trivial point. "Oh, never mind."

Golly, this dream was amazing. She'd never noticed so many details before, or heard such explicit dialogue. She would have to remember to record all this in the morning, fodder perhaps for a future book.

"Did you get paid already?" he asked as he replaced his gun in the holster and reached out a hand to pull her up off the bunk, and presumably shove her out the door. *The jerk!*

"The Oprah show doesn't pay. Well, only expenses."

"How much do you charge, sweetheart?" He dropped his extended hand and reached into the pocket of his snug trousers.

This entire conversation was taking a strange turn that Harriet didn't grasp. "I get two hundred dollars an hour for regular sessions when I'm back home, but—"

"Two hundred dollars! Honey, you'd better have some special talent to charge those rates." He thought a moment, then added with a wry grin, "Let me see your tongue." He chuckled when she clamped her lips together. "You're the one who does the buttermilk trick, aren't you? That's what I call expertise."

She sniffed huffily. "Of course I'm an expert. I've been in practice for more than ten years." She had no idea what he meant about buttermilk or tongue, but it sounded obscene.

"Ten years!" He peered at her closer, sweeping her body with a dismissive appraisal, which she found highly insulting. "You're a little old for this business, aren't you? Shouldn't you be on the cull pile by now?"

"I beg your pardon," she seethed, sitting up. She gave him back an equal head-to-toe appraisal.

"I can't believe I'm standing here talking to this dim-witted wench," Steve muttered under his breath. Using his gun barrel to tip the brim of his hat up higher on his head, he scrutinized her with an unflattering lack of enthusiasm. "Lady, you look like the back end of bad luck to me, and that's one card game I don't need."

She frowned with puzzlement. Hadn't he pitched his hat onto her briefcase? No, that had been in her other dream. Whatever. Now she was getting her first good glimpse, more distinct than ever before, of the brute that had plagued her of late.

His black hair, a tad too long, was brushed off his face and behind his ears. Day-old whiskers stubbled the dark skin of his face, but did not hide the sharp cheekbones, strong nose and jaw, or full—sinfully full—lips. Vivid eyes, blue as pure lapis lazuli, sparkled with a burgeoning interest that he couldn't suppress, headache or not. But it wasn't carnal interest.

She decided to take the offensive. "So when does the forceful seduction begin?" She plopped backward on the bed, arms raised above her head, her legs spread wantonly. "Could we get this over real quick, huh? I'd like to sleep sometime tonight."

"Forceful seduction? What in blue blazes is that?" he said, his eyes about popping out as he gazed at her outlandish pose.

"You know, where the guy forces . . . well, persuades . . . the woman against her will to have sex, and like it," she explained waspishly, squirming her tush a little to get more comfortable. "Really, let's get this over with. Haul yourself on over here, hon. Come on, jump my bones. Do the deed. Rock my world."

"Huh?"

"Do I have to spell it out? Let the fantasy begin." She scrunched her eyes closed, bracing herself for his sensual attack.

Nothing happened.

She opened her eyelids a bit.

He was gaping at her, his astounded eyes roving her exposed body. Then he let out a hoot of laughter. "Forceful seduction? Damn, I'm gonna kill those two perverts."

He was laughing so hard now, deep belly laughs, that he had to sit down on the opposite seat and hold his sides. He kept mumbling something about the biblical characters Cain and Abel and how he'd found his long-lost sense of humor, after all.

Harriet's eyes widened as Steve just laughed and laughed. At her. It was a textbook dream scenario—naked woman, laughing man, or vice versa—that insecure people had all the time.

Me? Insecure?

With utter humiliation, Harriet realized the X-rated picture of invitation she made. And for the first time she began to wonder if this was a dream, after all.

But then Harriet homed in on his one word, *pervert,* and inhaled sharply at his obvious hidden meaning. "You want to tie me up, don't you? No way! Uh-uh!"

"Tie . . . tie you up?" Steve sputtered and let loose with another burst of laughter.

Standing abruptly, she planted her hands on her hips and tapped a bare foot with indignation. She stopped tapping immediately when she noticed his eyes take notice of her loose breasts, which were bouncing along with her foot movement. So he wasn't dead below the waist after all. *The lech!*

"Listen up, lover, and listen good," she declared haughtily, tossing her hair back over her shoulder with a theatrical flourish. "I've put up with this forceful seduction business of yours for weeks, but I draw the line at bondage. Even in a dream."

"Bondage? Dream? Oh, God, oh, God!" Steve groaned, wiping at his eyes. "I haven't laughed so much since . . . well, in a long time. Next you'll be asking me to hang from the ceiling and you'll be bringing out the buttermilk."

Harriet clenched her fists and made a low, snarling sound.

"Did you growl? Did I just hear you growl like a *chatte*? Lord, what jungle did they find you in, little love leopard?" He chortled at his own joke.

He was making fun of her. Dr. Harriet Ginoza was the butt of this bozo's joke. No one had teased her or gotten under her skin in ages . . . not since she'd learned how to use her brains and her razor-sharp tongue on Frankie "the Frog" Harris way back in third grade at St. Agnes School.

"Now that I think about it, it all fits together," Etienne mused. "Leopards are cats. And Cain and Abel said you have a tongue like a cat. Oh, God, I hope you don't have a tail. Turn around and bend over so I can see, honey." He guffawed some more, then broke into another full-fledged bout of laughter.

She hoped he split a gut.

If she hadn't known it before, Harriet did now . . . her sweet savage lover was a sweet savage louse.

"No, I don't have a tail, but I damn well have claws."

She pounced on him, threatening, "I'm going to kill you."

Her attack was interrupted by three sharp raps on the door, followed by silence, then another three raps.

Steve's laughter faded, and he drew himself up alertly. When three more raps followed, he put a fingertip to his lips, cautioning her to silence—not that she'd been the one making all the noise—then moved to the door.

"Etienne," she heard a male voice whisper.

He promptly unlocked the door.

Two tall, exceedingly gorgeous black men—twins—dressed similarly to Steve, immediately slipped inside, and he locked the door after them. The black cowboys were packing pistols, too.

"Have you lost your mind, Etienne?" one of them exclaimed. "We could hear your laughter all the way to the end of the car."

"Yeah, but at least he got his sense of humor back," the other man pointed out, then cast a teeth-flashing, Dennis Quaid–style grin her way. "I guess your rooster has got his wings back, my friend," he observed, winking at Steve.

"Nice leopard skin," the first brother remarked, his admiring eyes taking in Harriet's scanty attire.

Harriet backed up toward the window. The compartment was hardly bigger than her walk-in closet at home, and these three six-foot-plus, well-muscled men took up most of the room. She forced herself not to panic. *It's only a dream, it's only a dream, it's only a dream.*

And, hey, wasn't this something new for her dream? More than one man.

A sudden thought occurred to her. *Oh, geez!* She hoped they weren't going to suggest something really kinky like a ménage à trois.

Even worse, she hoped she wasn't going to agree.

She'd never in a million years do such a thing in real life, but who knew what she'd countenance in her crazy dreams. After all, who would have ever believed she'd enjoy forceful seduction? Could she possibly be facing multiple sex partners?

But it wouldn't be a ménage à trois, she realized with a giggle. It would be more like a *ménage à quatre*.

All three men turned to stare at her when she giggled, which she never did in real life, either.

Harriet was so disappointed with herself. Really, she was wallowing in every ridiculous, stereotypical female fantasy in the world . . . ones that had never appealed to her before. *Damn, damn, damn. Next I'll be adding the old classic . . . oh, no!*

I wouldn't!

Would I?

She examined Steve more closely and inquired hesitantly, "How old are you?"

He said some guttural word in French, which she was pretty sure was the f-word equivalent, then snapped, "Thirty-one."

With a grunt of disgust, she threw her hands in the air. "That does it! I give up. The older woman–younger man fantasy, too!" She didn't care that the men looked at her as if she'd flipped her lid. She had. "I'm losin' it here, guys. My brain is regressing. I'm on a fast train to trailer-park bimbo-dom."

"Is she mad?" Cain asked Etienne.

"It would appear so," Etienne replied dryly. "I can't figure out if you two found her in a jungle, the opera show, or a lunatic asylum. But your prank is over. We've all had a good laugh. Now get this woman out of here."

"Huh?" the twins said. "What prank?"

"Yeah, what prank?" Harriet chimed in.

"*Merde!* This is the worst time to pull a stunt," Steve said, raking fingers through his thick hair. "I could see Abel trying such foolishness, but I expected more of you, Cain."

"What stunt?" the first guy, presumably Cain, asked.

"I'm offended," the other brother, Abel, added with a smirk.

"Danger?" she squeaked, thoroughly baffled. Harriet realized now that the biblical guys Steve had mentioned earlier must be these studs—Cain and Abel. She wondered idly if she was going to remember any of this in the morning.

The morning! she thought then. *If I don't get some sleep soon, I won't be able to put two coherent words together for my speech.* "Hey, Steve, if you're not going to do your forceful seduction routine tonight, I'm going back to sleep." With that, she did a backward swan dive onto the bench bed, then hitched down the hem of her short nightie. With a wide yawn, she closed her eyes. "See you tomorrow night, lover boy."

"Lover boy?" Cain and Abel whooped. "And what's forceful seduction?" Cain asked.

Her eyes shot open to see all three men gawking at her. *Now what?*

Etienne, to her surprise, did a brief recap of her earlier explanation of forceful seduction. Although his version was a bit more crude, and graphic.

"She wants you to do *that?*" Cain asked with skepticism.

"She wants you to do *that?*" Abel asked with delight.

Steve nodded. "She says the goal is to convince the woman that she wants something that she says she doesn't want. Perfect twisted feminine thinking! Hell, why am I even discussing it with you two?"

"And women *like* this forceful seduction?" Abel persisted with decided interest, turning to her.

"Yes, unfortunately," she responded, "although there has to be a clear line drawn, of course." And she proceeded to give her routine lecture on the female fantasy that would never die.

"Aaaarrrgh!" Steve interrupted, right at the good part where she was explaining the difference between S & S and D & D. "Get her out of here," Steve clipped out.

"Well, aren't you the grumpy one tonight!" she observed.

"That's just what I was telling him earlier," Cain told her.

Steve's blue eyes flashed angrily, but he made a determined effort not to look at her. Instead he ordered, "Cain, you take her away."

"Me?" Cain protested. "Why me?"

"Abel would probably stop in the luggage compartment for a quick dip of his overused wick."

"You don't want her?" Abel eyed her with decided interest, not at all upset by Steve's vulgar insult. In fact, he assured Harriet, "I'm never quick, darlin'."

"Now wait a minute," Cain said, narrowing his eyes at Steve. "Are you sayin' you think we brought this wench here for you?"

Wench? They'd better not be referring to me as a wench.

"Exactly," Steve said. "From the opera house."

If Harriet hadn't been lying down, she would have reeled with confusion. "I think I caught your headache, Steve. Would you mind getting me an aspirin from my briefcase?"

"Why does she call you Steve?" Cain inquired.

"How the hell should I know?"

"She wants you to give her an ass burn," Abel pointed out with glee. "Even I never heard of that. How do you do it? Can we watch? Does it have somethin' to do with ridin' her hard? Or spanking?"

"Tsk-tsk! What have you been hiding from us, my friend?" Cain chastised.

"Geez!" Harriet contributed to the crazy conversation.

"Out!" Steve demanded, pushing the two men toward the door. "I'll handle this whore myself. You two are going to get us all killed with this foolery."

"But I had nothing to do with this, Etienne. I swear," Cain said.

"Me neither," Abel added, but he was laughing so hard his words were muffled.

Whore? Did he say "whore"? Okay, so the rules have changed on this dream business, Harriet decided.

Steve slammed the door after the departing men. Once again, she was alone with him, and he was glaring at her with evil intent. As if *he* were the injured party here!

She stood and wound her right arm in a windmill warm-up exercise, preparing to belt him a good one. Thank goodness, one of her stepfathers had been a boxer. *Yep, it's time to let Steve Morgan know that this lady is no Ginny Brandon, virginal and acquiescent. It's time to turn the tables on the rogue of the century. It's time I take a step for all womankind in controlling my destiny, even if I'm only starting with a dream.*

Before Harriet could carry through on her windup, though, the creep grabbed her by the waist, hoisted her over his shoulder with a hand clamped on her almost-bare behind, and deposited her roughly on the floor of the empty corridor.

"Hey, you can't leave me out here."

"Watch me," he said grimly.

"But what am I supposed to do?"

"Find another customer, sweetheart." Then he noticed her briefcase sitting on the opposite seat and he flung that out, too, before slamming the compartment door shut, locking her out.

Harriet stood clumsily and eyed the closed door. Now what? She could scream or bang on the door, but in her nonattire she didn't really want to gain the attention of the conductor or other passengers. Hmmm. Pursing her lips, she narrowed her eyes and thought for a second. Then she smiled.

Stepping close to the door, Harriet said in a low voice, "Oh, Steve, what do you think the sheriff will say at our next stop when I tell him about the gold?" In *Sweet Savage Love*, Steve Morgan had confiscated a shipment of gold that he didn't want the authorities to know about. Harriet was betting that her threat would make Steve think twice about dumping her.

It did.

As the door began to open, Harriet moved to the side.

Steve stuck his head out, demanding, "How do you know about the gold?"

And Harriet walloped him over the head with her briefcase, knocking him stone-cold unconscious.

Yippee! Harriet exulted, doing a little victory dance around her prone victim. *Chalk one up for womankind.*

It was turning into the best damn dream Harriet had ever had.

Chapter Three

After her initial jubilation, Harriet tapped a forefinger against her lips worriedly. What should she do now? The big lug lay like a concrete block at her feet, on his back, out cold.

Well, she couldn't just let him remain sprawled half in and half out of her compartment. She should push him out into the corridor and lock the door on him—tit for tat.

But no, she wanted to put some closure on this nightly torment, once and for all. To know why Steve had switched gears on their crazy "relationship."

She huffed and puffed, to no avail. She was only five foot six and weighed a hundred and twenty-five pounds, but she worked out at the gym regularly. *Gosh, the brute must weigh at least two hundred pounds.* Finally, she saw a wooden luggage dolly sitting in the corridor and used it to haul him into the room. *Hey, I don't have a PhD for nothing.*

Kneeling at his side, she checked his pulse by lifting his limp wrist and pressing her thumb against the blue vein,

Sandra Hill

visible under his dark complexion. *Okay, pulse normal. The guy's gonna live. Ha, ha, ha! Live? He's a dream, for heaven's sake!*

She smiled to herself at the fanciful thought.

Then she frowned.

Because he did have a pulse.

Oh, boy!

She noticed something else. If Steve had had a headache before, she had news for him. That goose egg beginning to rise on his forehead spelled more pain to come.

"What in tarnation is goin' on here?"

Harriet practically jumped out of her skin and turned to see the conductor standing in the still-open doorway. But it wasn't Mr. Jessup, the nice conductor who'd been on duty earlier. This guy, wearing an antiquated railway uniform with a pillbox kind of hat, was tall, white and surly.

He held up the lantern in his hand to see better. It was the same kind as the one Steve had lit earlier.

Before she had a chance to puzzle over that oddity, the conductor repeated, "What's goin' on here? What's this man doin' on the floor? Is he dead?"

"No, of course he's not dead. Maybe he had too much to drink . . . or something."

The conductor's beady eyes took in her silk nightie, and a slow smirk spread across his pockmarked face. This was embarrassing, even in a dream. She was going to have to get her robe from the bathroom real soon with all the people parading in and out of her compartment. It was clear what he thought she was doing here. If she wasn't careful, he might just follow Steve's lead and toss her out on her rear, too.

Or worse.

Thinking fast, Harriet simpered, "Oh, that Mr. Morgan! He and I never met before; so I didn't recognize him." She waved a hand airily, the implication being that she was a prostitute having an assignation with an unknown client. "Oh, well, I guess it doesn't matter if you leave him there

44

till he wakes up. After all, he and I will be sharing this compartment, if you know what I mean, honey. All the way to New Orleans." She fluttered her eyelashes meaningfully. "You can just go now."

The conductor moved closer.

"Did you know Mr. Morgan is a gunslinger?" she added, glancing pointedly at the gun belt Steve still wore, low on his hips.

The conductor's eyes widened as they latched onto the two pistols, and he soon left, grumbling something about drunks and whores, the bane of a conductor's life.

Harriet shut the door after him. *Whew! That was close.* Her shoulders slumped then as she surveyed her surroundings. Everything was completely different from when she'd boarded the train several hours ago. The room was smaller, and a film of soot—coal dust—covered just about everything. Two upholstered bench seats faced each other, perpendicular to the windows. Steve's body took up just about all the space in between. There was no evidence of the small door leading to her private bathroom. So much for getting her robe!

And while her compartment had been stuffy before, now it was stiflingly hot. She stepped over Steve's body and tugged on the two wide windows, surprised when the frames moved upward, providing a blast of fresh air from the moving train. Harriet knew that windows in a modern Amtrak didn't open, for safety reasons, which she considered further proof that she was still dreaming.

She decided then and there that she was going to make an appointment with her friend, Dr. Julius Franklin, the minute she returned home to Los Angeles. Jules specialized in dream interpretation, and Harriet's dreams were becoming way too detailed and vivid. They must mean something.

Could she be having a nervous breakdown? Harriet had been pushing herself especially hard the past year. Meeting a tight deadline for delivery of her latest book. Lecturing at UCLA. Finding an apartment for her mother, who was husbandless once again, although Riff had soon bopped into the picture, vying to be spouse number six. Then this book tour.

Tears of exhaustion and frustration brimmed in her eyes. She needed to wake up from this damn dream. But to do that, she first needed to fall asleep. Not that she wasn't already asleep and dreaming, but she needed to sleep in her sleep. Even her fuzzy brain saw the contradiction in that logic.

Okay, so that's the plan, she thought, wiping at her eyes. *Sleep. Wake up. End of problem.*

Steve moaned softly and threw an arm up over his head, shifting slightly in the cramped space. She could tell by his even breathing that he now slept, no longer unconscious.

She was about to lie down on the bench seat, then hesitated. She'd better not take any chances, even if it was a dream. Reaching down, she carefully removed first one, then the other revolver from Steve's gun belt, placing the weapons out of his reach at the far end of the other seat, near the door.

Harriet tried lying on her side, then her back, her stomach, then her other side. She couldn't get comfortable. Geez, even in a dream, she couldn't fall asleep. But then, in her dreams, she was accustomed to sleeping with the rascal.

Do I dare?

Why not?

So Harriet blew out the lantern and slid down to the floor, nestling her body up against that of her dream lover. She rested her face on his chest, where she could feel his heart beat strongly against her cheek, and even wrapped his one arm over her shoulder. With a grin, she threw one leg over his thighs.

An outrageous idea occurred to her. *Maybe I should be the forceful seducer, for a change.*

Oh, yeah! Wouldn't that be a hoot?

Heck, why not? "Sluts 'R' Us" is apparently my motto these days.

But I'm too tired right now.

Wimp!

Maybe later.

She snuggled closer, relishing the familiar scent and contours of her lover's body. Strangely, she felt at home in this man's arms.

Within seconds, she succumbed to sleep . . . in her sleep.

Etienne opened his eyes to bright sunlight, and immediately shuttered them against the pain. He tried to focus on the ache throbbing behind his right temple, to will away the agony.

All those months in a dark hole, the repeated beatings . . . he'd have thought his body would welcome the sun's rays. But, no, his prison torment only took on another guise when he'd left the bars behind five years ago—the debilitating headaches.

After a few minutes of deep breathing and disciplined concentration, he felt the pain ease. When he cracked his eyelids slowly, he became aware of two important facts. First, he was stretched out on the floor of a railway compartment. Second, a sleeping woman had attached herself to him like barnacles on a sunken ship.

He couldn't see her face, but her warm breath tickled his neck. He blew out a few strands of her long, sable hair, which had managed to land in his open mouth—he'd probably been snoring—and sniffed deeply. Her hair smelled of lemons and fresh gulf breezes. But it didn't taste very good.

One of her hands lay possessively under his vest, over his heart. And a bare, creamy thigh had nudged its way between his legs so that she reclined half on top of him. His one arm encircled the woman's shoulders, cuddling her into his embrace.

Still sleep-hazy, he didn't know who she was; nor did he care at this stage. He just wanted to luxuriate in the sensuousness of the moment. To forget his past—the mistakes and regrets. To relax and not worry about the danger ahead. To find the Etienne Baptiste who'd been lost for so long.

Using his free hand, he examined the woman blindly, sweeping a callused palm over her shoulders, along the indentation of her small waist, to her curvy hips and long legs.

Instead of protesting, she sighed softly and nestled closer.

Had they made love?

Probably.

It wasn't too surprising that he wouldn't remember, either. Most of his sexual encounters in the past few years had been less than memorable. Ever since Vera had . . . no, he didn't want to think about that . . . about anything. He just wanted to luxuriate in the sybaritic sensation of mere feeling. Long years of suppressing his emotions had left him cold inside, but he was definitely thawing now.

He let his hand explore more. She was a small-boned female of medium height with a behind that would fit very nicely into a man's hands, he ascertained with a slow smile, palming said mounds appreciatively. It was the kind of well-rounded ass that petite women hated, but men loved. Men, of course, having a natural appreciation for the finer points of a woman's figure. Like a good ass.

That was when he added important fact number three to his list. He had a huge erection rising against the woman's inner thigh. Cain and Abel always said the morning rooster rose early. He had to say this rooster was about to crow, early or not.

Without thinking, he shifted the woman's body so she lay on top of him, her full breasts on his chest and the vee of her womanhood riding the ridge of his hardness. Her long, raven hair fell forward, screening her face. Lifting the hem of her tiny garment, he took one bare buttock in each of his hands and moved her against him rhythmically.

He groaned. The pleasure was so painfully exquisite.

She groaned, too . . . a soft, kittenish sound. Then she raised her head slightly, blinking at him through muddy green eyes, like a cat. "Again?"

"Again?" he repeated dully, transfixed by her eyes.

"Uh-huh," she purred, tracing a forefinger over his scratchy jaw, then over his lips.

As the vixen rubbed herself against him with feline persuasiveness, a red haze of arousal clouded Etienne's vision. He arched his neck, panting hard, in an effort to slow the pace. Lord, had anything in his life ever felt this good?

"How do you like having someone take you against your will?"

Against my will? Hell, if I were any more willing, I'd explode.

Etienne closed his eyes, trying to pay attention. But the hot blood churning in his brain wanted only one thing . . . his hardness imbedded inside the sweet cat's heat. He tried to tell her, but his tongue grew thick, barring words. Instead, he raised his hips up against her in silent invitation.

A low, seductive laugh of triumph trilled from her throat, and he opened his eyes slowly, waiting for an explanation.

"I decided last night that I should be the aggressor next time in this forceful seduction game," she murmured, the whole time nibbling at his neck. He could swear her tongue really was abrasive and catlike. "Would you like that, Steve?"

Etienne blinked as the words *forceful seduction* and *Steve* wormed their way into his foggy memory, jolting him. "Damn!" Etienne lost his lustful inclinations immediately as understanding hit him like a runaway train. "Damn, damn, damn!"

This cat-woman in the leopard-print chemise . . . this seductress turning him mindless with lust . . . it was the woman he'd booted out of his compartment last night. The one who'd . . . *Oh, my God!* He put a hand to his forehead where a bump rose ignominiously, explaining his throbbing headache. The woman had dared to strike him with her satchel. She must have knocked him unconscious.

She was still gazing at him with those huge, green, feline eyes, imploring him to . . . what?

"Are you going to surrender to me?" she whispered in a sinfully sexy voice, low and husky and full of enticing mystery.

"Surrender?" he choked out. Then he looked downward, which was a big mistake. Because he got a bird's-eye view of the prettiest pair of breasts this side of heaven—uptilted, with hardened pink nipples.

But no, something was wrong with this picture. Etienne forced himself to recollect. The woman had entered his compartment, uninvited, just as he and Cain and Abel were about to embark on the most dangerous assignment of their lives. She knew about the gold and his army background. She'd knocked him unconscious. Now she ogled him like he was a griddle cake, and she was the hot molasses. And she wanted him to . . . *surrender*?

Suddenly Etienne knew. Another person was about to slip the knife of betrayal through his vulnerable ribs. Like Vera. When the hell would he ever learn to be more cautious? His heart skipped a beat with alarm, then began to chug slowly with fury. Just as the sitting train was beginning to chug up its engines and build steam.

Sitting train? Etienne shot up off the floor, dumping the woman unceremoniously, and scrambled to look out the window.

That was when important fact number four dawned on him—the most important fact of all. Panicked, he peered out the window at the train station, which was becoming increasingly smaller as they moved away. With a silent curse, he recognized the black man standing, hands on hips, next to a wagon in the distance—Abel. And he realized that he'd missed his critical stop in Memphis. This woman—whoever she was—had ruined the entire mission.

"Am I still dreaming?" she said with a yawn as she crawled to her feet. With her arms stretched over her head, her little leopard-print chemise left nothing to the imagination.

"No, you are not dreaming," he said icily, advancing on the witless woman who was finger-combing her hair with disregard for the danger she had placed them all in. "But I assure you, my dear, you are going to wish this were a dream. Very soon."

Harriet's first attempt at forceful seduction had apparently fizzled. Not only was her lover no longer lying flat on his back, at her command, but his fists were clenched and his teeth gritted.

Harriet didn't have to be a psychologist to discern the signs of repressed hostility. The man would like to break her bones, not jump them. She backed away a bit. "Now, Steve, don't get your jockey shorts in a twist. I just switched roles on you, tried to show you how forceful seduction feels. It's called mirroring."

"*Sacrebleu!*" He inched closer. "My name is not Steve, and I have no idea what you're talking about. Who the hell are you?"

"Harriet Ginoza."

"Harry-Hat? What kind of name is that?"

"Not Harry-Hat, *Harriet*. Dr. Harriet Ginoza."

"A doctor? Not bloody likely!"

Harriet was beginning to notice an interesting thing about Steve's . . . rather, Etienne's speech. It changed. All the time. Thus far, she could identify a lazy, Louisiana drawl. An educated, almost British accent. Then a Southern cracker regionalism. Even an occasional French word.

Was it deliberate? The way he eased in and out of speech patterns might not be noticed by most people, but Harriet's job was to observe people's behavior, no matter how subtle. And this man was a consummate actor. The enigma puzzled her.

"Lady, you'd better explain what you're doing here, pronto. Because, frankly, I'm in a killing mood." He loomed closer.

"You know, Etienne, you emote entirely too much violence."

Taken aback, he snarled, "Emote? What kind of word is that?"

At least that stopped his progress for a moment. She'd have to talk down his anger, draw on her clinical skills. "I thought, at one time, that you suffered from the Don Juan syndrome," she went on blithely, "but now I'm beginning to see characteristics of the Genghis Khan syndrome. Genetic male aggression channeled into patterns of sporadic violence."

"Genghis Khan! Genghis Khan! First, you think I'm some man named Steve Morgan. Now, Genghis Khan. You must be sick. A fever perhaps?" He narrowed his eyes at her speculatively. "Dr. Ginoza, huh? Well, Ginny," he said, honing in on her last name, "perhaps you need to heal yourself."

"I'm a PhD doctor, not a medical doctor."

"Well, that explains it," he said, throwing up his hands as he moved another step closer.

She gulped as her back hit the door. "See. You must be Steve because you called me Ginny, even though my name is Harriet. And everyone knows that Steve and Ginny were legendary lovers in that book—"

He spit out an extremely foul word, grabbed her by the shoulders, and flung her down on one of the bench seats. The fingers of both hands circled her neck, pressing hard. "The truth," he demanded, relaxing his fingers only when he realized she couldn't speak.

Tears welled in her eyes, but she raised her chin with defiance. "You brute! I should have known that Steve Morgan would revert to savagery."

"I am not Steve Morgan," he said evenly. "Who sent you?"

His body lay heavily on top of hers, pinning her to the seat. And Steve, or whatever alias he used now, was back to strangling her again. Plus, a sharp object prodded her left thigh. Feeling blindly, she recognized the shape of one of the guns she'd placed there earlier. Grabbing it, she pressed the tip of the barrel between them, against his genitals. "Move it, buster," she ordered in a squeaky, choked voice, "or I'm gonna fill your crown jewels with lead."

Steve's blue eyes went wide and his fingers lessened their grasp on her throat. "Take it easy," he warned, easing himself off her and standing, then backing up slightly toward the window. "Don't do anything hasty." His eyes were cautious but admiring of her expertise in having outwitted him.

Harriet licked her dry lips, taking huge drafts of air into her burning lungs.

Meanwhile, Steve's eyes darted about the room, probably seeking an escape for himself, and halted at the pile of clothing she'd laid out on one seat. Picking up one of her Ferragamo pumps, he eyed it curiously. At first, she thought he was contemplating its possibilities as a weapon, but instead, he tossed it out the open window.

"Hey!" she screeched. "Those shoes cost me a hundred and fifty dollars."

"Oh, really?" He didn't look at all apologetic. In fact, his flushed face and tight jaw bespoke a boiling rage. "Well, here goes another seventy-five dollars, darlin'." And he lobbed the other shoe over his shoulder and out the window. Michael Jordan couldn't have done it better.

"You jerk!" she said, seething, and aimed the gun straighter, this time at his heart.

"What's this?" he asked with seeming unconcern, holding up her short red Dior skirt and jacket.

"A business suit. And it cost me eight hundred dollars; so don't you dare—"

Her favorite power suit joined her shoes on a stretch of countryside somewhere outside Memphis, Tennessee.

Now he'd gone too far. Forceful seduction. Violence. Harassment. Lack of proper respect for designer clothing.

It wouldn't really be murder if she killed a creep in her sleep, would it?

Steve was handling her black lace demibra now, inspecting it with infuriating detail. He glanced at the wispy half cups, then at her breasts, arching a brow with sudden understanding. Then he laughed mirthlessly as he discarded it, too, along with her second-best silk blouse.

"Why are you doing this?" she cried.

"Because you're holding a gun on me. Because you broke into my compartment and knocked me out cold. Because you expect me to surrender to you willingly. Because I am not *ever* going back to prison." He picked up her silk panty hose, held them out in front of his face, and shook his head in amazement.

But Harriet focused on one word. "Prison? Are you a murderer or something?"

"No, but I'm gonna be."

"Hold it. Now I remember about the prison. Steve Morgan concocted a scheme in *Sweet Savage Love* where he pretended—Ooomph!"

Steve had lurched forward, knocking the gun from her hand and slamming her back against the door once again. Now the gun barrel was pressed against her heart.

"Steve," she pleaded softly.

"Don't call me that name again," he sliced out.

"Etienne, then," she corrected. "Don't do this. You're not really a bad man. You're just—"

"Shut the hell up," he snapped, and turned her against the hard wooden door. Before she had a chance to realize what he was doing, he'd yanked her hands behind her back and tied them with her panty hose. Then he shoved her into a sitting position on one of upholstered bench seats. Grabbing her stretchy bikini briefs, which he regarded for only a moment with a flicker of interest, he used them to bind her ankles together. Finally he sank into the seat opposite her, knee to knee.

The whole time she was whimpering with disbelief.

Good thing it was a dream; otherwise she'd be screaming.

"Now, talk, or I swear I'm going to give new meaning to the expression 'skinning the cat.' "

"I already told you. I'm Dr. Harriet Ginoza, a psychologist. I boarded the Amtrak train in Chicago. I'm giving a speech in New Orleans tonight, and—"

"A sick-what?"

"A psychologist . . . you know, a scientist who studies the mind and human behavior."

He rolled his eyes. "And a ham track?"

She creased her brow over that question, then laughed. "I said Amtrak. It's the name of a railroad line."

He put one pistol back in its holster and the other remained in his right hand, which rested casually over his knee, but Harriet couldn't relax. She suspected the gun would be aimed at her heart again, in a nanosecond, if she made one wrong move.

"So tell me, Dr. Ginny, whose mind were you studying when you broke into my compartment? And why me?"

Okay, so Steve wasn't buying her story. She took a deep breath. "Listen, Steve . . . I mean, Etienne, the bottom line here is: This is just a dream."

"I beg your pardon," he said cynically and pinched his arm. "Ouch! *Oui*, I'm awake."

"It's the truth. Do you think I'd be prancing around in my nightie like this?" she pointed out, peeking down at her breasts that strained against the thin leopard-print silk because of her hands being pulled behind her back.

He looked, too, and despite his efforts to appear unimpressed, she recognized a faint glimmer in his eye.

"Not that you haven't seen everything I own, and then some," she said with a blush, "but I would have been mortified to have the conductor and your two friends see me like this . . . if it weren't a dream."

"Let me understand. You're saying I've seen you naked?"

"Sure. Lots of times. Every night for the past two weeks. Since my latest book went on sale."

He made a slight groaning sound of frustration. "And what book, pray tell, might that be?"

"*Female Fantasies Never Die*," she responded proudly.

His jaw dropped and his eyes about bugged out. When he realized he was gaping, he clicked his mouth shut. "Are you demented?"

She shrugged. "Probably."

With a snort of disgust, he put a booted foot on each side of her hips, slipped the toes behind her butt, and with an abrupt motion, drew her forward so that she fell to the floor on her knees. With her hands locked behind her, Harriet landed with her breastbone against the hard metal of the pistol on his lap and her face buried, for one split second, in his crotch.

His gasp and the flash of utter incredulity on his face told her that oral sex hadn't been his intention. But a movement under her cheek told her that another part of his body, far removed from his brain, had other ideas.

She righted herself briskly, kneeling between his thighs, which he promptly closed like a vise, rendering her immobile.

"You just crossed the line, mister," she seethed. "I've put up with enough of your crap these past two weeks. First it was crude sexual assaults, now violence . . . oooh!"

He'd just used the tip of his pistol to flick the nipple of first one, then the other breast. To her humiliation, they came instantly to life, hard and aching for further touch.

His full lips curved with satisfaction, but the somber grin never reached his eyes. He was touching her intimately as intimidation, not foreplay. Despite her squirming, he refused to let her rise from her knees.

He put the gun in his empty holster and, as if transfixed, he lifted her chin with a forefinger, then ran his thumb over her parted lips.

The feathery touch ignited a seismic shock that ran

through her body like a bolt of erotic lightning. Harriet was beginning to hate herself and her lack of self-control.

"Exactly how many times did we make love during these past two weeks?" he asked in a raspy drawl. Harriet couldn't tell whether his whisper was a sign of restrained fury, or arousal.

"Dozens."

"And I have no memory of the events? How extraordinary!" He let out a short laugh of disbelief. Then, "Was I good?"

"You were lousy," she lied.

He broke into a wide, lazy smile, and Harriet reeled under the impact. "God, you have a dangerous smile," she blurted out.

"So I've been told . . . a long time ago," he said in an oddly sad voice.

Harriet sensed pain and regret in Etienne's voice, and something deep inside her began to melt. She couldn't explain, but she wanted to hit the brute, and kiss away his hurts. She wanted to shake some sense into his male chauvinist head, and, at the same time, in some deep-seated, prehistoric part of her brain, she relished the fact that he was dominant and all man.

Was there a purpose to her dreams? Perhaps their erotic nature was a camouflage. What if she'd been given a mission by God to help this obviously troubled man? Harriet smiled inwardly at the prospect of any heavenly being designating her for such a celestial "Mission Impossible." She hadn't been in a church since high school.

Still, some part of her subconscious sensed the inevitability of her contact with this man. Fate, or the gods, had ordained her dreams for a reason, of that she was certain.

I could love him, she realized suddenly.

Oh, God!

"You have the strangest green eyes. Beautiful cat eyes," he remarked huskily as he brushed a strand of hair off her face. She could see by his hooded eyes and heightened breathing that he was equally affected by the curious chemistry between them. "Are you a gypsy? Have you cast a spell over me?"

She shook her head mutely. No longer struggling to rise, she was the one ensorcelled.

"Are you here to betray me?" His words were deliberately soft and casual, but she could tell the question was immensely serious. And that, somehow, she could hurt him with her answer.

She took her time before speaking. As awareness sizzled between them like an electric current, she studied the firm line of his jaw; his sad, blue eyes and gaunt cheekbones; the arrogant tilt of his chin; his full, passionate lips that she knew so well.

"I would never, ever betray you," she vowed as tears scalded her eyes. And she meant every word. "As much as I've tried to fight it, I think you're my soul mate."

Chapter Four

"Damn! Did you have to bring cold water?" Etienne griped at Cain as he attempted to shave. Not an easy task, Harriet observed, as the train chugged along at a relatively fast pace, swaying occasionally.

Cain sliced Etienne a glare, refusing to speak since their angry exchange of words a short time before. Cain blamed Etienne for some botched-up plan to leave the train in Memphis, and, of course, Etienne blamed her. The blame game . . . how juvenile!

Etienne was using a small basin and a square mirror from a portable shaving kit—a flat, wooden box-type affair like officers had used during the Civil War. Harriet had seen one at a Christie's estate sale for the descendants of Gen. Benjamin Butler.

Harriet was curled up in one corner of the seat near the window, still bound hand and foot. She watched with fascination as Etienne, bare to the waist—*Be still, my heart!*—lathered up with a brush and soap and wielded a straight razor with expertise. She forced herself to think of him as

Etienne, since that was the name Steve insisted on using now.

"And this razor is dull as a bayou soiree," Etienne continued to berate Cain. "I'll have more nicks than a butchered hog. How can I take on any believable persona without a decent shave?"

"Shut up and hurry, you dumb son of a bitch, or the only persona you'll be able to take on is that of a dead man," Cain seethed as he finished dressing.

"Who are you calling a dumb son of a bitch, you dumb son of a bitch?" Etienne spat out the indignant retort, along with some shaving soap. A thin line of blood trickled through the white foam from a cut on his right cheekbone.

"Speaking of dumb, do you know why Adam was the first dumb man?" Hey, if they were going to behave like idiots, she might as well honor them with a sampling of dumb-men jokes from her personal collection.

Etienne and Cain ignored her, as they had been doing for the past half hour. As if that would stop her.

"Because he thought Eve was cheating on him."

Cain grunted and Etienne gritted his teeth. Well, that was enough encouragement for her.

"And do you know what God said after he created Eve?"

Stone silence, except for the sound of razor scraping over whiskery flesh.

"Practice makes perfect." She beamed at Etienne and Cain.

"Are those riddles supposed to be humorous?" Etienne snarled.

"Are you saying that all men are dumb?" Cain asked at the same time.

"Bingo! On both counts. Try this one. What did Adam say to Eve during their first intimate moment?"

Etienne's face was turning purple with incredulity.

"Whoa! Stand back, Eve. Who knows how big this thing is gonna get!"

"You're pathetic," Etienne said and resumed shaving. But she thought there might be a little smile tugging at his lips.

"You're both pathetic," Cain snorted as he donned a nineteenth century–style suit—a nut brown, broadcloth outfit with a short jacket over a much-washed, off-white shirt. He was a devastatingly handsome man, right down to his well-toned flesh, which she'd seen a whole lot of since he'd shucked to his skivvies right in front of her. The immodest guy—probably an exhibitionist—could pose for *Playgirl* any day. "I'm surrounded by pathetic, sexually crazed, insane people. Good thing Abel isn't here. He'd no doubt be jotting the words to those dumb riddles down and setting them to song."

Etienne raised an eyebrow. "What flew up your chimney, Cain? Come on. Spit it out."

Cain complained mulishly, "Of all days you pick to dally with a wench! Dammit, Etienne, couldn't you keep your pizzle in your pants till we got in safe territory?"

"Pizzle? I haven't heard that word since we were boys," Etienne replied, wiping away the remainder of shaving foam with his shirt. "And I told you, she wasn't kneeling between my legs to . . . oh, damn, why am I even trying to explain to you?"

Harriet listened with amazement to the odd interchange. She had to admit that her position, kneeling between Etienne's legs, had looked suggestive when Cain had burst into the compartment an hour ago. He'd called Etienne names that made even her blush.

She'd tried to be helpful when Cain had unjustly attacked Etienne, but did her "lover" appreciate her efforts? No. Etienne had threatened to gag her if she didn't stop blabbing her opinions on everything from the repressed neuroses of hostile men to the psychoses of aberrant machoism. "I'd be willing to give you a free trial therapy session," she'd even offered.

Etienne's response didn't bear repeating.

"Hey, I get paid big money for my advice," she'd informed him haughtily.

"Your mouth opens more than a Tallahassee tart's."

Before she'd been able to respond to that crudity, Cain had proposed using his surgical expertise to suture her mouth shut. And she was pretty sure he hadn't been kidding.

So she'd wisely chosen to spare them her wisdom . . . for a while. That was, until Etienne had pulled out a small trunk of disguises—beards, makeup, wigs. And costumes ranging from gypsy to military uniform. They'd whispered furtively, arguing over which characters they should portray.

They'd been especially unappreciative when she'd said, "I feel like I'm watching Dumb and Dumber trying to pull off a madcap gold heist. Well, Dumb, Dumber and Dumbest, if you include that yahoo back in Memphis. Yep, the Three Stooges of the Old South." The other twin, Abel, was stranded back in Memphis due to their aborted plan, but they seemed to think he would make his way to New Orleans, where they would all meet.

Harriet had no idea why the two men were rushing now to change their clothing and appearance. They claimed some bad guys were hot on their trail, possibly even on this train, and that all their lives were in peril.

And somehow, for some crazy reason, Etienne blamed her for the whole mess. *Geez!* Apparently, her dreams were turning into adventure romps now, not just sexual fantasies.

Etienne had been about to release her ties a little while ago, after she'd told him he was her soul mate—*God, I can't believe I actually said that*—until she'd heard him and Cain discussing their current peril, which stemmed from some dude named Jim Pope, the Secret Service, master spies, and Etienne's incarceration in Andersonville Prison. None of it made any sense to her befuddled mind, but she'd made the mistake then of announcing that she knew all about Jim Bishop from *Sweet Savage Love*, although he hadn't been the enemy in that book, of course.

Unfortunately, *Pope* was close enough to *Bishop* in Etienne's dictionary to make him even more suspicious of her. Now the dimwit considered her his captive.

"Now what?" Cain asked, straightening. His head, as well as Etienne's, almost touched the ceiling of the compartment.

"Cut my hair." Etienne handed Cain a pair of scissors from the travel kit.

"The devil I will!" Cain stormed. "Have you lost your mind? We don't have time. If we don't get that gold to Texas by the end of the month, we'll never finish this job. Then what will President Grant do— "

"Cain," Etienne warned, looking toward her.

Both men turned to her, as if they'd forgotten she was there. *Some fantasy!*

"I still say we should toss her out the window," Cain said.

"The idea's gaining appeal by the second," Etienne agreed. "But we need to know where she got her information. And what her role is in Pope's organization."

"The only pope I know is in Rome," Harriet protested. "Any chance you guys work for Dumb Men, Inc.?"

They didn't even acknowledge her comment, although Etienne and Cain did exchange a pained look. She was getting tired of being the extraneous person in this dream. It was as if they didn't even care that she was there.

She soon learned otherwise.

As Cain quickly snipped Etienne's thick black hair till it was collar-length and parted, incongruously, down the middle, he quipped, "So, did you check her tongue?"

"No." Etienne laughed glumly. Then he added, "But she has an impressive posterior."

Harriet gasped. "This is sexual harassment, mister."

"Well, that's even more important." Cain glanced her way to see if he could perhaps see her backside.

"Show Cain your ass, honey," Etienne suggested sweetly.

"Oh! You are revolting. I'm never going to let you touch me again. Never!"

"Hah! Wait till I bring out the buttermilk. You'll be on me like catnip," he taunted.

"In *your* dreams, buster. Not mine!"

Cain's head was swinging back and forth like a pendulum as he watched the sharp exchange between the two of them. Amusement flickered in his dark eyes. "God, Etienne, I think you've finally met your match. Perhaps this woman is heaven-sent—a miracle sent to revive your dead . . . uh, spirit."

"God would not be so cruel."

Why was Etienne so disdainful of her? She knew better than anyone how to interpret hidden sexual signals, and this guy was sending zippo her way. He'd been telling the truth when he said he wasn't interested in her anymore. "Let's backtrack here a bit, guys. Start from the beginning. What's this tongue and buttermilk business? Can I get in on the joke?"

"No," Etienne stated flatly.

"Oh, it's a man thing, huh?" she snipped. "Even in a dream, men have to play sexist games."

"Why does she keep talking about dreams?" Cain asked.

"What sex games?" Etienne wanted to know.

"I said 'sexist' games, not sex games, you jerk."

"Huh?" Cain put a hand to his head as if disoriented. "All I did was ask why she keeps talking about dreams."

"Because this *is* a dream," Harriet asserted.

"Because she's a lunatic," Etienne said at the same time, "or a bad actress."

"Give me a break!"

"I'd love to break you. In two. Maybe later, sweetheart." He smiled grimly.

She made a face at the back of Etienne's head, which Cain caught. He grinned at her.

In the meantime, Etienne had put on a clean, blue, collarless shirt and a black suit jacket, which he buttoned up priggishly in Pee-Wee Herman fashion. He left the same black trousers on, rolled up at the ankle, but he put his scruffy boots, along with his other clothing and one of the guns, into the satchel. He slipped the second gun into the back waistband of his trousers.

"Be careful that gun doesn't go off accidentally and shoot you in the butt," she advised.

A low growl emerged from deep in his throat. The glare he cast her way could have melted concrete.

"Now, Etienne, hold your temper," Cain admonished. "There's no time to kill her now. Wait till New Orleans."

Well, that's comforting.

Etienne inhaled deeply, obviously forcing himself to relax, then bent to stuff his big feet into a pair of new, black leather shoes, which were apparently too tight. "I'm gonna have blisters by the time we get to New Orleans."

"Oh, goodie! They'll match the ones on your behind if that gun goes off."

"The only thing going off around here is your mouth," he said with distaste. Meanwhile, he raked his newly cut hair behind his ears, which called attention to the silly part down the center.

"Do you know why dumb men part their hair down the middle?"

Etienne's shoulders slumped and he closed his eyes as if praying.

"Why?" Cain asked.

Etienne's eyes shot open and he scowled at Cain for encouraging her.

"Because their heads aren't well balanced."

"Notice that I'm not amused," Etienne said.

"I'm not either, Etienne," Cain added ingratiatingly, and spoiled the effect by biting his lip to stifle its upward turn.

"Do you know that dumb men are proof that reincarnation exists?"

"Really?" Cain said playfully in perfect straight-man style.

"Oh, God!" Etienne moaned. "Please spare us."

"No one could get that stupid in one lifetime."

Cain hooted with laughter.

Etienne moaned louder. Then, disgusted with them both, he proceeded to smooth his jacket front. Bending his knees, he hunkered down so he was eye-level with the mirror propped on the upper window ledge and gave himself one last check.

"Be careful you don't split your pants," she remarked acidly, staring at the fabric of his trousers pulled taut over his behind. But what she thought was, *Man, oh, man!*

At first, his face reddened with affront. But then he flashed her a knowing wink, and asked Cain, "Is this enough of a disguise? How do I look?"

"Like a nerd," Harriet observed before Cain could answer. *A handsome nerd, though,* she added to herself.

"Fine," Cain disagreed.

They both ignored her opinion. At least she thought they had till Cain added with mock sympathy, "I don't think you look like a bird. Leastways, not much. Except perhaps a rooster."

"I'll show her a bird when I get her alone," Etienne promised, his eyes blazing blue fire at her.

"What did God get when he crossed a dumb man with a rooster?"

"Aaarrgh!" Cain and Etienne both exclaimed.

"A really dumb rooster."

"Do you really think she's working with Pope?" Cain asked Etienne then as they gathered the rest of their belongings. "I mean, she is really strange."

"If you think I'm strange, you ought to see how you all look from my viewpoint."

"Probably." Etienne shrugged, disregarding her cynical statement. "The Secret Service uses female spies all the time, as you well know."

Secret Service? A spy? Okay, this has gone far enough. "Why won't you listen to me, you lunkhead? I'm a psychologist, not a bloomin' spy."

"She says she's a doctor . . . a mind doctor," Etienne told Cain scornfully. "You two should have a lot in common, both being doctors and all. Maybe she'll let you examine her . . . tongue."

"Really?" A slack-jawed Cain addressed her. "You're a doctor?"

"You're a doctor?" Harriet echoed in amazement, then added before she had a chance to think, "What are you doing with *him*?"

"He's my best friend," Cain said simply. "More important, what are *you* doing with him?"

"I wish I knew."

"Don't you remember, honey?" Etienne recalled with an obnoxious snicker. "We're soul mates."

Harriet's face heated with embarrassment. She'd been hoping he'd forgotten her words. "I take it back."

"You can't take it back," he argued childishly.

"Yes, I can. A woman has the right to change her mind."

"In less than an hour?"

"Tsk-tsk!" Cain contributed. "Will you stop? You remind me of Dreadful and Bob when they used to go at each other."

"Who are Dreadful and Bob?" she asked.

"Childhood pets. A dog the size of a horse and a three-legged chicken," Etienne told her. Then he shook his head from side to side as if he couldn't believe he'd actually felt the need to answer her question. "You're right, Cain. I'm wasting time. Now go get a linen sheet from the conductor. Or better yet, see if you can filch one from the linen storage area, without anyone seeing you."

"A sheet? Why?" Cain's wide brow furrowed with puzzlement.

"A shroud," Etienne announced brightly. "For the corpse."

He and Cain turned as one to look at her.

"Me?" she squeaked out.

Etienne pulled a pair of wire-rimmed spectacles out of his jacket pocket and put them on. He beamed at her, the picture of an adorable geek.

"You know what the good thing is about men who wear glasses?" she blurted out. Harriet knew her jokes were ill-timed and inappropriate for the circumstances, but her life was falling apart, and she feared she might cry if she didn't laugh.

Etienne and Cain tilted their heads in question.

"When they take them off, you know they mean business."

Cain frowned with confusion, but Harriet knew the moment Etienne understood her flip remark. His eyes turned a smoldering shade of dark blue.

And Harriet wondered what he'd look like when he turned to a woman and took off his glasses, intent on *business*.

Immediately composing himself, Etienne then posed next to Cain. The black man slouched his shoulders a bit in a subservient posture, gazing at Etienne, but never making direct eye contact, as if Etienne were the master, and Cain a mere slave.

"Well, Dr. Ginny? What do you think?" Etienne inquired, a rascally glimmer in his somber eyes.

"I think Dumb and Dumber just got even dumber."

He wagged an admonishing finger at her. "Madam, let me introduce myself. I am Hiram M. Frogash, mortician. And this is my mortuary assistant, Hippocrates Jones."

"Gawd!"

"Our speciality is"—he wiggled his eyebrows at her in a lascivious Groucho Marx–style, which caused his spectacles to slip down his nose—"female cadavers."

A shiver of foreboding rippled over her skin.

"Oh, and did I mention I'm a taxidermist, too?" Then he crooked a finger at her. "Here, kitty, kitty."

"I can't believe I let you talk me into this," Harriet huffed out. "Dumb, Dumber and Dumbest just added a new gang member. The dumb-ee. Me."

She could barely breathe, wrapped snugly as she was in a linen sheet. Not to mention hanging over Etienne's shoulder with her butt in the air. They were passing through the corridors of the railway cars to the freight car near the end. The only good thing was that they'd untied her hands and feet, with Etienne pocketing her panties and stockings.

"Shhhh," he hissed. "You're supposed to be dead."

"Make way, make way. The undertaker is acomin'," Cain called out to no one in particular as he spearheaded their macabre procession. It was after noon, and most passengers were in the dining cars toward the front of the train, but there was always the chance they might run into someone. So Etienne had compelled her to make a choice . . . either cooperate in their screwball caper, or he'd conk her on the head with his revolver.

Some choice!

"Stop jabbering. Cain, we'll wait here while you check up ahead."

"Yassuh, master, suh," Cain replied sarcastically, then mumbled something that sounded like, "Up yours, master, suh."

Meanwhile, Etienne leaned against a wall and used the time to clamp a palm over her tush, chuckling. "Have I told you, you have a wonderful ass?"

"About fifty times," she muttered, "and if you don't stop touching it, I'm going to dislocate yours. Geez, it's hot in this sheet, and your shoulder is growing bonier by the minute. Can't you put me down for a while?"

"No. And I'd be willing to wager you've let me touch it, and much more, in those dreams of yours." His persistence on the subject of her tush was remarkable, especially for a guy no longer attracted to her.

Her silence spoke volumes.

So did his.

"Stop smirking," she chastened him.

"How do you know I'm smirking?"

"I'm an expert on body language. I even wrote a book on it, *Bodyspeak*. I can tell by the posture of your body."

"I thought you were an expert on women's fantasies."

"I am. I'm an expert on lots of things."

"I'll bet you are, darlin'."

"You're smirking again."

"I know."

"I swear, you're at the top of the list in my next book."

He said nothing.

"Don't you want to know what my next book will be?"

"Not particularly."

His supposed lack of interest didn't deter her. *"The MCP Scale: How to Identify a Male Chauvinist Pig."* When he still didn't respond, she went on doggedly, "That's why I know so many dumb-men jokes. I intend to weave them throughout the book."

"What do shove-nest pigs have to do with dumb men and scales? And how do you weave a riddle?"

"Shove-nest? Huh? Oh." She laughed. "Not shove-nest. Chauvinist. A male chauvinist pig exhibits the ultimate in obnoxious, crude, swaggering, oversexed, egotistical behavior of all the male species. A walking ape."

"Who says I'm oversexed?"

"And furthermore, since I've known you, you've done a whole lot of things that fall into a ten on my MCP rating scale."

"A ten being the worst, I assume." He didn't sound at all offended by her assessment of him.

Before she could educate him further, Etienne's body went tense, and he pushed away from the wall. Harriet heard rushing footsteps then, followed by Cain's worried voice.

"The conductor's approaching . . . in the next car . . . two government men boarded the train in Memphis . . . a search is on for three bank robbers," he panted out.

"Bank robbers?" Etienne snorted.

"Bank robbers?" Harriet repeated into his back. *Great!* Now Steve was robbing banks, too.

"That's the story Pope gave the railroad people in order to conduct a search," Cain explained hurriedly.

Just then, Harriet heard a door opening up ahead, followed immediately by the crack of a sharp slap close by.

"That'll teach you, boy. Where you been hidin'?" Etienne barked to Cain, easing smoothly into one of his dialect changes. "I told you to come back and help me carry this body."

"What's the problem here, folks?" another voice inquired.

It didn't sound like the same conductor as before. *Thank goodness!* He might have recognized Etienne, despite his disguise. *Though why I should care is beyond me.*

"No problem now, sir. But there ain't nothin' worse than a lazy nigger," Etienne remarked. "What he needs is a good whuppin'."

Cain whimpered dolefully.

"Ain't it the truth?" the conductor concurred. "Whatcha got in that sheet?"

"A corpse," Etienne apprised him matter-of-factly as he hefted her off one shoulder and onto another while he reached inside his jacket. She had to bite her bottom lip to keep from crying out at the rough handling. "And the damn body's growin' heavier by the minute. Deadweight, you know?"

I'll give him deadweight.

The arm wrapped around her thighs squeezed tighter in warning as if sensing her imminent protest. "Here's my business card. Hiram M. Frogash, mortician, at your service. And this no-good blackie here is my assistant, Hip-pocrates Jones.''

"I's sorry, master. Don't you be needin' to whup my no-good hide again,'' Cain whined. "I be good from now on.''

"Hiram M. Frogash, mortician. Richmond, Virginia,'' the conductor read aloud. "You're a long way from home, ain'tcha?''

"Yes, sir. I got me a commission to dig up the remains of four Reb soldiers what died at Gettysburg. We're bring-in' 'em back to their families in Louisiana. The corpses are in coffins in the freight cars.''

"Oh. Then what's in the sheet?'' The conductor sounded rather suspicious. And they were wasting a lot of time, especially if bad guys really were searching the train. Or were they good guys? Harriet was confused, probably from all the blood pooling in her head.

Etienne laughed conspiratorially. "I picked up a little extra business in Memphis. Got off the train for a nature call—hell, a man gets mighty sick of pissing in a chamber pot—when I saw these men arguin' over who was goin' to take the dead body of Sally Mae Benson back to Baton Rouge. 'Pears the gal ran away from home before her sad demise.'' Etienne's voice softened to an appropriately dole-ful undertaker tone. "They gave me ten dollars to take her off their hands.''

"Ten dollars!'' the conductor exclaimed.

"Well, we'd best be gettin' Sally Mae on her way,'' Etienne said, patting her rump as he shoved something soft and small, like an item of clothing, up under the folds of her sheet, between her knees. Perhaps her panties or stock-ings, which would cause undue questions if Etienne got searched. "Don't want to be spreadin' no fever.''

"Fever!'' the conductor cried out, and seemed to step away.

"Sally Mae died a week ago. Can't you smell her?''
Smell?
"No. Oh, Lordy, yes, I do. I smell her now.''

72

Immediately, Harriet heard running feet and a door slamming as the conductor made a hasty exit. She sniffed. There was, indeed, a strong odor, like moldy cheese.

Following a brief silence, Etienne and Cain burst out with relieved laughter.

"Could we get a move on it here, guys?" she interjected, raising her head slightly off Etienne's back but unable to see through her sheet. "Unlike you two hyenas, I am not having fun."

Cain guffawed. "What *is* that smell?"

"One of your dirty socks."

Cain made a choking sound of protest.

It took only a second for the words to sink in. "Why, you rat!" If her arms weren't restricted at her sides, Harriet would have pounded Etienne's back. Instead, she squirmed madly, trying to shake the objectionable sock loose from between her knees.

As he started walking again, Etienne commented, "I think I'm beginning to understand body language now, Dr. Ginny. Every time you squirm, your breasts rub across my back. I'm getting a mighty clear message that you want—"

She stilled immediately. "Oooooh! That was a definite ten on the MCP scale."

"I aim to please," he countered affably.

She felt a breeze; so, they must be on the small platform connecting the trains. No wonder he felt free to talk. There were no people about to overhear.

"Dammit, Etienne, you choose the damnedest time to get your sense of humor back," Cain snarled. "There are passengers in this next car. And they would definitely find it scandalous to see a randy mortician talking to an overripe female cadaver."

"I am not randy," Etienne said.

"I am not overripe," Harriet added.

Then she heard the squeak of the door opening and the low mumble of voices in conversation up ahead.

"Make way, make way. The undertaker is passin' through," Cain chanted out.

Maybe I'm not dreaming. Maybe I really am dead, Harriet thought. *Maybe, when the train derailed, I died.*

Etienne placed his hand over her behind once again. Not to tease her this time, she sensed, but more to assure her not to worry about the buzz of conversation around them.

To Harriet's dismay, despite his being a chauvinist to the nth degree, all she could think about was the tingle of sweet pleasure that vibrated from the brute's fingertips out to all the erogenous zones in her body.

Nope, I am definitely not dead.

Just dumb.

A short time later, the three of them stood in a freight car, the one containing four long wooden boxes . . . caskets.

They'd been stopped two more times along the way, but Etienne and Cain had their mortician routines down pat. None of their interrogators had been from Pope's gang . . . yet. His men might not be so easily duped, Harriet feared.

"What's in these things anyway? Besides the gold?" Harriet asked, walking over to one of the coffins with her sheet wrapped loosely around her body, no longer comfortable flaunting herself before two men in her skimpy nightgown. Even in a dream. "Real dead bodies? Ha, ha, ha!"

"*Oui,* of course," Etienne said, coming up behind her. He and Cain had been whispering over in the corner. Making more stupid plans, no doubt. "At least, one of them does."

"What?" she squealed, jumping back.

Slipping a deadly looking knife from one of his boots, Etienne pried open one of the boxes to show her a skeleton.

Harriet shrieked with horror. "You guys are nuts! Where did you get that . . . that thing?"

"A traveling medicine show," Etienne replied dryly. "And it cost me a hundred damn dollars, too," he said as he pounded the lid shut again, then opened another. It appeared to be empty, until he showed her the fake bottom, which hid a fortune in gleaming gold. His heavy-lidded eyes watched closely for her reaction, still not sure she wasn't the enemy.

Her mouth dropped open. There were dozens of bullion bars marked U.S. MINT, PHILADELPHIA lining the base of the casket, and presumably just as much in each of the others. "How much?"

Etienne shrugged. "A hundred thousand dollars' worth."

"Did you really rob a bank?"

His jaw clenched angrily. "No."

"Did you kill anyone?"

His lips twitched as he fought a grin. "Not lately."

That was good enough for her, for now, anyhow. "Now what?"

Etienne made a slight bow to her from the waist with a hand extended to the open casket. "After you, my dear."

"Huh?"

"You and I are going to hide in this casket. Cain will stand guard." The black man—could he really be a physician?—was already crouched in one corner, settling in.

"Don't get too comfortable, Cain. You have to nail the lid shut after we're inside."

"That's right," Cain grumbled, and stood again.

Harriet's eyes widened as she tried to comprehend what Etienne was saying.

He started to climb into the open casket, then hesitated, looking at her. Holding her eyes, he made a great show of removing and folding his spectacles, then slipping them into a pocket in his jacket. And she remembered her earlier remark about men who wear glasses.

Oh, no! He couldn't possibly think I would—

"Do you prefer top or bottom, honey?"

Chapter Five

"Don't worry," Etienne assured the woman when she balked at draping her body over his, face-to-face, in an inadvertently sexual position. "I lost all my . . . uh . . . male urges in the war."

He gave himself a mental pat on the back when he managed to get the words out with a straight face. Especially considering the fact that her trim body was covered only by a little leopard-print chemise and some sinfully charming undergarment he'd returned to her, which she called *panties*.

She nodded with understanding at his disclosure about male urges.

Understanding? Lord, I must be a better actor than I'd thought. Or a liar. All those years as a double agent, I suppose. The Secret Service trains us well.

Cain snickered.

To his chagrin, the woman, who claimed to be a mind doctor, pursed her full, naturally red lips—which he refused to view as kissable—and furrowed her smooth brow in serious contemplation. Which was ludicrous, considering the fact that she was lying on top of him in an open coffin—a most unserious situation. Even he, who'd lost his sense of humor—though it was coming back by leaps and bounds—could see how absurd they must appear. But, no, now she was bracing her arms on either side of his neck and raising her head to study him better.

"Impotence?" she inquired solicitously.

Cain, who'd been about to replace the lid sealing them in, hooted with glee, muttering something about him being hoisted on his own petard. *More like, hoisted on my own pizzle.*

But impotence? He gurgled with speechlessness. This time the woman had gone too far. "No, I'm not im . . . impotent," he asserted, barely able to say the word. "I just don't have the . . . uh, inclination all that often." Well, that was partly true. Unlike Cain and Abel, he didn't feel the need to part the thighs of every female in sight these days. He attributed it to his greater maturity and discrimination.

"Low sex drive," Dr. Ginny diagnosed, bobbing her head in confirmation.

"Low . . . low . . ." he sputtered.

"Oh, God, I can't wait to tell Abel," Cain chortled.

"Men place entirely too much importance on their sex organs. Really. They need to laugh at themselves a bit more. For example, did you hear what the elephant said to the naked man?"

"I don't care what the elephant said to—"

"It looks fine but can it pick up peanuts?"

He choked with incredulity.

"Now, now, I'm a psychologist, remember? You don't have to be ashamed," the infuriating woman rattled on. *Good Lord!* She was giving him a diagnosis from a coffin. "I heard you mention Andersonville. I assume you were a prisoner of war. Lots of POWs suffer postwar syndrome, or post-traumatic stress disorder. Sexual dysfunction is one of the traits. I can recommend—"

"Put on the damn lid before I kill her," he said seethingly to Cain, who'd stopped laughing and was listening to the woman with professional curiosity. When it seemed as if Cain might engage her in a doctorly discussion, he grabbed the witch by the nape of her neck, shoved her face against his chest, and glared at Cain.

"When was the last time you had sex?" her muffled voice persisted.

"That is none of your affair."

"Do you masturbate to orgasm?"

"Aaarrgh!"

As the lid was being pounded down, he heard Cain ruminating aloud, "Impotence? Postwar syndrome? Hmmm."

The woman continued to babble on, throwing out words like "sexual therapy" and "test-ostrich-own" and "creative visualization." He'd never met a woman who could talk so much in all his life. Or throw out so many big words.

Meanwhile, she was sucking up all the air provided by the knothole Cain had punched out of the side of the pine box, and squirming around to get comfortable. Not that there was much room to squirm in the tight confines.

Suddenly she went stone still.

"What now?"

"That hard object prodding my stomach had better be a gold bar."

He smiled. At least now he knew how to shut her up.

"Are you smirking?"

"Can't you tell by my body language, Doctor?"

"Oh, yeah."

"If you'd lie still, this wouldn't happen."

"Can't you control yourself?"

"I'm trying."

"Not very hard."

"*Hard* enough," he remarked dryly.

"So much for your impotence."

"*Mon Dieu!* I never said I was impotent."

There followed a long silence. Long for her, anyhow.

"What are you thinking about now?" he asked. An unwise question, to be sure.

"My MCP scale."

"What? Did I just tip the scale again? I didn't do anything wrong . . . well, deliberately wrong."

"Getting an erection with a woman in a casket clearly falls within the guidelines of a male chauvinist pig."

He chuckled. "A ten?"

"More like a ten and a half."

"Well, for your information, that's not an erection. That's just a little minor interest. A reflex. If I were really aroused, you'd know it, sweetheart."

"Oh, God," she groaned. "I still don't see why we couldn't have separate caskets."

"Because there's gold in the other boxes, too, and not as much empty space. Because I don't want you out of my sight till I know who sent you. Because I enjoy having you molt your hair into my mouth. Because drowning in our combined perspiration is preferable to being shot in the back. Because you have the sweetest ass this side of Opelousas. Because—"

"Enough already!"

"You two had better stop talking," Cain cautioned. "Much as I'm captivated by your entertaining conversation, you won't be able to see if someone enters this car unexpectedly. And I won't be able to warn you once they're here. So, for God's sake, don't say another word unless I give you the password."

"You're right, of course," Etienne said contritely, shamed at the way he'd allowed the woman to distract him when distraction could spell danger to them all. *Merde!* He was trained to be more careful. What was happening to him? Perhaps the headaches were causing his mental functions to diminish. "What's the password, Cain?"

There was a short pause before Cain replied, "Rooster."

Etienne didn't have to see his friend to know he was smirking.

"Are you sure you two aren't delusional psychotics? Perhaps there aren't any real bad guys following you at all. Perhaps, with your severe distortion of reality, you've created a danger that doesn't even exist. Perhaps—"

"Shut up, Harriet."

"Oh, all right. If you don't want my advice . . ." The woman settled down then with a deep sigh, followed by a yawn. "I'm so tired. I feel as if I haven't had a good night's rest in ages. If I fall asleep, are you going to attack me in my dreams again?"

Etienne stiffened. "I have never attacked any woman . . . not sexually, anyway. The women I make love to . . . they do not fall asleep. Furthermore, you and I have never made love, in or out of a dream."

"Yeah, yeah, yeah," she murmured, clearly not accepting his claims. "Men with sexual inadequacies always overcompensate by bragging of prowess they don't have. The superstud syndrome."

He gritted his teeth. *Don't strangle her now. You'll have plenty of time later.*

"Don't worry, though." She patted his cheek in comfort. "Intercourse isn't the only sexual game in town. There are other methods of—"

"Stick out your tongue."

"Why?"

"So I can cut it out."

"Geez, why are you always so grumpy? Frustration? No, that can't be it. You've been getting enough satisfaction from me to last a lifetime. Hey, maybe that's why you're having trouble getting the little soldier to rise. You've been wearing yourself out with me in my dreams." She yawned again.

Grumpy? Little soldier? The woman had a death wish. Before he could react to her latest outlandish statement, her body slumped, and she fell into a deep slumber. Instantly. Like a rag doll.

He hadn't done that since he was an innocent boy, tired out from long days exploring his beloved Louisiana bayous. He almost envied her.

"Did you hear that conversation?" he whispered to Cain.

"No, I'm laughing too hard," Cain said softly. "How's your 'little soldier'?"

"Fine. How's yours?" he grumbled.

"Seriously, Etienne. Laughter aside . . . this woman is rather strange."

"Hah! Tell me something I don't already know."

"Who the hell is she?"

"Damned if I know."

"If we get out of this alive, I want to ask her a few questions about that postwar disease. So curb your temper. Don't kill her right away."

"If we get out of this alive, you'll have to stand in line to ask her questions. I reckon there will be a line of people wanting to kill her, too."

"What's that noise? Sounds like purring. Oh, I don't believe it. What are you doing to her?"

Etienne made a *tsk*ing exclamation. "Give me a little credit for good sense, Cain. She's snoring."

"Oh," Cain responded with obvious disappointment.

"How long do you think we'll have to stay in these grave boxes? It's hotter than blue blazes in here, and Harriet— that is the name she's using, isn't it?—might look like a small package, but she's getting heavier by the minute. I feel as if I'm covered with a hogshead of sugar."

"I don't know, Etienne. Probably till New Orleans . . . about six hours."

He groaned.

"Do you think Pope will come?"

"Never!" Etienne sneered. "The bastard delegates his dirty work. And he's probably not even the head of this operation."

Cain exhaled loudly with resignation. "Can you breathe well enough to last that long? Here, let me poke out another knothole from the opposite side. And try to sleep. No sense both of us keeping watch."

"I couldn't sleep," Etienne said, and proceeded to nod right off.

"How long you been here, nigger?"

The loud voice was immediately followed by a crash—probably a body slamming against the metal side of the freight car.

" 'Bout three hours, suh," Cain replied with a cry of pain. "Why'd you punch me? I ain't done nuthin'. Just mindin' my boss's business here, suh."

More punching, slapping noises and grunts of pain.

Etienne came instantly awake. *Three hours!* Normally, he was a light sleeper, attuned to the slightest rustle. How could he have conked out for so long? And how could he have not heard, immediately, the racket of men entering their hiding place?

"Have you seen three men skulking about?"

"Three men?" Cain echoed.

"Yes, one white man and two blacks. Thieves."

Etienne blinked in the darkness of his coffin and realized that moisture coated his eyelashes. In fact, his entire body was wringing wet. The closed coffin was hotter than a sugarhouse during the *roullaison* boiling season.

He put a hand to the back of Harriet's head, sensing in her rigid posture that she, too, had been awakened by the commotion. Her hair was plastered wetly about her head, dripping onto his chest. Skimming his palm lower, down her back, he found her little chemise to be a sopping film—probably transparent—covering her body. Now, that was a sight he wouldn't mind seeing . . . later. If they survived the next few hours.

He squeezed her shoulder to signal caution, and she nodded. They both listened.

"Who's your master, boy?"

"Mister Frogash, suh. But he ain't my master. No sirree, I's a free man. Mr. Lincoln said so."

Oh, no! Cain's hackles are raised now. He should know better than to react to mere words. Damn!

"Mr. Lincoln's dead," the first voice spat out with a cruel laugh, followed by another crash and the smack of flesh meeting flesh—from more than one set of fists, he'd wager. Listening carefully to the voices and placement of moving feet, Etienne concluded there were only two of them . . . thus far, anyhow.

"Yep, ol' Abe's eatin' maggots," the second man cackled, "an' you're gonna be joinin' him if you get uppity again, nigger. Do you understand?"

The only response from Cain was a moan. Then he gasped out, "Choking."

A short, mean laugh erupted from one of the men. Etienne recognized the sound of fabric passing quickly over metal and the thud of a heavy weight hitting the floor. Cain had probably slid to the floor when the thug released a choke hold on his throat.

Etienne would relish nothing more than to jump from his box and beat the two villains bloody, which was impossible with the nailed lid. Besides, they'd discussed the risks in detail. If one of them were in danger, the others were to consider the mission of more importance than any of their individual lives.

They'd worked together on other assignments before, for the Secret Service during and after the war, and now for President Grant directly. Cain had served well in "the doctors' line," a network of physician spies. Abel had entertained Rebel troops with his music in hotels and brothels throughout the South, where he'd picked up invaluable military information. And Etienne had been a much-prized double agent for four years before his incarceration, and an agent in the Secret Service since the war. But not much longer. Once they closed down this government corruption ring, he would be free and clear. And President Grant had promised to intercede on his behalf, releasing all the back pay for years spent as a double agent.

Yes, they had the procedure down pat, Etienne reminded himself, returning to the present. Carry no identification. Confess nothing. Avoid provocation of captors. Wait for the right opening. Never let emotion guide actions.

Besides, these men were probably just blustering bullies. A needless death wouldn't be the style of Pope's men. The dishonest ex–Secret Service agent wanted no bloody trail that might lead to him. And, more than anything, he'd want to recapture his gold.

Still, Etienne barely restrained himself from banging on the lid to help Cain.

"Who's your master?" the first man demanded again. "And what are you doin' back here? Stealin' property from good white folks' trunks, I reckon."

"No, suh, I's not a thief. I work for Mr. Frogash. He's a mortician."

"A mor-mortician," the second man stammered, clearly surprised.

"Yessuh. He has a fine funeral parlor in Richmond. We're taking those grave boxes back to Loo-zee-anna for burial. They's dead Confederate soldiers what died at Gettysburg. I's standin' watch till Mr. Frogash comes back from the dinin' car."

"Gettysburg, huh? Hell, it's no more'n them Johnny Rebs deserved," the first man said. "We shoulda shot 'em all. Left 'em for buzzard bait. Like we might just do for you, woolyhead."

Etienne's heart raced and raging blood boiled within him. It was Harriet who signaled caution now by gripping his shoulders, then placing a surprisingly gentle hand on his cheek in empathy.

He forced himself to calm down.

"Do you think we should check them out, Luther?" the

second man asked. The voices were closer to the caskets now.

Luther? It must be Luther Brisk. He's the meanest son of a bitch working for Pope. Learned all his dirty tricks riding with Sherman's Bummers.

Most people knew of "Sherman's Hairpins," the heated and deformed railroad tracks the general had left in his wake as he marched through the south, and "Sherman's Monuments," the chimneys that were the only remains of the civilian homes he had burned to the ground. But few talked about "Sherman's Bummers," the lawless gang who performed fiendish outrages as they followed on the flanks of the regular army.

"Oh, hell! I s'pose so," Brisk said. "That's the first thing Pope'll ask us...if we checked all the hidin' places."

"You're right," the second man agreed. "Come on over here, boy, and open these lids."

Without any warning, several loud gunshots reverberated through the freight car. Etienne suspected that the bullets had hit one of the coffins in front of them.

"What'ja do that for?" Cain whined.

"Just shooting me another Reb soldier," Brisk boasted.

"Lordy, Lordy, my boss is gonna have a hissy fit. Them pine caskets cost good money to build. You splintered the wood on that one worse'n a Virginny woodpecker."

The woman began to shiver with terror. He placed a hand over her back and patted her in reassurance, though he had to admit he wasn't feeling too calm himself. Especially when he heard Cain rise and shuffle over toward them.

"Mr. Frogash ain't gonna be too happy 'bout this, no sirree."

"Shut up," the second man snapped. "Now open the damn box so we can get on with our business."

A squeaky noise followed, as Cain pried up the nails, one after another, in the nearest casket. He and Harriet were in the one at the back of the car.

"Godamighty!" Brisk exclaimed as Cain presumably lifted the lid. It sounded as if he'd jumped back.

"Holy thunderation! It really is a Reb soldier. And take a gander at that bullet hole in his jacket, right over the heart, and the bloodstain."

"The Yankee that downed this one musta been a crack shot," Brisk observed with morbid enthusiasm.

"Should we open the other ones?"

"I dunno. Let's look in these trunks first," Brisk said.

"Oh, Lordy!" Cain muttered. "You shouldn't be openin' people's private property."

"Shut up, nigger," Brisk snarled again, "and do as you're told."

Etienne felt the body pressing down on him begin to tremble and he knew, he just knew that Harriet was about to scream. Panic had a way of turning the brain to mush, as he well knew. He'd screamed himself on more than one occasion.

She made a little squeaky whimper, presaging a full-blown howl to come.

He clamped a hand over her mouth, moving it only when he felt her body relax.

"What was that?" Brisk asked.

"Rats," Cain answered with his usual quick thinking. "They're attracted by the corpses. That's why my boss wanted me to stand guard."

The other man gagged.

"Damn, Franklin, you must have the weakest stomach in the world. How can you strangle a man without blinking, and lose your breakfast over a puny dead body?"

"It's the rats," Franklin choked out.

Etienne understood only too well about the rats and Franklin's horror of the vermin. With a shudder, he banked his repulsive memories and honed in on the name *Franklin*. So, it was Luther Brisk and "Mad Brad" Franklin. Not too bad. He and Cain could handle these low-level ex-agents. But Pope surely had more of his men—those sharper and more adept at spy-catching—waiting for them down the line. This was only one danger they had to face.

Harriet chose that moment to go rigid, her heart pounding rapidly against his—*thud, thud, thud*. He was surprised everyone didn't hear. She raised her head slightly at the same time he placed a hand on her jaw and felt her mouth begin to open.

Acting quickly, Etienne took steps to stop her scream. Sensing protest, he imprisoned both of her wrists in his one hand, behind her back, and he snaked both of his legs around her calves, locking her in place. Then he moved his other hand to her nape and clamped her mouth over his in a rough kiss.

It was the most dispassionate of kisses, the most unsexual embrace.

At first.

While Brisk and Franklin rummaged through the clothing and personal articles in the trunks, Etienne loosened his pressure on Harriet's neck, still holding her firm but allowing for movement. He shifted the position of his face so their lips were slanted for a better fit. With a silent groan of pleasure, he moved his mouth against her lips, shaping and coaxing till she parted for him.

"They must have jumped off the train right after Memphis," Brisk concluded with disgust. "Hell, we've checked every damn car on this train."

Etienne ran his tongue along the seam of her lips, tasting. Then slowly . . . ever so slowly . . . he tortured himself with the exquisite pastime of riposte and retreat. And, damn, but his sword was made for her welcoming sheath. Instantly, he was on fire, but not from the temperature. He wanted the woman with a fierce need. And all he'd done was kiss her thus far.

"If they jumped off, what do you think they did with the gold?" Franklin wondered.

Etienne barely registered the words through the blinding haze of his passion. Especially since the witch in his arms

87

was reciprocating his deep kiss, pressing her little cat tongue in and out of his mouth in counterpoint to his own strokes. And, damn, Abel had been right. It was abrasive.

"Franklin, your skull's gotta be thicker'n a fence post. They wouldn't be dumb enough to bring so much gold on a train!"

"You think you know everything, Brisk. They could have brought it on board, easy. Why, it could even be in those caskets over there."

"Well, then, why don't you just go on over and open 'em up? 'Cause I ain't rummagin' through a bunch of bones."

Etienne stiffened at the renewed danger, though how he'd managed to hear the new threat amazed him. The woman was drawing rhythmically on his tongue, which he'd just discovered had an invisible, inner connection to another body part. Every time she sucked, it pulsed. Could a man die from ecstasy?

"And bottle flies," Cain interjected. "Don't forget the bottle flies."

"Huh?" the two men exclaimed.

"The other bodies are still ripe. Them cold northern winters must preserve a body some, I reckon. Last I checked, they was covered with those pesky bottle flies."

Franklin gagged again, and Brisk spat with revulsion.

The war had been over for five years, and the Battle of Gettysburg had taken place two years before that. If these two dunderheads were thinking, they'd know corpses would have long dried out and withered to dust by now.

"Let's get the hell out of here," Franklin suggested.

Brisk must have agreed, because Etienne heard departing footsteps, then Brisk giving Cain one final parting shot. "If you see those men . . . or anything suspicious . . . you come get me right away. You hear me, boy?"

"Yessuh," Cain replied docilely.

Etienne almost shot up against the lid of the coffin when the woman, who now moved her lips slickly against his from side to side, added a new facet to her assault. She was moving her hips against him with little jerky spasms.

Or am I the one assaulting her?

Who cares?

Not me.

Etienne couldn't remember the last time he'd been so hard and eager. Excitement throbbed throughout his body, centering on his sex and rippling outward in waves.

It must be madness.

Breaking the kiss, he fought for control, panting into her ear. He still held her firmly by the neck with one hand, her hands imprisoned behind her with his other hand and her legs enveloped by his thighs.

He should release her now.

He smiled against her ear. He wasn't that mad yet.

Harriet was absolutely terrified and burning up with arousal. This was the worst of her sexual dreams thus far. In the past, she'd never been so wanton and needful. Steve had been the aggressor, she the passive recipient of his raging passions.

She was practically melting in the close confines of the hot casket. Maybe it was just the heat generated by the tight space and the high outside temperatures of the semitropical South.

No, she had to be honest. The rogue in the undertaker's suit was responsible for her present dilemma. The one who was licking the whorls of her ear and then—*oh, mercy!*—thrusting the hot tip of his tongue in and out with erotic rhythm.

She sighed. She couldn't resist him, even in the midst of danger, although she was pretty sure the two psychopaths attacking Cain had left. But even if they hadn't, she was beyond rational thought. Locked in Steve's . . . rather Etienne's . . . tight embrace, Harriet couldn't move. She was a prisoner to the tantalizing sensual ravishment, and was not surprised when the ache between her legs began to grow under the seductive foreplay.

At first, she thought the blinding light resulted from the overpowering orgasm that pounded out from her center in increasingly stronger waves as Etienne bucked his erection against her. Short strokes because of their space limitations, but hard.

His rasp of sweet torment broke the silence, and that was what pushed Harriet over the edge. Arching her neck back, she cried out her release.

"Well, if that don't beat all. No wonder you two didn't hear the password. I said 'rooster' so many times, hens from miles around are cluckin' to high heaven. They heard me, but not you two cotton brains."

Harriet blinked, adjusting to the harsh light after being in the dark for so long. Raising her head slightly, she gazed down at Etienne, whose passion-misty eyes regarded her with bafflement. She could sympathize with his confusion. This instant chemistry between them was a puzzle to her, too.

And, golly, even in his sweat-soaked condition, with his black hair hugging his head wetly, he was heart-wrenchingly handsome.

Was that swelling of his lips from her kisses? Was that bite mark on his neck from her teeth? Was the tense set of his jaw a sign of the arousal that still racked his body?

"Whoo-ee! So this is the forceful seduction the wench has been harping about," Cain whooped, pointing at Harriet's still restrained hands and legs. Etienne loosened his grip, as if her flesh suddenly scorched him.

Addressing Etienne, Cain inquired, "Was it as good as it appeared?"

A lazy male smile spread across Etienne's face as he came slowly back to the present. "Better," he drawled. "Much better." He winked at her.

With utter mortification, Harriet became aware of her position and what she'd just done. She hid her face against Etienne's chest, which was rumbling with laughter now. Whether at his own actions or hers, she couldn't be sure.

Cain muttered something about roosters coming back from the dead.

"Are you all right?" Etienne asked Cain, suddenly remembering the beating they'd heard from the casket. He sat up in the box, taking Harriet with him to rest on his lap.

"I'll be fine," Cain said, "though I wouldn't mind being the one in the coffin next time." He waggled his eyebrows at Harriet, whose damp nightie left little to the imagination.

Embarrassed, she buried her face again in Etienne's shirtfront.

"Are you sure?" Etienne questioned as he automatically pulled off his jacket, wrapping it around her. "You're going to have quite a black eye and a swollen lip."

Cain shrugged. "The worst is my ribs, but I think they're only roughed up a bit, not broken. I'll check later." Then Cain said he was going to go see if he could find some food and water. "I don't think Brisk and Franklin will be comin' back, at least not right away. But be careful anyway."

Etienne nodded in agreement.

When Cain was gone, Harriet rose from the casket. The jacket parted in the process, exposing her wet nightie.

Etienne's eyes about bugged out, and he gasped for breath.

Harriet couldn't be concerned about modesty now. She had a much more important problem. All her principles were shot to hell. Dr. Harriet Ginoza had just succumbed, willingly, to forceful seduction with an oversexed ape in a coffin. "I just want you to know," she said in a strangled voice, "that I don't usually do things like this."

"It was a first for me, too, darlin'." Etienne was standing beside the coffin, trying to adjust the bulge in front of his trousers. The man had no shame at all.

"I haven't been with a man for a long time . . . except for you, in my dreams. That must be why—"

He raised an eyebrow at her. "How long?"

91

She blushed. "Two years."

"Two years! I thought six months was a long time for me!"

"Anyhow"—she gulped—"I've never done anything like this before. And my only explanation is that I was . . . I was . . ."

"Deprived?" He grinned at her discomfort.

"No, deranged is more like it." Harriet cringed with humiliation. He wasn't making this easy for her.

His eyes were raking her clinging leopard-print nightie every time the jacket flapped open. Somehow, the jacket's contrast with the nightie created an even more titillating image.

Harriet realized she had to cover herself better before Etienne decided to do something about that bulge. Right now. On the floor. With Cain coming back any moment. And, considering the way her heart continued to race, she feared that she might just welcome him.

Scanning the old freight car, Harriet took in the gowns and button-hook shoes on the floor and spilling from antique trunks. Some Southern lady was going to be awfully peeved at this mess.

But, no, this is a dream, she reminded herself.

She noticed the whoosh of air coming from the open door of the freight car and scanned the passing countryside. Not a skyscraper or modern building in sight.

A weird thought niggled inside her head.

The sound of the train chugging along hummed in her ears. *Choo-choo, choo-choo, choo-choo, choo-choo . . .*

The thought niggled stronger.

She turned then to Etienne, who was wiping perspiration from his face and hair with a shirt he'd picked up from the floor.

"What year is this?" she asked hesitantly.

His eyes widened with surprise. "Eighteen seventy."

She closed her eyes and moaned softly. The niggling thought unfurled, like a banner, into an outlandish idea.

When she opened her eyes again, Etienne was staring at her oddly, taking in her near-naked appearance with raw, masculine interest, which he quickly masked with a frown.

"This isn't a dream, is it?" she whispered.

"Really, your continual prattling about dreams is tiresome. And very unoriginal." Now that he'd gotten his arousal under control, he was picking carefully through the clothing in the trunks and tossing various items toward her—a pale marbled lavender gown with a tight bodice and full, stiff underskirt of a deeper purple; a pair of black velvet slipper shoes; a straw hat with lavender satin ribbons; ivory combs; even a frilly parasol. "Put them on," he demanded.

When she handed his jacket back to him, he hung it and his shirt to air dry on a nail near the doorway. Meanwhile, he wiped his perspiration-damp body with another clean shirt from the floor. The men's apparel was plainly too small for his much larger frame.

Harriet clutched a fringed shawl in front of her, fighting back tears of panic. All the niggling thoughts and ideas in her head were too much for her to handle in her distraught state. What she was thinking, what she now feared, it just couldn't be possible. Could it?

Etienne snorted at the woman's belated delicacy. As if he hadn't seen all she owned already in that wet, nearly invisible chemise. The flimsy shawl only called to mind what he'd already viewed. He forced himself to look away from her enticing body, but he couldn't force away the memory of how that body had felt in his arms a short time ago. How she'd responded to his kiss. How he'd bloomed hot and hard within seconds. How—

"You don't understand. This is 1997. It has to be," she whimpered.

Startled, Etienne turned back from where he'd moved to lean against the doorway, inhaling deeply of the fresh air. He lifted his eyebrows scornfully. What game did she play now? "No, my dear, it is not. This is 1870. Of that I am certain."

"I'm not saying it's not. Eighteen seventy, I mean. It's just that I come from 1997. Oh, don't look at me like that. I have no idea what's happening to me, or why, but I'm not crazy. All I know is that after the train derailed, everything around me changed. It's almost as if . . . as if the train derailment opened a door to another century."

His eyes widened. "Oh, darlin', surely you can come up with a more plausible explanation. Because if you don't, that means you have some devious reason for being here, and I'm going to have to kill you." Etienne spoke the truth. If she was a spy, working with Pope, he might very well have to commit murder. His mission was more important than any mere woman.

The nitwit waggled her fingers in the air, waving his threat aside as of no consequence. Obviously she was unafraid of him, but at the same time, it was equally obvious that the bizarre circumstances surrounding them shook her composure.

"Do you think God sent me here?" she asked, as if desperately grasping for answers.

Huh? "For what reason?" he scoffed.

"I don't know." She groaned. "Maybe as a punishment for succumbing to those horrible dreams about you."

He gave a short laugh of derision. *Oh, wonderful! She's back to the sexual fantasy again. Lord, she's like a yipping puppy clinging to a man's pant leg when she gets an idea in her head. She could wear a man down with her nagging.* "God is punishing you by sending you through time to be with me? Seems to me as if I would be the one punished in that hellish scenario."

She scowled at his interpretation of her words. "Don't be silly."

Etienne narrowed his eyes at her. It was the second time she'd called him silly, and the word didn't sit well with him.

"Let me explain this in real simple terms," she said slowly, as if speaking to a moron.

He gritted his teeth.

"I've been praying for those pesky dreams to stop. I'm a grown woman . . . a trained psychologist, for heaven's sake. I should be above erotic fantasies of"—she gave him a disdainful assessment that put him in the same class as frog spit—of forceful seduction.

Not that again.

"One of the best ways to overcome an addiction is to face it head-on, wallow in it till its ugliness overshadows its appeal," she blathered on, this time in her lecturer mode. "Yep, I think God answered my prayers. He sent me here for the cure."

Etienne put both hands on his hips and gaped at her. *I'm a cure for what ails her?* Harriet averted her eyes, but not before he noticed her quick glance of appreciation at his bare shoulders and chest—a glance that followed the path of black curls leading down in a vee to the waistband of his trousers.

A slow grin began to replace his frown. "You're upset about some sexual fantasy you've been having of late, with me as a partner? And you think the answer is for us to make love, over and over, till you're sick of me?"

"Yes," she said enthusiastically, clearly pleased that he agreed with her.

"Lady, I've been propositioned by all kinds of women, in all kinds of places . . . even some that were mighty peculiar. But I have never, *ever*, had a woman beg for my lovemaking as an exorcism."

"So?" she said, tapping her foot impatiently.

She probably yearned to clout him a good one, but was restraining herself to stay in his good graces. Till he could play stud to her perverted whims. *Merde!* "Thank you, but . . . no, thank you." He made the mistake of laughing then.

With a growl of outrage, the red-faced witch unrestrained

herself, and before he could react, whacked him on the side of the head with a lace parasol.

It didn't help that she whisked her hands together and remarked, "Laughing at a woman is a six on the MCP scale, you jerk."

Chapter Six

"Sweetheart, this is M'sieur Gautier," Etienne said with the slick charm of a snake-oil salesman. "M'sieur, may I present my wife, Mrs. Frogash. She's . . . mute."

Mute? Harriet bit her bottom lip to stifle the impulse to tell her "husband" what she thought of his latest lame-brained scheme. Not that she hadn't already voiced her opinion to him repeatedly in the hour since they'd left the train. But, considering the fact that she'd knocked him practically unconscious, for a second time, and that Cain had arrived just in time to prevent her being strangled after Etienne woke up, Harriet decided that silence might be warranted . . . for a while.

Except that if she didn't talk, she'd have to think. And if she thought for even a second, she'd have to face the reality of the nightmare she'd landed in. And accept that it wasn't a dream, after all.

Could it be time-travel?

No, no, no! I don't want to think about that insanity.

Etienne, back in his undertaker mode—hair center-parted

and slicked back with Macassar oil, spectacles, the whole nerd nine yards—waxed doleful—over her being his mate, or mute, she wasn't sure—as he introduced her to Vincent Gautier, the owner of a warehouse near the railway station in New Orleans. But the speaking glance he cast her way was anything but doleful. It said, loud and clear, "Say one word and you are dead meat, babe."

"Gaaa," she gurgled, a la Helen Keller, in greeting to Mr. Gautier, ignoring Etienne's warning glower.

"Madame Frau-gawsh," Mr. Gautier acknowledged with a polite bow of his head in her direction, apparently understanding her wordless hello. Then he patted Etienne on the arm with sympathy.

And Etienne—the jerk—confided to the man, loud enough for her to hear, "Deaf *and* dumb."

"Fuggu," she grunted to Etienne in a guttural comeback.

The flash of surprise, then irritation, in his baby blues told her that he knew just what she'd said. "Later, darling," he promised sweetly and made a little slicing gesture across his neck that only she could see.

The late-morning sun beat down unmercifully on Harriet as she sat perched on a seat of the buckboard-type wagon they'd used to cart the caskets of gold from the freight car. The lavender walking dress Etienne had given her to wear was a magnificent confection with a rounded neck and cap sleeves—pure Southern femininity, and hotter than hell. Her only protection from the sun's rays was the whimsical straw hat with ribbon streamers. Etienne had taken the parasol away from her, deeming it a weapon.

Etienne and Mr. Gautier were back to negotiating their business arrangement, a conversation conducted in rapid, hand-gesturing French. Finally, Etienne pushed his spectacles up on his nose—*Geez, he's a doll, even with glasses and that stupid center part*—and fished a roll of antiquated paper currency from his pocket. Peeling off several bills, he handed them to the warehouse owner.

Meanwhile, Cain and one of Mr. Gautier's workers were

unloading the caskets and carrying them inside. Harriet put a hand over her heart in dismay as she watched Cain wince when he hefted one end of a heavy casket onto his shoulder. In the short time Pope's men had been there, they'd worked him over horribly. Two bruised ribs, which Cain had instructed Etienne on wrapping with tight strips of linen from some lady's crinoline, a black eye which was already swollen shut, bruises on his back and arms, and an ugly cut on his chin from Brisk's beringed fist.

But Cain dismissed her concern and quipped, "Don't pay no never mind to these li'l bruises. At least they didn't loosen my teeth. One thing my women are right partial to is a full . . . set of teeth." He'd wiggled his eyebrows at her then. *The rogue!*

Business concluded and gold safely stashed, the *two* rogues now climbed up onto the seat of the empty wagon, bracketing her between them. Clicking his tongue, Etienne gave the reins a brisk shake, then exchanged a worried, silent look with Cain.

"Let's make tracks. I have a bad feeling," Etienne said, using a short whip lightly on the horse's rump.

"Me, too," Cain said as his eyes made a wide sweep of the busy street.

"Au revoir," Mr. Gautier called after their departing wagon.

Harriet turned and waved a hand at Mr. Gautier in a limp-and-languid, exaggerated Scarlett style. The idea for a new book was already churning in her brain—*The Scarlett Syndrome: Southern Body Language.*

"Merde!" Etienne muttered, gawking at her as if she were two mint leaves short of a julep.

Ignoring him, Harriet whispered to Cain, "What does *merde* mean?"

"Shit." Cain's terse reply was accompanied by a grin.

"Tsk-tsk!" She elbowed Etienne in the ribs reprovingly. "You should appreciate the fact that, since I landed in Southern belle hell, I'm trying to adapt . . . act the part. You know, when in Rome, do as the Romans do."

"Hmpfh! Now she thinks she's in Italy."

"Y'all come on over to Tara sometime, darlin'," she drawled in further demonstration, batting her eyelashes. "Ah do declare, ah might just swoon."

Etienne shook his head at her antics.

"So, husband dear, what do you think of my South mouth?"

"I liked you better mute."

"Oh, you can't fool me. You act annoyed, but you're really turned on by me."

"Hah! When gators roost in trees!"

"And I amuse you. Yes, I do. Don't deny it. I can read your hidden body signals."

"Read this signal," he snapped with exasperation. And the gesture he flicked at her was not nice.

"What's a sure sign that a dumb man is going to be unfaithful?"

"I warned you about those dumb-men riddles, Harry-Hat," Etienne gritted out.

"And I told you my name is Harriet."

"So, what's a sure sign that a dumb man is going to be unfaithful?" Cain asked, pulling her back to her joke.

"If he has a penis," Harriet said.

Etienne and Cain both gasped.

"You should know the answer to this one, Cain . . . being a doctor and all. What do you call the soft, fleshy tissue surrounding a penis?"

Cain seemed to be seriously considering her question.

"A man," she hooted.

"Harriet, nice girls . . . *ladies* . . . don't ever say that word out loud," Etienne told her with exaggerated patience.

"What word. *Penis?* Oh, give me a break. Penis, penis, penis, penis. There! Did the sky fall down?"

"She has a point, Etienne," Cain said. "When you think about all the rules that society imposes on—"

"*Mon Dieu*, we have two sorry lunatics with guns close on our tails, who knows how many more closing in for the kill, and her tongue won't stop flapping with nonsensical jokes. And my best friend decides to jump on her side."

She was about to tell the ingrate off, but he stopped the wagon abruptly in a narrow alley a short distance from the warehouse. Without talking, he and Cain quickly took their gun belts and weapons from the satchel in back and strapped them on.

Alarmed, Harriet stood. "Etienne, don't you think—"

"Damn to blue blazes! Sit still and hush your mouth."

"But—"

"Mind what I say, or I swear I'll hog-tie and gag you faster'n you can say your prayers."

"You wouldn't dare," Harriet said, but she stayed put and decided to ignore the jerk and pay more attention to the sights, perhaps find some insight into her odd adventure. Etienne soon had the horse moving them into the city proper—the Vieux Carré.

Harriet knew the area well. The picturesque French Quarter of old New Orleans, nestled at the inner curve of the wide Mississippi, was laid out in a block pattern with more than a dozen streets leading from the river to Rampart Street and a smaller number crisscrossing from Canal Street to Esplanade. The famous Place d'Armes, later called Jackson Square, and the Cathedral of St. Louis, sat directly at its center. The wide streets were bordered by brick sidewalks, or banquettes, with lovely shade trees.

The Creole homes that abounded there, removed from the newer American sector, were two-or three-story affairs with overhanging roofs and wide galleries ornamented with the famous iron lace—cast iron formed into delicate decorations. Tall shutters—mostly forest green—protected the mysterious interiors and hid the bubbling fountains of the center courtyards, while the exteriors boasted such gay colors as grand rouge, which came from a combination of brick dust and buttermilk.

Etienne and Cain grew more and more tense as they scanned the busy streets. And the fine hairs stood out all over Harriet's body as she was forced, despite her best efforts, to accept her new surroundings. She saw nothing but men in Yankee blue army uniforms or nineteenth century–style suits and work clothes, or females in long gowns, some of plain homespun materials, other, fancier outfits beribboned and flounced with expensive fabrics. The black women wore kerchief-style turbans. The whole scene was authentic down to the finest fringed parasol and the most intricate opaline buttons.

Instead of the usual cars and tour buses seen in the center of the city, only horses and horse-driven omnibuses were in evidence. An occasional mule or ox pulled produce-laden wagons toward the French Market or the ships docked near the Mississippi levee.

What does it mean? No, I can't deal with this now.

Blindly, she sought for some way to break the strained silence and avoid the inevitable truth. "One of my stepfathers, Vincent Lafour, is from Louisiana. My family lived outside the city, near Lake Ponchartrain, when I was eight years old," she said irrelevantly.

Neither Etienne nor Cain responded to her disclosure . . . at first.

"Over there," Etienne told Cain. "Did you see Brisk going into the Cabildo?"

Cain nodded, his face grim. "He'll have the sheriff bird-dogging us in no time. Let's get out of here."

Back on their wagon seats, Etienne shook the reins, directing the horse in the opposite direction from the jail.

"Somebody had better give me a gun or a knife," Harriet decided.

"I wouldn't trust you with any weapon."

"Are you still pouting over that little bop I gave you with my umbrella?"

"No, I'm pouting over the *two* 'little bops' you gave me. Be forewarned, darlin', I intend to pay you back, bop for bop. After I've tortured all your secrets out of you. And believe me, I know some very interesting torture techniques.''

I'll bet you do, honey. I've experienced a few of them already. "I'm not afraid of you."

"That's because you're demented."

"Besides, you've been torturing me for weeks with that forceful seduction routine of yours."

"Well, wait till I hang you upside down from a tree and slather buttermilk all over your naked body."

Cain leaned forward to scrutinize Etienne with astonishment. The grin he gave his friend translated into a twentieth-century version of, "Way to go!" Normally, it would be accompanied with a high five.

"Buttermilk?" she squeaked. "I hate buttermilk."

"You're not the one who'll be licking it," Etienne informed her coolly.

Licking? Every erogenous zone in Harriet's body came alive. "That's a five, buster," she blustered. "Keep it up, and I'll be able to fill my whole book with your macho, sexist tripe."

"My pleasure to oblige," he snickered.

"Ahem," Cain coughed to halt their ill-timed bickering. Then, in a deliberate attempt to change the subject, he picked up the thread of Harriet's earlier conversation, asking, "*One* of your stepfathers lived here?"

Harriet gave Etienne one last scowl and shifted away from him slightly to show her distaste for even the brush of his shoulder. Then she smiled at Cain, indicating he wasn't quite as much of a creep as his friend, and explained, "Yes, my mother was married five times. In fact, her marriage to Vincent lasted only two years, but I came back to Louisiana lots of times to visit with my sisters, Sheila and Blanche, who are Vincent's daughters."

As she thought back now, the gentle Cajun restaurateur was one of the few stable influences in her young, shaky life and that of her two younger sisters. Their summer vacations with him had represented much more than child-hood visits.

She started to ask if they'd ever been in Vincent's lake-side restaurant, but stopped herself when she realized that, of course, they couldn't have. It hadn't even been built yet.

Or had it?

Oh, God!

"And how many times have you wed?" Etienne asked, although he didn't seem particularly interested.

For some reason, his indifference bothered Harriet. Didn't he even care that she might be involved with another man? For all he knew, she was married. And how about him? Oh, geez, what if he was married? What if she'd been making out with a married man in a casket? That made her indiscretion even worse.

"Are you married?" she snapped, more brusquely than she'd planned.

"No," he said, his tone redolent with distaste.

"Ever?"

"Never." He laughed.

She breathed an inner sigh of relief, feeling an inordinate pleasure at his single word.

"You didn't answer my question," Etienne reminded her. "How many times have you been wed?"

"None," she answered. "My mother's husband-hopping taught me one thing . . . never depend on a man for my identity. Be independent. Financially and personally. Always in control."

"Sounds logical," Cain assured her with a pat on the knee.

"Sounds boring," Etienne said at the same time. If *he* dared to pat her knee, she swore she would break his hand.

She glanced at said hand, holding the reins loosely, and noticed he had a missing fourth appendage. "How did you lose your finger?" she asked bluntly. "Did you stick your hand in the cookie jar at the wrong moment?"

Cain inhaled sharply, and Etienne stiffened.

At first, she didn't think Etienne was going to reply. Eventually, he shrugged. "Someone wanted my ring."

Cain squeezed her knee in caution, but Harriet blundered on. "Someone cut off your finger to get a ring?"

Etienne looked at her then, and she reeled at the brief pain that flared in his luminous eyes, immediately replaced with contempt. "The man . . . a Confederate guard at Andersonville . . . thought I was dead. I'd been mistakenly put on the refuse pile with the corpses." His voice was cold.

Andersonville Prison? Harriet felt awful. "Oh . . . oh, Etienne! I'm sorry. I shouldn't have asked. It's just that –"

"Have you ever been covered with maggots?" he went on. "God, that swampy hellhole was a breeding paradise for the slimy suckers. They grew to an ungodly size, and they were everywhere. In our beds, our food, our hair, up our noses, in our ears . . ." His words faded off as he realized how much he'd revealed.

And Harriet couldn't speak for the tears that choked her throat. Without thinking, she laced her right hand with his left one, the one with the missing finger, and refused to let him tug away. In the end, he relaxed and they lapsed into silence again.

She imagined, with impossible logic, that their hearts communicated at that spot where their two wrists pulsed against each other. As if in confirmation, Etienne jerked his hand suddenly, his eyes locking with hers in question. She held tight, needing a connection with someone familiar in this strange world she'd entered. At least, that was why she told herself she held his hand so tightly. A familiar soul . . . that was all Etienne represented to her.

Familiar? Harriet gazed about her once again. Alarm shook her as she was forced to accept the fact that, while she was familiar with all the nooks and crannies of the Crescent City, what she saw now was in no way familiar. She recognized the typical Louisiana assault on the senses— myriad smells, vivid colors, shimmering heat, raucous sounds—and yet this New Orleans was vastly different from the one she knew. It was a city shabby with neglect from years of wartime occupation and Reconstruction poverty, but now undergoing a major overhaul by carpenters, masons and painters, no doubt from Northern carpetbag money.

It was a living nightmare.

But, unfortunately, it wasn't a dream. Harriet knew that now. Too much time had passed. It was all too real.

With a droop of resignation, Harriet inspected her companions further. Their tense demeanor bespoke the danger that still hovered over them like a black cloud.

But Harriet couldn't obsess over the supposed danger from Pope's men, or government agents, or the whole gold theft situation. She was more concerned, and more frightened, than she'd ever been in all her life, about a different kind of danger. In shock, Harriet had tried to avoid thinking about the unbelievable evidence assaulting her at every turn, ever since Etienne had told her more than two hours ago that this was 1870. But the reality of her time-travel, or whatever it was, blasted her at every turn. She had to accept facts.

Somehow, some way, she had landed in another century.

If Harriet hadn't been convinced before, she was now, as the colorful, post–Civil War city unfolded before her with infinite, way-too-authentic detail.

"Is this really 1870," she whimpered.

Etienne clucked his displeasure and shook off her hand.

Cain turned to her with surprise. "Yes, it's 1870. Why do you ask?"

She hadn't realized she'd spoken aloud.

"She claims to come from the year 1997," Etienne informed him dryly. "On a broom, no doubt."

"No, a train," she said. "And it's not funny."

Both men were grinning.

"I've been thinking about this, and I've come to the conclusion that my time-travel, or whatever it is, has something to do with the train derailment and that railroad bridge over the river that you told me hadn't been built yet."

"Huh?" Cain said.

"She claims to have been on a 1997 train that runs straight through from Chicago to New Orleans," Etienne explained to Cain.

"Well, that will be possible when the railroad bridge is completed later this year," Cain pointed out.

"Oh, God! That's it," Harriet exclaimed, feeling a ray of hope for the first time since she'd fallen through this time hole.

Etienne put a hand to his forehead. She'd probably given him another headache. "Please, Cain, I beg you, don't ask—"

"What is *it*?" Cain asked.

"—her what she means." Etienne continued to rub his forehead, being careful to avoid the goose egg.

"Don't you see, all I have to do is board that train when it takes its first nonstop ride back to Chicago. Somehow, I just know that's the key to my return to the future. When will that be?"

"The end of October, I think," Cain said.

"Two months! What am I going to do here for two whole months?" Suddenly she brightened. "I know. I'll take lots of notes. Think of all the books I'll be able to write. Maybe this nightmare isn't really a nightmare, after all. I should consider this an opportunity." She smiled brightly at both frowning men.

Neither Etienne nor Cain looked any more convinced than if she'd said she came from the moon.

"There's a new insane asylum in Chicago, Etienne. I visited the facility yesterday. Perhaps she escaped from there."

"You visited a hospital yesterday?" Etienne inquired with raised eyebrows. "I thought you and Abel spent the day in bed with those whores at the opera house."

"Only half the day."

"I think that's where she came from, Cain. Madame Dubois's Opera House. She told me she was at the opera house. Are you sure you didn't see her there? Maybe let something slip about our . . . work?"

"Good heavens! And you two think I'm nuts?" Harriet interjected. "No, I'm not insane. And I never said I was a prostitute at some opera house. I said I was on the Oprah show."

"Oh. What did you do at this . . . Oprah show?" Cain wanted to know. "Madame Dubois puts on a show with an Egyptian girl who's so limber she can dance and . . . ah, fornicate at the same time. Her backbend is something to behold. I don't suppose you . . . ?"

Etienne's lips twitched with suppressed mirth.

"Aaarrggh!" Harriet screeched. "Will you two listen? Something strange happened. I am a psychologist . . . Dr. Harriet Ginoza. I was on the train from Chicago to New Orleans—where I was supposed to give a lecture today related to my new book—"

"What new book?" Cain asked, his forehead creased with puzzlement.

"Don't ask," Etienne advised him.

"*Female Fantasies Never Die.*"

"Too late," Etienne groaned.

"Really?" Cain remarked, clearly interested. "What fantasies might those be?"

"That's irrelevant. As I was saying . . . I was on the train. There was a minor derailment. I woke from one of those blasted dreams of mine"—she cast Etienne a condemning glare—"and next thing I knew it was 1870."

Etienne and Cain exchanged a look that said, "Yep, insane asylum."

"I know that time-travel's impossible," she went on, "although now that I think about it, I had a client a few years ago who claimed to have traveled from ancient Rome to 1993. Thought he was a gladiator, and his chariot was a vehicle of time-travel. Gee, I wish now that I'd listened more closely, been more open-minded. Of course, I also had another client who wore a space suit and said he was an alien from another planet, come to study earthlings.''

Etienne rolled his eyes.

''Do you reckon Pope would have hired an agent like her?'' Cain asked Etienne, obviously not buying her story.

''Possibly. Her tale's so far-fetched it's almost believable. I think he means her to be a distraction to us, especially sending her in that leopard-print chemise. He's hoping our brains will be led by the divining rod between our legs.''

Cain peered down in the general vicinity of his divining rod, probably considering it more like his ''divine rod.''

''I am not a spy,'' Harriet said between gritted teeth. ''Nor am I a prostitute.''

Just then a loud shot rang out, followed by another, which hit the side of the wagon. Etienne and Cain ducked, pushing her down into the well of the seat. In delayed shock, Harriet felt the pain in her shoulder. Glancing to the side, she saw blood beginning to run down in rivulets, marring her beautiful gown.

She moaned, drawing Etienne's attention.

He inhaled sharply as he took in her condition. Wrapping an arm around her waist, he pulled her from the wagon and began running down the crowded sidewalks. Cain grabbed Etienne's satchel, his medical bag and her briefcase from the wagon bed and soon caught up.

Several shots followed, and Harriet heard some women scream and men shout in outrage at the men who chased after them.

In and out of the crowded streets, through some private courtyards, in the front door and out the back of a busy mercantile they ran, never stopping as they headed out of the French Quarter. Harriet had a stitch in her side, her lungs burned, and she'd lost her pretty hat along the way, her hair flying every which way. But she didn't care, being too concerned about the wound in her shoulder and the danger closing in on them.

Ultimately, they stopped behind a distillery, which

reeked of heavy spirits and other unpleasant smells. Slumping against the wall, all three of them panted heavily, especially Cain, whose bruised ribs must have been killing him.

Regaining his breath, Etienne took her by the upper arms and hunkered down at eye-level, asking, "Are you all right?" Somehow, he'd managed to retain his spectacles, and the center part in his hair was arrow-straight.

"Yes," she said, barely able to get the word past her heaving chest. Her heart was beating so fast it felt as if it were lodged in her throat.

Taking hold of the rounded neckline of her gown, Etienne tore it to the left, exposing her wounded shoulder. She gasped, then cried out in pain when he used a handkerchief from his pocket to wipe away some of the blood.

Cain stepped forward and took the cloth from Etienne's hand. Wielding it in a more gentle, doctorly manner, he cleaned her off, examining the area thoroughly.

"How bad?" Etienne asked with surprising tenderness.

"The bullet creased the skin. Nothing serious. Won't even need stitches."

Etienne ran his hand over his mouth distractedly. "We've got to get out of the city, go into hiding for a few days."

"Bayou Noir?" Cain inquired as he took his own handkerchief and made a makeshift bandage around her shoulder, tying it under her armpit.

"Probably. But we have to find a room in the city for tonight. Pope's men will be watching the outskirts like vultures." Making a decision, Etienne grabbed his satchel and took her uninjured arm, yanking her in the opposite direction from which they'd come. Cain picked up his bag and her briefcase.

Harriet wasn't sure she should be moving so far away from the train, her vehicle of time-travel. Digging in her heels, she asked, "Where are we going?"

"Simone's Sporting House," Etienne replied. "It's as

good a place as any to hide out for the night. Perhaps Abel will catch up to us by morning.''

"An athletic club? Now? You haven't had enough exercise today?''

"Huh?'' they both said. Then Etienne laughed. ''Simone operates a . . . uh, parlor house.''

"Oh, you two are incredible. You're going to a house of prostitution,'' she accused.

"Yes,'' Etienne admitted with no shame whatsoever.

"Uh-uh! You can drop me off right here. I'm going back to the train station.''

"I beg to differ, mam'zelle. You're coming along with us,'' Etienne told her. ''I still want to know who sent you.''

"Well, it should be obvious to you now that I'm not in cahoots with that Pope guy. I've been shot, for heaven's sake.''

"They were aiming at me and Cain, not you.''

"Well, I'm not going to some . . . cathouse.''

Etienne cast a sidelong glance of amusement at her choice of words, maneuvering her along by the waist now. His lips were way too close to hers when he whispered, ''And maybe we'll find a good use for that mouth of yours yet in the right setting.''

Red-faced, she clamped her lips shut tight, irritated with the laughter rippling from the two lugs at her sides.

"I still think you should check out her tongue,'' Cain said as they continued walking, skirting in and out of alleys and courtyards, obviously well acquainted with the backways of the old city.

"I did. And she does have a cat tongue. Really. You can just imagine the attraction she would be for Simone.''

"The most popular bordello in the south,'' Cain supplied.

Harriet stared straight ahead, refusing to rise to their teasing. At least, she hoped they were teasing.

Then she thought of something else. ''Steve Morgan took

Ginny to a brothel in *Sweet Savage Love*. Against her will. And he was hiding out, too.''

Etienne groaned. ''*Sacrebleu!* The book again!''

''Hmmm. You know''—she returned her gaze to Etienne—''I'm beginning to think, more and more, that I'm here because of that book and that blasted dream. And you.''

Etienne groaned louder. ''The dream again!''

''Really. Think about it, Etienne. Maybe it's a reincarnation kind of thing. Destiny. Fate.''

He responded with a terse one-word expletive.

''What did you and Etienne . . . I mean, this Steve and Ginny . . . do in that bordello?'' a confused Cain asked, huffing along beside them.

''Yes, what did we do?'' Etienne chimed in. He tucked her in even closer to his side, his right hand riding high above her waist, almost to the underside of her breast.

Oh, my God! Forbidden images of her sexual fantasies flickered through her mind at his insinuating question. She lifted her chin and declined to answer, unable to decide whether she was more embarrassed by the picture in her head of all the outrageous things she'd done with this brute in her dreams, or by the outrageous things she'd like to do.

Etienne and Cain burst out laughing.

Simone's house of ill repute was a camelback mansion of gaudy splendor—two stories in the front rising to four in the back—located in New Orleans's red-light district, aptly named for the ruby glass or red lanterns hanging on each building's front.

They entered clandestinely by the rear door, bypassing a young stable hand who recognized them.

Harriet thought briefly about escaping from her ''captors,'' but where would she go? No, it was better to wait things out. Especially if she had two months to wait until her time ''hole'' opened up again, as she suspected.

They strolled through the kitchen, walking by the startled

cook and maid, who were peeling shrimp on a wide oak table. Obviously knowing their way around, the two men led her into a pristine, walnut-paneled hall whose fine Brussels carpeting cushioned their steps. The air held the scent of talcum powder, freshly ironed linens, liquor, and an indefinable something, which Harriet quickly recognized as sex.

"Mon cher!" exclaimed a tall, slim woman with auburn hair piled into a knot atop her head. She rushed through the sliding wood doors of a parlor and into Etienne's open arms, hugging him warmly.

"Simone, *chérie!*" he greeted her as he whirled her in a circle.

Unlike the hardened soiled doves Harriet had expected to meet in a brothel, Simone could pass for a well-bred Creole virgin . . . pure as the driven snow. Well, more like pure as the driven slush, Harriet quipped to herself. The woman's long black skirt and high-necked, white blouse was more what Harriet would have expected of a schoolmarm, not a madam. But her large breasts and slim waist, prominent in the close-fitting garments, would be an asset in her line of work, Harriet observed, perhaps unkindly.

Leaning back slightly, Simone appraised Etienne's appearance with an uplifted brow, taking in his spectacles and center part, then giggled at Cain's equally out-of-character garments. "My, my. Who are we today?"

"Morticians," Etienne said flatly.

"Tsk-tsk!" Simone shook her head at their seeming foolery.

"We need to hide out for the night," Etienne told her and briefly explained about the men following them.

Simone, immediately serious, assured them she had guards aplenty and all of her employees were close-mouthed. They would be safe, at least for a short period of time. After they were safely ensconced in their rooms, she'd go talk to her girls and the guards, she said.

Then, relaxing, Simone moved into Cain's arms. *"Mon*

coeur," she sighed, looping her arms around his neck and peering at him through sultry, lowered lids. "So, the swamp doctor returns."

"He does," Cain said, smiling widely as he laid wide palms on the woman's buttocks, pulling her closer.

She immediately moved his roving hands higher to the safe territory of her waist. "But what has happened, *cher*?" she fretted, passing fingertips over his bruised eye and cut chin.

"I ran into a little trouble, love."

"What? One of your corpses attacked you?" She clucked. "Oooh, that cut needs some stitching."

"No, it'll heal on its own," he said.

"Will you have time to examine my girls for the pox? And did you bring more of those French letters I asked you to order from Paris?"

He nodded. "They're in Etienne's satchel. Don't you have any of the quinine sponges left that I sent you last month?"

"*Certainement!*" Then Simone fluttered her eyelashes flirtatiously. "I have the strangest . . . itch. Do you think you have a cure for *that* in your medical bag, too?"

"I have just the cure," he assured her, "but, Simone, my dear, I thought you were saving that . . . itch for my brother. He would cut off certain of my favorite body parts if I stepped within two feet of your bedchamber."

Simone laughed, a feminine, rippling sound.

"Where is the scamp?" she asked lightly, but her air of unconcern was belied by the anxious wringing of her hands.

Cain patted her arm. "He should be here soon."

She nodded, but one hand trembled nervously over her heart.

Hmmm. There was a story here.

Then Simone's attention moved to her.

And it was about time. Harriet was practically swooning from loss of blood and all that running and Etienne's suffocating hold on her as he'd dragged her along.

"And this is?" Simone inquired. *"Une fille de joie?* Oh, *bon Dieu,* I did not notice before. The woman has been injured and you two oafs stand about bantering with me."

Harriet flashed the two oafs a satisfied smile as Simone fussed over her shoulder, then declared she would soon have the wound cleaned and bandaged properly.

"Simone, may I present Dr. Harriet Ginoza," Cain said finally.

Simone arched a brow at him.

"She's a sawbones like me," he explained "but she's Etienne's soul mate, come to rescue him."

She and Etienne both groaned. That *soul mate* remark of hers was going to stick like Krazy Glue.

"C'est vrai? Really?" Simone linked her arm with Cain's.

"Really. She's already brought his sense of humor back."

"Très bien!" Simone exclaimed, smiling a welcome to Harriet. "He was becoming such a dour fellow."

Etienne, leaning casually against a wall, snorted with disgust at all the ribbing.

"And I'm fairly certain the male urges he lost in the war are coming back, too," Cain confided with exaggerated solemnity, despite Etienne's warning glare.

"What lost urges?" Simone inquired with professional interest as she motioned for the three of them to follow her up the stairs and through the strangely silent house. Non–business hours, Harriet supposed. "He stopped here last year, and Francine never complained," she told Cain. "In fact, they broke the rope supports on one of the beds. His disguise then was a pirate. Eye-patch, hoop earring, parrot. *Alors!* I never heard so many 'Land ho, maties' in all my life. Now that I think on it, the parrot is still here, a pet of Francine's."

Harriet heard a choking sound behind her, but she didn't turn to see if Etienne was amused or outraged this time. She was too busy imagining what kind of strenuous exercise would have resulted in a broken bed. And how he would look as a pirate.

"Which would you prefer first, *mes coeurs*? A bed or a tub?"

"A tub," Etienne put in quickly, still following Harriet up to the third floor. "Harriet and I need to take a bath. For some reason, she smells like an old sock."

It was Harriet who choked then.

Etienne came up beside her in the hall and grinned.

He had a killer grin. And Harriet had a sudden hatred for killer grins. *Pirate, indeed!*

She swallowed hard to keep from grinning back.

"And would that be the single tub you want, or the large double one I've installed for my clients' pleasure?" Simone asked, a mischievous gleam in her hazel eyes.

Cain slapped his knee and chortled gleefully.

Harriet ground her teeth.

"Double, of course," Etienne said.

Harriet was about to protest, even though images of her in a tub with the dark-skinned scourge of her life tantalized her senses. But she failed to get the words out before Etienne came up with another bright idea.

"Simone, darlin', I don't suppose you have enough buttermilk to fill a tub?"

Chapter Seven

Simone and Cain continued down the hall, chatting amiably, while Etienne shoved her into an outrageously decorated room on the third floor, complete with red velvet drapes and an overabundance of gilt mirrors.

"You don't have to push me," she grumbled. "I want to go with Cain and Simone."

"To help Cain check Simone's girls for the pox? *Mon Dieu!* Why? Do you have some advice for whores, too?"

"Well, actually, I might. Prostitution is the most gender-oppressed profession in the world. I'll bet if those women had a support group to vent their frustrations, half of them would hop the next train out of here."

"And you think Simone would thank you for that?" He pointed a finger at her menacingly. "Don't interfere with Simone's business. I don't want her to suffer for our being here."

"If you weren't so stubborn, you'd recognize that I have valuable information to impart."

He braced both hands on his hips and pressed his lips

together—body signals that he wasn't receptive to her advice.

She narrowed her eyes at him. "Did you hear about the dumb man who stopped another man from beating a donkey?"

"I warned you not to tell any more of those dumb-men jokes."

"It was a case of brotherly love," she quipped.

He clenched his jaw and glared at her.

"Speaking of fallen women . . . did you hear about the dumb man who saw an old woman fall down and didn't stop to help her up?"

"I'm not listening," he said, staring up at the ceiling.

"His mother had warned him against picking up fallen women."

"Your jokes are not funny."

"I think they are. And if you had a sense of humor, you'd think so, too. Lighten up, Larry."

Satisfied that she'd gotten the last word in, Harriet lifted her chin haughtily. Until she got a glimpse of herself in one of the mirrors, that was.

"Eeech!" she squealed, recoiling with disbelief at the sight of herself in a ripped gown hanging off one shoulder practically down to her breast. Not to mention finger-in-the-light-socket hair and smudges of dirt and blood on her cheek. No wonder he'd lost interest.

Glancing to see what was wrong with her now, Etienne's spectacles slipped down his nose. In all the rush, he must not have realized that he still wore them. Now he took them off and slipped them into his jacket. He probably thought that would be her cue to jump his bones. *As if!*

Peering closer at the mirror, she examined the filthy bandage. The wound didn't really bother her much; it only needed a good cleaning, which she could do herself. Not that she'd tell that to the skunk standing across the room, glaring at her as if she were nothing but trouble for him. She planned to bleed this injury for all it was worth.

But first things first. Harriet had never visited a whorehouse before, and she had to admit to a mild interest.

"Tacky, tacky," she commented as she sashayed around the room, fingering the satin coverlet on the high, four-poster bed, flicking her fingernail against the ornate crystal wine decanter on a side table, trying to imagine how a low, one-armed velvet fainting couch would fit into the scheme of things, averting her eyes from too close a scrutiny of an oil painting of a nude man and woman over a small mantel. She picked up a stereoscope and casually peeked inside. *Oh, my!* Red-faced, she immediately put it back down.

A blue booklet caught her attention then . . . appropriately called *The Blue Book*, an annual publication listing all the sporting houses in New Orleans. On each page the "landladies" of the different establishments spelled out the special attractions of their houses, including multilingual prostitutes. *Geez! That must come in handy when moaning, "Ooooh, oooh, oooh, you stud, you."*

Harriet tossed the book aside with disgust and scanned the room again. "The only thing missing is the whips and chains."

Etienne looked up from where he was dumping his leather satchel and her briefcase in a far corner. "I'll bring them when I come back. They should prove useful in your torture."

"Torture schmorture," she scoffed, then focused on something else he'd said. He was riffling through his bag for clean garments. "Where are you going?"

"It's none of your concern where I go . . . unless, of course, you intend to report it back to your superior." He slitted his eyes at her menacingly. "Now, if you'd like to confess to your spying, perhaps I would consider leniency."

"I spy. You spy. We all spy," she replied in a singsong chant. "Gosh, you've got a one-track mind."

"Did you just admit to being a spy?"

"No, I didn't admit to being a spy. I was joking. Can't you take a joke?"

"A joke," he sputtered. "I'm seriously contemplating murder, and you think it's a joke?"

"You'd better watch that vein in your forehead. All that repressed hostility could result in a stroke," she told him bravely, refusing to cower under his continual accusations. "On the other hand, it's kind of a nice complement to those two lovely black-and-blue goose eggs." He had a lump the size of a small golf ball on his forehead and another on top of his head, right in the middle of his ridiculous center part. It made the cowlick stand up straighter.

Etienne clenched his fists and said through gritted teeth "Know this, you foolish wench, you will either tell the truth when I come back, or I'll torture it out of you. Don't think I won't. And you'll pay for the *lovely* bumps on my head, as well."

She stuck her tongue out at him, which was a mistake, not to mention juvenile and totally out of character.

"Later, darlin' ''—he laughed, despite himself—"provided you've got a lily-white past. Well, not lily-white, but spy-free. I can't say you're the type of woman I usually fancy, but you'll do in a pinch, I reckon."

"In a pinch? Like I would even let you touch me with a ten-foot pole!"

"Oh, I'll touch you with a pole, all right, but I would never claim ten feet." He wiggled his eyebrows meaningfully.

She was too revolted by his crude double entendre to speak.

But he was so cute when he did that eyebrow thing. *Jeesh!* Harriet damned herself for the way in which this vulgar, chauvinistic Neanderthal flustered her.

Oh, God! I'm falling apart at the seams here. Next he'll blow a raspberry at me, and I'll think that's cute, too.

Harriet had never been a weak woman. Far from it. But this man . . . this infuriating man . . . had an effect on her that she abhorred, one she couldn't seem to control or pigeonhole as she did all other aspects of her life.

He was responsible for her being caught in this time warp, or whatever it was. And he must be the key to her solving the mystery and returning home. So she couldn't alienate him. Not totally, anyhow.

He smiled at her knowingly. But it wasn't a cruel, mocking smile, as some of his were. It was open and warm and appreciative, as if he enjoyed bantering with her and considered her equal to his challenges.

There I go again. Practically swooning. "Oooh, don't think you can flash that killer smile at me and everything is peachy keen again."

"Killer smile?" he asked, and smiled even wider.

"You know what I mean. The flick-my-Bic, I-know-how-to-light-your-fire-anytime-anywhere smile."

At first, he frowned with confusion. Then the smile returned, slow and lazy. "Does that translate into your being attracted to me?"

"Attracted? Attracted? Haven't you been listening to me for the past ten hours? Why do you think I've been engaging in those loathsome dream bouts with you if I wasn't attracted?"

"Oh, no, not the dream nonsense again!" he complained, then put a hand to his chin thoughtfully. "How loathsome?"

Harriet clamped her mouth shut. *Add motormouth to my list of sins.*

Seeing that she wasn't going to divulge anything more, Etienne started for the door. He rubbed his forehead as he walked, no doubt trying to massage out a migraine.

"I could get rid of your headache for you," she blurted out.

Etienne stopped with his hand on the doorknob. "Lady, you're the one who gave me this headache."

"You deserved both of those whacks, but that's beside the point. I often use hypnotherapy in my practice to cure clients of migraine headaches. My success rate is very high.''

"Forgive me, God, for asking," he muttered, rolling his eyes heavenward, then addressed her. "Hypnotherapy?''

"I hypnotize my patients into a trance and then talk them through the cause of their pain.''

"You get rid of headaches with your talking? I don't think so.'' Etienne put a hand to his head as if she were giving him an even bigger headache, just by offering to help.

"Really. Most headaches aren't caused by physical disorders. Work stress and marital problems are two of the biggest culprits, but, of course, there can be any number of other factors.'' She brightened. "Even impotence. Although it's six of one, half dozen of the other whether impotence generates the migraines or vice versa.''

"Aaarrgh! I am *not* impotent. And you are truly demented if you think I would allow you to mesmerize me into a helpless trance. Not that I think you could.'' He closed his eyes for a moment, as if counting to ten. When he opened them, he wagged a finger at her, ordering, "Stay right there. I'll be back shortly, and then you will answer all my questions, truthfully, or I'll be the one putting you into a trance. A permanent one.''

"I'm coming with you," she decided.

"No, you are not." He folded his arms across his chest. The mulish expression on his face did not bode well for her.

"You can't make me stay here," she asserted.

He raised his eyebrows, then jauntily tossed a large key into the air, catching it deftly. Before she could register that it was her door key, he began to exit.

"Oh, *merde!*" Etienne swore as he almost ran into a fortyish, six-foot-tall woman with the shoulders of a linebacker who filled the doorway. The no-nonsense glint in the amazon's eyes said she wouldn't think twice about using the pistol stuffed in the gun belt she wore over her blue calico gown.

With a mocking bow, Etienne introduced the two women. "Harriet, *honey,* I forgot to tell you. This is your . . . guard. Joleen, do you think you can keep my captive here till I return?"

Joleen raised her chin with affront. "Better'n you could any day, you swamp weasel."

Weasel? Oh, yeah!, Harriet thought.

With a dramatic flourish, Etienne handed the door key to Joleen. "Guard her well then. And don't turn your back on her. She has a fondness for whacking."

"Whacking? What's whacking? I don't do perverted things with women," Joleen told Etienne.

He let loose with a hoot of laughter.

Harriet tried to step around the woman, who snorted with glee at her daring and gave her a shove in the chest. Harriet lost her balance and staggered backward, landing against the bed. She sat down with a whoosh, then stood huffily.

Time for a switch in plans. "I thought I was going to get a bath," she reminded Etienne, who didn't even chastise the woman for her rough treatment.

He grinned, obviously thinking she was anxious to jump in a tub with him.

Hah! That would be the day. Just because she'd admitted to an attraction didn't mean he could have her. Not anymore. She'd changed her mind about making love till she got bored with him. "We need to talk, Etienne."

"Later." With that single word, he spun on his heel and was gone, leaving a stunned Harriet to face the woman who might as well be a brick wall. The weasel had actually left her here to fend for herself. Well, she'd show him.

Her guard was about to go out the door, as well.

"Did you know that Etienne is a necrophiliac?"

The woman turned, trying to appear uninterested, but finally she gave in to her innate curiosity. "What's a neckrow . . . whatever you said?"

"A person who likes to have sex with dead people," Harriet explained with a great deal of satisfaction.

"Really?" Joleen exclaimed. "Mr. Baptiste is one of them?"

"Really." Harriet crossed her heart for emphasis. "I know for a fact he was screwing around in a coffin back on the train just a few hours ago."

By the look on Joleen's face, Harriet just knew the word would pass along the whorehouse grapevine faster than the juiciest gossip. The weasel deserved it.

"Hey, some men feel the need to make love with anything that moves. Then there are those who don't want to limit themselves."

"Ain't that the truth!" Joleen agreed.

Then, recalling her guard job, Joleen plastered a glower on her face. Once again, she was about to leave.

"Who are you?" Harriet asked, ambling closer, thinking she might establish a friendship with the woman and thus find a way out of this place.

"Huh? I'm Joleen. Your man already told you that." The woman was clearly uneasy standing there talking with her.

My man? "Are you a . . . a . . . " Harriet felt her face redden as she searched for the right word.

"Hooker?" the woman offered, amused at Harriet's discomfort. "I usta be, but I ain't serviced a man, for coin, in more'n five years. Got plum tuckered out durin' the war. Practically got calluses on my backside." She chortled at her own jest.

An ex-hooker? "I didn't know they used that word now. Hooker, I mean." Harriet was rambling, trying to distract the woman and ease her way out the still-open doorway.

"Ain't you ever heard of General Joe Hooker? Durin' the war, all the soldiers was huntin' for a bit of it, but Joe Hooker . . . he was a real handsome figure of a man . . . he visited so many of the bawdy houses in Nawleans, they renamed it Hooker's Division. Hee, hee, hee! An' they named us gals after 'im." Joleen laughed heartily in remembrance, then proceeded to describe in graphic detail the size of the general's equipment, and she didn't mean his cannon. She probably hoped to shock Harriet.

Instead, Harriet informed her, "You know, a man's virility is not commensurate with the size of his bodily appendages."

Joleen gaped at her, then chuckled, "Well, tarnation, don't I know that better'n most."

With a grin, Harriet asked, "Do you know what men and snowstorms have in common? You never know how many inches you're going to get or how long it will last."

Joleen slapped her knee with a whoop of appreciation. "Best time I ever had was with a private that had a pecker the size of my thumb, 'ceptin' when it got to salutin'. Whooee!"

Harriet was having second thoughts about having encouraged Joleen with a dirty joke.

"But General Hooker, he was a different can of beans all t'gether. Yessiree, he was built like a stud bull."

This was all very enlightening, but Harriet was more interested in the other stud. The one who ordered her about as if she were a real captive. They'd come a long way from forceful seduction. All she'd gotten from him lately was force. "Can I at least take a bath?" she asked with a sigh. "You could stand guard outside the bathroom door."

"Well, I don't know." Joleen hesitated.

"I promise I won't escape . . . while I'm in the tub anyhow."

"Girly, you ain't gonna escape nohow while I'm watchin' over you. And Mr. Baptiste didn't say nuthin' about no baths."

"He didn't say I couldn't have a bath either," she coaxed.

"Well, you do smell like an old sock."

While they walked to the end of the corridor where the bathing chamber was located, Harriet regaled the seasoned whore with graphic details of all the distasteful things

Etienne liked to do with female cadavers. Harriet never knew she had a talent for obscenity. Until now.

Harriet leaned her head back against the rim of a deep copper tub encased in a magnificent mahogany cabinet. The scent of gardenias filled the air from the huge dollop of bath oil she'd dumped in the warm water.

It wasn't the double tub Simone had offered. Harriet doubted that one existed, realizing belatedly that a wood-paneled, brass-fixtured bathing room such as this would be a luxury in itself for this time period. Simone and Etienne had been teasing her, she concluded now.

Now that she was relaxed, she had time to think, and wonder what had brought her to this incredible juncture in her life. Tears welled in her eyes as she tried to understand.

These were the facts: She was in the year 1870. Time-travel of some sort had taken place.

But how? Could the train derailment have resulted in a more serious accident than she'd perceived? Perhaps she'd died instantly. Could this be a form of reverse reincarnation?

And why? There was no scientific explanation for time-travel. But Harriet did believe in miracles. Maybe some heavenly being had brought her here for a purpose.

Etienne! she concluded with sudden insight. *He must need me. God must have sent me here to help Etienne.* She bit her bottom lip as an unbidden idea wormed its way into her head. *Or do I need him?* Now that was a thought to give her nightmares.

No logical answers were forthcoming.

Harriet had been in worse fixes before in her life—well, not worse, but bad—and she was confident that her intelligence and determination would pull her through this one, too. It was important that she put a positive spin on this experience.

So Harriet let her tense muscles loosen in the warm water. Perhaps she'd take a short nap when she got back to her hooker-heaven bedroom, to further energize her for Etienne's "torture" to come. She had a feeling it would be of a sexual nature.

Suddenly, the water felt a lot hotter.

By late afternoon, Harriet paced angrily across the opulent bedroom. A prison, really, since the door was locked and there was a guard outside in the hall.

Her full-length silk wrapper swished about her legs as she stormed back and forth, muttering livid imprecations against the domineering man responsible for her dire straits. The only people she'd spoken to for the past four hours had been Joleen and the young maid, Charity, who'd brought her a meal hours ago—a delicious shrimp gumbo with homemade bread and butter, sweet, crisp pralines for dessert, and a glass of buttermilk. Neither woman would answer her questions, or listen to her lecture on the perils of the most degrading profession in the world.

"How many men do you . . . uh, service in one night?" Harriet had asked.

Charity had shrugged. "Five. Once I did eight, but that was 'cause it was Mardi Gras. All the Creole men gets a bit of religion during Lent. So I guess they was storin' up." She grinned at Harriet.

Harriet hadn't been amused. "You women need a good union."

Joleen had told her she needed a good something else.

"Well, I never—"

"That's for certain! Too bad General Hooker's not around anymore. He could have done the job good and proper."

Charity had come back one other time, at Etienne's instruction, to clean their clothing. The only response Harriet had been able to get out of the timid girl then was a gasp when she told her about Etienne being a necrophiliac.

Later Harriet realized she was left practically naked, with only the thin, belted gown for covering. Just like Ginny in

Sweet Savage Love, she thought. Except that Steve Morgan had locked Ginny in a brothel, totally naked, so that he could have his carnal way with her. Thus far, Harriet's version of good ol' Steve hadn't exhibited all that much interest in her, carnal or otherwise. Except to accuse her of being a spy. *Harriet the Spy! Golly!* If she were really a spy, she'd have figured out this whole mess by now and been on her way home.

Where was Etienne?

Harriet wasn't used to idleness, and her lack of physical or mental activity was driving her crazy. On her fiftieth loop of the room, she noticed her briefcase and his satchel. *Okay, master spy, time to test your James Bond talents.*

Sinking to the floor, Harriet opened Etienne's satchel and began to rummage through the contents. Some clothing, a man's blond wig and mustache, her panty hose, ammunition, a leather pouch holding some primitive condoms, a velvet case the size of a deck of cards, and a small book called *French Letters*—a Bible. *A Bible?*

Harriet sat back on her heels and opened the miniature Bible. On the flyleaf, in flourishing script, was written, *To Etienne. God be with you. Love, Papa. December, 1861.*

Well, well, well. The lout had a father. He must have given him the Bible when Etienne went off to fight in the Civil War. Harriet felt a peculiar sadness as she held the well-worn book in her palm, caressing its cover.

She put the Bible down and picked up the velvet case. Pressing the tiny catch on the side, she opened it to see a trifold frame, holding three sepia-toned photographs.

One was of a man and woman, standing before a California-style ranch of the previous century. The man was an older version of Etienne, dark and broodingly handsome. He had his arm wrapped around the waist of a beautiful, brunette woman, also tall, who stared up at him adoringly. The wicked smile on the man's face as he regarded the woman bespoke humor and great love.

Harriet's heart swelled just looking at the photograph,

and for some reason, tears filled her eyes. "I want that kind of love someday," Harriet whispered, and the thought just about floored her. When had she started yearning for love?

Forever, a voice in her head said.

Pushing that uncomfortable realization aside, Harriet slipped the picture out of its frame and turned it over. A different handwriting—bold and without fuss—proclaimed, *Papa and Selene, Last Chance Ranch, California, 1855.*

She replaced the photo and directed her scrutiny to the next frame. A lovely old plantation home, showing signs of disrepair, stood at the top of a rise, highlighted by an alley of arched oak trees, dripping moss. In the forefront was a bayou stream. The three-story mansion with its wide center staircase had deep, roofed galleries and massive columns. The picture was a poignant vignette of the Old South, and Harriet felt an odd pulling sensation when she gazed at it.

Home, she thought, and couldn't explain why the place felt like home to her. She'd always lived in cities. Highrises. Concrete. Crowds. She would never feel comfortable in a war-ravaged place like this. It appeared desolate and neglected.

And she wished, with all her heart, that it belonged to her. Or rather that she belonged to it.

The heat must be getting to me.

Pulling that photo from the frame she read in the same script as that in the Bible, *Bayou Noir, 1845.*

Setting the picture aside, Harriet turned to the last one. Eight children and a humongous shaggy dog posed on the porch and steps of the same ranch as in the first photo. The three oldest boys, aged about twelve, stood with arms linked over each other's shoulders, grinning impishly. It wasn't hard to identify the two identical black boys as Cain and Abel, and in the center stood Etienne. He was darling, even then showing promise of a sinful handsomeness.

Next, Harriet studied the remaining, much younger children—two boys and three girls. They ranged in ages from about two to six and resembled Etienne in one way or another, even the smallest blond girl. Harriet smiled at the charming picture. But then she pulled this photo from its frame, too, and almost reeled with shock at what she read: *California, 1852. Cain, me, Abel, Rhett, Ashley, Scarlett, Tara, Melanie, and Dreadful.*

Dreadful? Harriet smiled. She just knew that Etienne had dreamed up that name for a dog.

But how was it possible that someone had given children those *Gone With the Wind* names in 1852? Something was wrong with this picture. Drastically. Harriet put her fingertips to her forehead and pressed tightly, trying to figure out the puzzle. Margaret Mitchell hadn't written her famous novel until the 1930s. This photo said 1852. Now, the name Rhett or Scarlett or Ashley or Melanie, even Tara, might have been used in the 1800s, but not all together. That was too much of a coincidence.

There was something else. Harriet returned to the first photograph and peered closer. The woman looked vaguely familiar. Oh, no! It couldn't be. Yes, it was. Sandra Selente . . . the famous model who was known by the single appellation *Selene*. She'd disappeared suddenly last year during a photo shoot in . . . oh, geez . . . New Orleans.

Goose bumps stood out all over Harriet's body as she tried to comprehend what she saw before her very eyes. Was it possible . . . no, it couldn't be . . . was it possible that time-travel really could occur? And that she wasn't the only one who'd traveled back in time?

It was just too much to take in, and accept.

Seeking something familiar to anchor her, Harriet turned to her briefcase. Carrying it to the bed, she crawled up onto the high mattress and sat cross-legged in the middle, setting the leather Louis Vuitton attaché case in front of her. It had been a gift to herself on getting her doctorate degree from Stanford three years ago. Turning the combination lock, she flipped it open.

First, smiling smugly, she took one item out of the briefcase and slid it under the mattress for safekeeping. She'd forgotten about that little bit of insurance she'd stashed away. It might make the difference in her survival here in the past.

There was another item or two she'd forgotten as well in her briefcase . . . the two books. When she wanted to convince Etienne that she came from the future, all she would have to do was pull out *Sweet Savage Love* or *Female Fantasies Never Die.*

A short time later, she sat engrossed in mind-numbing work, taking notes, dictating into her recorder. Although she operated intelligently on one level, Harriet knew she was in deep shock.

"God, help me," she whimpered more than once. Harriet hadn't prayed in years, but she did now. "Please, please answer my prayers."

She thought she heard a celestial voice in her head say, *I already have.* Harriet groaned. Because she was really, really afraid that the answer to her prayers had black hair, blue eyes and a killer grin. A mortician-pirate-gunslinger-rogue. Talk about divine justice!

Chapter Eight

"So what're you goin' to do with your Dr. Ginny?" Cain slurred.

"*My* Dr. Ginny?" Etienne peered up over the rim of his glass, and even that effort caused the sweet buzz in his head to intensify. This was only his third glass of absinthe, but it came from Simone's potent private stock.

Exhausted from spending the entire afternoon covering their tracks and making plans to leave the city tomorrow, he and Cain sprawled lazily in Simone's second parlor on the first floor, their long legs propped on a low table. It wasn't yet time for the evening trade to arrive.

Cain belched lustily. Disdaining the licorice-flavored liquor, and lacking his usual finesse, he drank straight from a bottle of bourbon.

They weren't yet knee-walkin' drunk, but well on their way. That must have been why Etienne's thoughts kept returning to the woman upstairs. A dozen willing whores sold their wares in Simone's house, and he kept picturing the talkingest wench in the South. Naked. Soaking in a tub.

Reclining on the big tester bed. Posing in front of the triple mirror. Stretched out on the fainting couch just high enough off the floor for a man to . . .

Something else even more alarming nagged at him. All her talk about time-travel. *Ridiculous!* And yet he found himself asking, "Cain, do you remember that magazine of my stepmother's we found when we were boys?"

At first, Cain frowned. Then his face brightened. "You mean the one that had her picture in it? The one with the year 1996 on the cover?" Before Etienne could answer, Cain protested, "Oh, no! Don't tell me. You're startin' to believe that doctor woman's stories?"

Etienne felt his face redden. "Of course not."

"You don't sound sure. You're drinkin' mash and talkin' trash, boy. How much you had to drink?"

"Not as much as you, *boy*," Etienne snapped. "And it's not liquor logic. I wondered about Selene lots of times. She was . . . well, different."

"Different doesn't make her a time-traveler," Cain scoffed.

"Remember those arrow-backs classes she taught the slaves for exercise? And the stories she told us about other planets?"

"Yes. For a long time, you made everyone call you E.T. after that one nursery-tale character . . . a visitor from outer space." Cain grinned in memory. "Did you ever ask Selene?"

Etienne shook his head.

"So there! You couldn't have been too convinced."

"You're right." Etienne sighed, then took another sip of the Creole liquor. "But I'm wishing now that I'd left Harriet, or Ginny, or whatever the hell her name is, back on the train."

Cain nodded. "You prob'ly should have slit her tongue so she couldn't pass on information. And maybe cracked a few bones in her fingers to keep her from writin' any notes."

"That's not very doctorly of you," Etienne observed, knowing Cain wasn't serious. Cain was a formidable foe when backed into a corner, but he never caused pain except in defense.

Cain shrugged. "I don't feel much like a doctor anymore."

"You *are* a doctor. A good one," Etienne declared fiercely, "and you're going to resume your doctoring this time. The bayou needs you."

"The bayou needs you, too, my friend," Cain challenged him with a level look.

Etienne prepared to argue, but then he slumped lower in his chair. He had no energy for enumerating all the reasons why Bayou Noir was no haven for him anymore. Or anywhere else that he could think of. "Ah, Cain, how did we become so crippled inside? You're as wounded as I am by that damn war."

"We both should have stayed in Europe."

"Well, we didn't. And now we have to move on. At least I'm getting my sense of humor back," he quipped.

"And your rooster," Cain pointed out drolly.

"You're uncouth." Etienne laughed.

"Yes, and I learned it all from you." Cain took another long swig from his bottle. "So, back to your Dr. Ginny. Even if she is working for Pope, I can't see you killing her outright."

"Because it would be too messy?"

"No, because she's your soul mate." Cain winked at him, or tried to. His eyelid just twitched.

Etienne snorted with disgust. "At least Pope doesn't yet associate our names with the gold shipment. That was one bit of good news we found out this afternoon at the Exchange," Etienne said. "That should give us a few days' headway. If we lie low at Bayou Noir for a week, he'll probably think we took the gold out of the city. We don't want to lose him totally, but we have to lead this chase to our ultimate destination. The final confrontation has to take place in Texas, not Louisiana.''

"That still doesn't address the woman. Joleen told the kitchen maid that the wench is pacin' her room, callin' you names that made even Joleen blush.''

"I find that hard to believe . . . that Joleen can blush.''

"And Simone says she's trying to advise her girls.''

Etienne groaned. "I suppose I should go up, but . . . well, I told her that I'm going to torture her.''

Cain grinned.

He grinned back.

"Forceful seduction?''

"Hell, how should I know? I've never tortured a woman before,'' Etienne grumbled, "and I sure as sin wouldn't know how to forcefully seduce a woman.''

"I could instruct you,'' Cain offered obligingly.

"Hah! Everything you know, I taught you.''

"Not everything,'' Cain disagreed.

"Hmpfh! You're all vine and no taters when it comes to sex. Talk, talk, talk.''

"Oh, really. Well then, how 'bout I go up and 'torture' the secrets out of the little leopard lady?'' Cain licked his lips with anticipation. "I think I'm 'up' to the task.''

"No chance!'' Etienne's too-quick response caused Cain to hoot with glee. "I'm thinking of leaving her here and paying Simone to keep her locked up till this job is completed. After that, it won't matter what she divulges. We'll be safe by then.''

"That could take weeks. The woman is all fired up and full of git now. I can't imagine what she'd do if you imprisoned her in a fancy house for a month.''

"Probably lead a posse after me. Or whack me another time.'' Etienne chuckled, touching the tender lumps on his head. "You're not suggesting we take her with us?''

"Through the swamps? No. But I do think you should tumble her a few times before we leave. She's cute as a speckled pup.''

135

"A speckled pup? Hah! More like a sharp-clawed cat." Then he added with a smile, "A few times?"

"Yup. I reckon five or six ought to cure what ails you."

Etienne choked and set his drink aside. "I haven't gone six rounds in one night since I was eighteen."

"See," Cain soothed, "it's just what the doctor ordered. Get your wick trimmed, good and proper, and those blue devils of yours will fly out the window."

The young maid, Charity, knocked on the door then and brought in a light dinner. All of Simone's girls did double duty, on their backs and on their feet around the house. Within seconds, he and Cain were wolfing down shrimp gumbo, fresh bread and butter, pralines . . . and buttermilk.

The whole time she served them, the girl kept casting nervous glances at Etienne, making sure she never got too close to him. He'd noticed the same reaction from Lily Sue and Erline when they'd passed him in the hall, but he'd figured then that it must be his smelly condition. He'd since had a bath.

Etienne's brow furrowed and Cain's did the same when their eyes connected. With a silent signal, Cain stood and followed the girl when she left. Actually, he staggered, muttering something about the floor being uneven.

Etienne heard Cain and Charity murmuring in the hall, followed by a high-pitched squeal. Cain had probably pinched her bottom. Then Cain erupted into laughter. When he returned to the room, he was still chortling.

Before he closed the door, the sound of a sudden, piercing trill of music spilled into the room, coming from the front parlor. A poignant trumpet melody played out, and Simone's clear soprano voice sang the words Abel had been writing down back on the train.

"Abel," he and Cain said at the same time. Even though they hadn't been particularly worried about Abel's safety, a wave of relief washed over Etienne. They wouldn't go to him yet, though. Abel and Simone would have some catching up to do.

Cain resumed eating, looking up at Etienne repeatedly and smirking.

"Well, spit it out," Etienne snapped. "What'd she say?"

Cain paused dramatically, then announced, "Everyone now knows about your perversions." He tried to speak solemnly but was unable to hold a straight face.

"Perversions? Which ones?"

"Just one. Seems you've become a . . . let's see . . . what did she call it?" Cain tapped his head dramatically. "Oh, yes, a neck-row-filly-act."

"Filly-act? Does it have something to do with horses?"

Cain laughed so hard tears filled his eyes. "Oh, oh, oh . . ." he sputtered.

Etienne glowered till Cain finally stopped howling and explained with great relish. By the time he finished, Etienne's jaw had dropped practically into his empty bowl.

"Corpses?" Etienne stood and threw his napkin on the table. "I'm going to kill the wench, after all."

A short time later, Etienne stomped up to the third floor. Joleen flashed him a disdainful scowl, mumbling something about "bloody perverts," thus confirming she'd heard the story, too.

"Go and have dinner," he ordered.

She scurried past him so fast that the hall curtains fluttered.

Etienne inserted the key in the door and entered, primed for a fight. Instead, the room was quiet. He saw that the woman was asleep on the bed, her travel case and papers strewn around her as if she'd dozed off. One arm was thrown over her head. Masses of black hair spread about the pillows in seductive display. Wearing only a thin wrapper, which had parted, she slept on her back with one long leg exposed from bare foot to upper thigh.

A sweet swelling flared in his groin. *Hmmm. Maybe I could go a bout or two, after all. Or three or four.*

He was already unbuttoning his shirt, heading for the

bed, when he tripped over something on the floor. He glanced down and his burgeoning arousal died an instant death, replaced by blood-boiling fury.

How dare she? How dare she go through my bag? Could she be a spy, after all? Oh, I should have broken into her travel case and investigated further. Careless! I've been too careless.

He picked up the Bible his father had given him before he'd left to fight in the war. His throat closed as he flipped open the cover, reading, *To Etienne. God be with you. Love, Papa. December, 1861.* Hah! His father had given him the gift on his departure from California, but that was before he'd discovered which side Etienne supposedly fought for—the wrong side. They hadn't spoken since. He slammed the book shut before he disgraced himself by crying, and put it carefully back into the bottom of his satchel.

Then he contemplated the photos the intrusive woman had riffled through. Checking to make sure she'd done no damage to his precious mementos, he ran a fingertip caressingly over the three frames. Papa and Selene—he couldn't even bear to look at that photograph. Bayou Noir, which tugged at his heartstrings like an anchor in the raging sea of his life. And his brothers and sisters, whom he missed so very much.

He smiled, despite his sadness, and wondered how they would look now. Almost ten years had passed since he'd seen them last. Rhett would be twenty-four and helping Papa run the ranch. Scarlett was twenty-one and a raving beauty, according to a miniature portrait shown to him last year by Blossom, his old cook at Bayou Noir. Ashley, at twenty, was still studying law at Harvard. Tara, only nineteen, had married early and already had two children, both boys, with her farmer husband. Melanie, the youngest at fifteen, with her incongruous blond hair, would probably still be in the schoolroom.

With a sigh of regret, he put the velvet case into his satchel, and directed his attention to the bed. Eyes narrowed, he sat down gently on the side of the mattress and began to examine the items the witch had scattered so carelessly.

A small black box that he couldn't identify; he set it aside for now, along with a strange, flat green case holding twenty-eight pills in slotted rows of seven.

Next, he picked up two books. *Sweet Savage Love* by Rosemary Rogers had a paper cover depicting a man and woman in a close embrace. *Steve and Ginny?* He turned a few pages and read the copyright page. The latest date, following numerous reprintings, was 1997.

Etienne felt a roaring in his ears as the implications of that date hit him with full force. She hadn't been lying. She really did come from the future.

No, no, no! It isn't possible. It has to be a trick.

But who would go to such lengths? Pope? His superiors? It hardly seemed credible.

He put a hand to his head to ward off an impending headache. If anything could cause his migraine to explode, this distressing discovery would.

He turned to the other book, which had a hard cover. *Female Fantasies Never Die*, by Dr. Harriet Ginoza.

The headache hit like a knife through his forehead. Inhaling and exhaling deeply, he finally managed to control its force. He turned the book over then and stared at a photograph in shades of black and white of the woman sprawled out next to him. Wearing a severe dark suit jacket over a white shirt, she looked straight ahead, chin lifted haughtily to its usual elevation. The only concession to her femininity was the pearl earbobs exposed by her upswept hairstyle.

Etienne flicked to the copyright page, but he already knew what he would find. The year 1997.

Maybe I'm going insane. Maybe my mother's mental illness passed on to me, as I always feared. Maybe the prison dementia I fought off for so long has finally claimed me. Maybe this is God's punishment for all my sins. Maybe none of this is real and I'm just dreaming, as the lady has been claiming to be all along.

Setting that book aside as well, Etienne picked up the notebook and began to read. Apparently, she'd decided to start a journal of some sort.

August 25, 1870

Today I met my soul mate, and he's a jerk...

Etienne smiled. *Jerk.* Selene had often used that word to describe his father. He supposed it was equivalent to that *male chauvinist pig* term Harriet had mentioned. Probably her cantankerous version of *dear* or *darling.*

He read further.

... At first, I thought Etienne Baptiste was Steve Morgan, that MCP who's been plaguing my dreams so much lately. But he's not. He's worse.

Etienne frowned. He was the aggrieved party here, not her. He was the one who'd been knocked unconscious, twice. He was the one whose personal property had been ransacked. He was the one saddled with an unwanted, opinionated, endlessly chattering responsibility.

... He has a killer smile and a body to die for, just like the Steve of my dreams....

Etienne decided that he might not strangle her after all for her slanderous remarks about his sexual inclinations. He sucked in his stomach; being on the run one way or another did keep a man lean and well muscled.

... but, unlike Steve, the crud stud has no interest whatsoever in me....

Well, he wouldn't say that precisely. And what the hell was a crud stud? Probably the same as an MCP.

He skimmed through the other pages, and there were lots of them. Apparently Harriet liked to write almost as much as she liked to talk. He would return to them later, his headache making even the process of reading a painful chore. Besides, for now, he was most interested in her reaction to his Bible and the three pictures. He flipped to those sections of her journal.

Just as her two books had him wondering if time-travel was actually possible, his personal belongings—the Bible and the three pictures—had done the same to her. She was confused and frightened, as well she should be. Unfortunately, she looked to him for answers and a way out of her unwanted adventure.

And he had no answers.

Tossing the notebook to the floor, he removed his boots. Then he padded over to the table, where he poured a small glass of water from a carafe, dropping in one of Cain's headache powders.

It was only six o'clock, still light outside, but Etienne felt a debilitating weariness. He needed to lie down. Until his headache passed. Until he slept a little. Until he understood who this woman was and why she'd landed in his life.

Should he wake her?

No, not yet. With the hammer pounding behind his eyeballs, he didn't think he could stand her jabbering right now. She'd probably start right in lecturing him. Or want to talk about her theories on time-travel. Or hit him over the head again.

Just a little rest. Should he plop down on the fainting couch, which would be uncomfortable for his large frame, or should he ease into the ample empty space left on the bed? He had no trouble deciding.

What about clothing? Should he remove his garments, as he usually did?

Hell, why not? She talks a great game. Let's see if she throws in her chips or bluffs her way to the end when con-

141

fronted with a real man in all his glory. Besides, I'd like to show her my full house, and my royal straight isn't so bad either. Etienne chuckled to himself. His headache must be melting his brain. Either that, or his sense of humor had been absent so long, it was making up for lost time.

Soon his headache eased. He lay on his back under the crisp sheets, his arms folded behind his neck, studying the ceiling. It was a moment out of time and he took great pleasure in it—a soft bed with goose-feather pillows, clean linens smelling of fresh air, a mild breeze rustling through the two open windows, the sound of a dove calling to its mate in the distance. He hadn't always been so appreciative of the little things in life. A brutal war and a horrific prison had taught him well.

And there were other little pleasures in life that he cherished now, Etienne thought with a smile as Harry-Hat—he knew Harriet rankled when he misspoke her name—grew restless in her sleep and cuddled closer. Yes, there was the scent of gardenias in a woman's hair, the feel of satiny skin in mysterious places, the wonderful purring sound a female made when she was pleasured, or the even more wonderful scream she released when satisfied.

So many little blessings in this world, and yet Etienne was so unhappy. Why? he wondered as a wide yawn overcame him. Why couldn't he go back to the way he used to be?

Harriet threw one leg over his and squirmed against his side. With a resigned sigh, he put an arm around her shoulder and drew her warm body closer, her head resting on his chest.

She would be furious when she awakened in this position.

Good.

In the meantime, he hoped he had one of her famous erotic dreams.

* * *

"*No!* Get them off! Get them off!''

Harriet awoke with a jolt to find herself in bed with Etienne. Dusky evening approached, but she could still see in the fading shadows. He was flailing his arms and legs about as if trying to whisk something off his body. In the process, he kicked off the sheet.

He was stark—*be still my heart*—naked. And she wasn't much better, her silk wrapper having come unwrapped.

But she couldn't be concerned about that now. Etienne was having a violent nightmare, and it must involve those Andersonville maggots he'd mentioned earlier. *The poor man!*

She soothed him with whispers—"It's all right now. Shhh. It's only a dream''—and light caresses over his clenched jaw and jerking shoulders. Eventually, he whimpered and slumped into an exhausted sleep.

She tried to rise, but her long hair was caught under his outflung arm. And he'd managed to trap one of her legs between his. Wide awake now, she figured she must have slept at least four hours. Remembering how angry she'd been with Etienne for locking her in this room, she tried to call up the rage. But it had all drained out of her in witnessing his nightmare.

As he slept, his face showed a vulnerability that he masked with cynicism when awake. His full lips parted slightly. Like most dark-haired men, he had a five-o'clock shadow, even though he'd shaved that morning.

I hate that he's been hurt. By a war, or people, or just circumstances. But that's crazy. I have no connection to him.

She put a hand to her mouth to stifle a moan as she realized, *Yes, I do.*

Moving her hand from her mouth to his chest, she felt his heart beating strongly. And that touched her, too. He was a virile, healthy man. And he was hers.

Huh? He's not mine. And I don't want him to be mine. No, no, no!

Even so, it was with a proprietary air that she ran her fingertips lightly from the silky black hairs on his chest down to the vee at his waist, and lower. He was a big man—tall and slender and well muscled, but not pumped up like a bodybuilder.

So many scars! Were they the results of childhood scrapes? Or much worse?

Tears welled in her eyes at the pain he must have suffered. And she wished, for the first time in her life, that she could take another person's suffering on herself.

Her hand had been resting, palm downward, on his flat stomach, very close to another interesting part of his body. And it wasn't his long, furred legs that drew her now. Or the big, narrow, high-arched feet with the beginnings of a blister on each heel. His manhood had a beauty all its own.

She was about to touch it—she couldn't help herself— when a hand clamped over her wrist. She glanced up, with dismay, to see Etienne's eyes, wide open, and staring at her.

Using his grasp on her wrist as leverage, as well as fingers burrowed into her hair, Etienne drew her up so she lay half on her side, half on his chest, eye to eye with him. Her hair spilled out around them.

"Why are you weeping?" he asked softly.

"For you. For your pain. And your beauty."

"Pity?" His eyes glinted with hurt, and his body tensed defensively.

She shook her head from side to side. "Not pity."

He studied her face for a long moment, his chin lifted pridefully. She knew the instant he accepted her words, because his entire body relaxed. Then, releasing her wrist, he put his hand to her face, brushing a strand of hair back behind her ear.

"I want to kiss you," he said huskily. It wasn't a request.

The words were like pellets in a pinball machine, racing to all the important targets in her body. *Ping, ping, ping,* her defenses were crumbling. "I think I'll die if you don't."

A small smile spread over his lips as he raised his head slightly, narrowing the distance between them. She smelled licorice on his breath—not an unpleasant odor. His lips were a hairbreadth from hers when he whispered a command: "Open."

She complied instantly, never questioning his authority.

His kiss was violent in its tenderness. He used his lips and teeth and tongue to learn her mouth, turning her pliant and mewling for more. When she tried to deepen the kiss, demanding, "Harder," he refused, nipping her jaw to show who was in control. He would obviously set the pace.

"Are you punishing me?" she moaned, though some remote portion of her brain reminded her that she was the one who had reason to be angry.

"Yes."

"For what?"

"I can't remember," he rasped out with a laugh.

In a flash, before she could blink, he flipped her on her back and moved over her. Without breaking eye contact, he tore off her robe and tossed it to the side.

This time, when he kissed her, Harriet felt as if a storm had invaded her bed. He ravished her with hard kisses, then drained the life out of her with the heat of his thrusting tongue. Just when she thought she could bear no more, that things were happening too fast, he slowed and gentled. Then his kisses melted her with coaxing expertise.

Oh, he was a good kisser. A really good kisser.

She wanted to put her arms around him, to participate more fully, but he denied her efforts with a masculine growl. Harriet didn't like being dictated to and she balked, wrapping her arms around his wide shoulders. "Steve," she protested.

In a heartbeat, her hands were imprisoned above her head, pinned to the mattress by their interlaced fingers. Holding her eyes, he used his knees to spread her legs wide.

With slow, slow insinuation, he let his body weight settle over hers.

"I am not Steve Morgan. I am Etienne Baptiste."

"Oh." She hadn't realized she'd spoken Steve's name.

"Say it."

"Etienne," she breathed.

"This is not a dream," he said between gritted teeth.

"I know," she whispered. She could feel his arousal growing against the apex of her thighs, and it was nothing like her fantasies. This was so much more.

Her breasts peaked and ached. She tried to move from side to side to abrade them against his coarse chest hair.

He wouldn't let her move.

"You don't like losing self-control, do you, Harriet?"

She gasped at his too-perceptive assessment. That kind of knowledge gave him power, and Harriet grew alarmed. This was alien territory for her. Dangerous.

"What are you afraid of, *chérie*?"

"Nothing." Why didn't he just stop talking and do it?

"Did I tell you that I'm an expert in body language, too, Dr. Ginny?" he said smoothly.

Uh-oh! She shook her head. She couldn't speak.

"The pupils of your strange cat eyes are enlarged and very dark," he whispered as he ran the tip of his tongue around his lips to moisten them. She followed its path like a hungry wanton. "Do you know what that means?"

"What?" At first, Harriet forgot what he'd asked. Then she remembered his question about dilated pupils. She should know the answer. But she was beyond rational thought.

"It means you're about to climax," he said boldly and bucked against her once. Only once.

That was all Harriet needed. To her shock and humiliation, she began to climax. A wild explosion of feeling rippled out from that place where he pressed against her, unmoving now. And all the time he watched her like a hawk with its prey.

She tried to escape his imprisoning hold—to force a response from him, or to escape.

He wouldn't budge.

"Relax," he coaxed. "Let it happen. I want to watch. You're beautiful when you're aroused. Your cheeks are flushed. You're panting. . . ."

Panting? Me? She clamped her mouth shut.

He nipped her chin in playful chastisement. "So beautiful. Come for me, *chérie,* come . . ."

"No." She resisted. Harriet had to be in control. She always had been in the past. If she surrendered now, she would be vulnerable. Dependent. "No, no, no."

Determination sparked in his pale eyes. He moved himself against her slickness, side to side. Once, twice, three times.

Tears streamed down her face as she fought against this shameful weakness. It wouldn't be so bad if he were as out of control as she. It wouldn't be so bad if it were dark and he weren't witnessing her vulnerability. He would use it against her, she just knew he would.

Leaning down, he kissed the side of her lips. Gently. A soothing caress meant to comfort her distress.

It only pushed her closer toward the edge.

"Not like this. I don't want it like this," she cried out. "Inside . . . I want you inside me."

Oh, this was the worst kind of forceful seduction. Harriet felt like a traitor to herself and all womankind. She was actually begging a man to make love to her.

"Like this?" he teased, taking his erection in hand and placing himself at her entrance, no further.

Harriet screamed. She arched her breasts against his seemingly immovable chest and rocked her hips against him in fast, rhythmic, involuntary undulations. Flinging her head from side to side, she surrendered to the most cataclysmic orgasm of her life. Every inch of her skin was an erogenous zone, convulsing in ever-widening circles of ecstasy.

And when it ended, when she felt she had nothing more to give, she glanced up at Etienne, who watched her expectantly. To her alarm, his eyes were darkening into pools of arousal. His lips parted with soughing breaths.

And, God help her, she wanted more.

Chapter Nine

He released her hands and braced himself on outstretched arms. Slowly, with a long, drawn-out groan, Etienne entered her. And her traitorous inner muscles expanded to accommodate his girth and grasp him in welcome.

"Oh . . . oh, my God!" To her surprise and his obvious pleasure, she climaxed again.

Panting heavily himself now, Etienne raised himself up so that he sat on his haunches, taking her with him to straddle his lap. He was still imbedded in her.

Through the crimson haze of her nonstop arousal, Harriet saw that sweat beaded Etienne's brow and his teeth were bared and gritted, as if in agony. The man was just as excited by this loveplay as she was, except that he exercised much greater restraint. *Darn it!*

Placing a wide palm between her shoulder blades for support, he forced her to arch backward so that her breasts lifted like twin sacrifices for his worship. And worship he did. With the first flick of his tongue, he relit the fire between her legs, and, unbelievably, the erotic spiral started all over.

"Noooo," she wailed. "It's too much, too soon."

"Ah, I'll prove you wrong, *chérie*," he promised and spread his knees wide, taking her thighs as far apart as they would go. The whole time, he tongued first one breast, then another, followed by the fiercest, sweetest suckling on her nipples. Nipples that had magical threadlike connections to every pore and muscle and blood vessel in her over-sensitized body. She didn't look, but she had a sneaking suspicion her toes might be tapping.

From then on, Harriet couldn't tell where one orgasm ended and another started. She lost count.

During one of the few pauses, she recalled him mentioning something about the need to go get his *French Letters* and her telling him she was protected by birth control pills. She'd clamped her legs around his waist to prevent his leaving the bed. *Oh, geez! Did I really do that?*

After that, everything became fuzzy. All she knew was that she'd time-traveled herself to feminist hell, plaything to a macho man's every whim. And she was loving every minute of the blitz. *Gloria Steinem, eat your heart out.*

"Why are you grinning?" he whispered, taking a small, teasing bite at her lower lip.

"Because I—" Harriet never finished her sentence because she realized, with shock, that she was flat on her back—though how she'd arrived there, she had no idea—and the brute hadn't yet begun to move inside her. How did he do it?

Oops! Correction. The grand finale is about to begin. Hold on to your hair net, Harriet. Here comes big trouble.

Levering himself on straightened arms, corded neck arched, Etienne pulled himself out and then eased back in with slow, excruciating abrasion. Over and over, he repeated the procedure.

Her eyes were probably rolling in their sockets like slot-machine fruits. She was pretty sure her tongue wasn't hanging out, but she clamped her lips together just to make sure.

Harriet remembered reading a statistic one time that the average man thrusts sixty to a hundred and twenty times during sexual intercourse. She hadn't believed it then, but now she thought a new world record was being set. By a not-so-average man. *Oh, my!*

She raised her knees to better accommodate him. She caressed his perspiring face, his wide, tense shoulders and his heaving chest. But this was Etienne's show. He was the maestro calling the tunes. She was the mere instrument. And, amazingly, she didn't mind.

When his strokes finally became shorter and harder, hammering her, actually moving her across the bed, he began to groan. And it was the most glorious, primal male sound in the world. When he exploded inside her continually convulsing folds, Harriet splintered with him.

For long seconds afterward, she lay stunned, her head mashed against the headboard, her legs spread wide with wanton abandon, an embarrassing wetness—his and hers both—spreading under her. And Etienne was sprawled over her like a clump of Mississippi mud, his face pressed between her breasts. The only sound in the room was the loud, mingled soughing of their burning lungs.

"I have never, ever experienced anything like that before," she gasped out.

Etienne, whom she'd thought asleep, raised his head to peer at her incredulously. "And you think I have?" He burst out laughing and wouldn't stop. Even when she pummeled the brute's chest, he kept laughing. Even when she shoved him over onto his back and straddled him and tried to clamp a hand over his mouth.

Only when she stopped and her face brightened with a sudden idea did he still. He regarded her suspiciously.

She hated the way she'd lost her beloved self-control, but now she was in the driver's seat, so to speak. She wriggled her bottom on his hard stomach for emphasis. The guy had a thing about her behind, or so he'd said a hundred times or more since they'd first met, and she wasn't above using it against him. Perhaps she could retain some self-respect if she showed the lout that she was capable of remaining calm while directing *his* sexual agony. *Hmmm.* Who said a maestro needed a baton? Who said the kitten couldn't teach the tomcat a thing or two?

"Etienne, darlin'," she cooed.

He immediately sensed her plan. "Oh, no. I couldn't." Throwing up his hands in mock defense, he chortled, "Not yet."

Harriet smiled, a pure feline curve of the lips, and proceeded to prove him wrong.

Ten minutes later, she had him purring. In another ten minutes, he was hissing. In the final ten minutes, when he bowed his back and dug in his claws, it was too late. He was putty in her cat paws.

Forceful seduction really wasn't so bad, she decided, when the shoe was on the other foot . . . uh, paw.

For the next two hours, give or take an eternity, Etienne found he actually was capable of fulfilling Cain's outrageous prescription. Although one "tumble" became indistinguishable from another, he figured there must have been at least four.

The woman was amazing.

He was amazing.

He couldn't wait to see what amazing thing she did next.

He couldn't wait to see if his amazing rooster could raise its tail feathers again, or if it was in rigor mortis.

"August Twenty-fifth, 1870. MCP File. Subject A, Etienne Baptiste. Today the subject exhibited symptoms of sexual obsession, and deviant syndrome patterns of exhibitionism."

Oh, no! he groaned inwardly. *She's going to start talking again. You'd think her tongue would be numb from all the exercise it's had this evening.*

Reluctantly, Etienne raised his head from where he lay,

facedown, spread-eagled in the middle of the bed.

Harriet was speaking into her hand. *Her hand? She must be demented, after all.*

On closer examination, he saw that Harriet was speaking into the small black box he'd seen earlier. Not that speaking to a box was any better.

Rolling over onto his side, he braced his elbow on the bed to support his head. Then he scrutinized her in the golden glow of a half dozen candles he'd lit sometime between her riding him and his showing her the real purpose of a fainting couch.

She sat propped against the pillows at the headboard, a sheet drawn up almost to her neck. The whole time, big words—which no doubt couched insults to him—rattled from her mouth like a drum, *rat-a-tat-tat.* The words he dismissed. He'd rather pay attention to the bruised puffiness of her lips. He loved kissing those lips, he really did. But, taking note of the glare she cast his way as she continued to talk to her box, he stifled the impulse, for now. She might just bite him, *deviant sin-drone* that he was. In fact, she already had, in some less than delicate places, far from his mouth.

He couldn't resist a different temptation, though. Stretching out his free hand, he trailed a forefinger up her linen-covered leg from ankle to thigh.

She shimmied away from him slightly, as he'd expected she would.

"Subject A also exhibits symptoms of *délire de toucher.*"

"Hey! I know what that is. And I do not have a compulsion to touch. Well, at least not a compulsion to touch everybody." He smiled at her.

Harriet moaned.

He took that as a good sign.

"Subject X, Harriet Ginoza, regressed today under the duress of forceful seduction . . . and hormone madness," the wench prattled on. "By surrendering her will to an

Sandra Hill

MCP, she discovered that sex can be a great equalizer. With two winks of an 1870 rogue, she sank to the crude level of aforementioned Subject A, wallowing in the degradation of meaningless sex. Now exploring the possible existence of a *Female* Chauvinist Pig Syndrome, or FCP."

Wallowing? I don't wallow. And meaningless? It meant a lot to me, for a certainty. "What in blue blazes are you doing?"

"Dictating," she answered absently.

"To whom?" he asked huffily. *Not me, honey. No matter how hard you try to hold the reins, I'm driving this wagon.*

"Not 'to whom,' silly. To my recording machine."

"That's the third time you've called me silly," he said, his eyes narrowing. "It's not a name I appreciate."

"Oh, pooh!" she said, dismissing his complaint.

Pooh? Did she really say "pooh" to me? Then, before he could ask her what "pooh" meant, she held up her little black box in demonstration. By pressing a button, the words she'd just spoken, as well as his question, came rumbling out of the box.

He jerked back in surprise. *"Qu'est-ce que c'est?"* he exclaimed.

"A tape recorder."

A tape recorder? What the hell's a tape recorder? One more item added to the mystery of this woman, who was already back to conversing with her magic box. He would study the box later to discover its secrets, but for now, magic of another type was starting to ruffle some feathers . . . rather, one feather that was not so limp, after all.

Mon Dieu! She was beautiful with her love-mussed ebony waves. Pink bruises and whisker burns already stained her creamy skin. What he could see of it, that was.

The woman was a strange contradiction he hadn't yet figured out. She was hotter than a June bride in a feather bed, but, in between their bouts of bone-melting sex, in which she was the most uninhibited lover he'd ever experienced, Harriet always withdrew into herself. And blamed

154

him for her lack of control. *Merde!* Who ever heard of an exprienced woman who worried so about surrendering herself to a man?

"I think I'll order some buttermilk sent up," he said, having a sudden inspiration.

She leveled him with one of her I-am-superior-and-you-are-a-scurvy-male looks. After all he'd done for her, too.

He chuckled. "Come on, honey. A little buttermilk will do you good."

"Buttermilk's bad for digestion."

Digestion? At a time like this, she's worried about her digestion? "What's really the matter, darlin'?"

"I'll tell you what's the matter, you . . . you jerk. You're turning me into a brainless bimbo." She pressed a button on the box and set it on the bedside table. "I don't recognize myself anymore. This is worse than those forceful seduction dreams. Now I'm an active participant, and I just can't let it continue."

"Oh?" *We'll see about that. Never underestimate the determination of a Creole man, sugar.* His fingertips were exploring other territory now with seeming idleness, like the sensitive skin running from her wrist to her inner elbow where goose bumps broke out like quicksilver. He loved the way she shuddered involuntarily at just that mere touch. She was so responsive. Or was he that good?

Probably both.

He grinned.

"And stop touching me," she snapped, slapping his creeping hand away.

He grinned wider. And before she could react, his hand darted out and grabbed the hem of the sheet near her neck, flicking it down and off to the side. She tried to slip away but he lunged for her. Because their bodies were slippery, he almost slid right over her.

Laughing, he managed to grab the spindles of the headboard and right himself over her squirming body. *If you only knew how much I enjoy your squirming, honey!*

Sandra Hill

Shrieking madly, she berated him with all kinds of love words, like *pond scum, sex pervert, Andrew Dice Baptiste,* and, the one he liked best, *You damn sex machine!*

Finally, he got her under control by forcing her hands over her head and onto the spindles where he secured them with two tassels from the mosquito net. The rest of her flailing body he pinned to the bed with his own much heavier weight.

"See," she sputtered. "You are into forceful seduction."

He shrugged. "I never had a taste for it before, but I must say you have whetted my appetite."

"Let me up. Now."

"I have a better suggestion." He wiggled his eyebrows at her. Unfortunately, it didn't draw the usual response. Instead, she bucked up against him angrily.

Bucking was good, too, he decided.

She realized her mistake instantly and groaned.

Did the groan mean she was weakening?

Hoping it did, he tested the slickness of their bodies by rubbing his chest hairs across her breasts. Pink nipples—hardened into pebbles from his earlier ministrations—were the crowning glory of the most beautiful cone-shaped breasts. Not too large, not too small. Just right for a man's hand.

"Don't you want to know what my suggestion is, honey?"

"No!" She scrunched her eyes tight, but not before he saw her involuntary reaction to his caress. "Why are you doing this?" she cried.

"Oh, darlin', isn't it obvious? Because I want to."

"We need to talk about this time-travel business."

He hooted with laughter. "If you think that you and I are going to carry on a rational discussion now, you really are demented. Now, my suggestion is this . . . since you don't want buttermilk, I was wondering . . . how do you feel about wine?"

Her eyes shot open. "Wine?" she squeaked out.

With a wink, he lifted himself off her now poleaxed body and walked over to the sideboard, where he picked up the crystal wine carafe. When he hovered over her once more, he held the cool glass against first one breast, then the other.

He traced a fingertip over the carafe's design. "Oh, look at this, Harriet," he said silkily. "Isn't this ornate beadwork on the rim interesting? I wonder if . . ."

Harriet made a gurgling sound, which he took for another good sign.

A short time later, he husked out, "Who knew wine could be drunk in so many interesting ways?" Then, "Did you know you have gasping down to an art, sweetheart?"

Harriet was speechless, for once. He suspected it was the beadwork that did the trick. The pièce de résistance.

Eventually, Harriet regained her power of speech. The first words out of her mouth were a complaint.

"I'm sticky and hot. I need a bath," she whined, swatting away his hand, which was measuring the curve of her buttocks.

"Maybe we should find Simone's double tub."

"I'm not getting into a tub with you," she asserted. "Who knows what perversions you'd have lined up there."

"Darlin', you love my perversions. I've counted every little appreciative squeal of yours, and there were hundreds."

"I do not squeal."

"Ooh, ooh, ooh," he mimicked.

She couldn't hold back a grin.

Well, that was progress. He was learning to read her body language so well he could probably become a mind doctor, just like her.

Climbing off the bed, both sets of their knees proceeded to crumple. His had brush-burns. In fact, another part of his body was a bit brush-burned, too, from overuse.

And Harriet's skin, from forehead to toes, was one big whisker-rasped flush. Her hair was a wild mane of black

157

curls, which had frizzed in the humidity. Her lips—her wonderful, deliciously full lips—were swollen and red from his kisses.

He was about to step into his trousers and hand her the silk dressing gown when they passed a large, beveled mirror hanging on one wall. Stopping, he dropped the garments, looped an arm over Harriet's shoulder and posed them in front of the huge reflection. "Damn, we look fine."

She moaned.

He wasn't sure if the moan meant "Oh, no!" or "Oh, my!" But the end result was that they didn't make it to the bathing chamber for another half hour.

Who knew the cock could crow so many times before dawn? Or that the South could, indeed, rise again. And again. And again.

In the middle of the night, Etienne awakened to the wail of Abel's trumpet. Abel's expert fingers and mouth evoked almost human voices and emotions from his instrument— a child's sob, a man's belly laugh, and a woman's sigh of pleasure. Also filtering up were the sounds of muted laughter, both male and female voices. Apparently, Abel was entertaining the "troops" in Simone's parlor; so it couldn't be much past midnight.

It was astonishing that so much had happened since he'd come upstairs less than six hours ago. He glanced sideways at the woman cuddled into the curve of his arm. In sleep, her full lips were closed—*thank God!*—and pouty from all his kisses. Her stubborn chin wasn't quite so rigid. And her hand, which rested on his chest, looked small and vulnerable.

Etienne's heart lurched.

It was lust, of course. Harriet, the curious woman who claimed to come from the future, had more than made up for the years of sexual deprivation he'd suffered during the war. He felt renewed now, and for that he had to be thankful.

She wasn't a spy. He was convinced of that.

So, what to do with the wench?

Easing gently out of the bed and pulling the bed linen up over her sleeping form, Etienne tapped his chin thoughtfully. He and Cain and Abel were leaving early in the morning for Bayou Noir, by separate routes. They would meet up near Bayou Barataria and head down to Bayou Vilars before nightfall.

As to the woman, well, he would follow his earlier plan and leave her under guard with Simone for the next month. He could send word by way of Abel when it was safe to release her, once the gold was back in President Grant's treasury and the massive government corruption ring was uncovered. By then, he would also have obtained his back pay and gained the much needed information on those who'd betrayed him during the war.

Then what?

Well, he supposed Harriet could make her way back to her time, or wherever she'd come from. It was her problem, not his. He would leave enough money for her care; that was as far as his responsibility went.

Ignoring the niggling tug of guilt on his conscience (truth to tell, he felt lower'n a doodlebug), he dressed quietly, donning the blond wig and mustache and the garb of a Mississippi riverboat gambler just in case there were strangers in Simone's parlor who might recognize Etienne Baptiste from the old days.

He gave her one last, lingering look. He would remember her like this, one arm thrown over her head in carnal satisfaction—she would hate that image, he knew—her face and body posture that of a woman who had been loved, long and well.

That odd lurching of his heart occurred again.

It was probably the wine he'd consumed. In a most unconventional manner.

With his hand on the doorknob, he paused. Would he ever see her again?

He doubted it. *C'est la vie.*

She'd been great entertainment to slake a man's lust, but he had no intention of muddling his life with a woman.

Au revoir, chérie.

Harriet's life was muddled beyond repair.

That was her first thought when she awakened hours later, even before she opened her eyes. The events of the past few hours flickered behind her eyelids, like an X-rated fast-forward video, and she cringed.

I am a disgrace to my profession. I am a disgrace to every woman of the nineties. I am a spineless, oversexed slut . . . well, at least where one persuasive, oversexed jerk is concerned.

She cracked an eyelid to look at said persuasive, oversexed jerk, and immediately sat upright. *Gone!* The jerk was gone.

Calm down. He probably just went to the bathroom, or something. Maybe, considerate guy that he is, he's getting us a little snack from the kitchen.

Yeah, right.

Dragging her battered body out of the bed, Harriet assessed her situation in a glance. The candles Etienne had insisted on lighting were burned down halfway. That fact, combined with the sounds of music and laughter and muffled voices coming from downstairs, told her it must be about two A.M. Joleen had told her that the girls worked from about nine P.M. to four A.M.

Glancing around the room, Harriet gasped. All of Etienne's belongings were gone, along with her two books and tape recorder.

He had abandoned her. Why that should surprise or hurt her so much, she couldn't imagine. All she knew was that her heart was shattering.

How could he engage in the most overpowering sexual experience she'd ever had and just walk away? And there was no doubt in Harriet's mind that the chemistry between them was phenomenal.

Because it was just lust for him, she concluded.

Harriet slumped wearily to the edge of the bed and let the tears flow freely, something she hadn't done in a long, long time. She cried for the weird detour her life had taken. She cried because she was lost in time, and didn't know what to do about it. She cried for her missing self-control and self-respect. But mostly, she cried because she'd thought, foolishly, that she'd found a soul mate . . . a prince.

Unfortunately, her prince had turned into Super Toad.

After she'd cried her eyes out and started hiccoughing, Harriet decided she'd had enough self-pity. She was a strong woman. She would survive, even in the past. With any luck, it would only be two more months until the railroad bridge was completed. There had to be work opportunities for women here, too. Intelligent, thinking women who, once burned, never, ever again succumbed to the charms of a blue-eyed rascal.

A plan . . . what she needed was a plan. With all the men killed in the war, and the large number of widowed or single women, she could probably set up a relationship service—sort of a matchmaker. And how about the men suffering from postwar syndrome? She could definitely help them. And, dammit, there were way too many prostitutes in this war-torn city. Yep, possibilities abounded for a bright, ambitious woman.

I am down, but I'm not out, Mr. Baptiste. You may have thrown me a sucker punch, but I'll be up before the count of ten. Just watch me.

A short time later, dressed in the lavender marbled gauze gown, which one of Simone's employees had repaired and laundered, Harriet packed her few belongings in her briefcase, including her journal and her leopard-print nightgown. Then she proceeded to the door, which was locked, as she'd

161

expected. Rapping lightly, she called out, "Oh, Joleen. Are you there?"

At first, there was silence. "Yeah, whaddaya want?" a voice finally mumbled. She must have been sleeping up against the door.

"Could you come in here a minute, please?"

Harriet heard some shuffling noises, followed by several curse words, but the door opened.

"What?" Joleen barked as she entered the room.

"Don't be mad at me, Joleen," she implored. "I'm just feeling so down and blue. Etienne left me, you see, and I . . . I . . ." She burst into sobs. One big crocodile tear slid out of her eye and ran down her cheek.

"Ah, now," Joleen said, "ain't that just like a man? Plows the field, then leaves the furrows to wither in the sun. Or be tended by some other farmer."

Harriet almost giggled at the analogy.

"Could you sit down and talk to me for a little while?" Harriet pleaded, eyeing the open door behind Joleen. "I need . . . I need to talk to another woman. Did Etienne leave or is he downstairs? Will he be coming back to me?" She batted her eyelashes hopefully.

"Now, honey," Joleen soothed, plopping down on a straight-backed chair near the door. *Heck!* "Don't be countin' on that swamp rat. He's leavin' here at first light."

That's what I thought. And, yeah, swamp rat about describes him. "But what about me?" she wailed, though what she'd like to do was make a mad dash for the door.

"It's not too bad. You're to be locked up for a month, till he sends word to release you. But don't go gettin' all fretted up. You don't have to service no men. Lessen you wants to."

"Me?" Harriet choked.

"Don't be puttin' on those la-de-da airs. Workin' for Simone ain't bad. The whores gets to keep a third of their take and they only have to pay for their rooms and meals and linens. And the Catholic girls can even go to mass on Sundays.''

Harriet was horrified.

''And girls like Charity gets paid extra, of course.''

Harriet shouldn't ask. ''Why?''

''She's a 'self-starter.' She gots a talent for helpin' young men get their cherries popped. Or sparkin' some life in men what can't get their sun to rise no more.''

But then Harriet focused on something else Joleen had said. *A month? Etienne expects to keep me locked up for a month?* Harriet gritted her teeth. Oh, someday she was going to find that jackass and put his tail in a sling. But first things first. She had to escape.

''I don't know how I'm going to survive the pain, Joleen. Have you ever felt like this? I mean, my heart just swells when I think about Etienne.'' *I think I'm going to gag.*

''Honey, at my age, just about everything swells. Don't you be moanin' and groanin' over that Baptiste fella, though. They's plenty more men in this city, and most of 'em don't favor pokin' their private parts in dead women.''

''Really?'' Harriet said and batted her eyelashes some more. She pulled another chair up close to her guard so that they were almost knee to knee. ''Joleen, you have the most beautiful eyes. No, really you do. They're greenish, like mine, but much different. Look at mine. Look closely. See the pupils.''

Harriet's voice took on a monotonous, tranquilizing tone. The eye method was one of her best hypnotherapy techniques. Within seconds, Joleen, who was probably exhausted to begin with and in a susceptible state of suggestion, lolled against the back of her chair in a deep trance.

Okay, step one accomplished.

''Why is Joleen sleeping?'' a female voice asked.

Oh, great! It was Charity, strolling down the hall. By the looks of her wrinkled, red satin gown hanging half off one shoulder, she must have just finished with a client. Harriet instantly berated herself for her harsh assessment. Right now, she didn't feel much better than a whore herself.

"Oh, Joleen just dozed off," Harriet lied blithely. "Would you come in for a second?"

"Ain't you s'posed to be locked up?" Charity asked dubiously.

"Oh, Etienne trusts me now," She waved her hand airily toward the rumpled bed. Then, seating Charity on the chair, Harriet sank down to the bed and proceeded to tell the softhearted girl her sob story.

"Ain't men the worst sort of rats?" Charity commiserated.

"Absolutely. By the way, Charity, do you know that you have the most unusual eyes?" Within minutes, Charity had joined Joleen in la-la land.

Hmmm. What to do with them?

Harriet smiled.

Carefully, she gave the two women their separate posthypnotic instructions. Joleen was to strut around the room, flapping her elbows like a chicken and clucking, "Cock-a-doodle-do." Charity was to clasp her hands over her head and chant, "Etienne is a jerk, Etienne is a jerk, Etienne is a jerk. . . ."

The password given to both women, which would end their trances, was, naturally, *rooster*.

Well pleased with her efforts thus far, Harriet whisked her hands together. Then she went over to the bed and lifted the mattress to obtain the most important element in her escape plan—the single bar of gold she'd filched from the coffin back on the train when Etienne and Cain had turned their backs on her for one fortunate moment. Her insurance policy. Her ace in the hole. No way had she been going to leave that train, her anchor to the future, without some financial security.

Hey, she wasn't a total nincompoop.

Putting the bar in her briefcase, along with Joleen's gun belt and pistols—though what she'd do with those, Harriet had no idea—she headed for the door and freedom.

Even so, just before Harriet closed the door and turned the key in the lock, she felt tears well in her eyes. With painful insight, Harriet realized that she'd held something precious in her hands in this room, and somehow it had slipped through her fingers.

Chapter Ten

Etienne took one last sip of the thick chicory coffee, a Creole mainstay, and pushed his chair away from the table. It would be dawn soon. Time to leave the Crescent City.

"What the hell is taking Abel so long?" he grumbled.

"Need you ask?" Cain responded with an arched brow.

They'd long since finished the huge breakfast Simone had laid out for them before going off with Abel more than an hour ago. The fancy house customers had departed by now and the girls had retired after a tiring night's work.

He stood and walked over to a side mirror, checking his disguise again. The blond wig and mustache changed his appearance dramatically, not to mention the pleated shirt, brocaded vest and frock coat left behind by one of the brothel's customers.

This whole parade of disguises was wearing thin, and bordered on the ridiculous. But it was a game Etienne played to divert Pope. In order to win the game, they had to lead Pope and all the game players to Texas—the lair of the prime player in this charade. No sense killing ants if the main nest stayed intact.

"How come I never get to be the riverboat gambler?" Cain complained behind him. He was dressed in the blue uniform of a Yankee army corporal.

"A blond Negro?" Etienne inquired with a grin.

Cain shrugged. "I've seen a few."

"Next time, then."

"With any luck there won't ever be a next time." He stowed his medical bag in a knapsack and asked, not for the first time, "Aren't you going to say good-bye to the wench before we go?"

"*Mon Dieu*, no!"

Cain laughed. "Afraid, are you?"

"For a certainty. The witch has worn me down to a nub as it is. I don't trust her strange allure."

"Nubs have a way of coming back. Trust me on that. We doctors know these things," Cain teased. "Perhaps you fear yourself, my friend."

"Perhaps," Etienne agreed with a grimace.

Then Cain exclaimed, "Would you look at that? Here comes my wife."

"Well, heavens above, why are you-all dawdlin' heah? Tain't nothin' like an uppity nigger!" a high-pitched feminine voice addressed them from the hall. Abel sashayed into the room with a flourish, wearing a long calico gown of faded gold that no doubt belonged to Joleen. A bucket-style bonnet adorned with silk buttercups crowned a head of shoulder-length, black curls. He carried a yellow parasol, and matching gloves covered his rough hands. Two melon-sized mounds stuck out from his chest.

"*Merde!* You look like a sunflower," Etienne observed.

"Nice bosoms," Cain remarked.

"Touch my tits and you're gator bait, you randy buck, you," Abel hissed, narrowing his eyes at his brother.

Chortling, they all walked toward the front door.

"Stop right there! All of you!"

They spun around to see Simone standing at the top of the stairs, hands on hips. She wore only a dressing gown, and her mussed hair bespoke her recent activity with Abel. The flush on her face was from anger, not lovemaking, though.

"What'd you do? Refuse to marry her again?" Cain asked Abel.

For years, Abel had been besotted with Simone, and vice versa. It didn't matter to him that she'd once been a harlot, that she ran a house of ill-repute. Or that she was white. It didn't matter to her that he was a musician with less than spectacular financial promise. Or that he was a Negro.

But Abel knew that, despite the war and the Emancipation Proclamation, a mixed marriage would never be accepted. As it was, Simone had received more than one threat from the Knights of the White Camellia just for allowing blacks into her establishment.

"She always asks. I always say no. Maybe it would be best if I went travelin' with Billy Bolden's Brass Band. At least then our inevitable separation wouldn't hurt so bad," Abel replied in a subdued voice. Then he straightened. "But it's not me she's starin' at with fire in her eyes now."

Cain and Abel both glanced at Etienne.

"Me? What did I do?"

"Not you," Simone said, storming up to them. "It's that . . . that woman you brought here. She's gone."

"Gone?" they all said.

"What? Have you turned into a chorus of parrots? *Oui*, the woman is gone and she has put a voodoo curse on two of my girls."

"Voodoo? Are you sure, *chérie*?" Abel asked. "She's not even from the South."

"Well, actually, she has lived here," Cain corrected. "Remember, Etienne, she said her stepfather was from Louisiana?"

"Aaarrgh!" Simone stamped her foot. "Would you all

listen to me? The witch has put two of my girls into a trance. Joleen is upstairs squawking like a chicken, and Charity keeps chanting the same refrain, over and over, 'Etienne is a jerky, Etienne is a jerky.''

"What's a jerky?" Abel asked. "I mean, I know what hardtack is, but what does it mean when a woman calls a man a jerky? Oh, I see, I s'pose it has something to do with his *hard*tack.'' He made a gesture at Etienne's groin.

"Aaarrgh!" Simone shrieked again.

"Good Lord!" Etienne put a hand to his forehead in disbelief. *What next?*

"Not *le bon Dieu*. Damballa," Simone told Etienne.

He shook his head, convinced that Harriet wasn't involved in the black arts. "She did tell me that she uses something called hypnotherapy with her customers," he recalled. "In fact, she wanted to cure my headache by putting me in a trance."

Simone leveled an angry glare at Etienne, as if he were already in a trance. "So, M'sieur Baptiste, what are you going to do about this situation?"

He tossed his satchel to the floor with disgust and headed back up the stairs.

Behind him, Etienne heard Simone comment to Abel, "You look pitiful."

And Abel asked her, "Do you want to touch my bosoms?"

It took two hours before they were able to break the trance. That was when Cain berated him, "None of this would have happened if you'd kept your damn rooster in its coop."

"Rooster," Joleen and Charity murmured then, coming instantly alert. They didn't remember a thing, except that Harriet had admired their beautiful eyes. Then they proceeded to lambast Etienne for abandoning the poor, helpless woman.

Helpless? She's no more helpless than a wildcat in a henhouse.

After that, they gave him a tongue-lashing over his unusual sex habits. "No wonder the sweet lady left you, you slimy swamp rat," Joleen declared. "Can't ya get it up for any live women no more?"

Cain and Abel dragged him away before he attacked the blathering Amazon, and probably got himself walloped in the process.

"Are we going to search for her now?" Cain asked as they left Simone's house, hours later than originally planned.

"No."

"No?"

"I don't ever want to see that woman again," he said, seething. "I fear what I'd do to her." Despite himself, though, an image flitted through Etienne's mind of just what he'd already done to her. And a small part of him—the part not blistering with blood-boiling anger—had to admire the woman's ingenuity. She'd outwitted him, good and proper.

In some ways, he wished they would meet again someday. She wouldn't find him such an easy target a second time.

Etienne leaned against a levee piling, smoking a thin cheroot. He'd just purchased a steamboat ticket and was waiting for the passenger boarding to commence. A discreet glance across the wide street confirmed that Cain and Abel still stood in front of the Lousiana National Bank on Decatur Street.

He had booked a short passage on the *Dixie Belle*. Mademoiselle Abel, in Sunday finery, had done likewise. "She" pretended to be going to visit her sister Sula Mae down in Terrebonne Parish and would board after him, as was the custom for black travelers. Abel had already warned Cain that if he tried to kiss "her" good-bye, there would be hell to pay.

Cain planned to maneuver a large pirogue he'd purchased up to Bayou Barataria, where they would all meet later that day to continue their journey to Bayou Noir. In all, the trip should take four days.

It wouldn't be the most comfortable mode of travel. Steamboat packets navigated many of the interlocking bayou waterways, but none could penetrate as far as the remote Bayou Noir, especially during this low season. Flatboats did make the rough trek, but Etienne was exercising extreme caution. He didn't want the three of them to travel together among strangers who might later identify them to Pope's men and bring a premature ending to the staged chase.

So now Etienne put his finger to the side of his nose. It was the signal to break ranks and commence their plan.

Unfortunately, Cain put his thumb to his nose and wagged his remaining fingers. It was not the agreed-upon return signal.

Really, for a serious physician, Cain went too far with his foolery. Especially of late.

Abel didn't appreciate his brother's games, either. He poked Cain in the ribs with an elbow. Then he made eye contact with Etienne and pointed his parasol toward the bank entrance.

Etienne's jaw dropped.

Strolling out, large as life, was Harriet, the bane of his life.

With the skirt of her gauzy lavender gown swishing from side to side, she walked right by Cain and Abel without recognizing them. She was too busy counting a wad of paper money, which she tucked into a side flap of her travel case. Then, smiling with a feline I-got-the-cream satisfaction, she flicked open a parasol and proceeded down Canal Street toward the railway station.

His first reaction was to let her go. Even though he was madder than hell at her, he couldn't risk accosting her on an open street.

But how had she gotten so much currency? He'd examined the contents of her satchel. She had nothing of value to barter in a bank.

Suddenly, the hair stood up on the back of his neck in warning. Well-honed instincts advised him to investigate further.

Using silent signals, Etienne directed Cain and Abel to follow him. Then he tossed his cheroot to the ground and strode after Harriet.

"*Salut,* mademoiselle," a man greeted her, edging in close to her side.

She gave the tall fellow in the dandified attire of a riverboat gambler a haughty scowl at his familiarity. He wasn't the first man to accost her today. A few had even tried to cop a feel. Thank goodness, she'd had the foresight to grab a parasol from the umbrella stand at Simone's. She'd soon discovered that a parasol was better than Mace. Apparently single women on the streets were considered fair game.

But she wasn't a frail little Southern belle. She would get rid of this creep, just as she had the others. A cursory glance revealed a version of Kevin Costner with blond hair and mustache and a rakishly tilted hat.

Oh, my! She did have a thing about Kevin Costner.

But, no, no, no . . . a handsome man was the last thing she needed in her life right now.

"Slow down, *s'il vous plaît.* I just want to talk with you, *chérie.*"

Uh-oh! She would recognize that voice anywhere.

Her only outward reaction was a slight stumble in her stride, which she immediately corrected. "You are pitiful," she murmured and kept walking.

"Now, darlin'—"

"Go away."

"Why did you run away, *chérie*?" he asked in a low tone, meanwhile nodding to passersby to maintain the impression of normalcy. A grimace passed over his face a the warning whistle of a nearby steamboat, which would be departing soon.

Harriet stared straight ahead as she accelerated her pace, hoping he would give up his pursuit.

Instead, he kept in step with her.

Coming to an abrupt halt, she confronted him. "You want to know why I left? Well, I want to know why you locked me up."

"Safety."

"Safety?" she scoffed. "Whose? Mine or yours?"

"Both."

"Liar. You know, you can always tell when a man is lying. He moves his lips." Neither of them smiled at the joke. Her voice carried a wealth of venom. "I detest you."

"I'm not so fond of you right now, either, Harriet."

"Just like a man! Sweeps a woman off her feet when he's horny, then sweeps her out the door afterward."

Etienne rolled his eyes with exasperation. "Come into this restaurant with me where we can talk in private," he suggested.

"I may have suffered a brain blip, but I'm not totally stupid. You had your chance to talk last night, buster."

"I was busy communicating in other ways."

Her face flushed. "I'm not going anywhere with you, ever again. And stop touching me, you . . . you lech." She shrugged off the hand that he'd put to her elbow to assist her into the cafe.

"I have no time for this nonsense," he muttered to himself. Then he sliced her with a glare. "How did you get the money?" he hissed out, ditching subtlety.

"What money?" She averted her eyes.

"The money you put in your travel case."

She exhaled with resignation, realizing that there was no sense denying an obvious fact. "From the bank."

"Aaarrgh! I already know that. What I want to know is what you gave the banker to get the money?" He spaced his words evenly as if addressing a thickheaded child.

Harried snapped her parasol shut, and braced both hands on her hips belligerently. "A gold bar."

Her answer obviously stunned him.

"Wh-what? You stole one of my gold bars?"

She waved a hand airily with disregard.

"Now you've really done it, Harriet. I'm going to have to kill you."

"That's right, violence is the answer to everything in your dictionary. First forceful seduction, now physical threats. Don't try to paint me guilty. You stole the gold in the first place. So you're the real thief in this picture."

His eyes widened with astonishment at the accusation. "I *recovered* the gold shipment from men who stole it from the U.S. government. I work for President Grant."

"You do?" She blinked in surprise. Actually, he'd alluded to this mission before, but was he telling the truth? Probably. But it didn't make any difference to her. "Well, that's beside the point. Since I didn't steal it from the government, the crime isn't mine," she deduced.

"That's the damndest feminine illogic I've ever heard."

"Makes sense to me."

"Do you have any idea what you've done?"

"You're boring me. Go away," she said, and resumed walking. "I've got a train to catch to Chicago."

"Chicago? Not bloody likely."

She stopped again, and tried a more even-tempered approach. "Listen, Etienne, you locked me up. I escaped. No harm, no foul. We're even. So, hit the road, Jack. I'm not your problem anymore."

"Oh, you most definitely are my problem. Showing that gold bar in public is comparable to waving a red flag. Pope's men are going to be swarming all over this city within hours. And you, my dear, will be considered my accomplice."

A brief spark of fear almost made her gasp, but she bit her bottom lip to halt any outcry. Unfortunately, that simple action caused Etienne's eyes to linger on her lips. And she knew by the parting of his lips and the dilating of his pupils that he was remembering way too much about her mouth and its wicked talents, talents even she hadn't known she possessed.

"I can handle myself," she said weakly, her fist instinctively clenching the handle on her briefcase.

He understood immediately. "Joleen's pistols? Do you have any idea how to use a gun?"

"No, but I'm thinking about practicing on you. Guess which body part I'm going to aim at?"

"Guess which body part of yours I'm going to wallop once we get out of this city?"

"Another one of your perversions?" she cooed sweetly.

"God, I'd like to twist your sharp tongue into a knot."

"I'd like to see you try."

Stroking his fake mustache, Etienne seemed to come to a decision. "You'll have to come with us now, of course. Not that I relish the prospect of another moment in your company."

"Thank you for the heartfelt invitation, but no thanks. You had your one-nighter. Go carve a notch in your bedpost and ride off into your MCP sunset." She stopped walking and scowled at him. "I gave you your walking papers, mister. Scram."

"So that's what this is about. A woman scorned and all that?" He grinned.

The grin was the last straw. Harriet raised her closed parasol.

Etienne reacted just in time, deflecting her aim so that she hit him on the shoulder, not the top of his head. Passersby were watching, but she didn't care.

"Calm down, Harriet. Men have been sowing wild oats from the beginning of time."

She growled. "I refuse to be your wild oats."

Etienne laughed. He dared to laugh at her.

She raised her parasol again. In the haze of her anger, though, a large black woman in a tacky yellow dress accidentally walked into her, and then, not so accidentally, grabbed her briefcase. She and her companion, a black man in a Yankee uniform, rushed away.

With parasol still raised, Harriet shrieked her outrage and began to pursue the thieves. Her money was in that briefcase.

"Harriet, stop!" Etienne called after her. "It's not what you think."

Just before he tackled her from behind and hefted her into his arms, Harriet got a glimpse of her attackers up ahead. They'd slowed down at the corner and glanced back at her.

She started to laugh hysterically. It was Cain in the army uniform. And, oh, good Lord, Abel was dressed as a woman. While Cain looked debonair and dashing in the Union blue, Abel looked like a six-foot-plus Chiquita banana.

Her attention was diverted by the brute whose arms were locked around her flailing legs and shoulders, pressing her face into his chest so her words came out muffled and indistinguishable. He was explaining to a police officer who'd just walked up, "There is no problem, *capitaine*. My wife swooned. Her monthlies, you know." He confided that last with a manly cough.

Then he whispered in her ear, "Hush, sweetheart. You have been checkmated." Pinching a spot on the back of her neck, he added, "I'm not a hypnotherapist, darlin', but I have a few tricks up my sleeve, too." He pinched harder, and she felt really strange. If she didn't know better, she would think that she was experiencing her first true-blue Southern-belle swoon. Either that, or Etienne knew about the carotid artery.

The last thing she heard Etienne say was, "I sure hope you can row, honey."

Harriet was curled up almost in a fetal position, her face resting on some fabric that smelled vaguely familiar.

Etienne. The cloth carried the scent of Etienne's skin.

With her eyes closed, she smiled and burrowed her face deeper. She must still be in the brothel with Etienne. He hadn't abandoned her, after all. She drifted in and out of sleep then, incongruously comforted by his presence.

Awareness tugged at her consciousness. Harriet couldn't be sure if minutes or hours had passed. An excessive heat bore down on her, and her body began to ache from its cramped position.

She yawned and tried to stretch. But couldn't.

Geez, did the lout have to take up the whole bed? Typical of the male species exerting its subliminal force.

But she liked his maleness, she decided. Running her fingers caressingly over the rough surface of the cloth that pillowed her head, she encountered several buttons and realized that it must be his jacket.

When had Etienne dressed?

Ribet, Ribet!

Harriet jerked awake. She was hungry, but surely her stomach wasn't rumbling that loud. Was it?

Ribet, Ribet!

"What is that?"

"A bullfrog," Etienne told her matter-of-factly.

"A bullfrog? In a brothel?"

Etienne laughed. And she thought she heard two other male voices laugh, as well.

Now fully alert, Harriet sat up and a blinding heat struck her. Opening her eyes slowly, she saw the most amazing sight. Overhead, bright sunlight barely penetrated a thick green canopy of ancient oak trees dripping moss. And the canopy was moving.

Confused, Harriet leaned back on her elbows and saw Etienne in his shirtsleeves, paddling a big canoe that resembled a hollowed-out tree trunk—a pirogue. Behind him was Cain, also rowing. Stretching her neck to peer behind her, she saw Abel in a yellow dress at the front of the canoe, his sunflower bonnet hanging down his back by its streamers. She was stuffed into a narrow space on the floor of the canoe between Etienne and Abel.

She put a hand to the back of her neck, which ached, and memory hit her like a two-ton truck. Etienne had pinched her there, on her carotid artery, just before she'd blacked out.

Oh, God! The slimeball really had dumped her at Simone's. And now he was kidnapping her. Furious, Harriet pushed herself upward to get to her feet. "Why you no-good, son of a—"

"No!" all three men yelled at once.

"Don't stand," Etienne warned.

But it was too late.

Harriet jumped up. The canoe swayed, then tipped over. Within seconds, they were all in the green, murky water, swimming for shore.

As she stood on the shoreline, her feet sinking in mud up to her calves, Harriet watched an alligator the size of Vermont cruise by with her briefcase in its snout.

"Go get that alligator," she shrieked to Etienne.

He was tossing his satchel, Cain's medical bag, and the case holding Abel's trumpet onto the bank, while the two cursing brothers were righting the canoe. The icy glare Etienne shot her was not promising. Geez, how was she expected to know that the canoe would tip over?

"Okay, I'll do it myself," she said huffily. Slogging out of the mire, she grabbed one of the paddles floating by. Then she stomped along the river's edge through mud the consistency of pudding, which quickly swallowed her tracks. The whole time, she kept in her sights the alligator, who was swimming near shore with her briefcase.

"Harriet, come back here. It's not worth the money. Besides, Abel put your money in his trombone case."

"Hah! Who cares about the money? That's a Louis Vuitton briefcase. Besides, my birth-control pills are in there."

"Birth . . . birth-control pills! You're chasing a dangerous animal over pills?"

"Yep!" Raising her paddle overhead, she brought it down hard on the alligator's head. The surprised animal gave her an astonished once-over with its protrubent eyes, then released its booty. She used the handle of her oar to maneuver her briefcase closer. Stunned, the beast continued to gape at her through its big, lidless eyes.

She turned to go back and saw immediately that the alligator wasn't the only one stunned and gaping.

"Hey," she explained to the three men who clearly had never seen a real woman in action, "a girl's gotta do what a girl's gotta do to survive in the jungle."

"This isn't a jungle," Etienne informed her when he finally got over his shock. "It's a bayou."

Tucking her teeth-imprinted briefcase under her arm—the handle hanging by a thread now—she looked up at the plague of her life. "Same difference, hon. Jungle, bayou, Wall Street, the dating scene . . . you need a machete to get through all of them." She tapped his chin as she passed, just to annoy him. What she'd like to do was punch out his lights.

"Aaarrgh!"

"Perhaps you could channel some of that hostility into a hobby. Do you have a hobby?"

He spun on his heel and stomped away in front of her.

She followed him. "Anger is just an emotional reaction to a frustrating event," she explained to his back. "A defense mechanism."

"Someone must have put a curse on me," Etienne grumbled.

"I've noticed that you're often stressed out, and that's unhealthy. Taking more than eighteen breaths per minute is the stress factor I always use for diagnosing—"

"You've been counting the number of breaths I take?" His eyes flashed with consternation as he turned on her.

"I do it reflexively," she admitted.

"How have you managed to live so long?" He pulled his own hair with exasperation.

Geez, the guy really did need an anxiety overhaul. Being a softie at heart, she decided to help. "I've developed a good exercise for recovering from an energy drain of negative emotions."

She waited for him to ask her to elaborate. When he didn't, merely rolled his eyes heavenward, she went on anyhow. "With your mouth closed, curl your tongue under, and hum for three minutes. It works every time."

At first, he seemed to consider her words, probably testing how to curl his tongue.

"You have to hum, too."

He made a grunting sound of disgust. "The first thing I'm going to do when I get to Bayou Noir is find a voodoo priestess to remove the curse."

Abel, who'd just come up, must have overheard. He appeared to be trying out the tongue routine. Or maybe that humming sound was suppressed laughter.

Actually, all three men were laughing now.

"Do you understand half of what she says, Etienne?" Abel choked out.

"No. Just smile and nod. That works with most women."

The jerk! "I've decided to make you three the control group for my MCP study. Jerks Anonymous, that's what I'll call you."

"What's an MCP?" Abel inquired of Cain.

"Male chauvinist pig," Cain answered, to her amazement. She hadn't realized he'd been listening so closely.

"You missed all the good lectures Dr. Ginny's been giving us while you were off cavorting in Memphis," Etienne added.

"Cavorting?" Abel snapped. "If someone hadn't been havin' his rooster groomed at the wrong time back on that train, we would all have been on our way to Texas by now."

"Texas? You're going to Texas? Oh, no! I am not going to Texas. That's too far away from the entry point of this time hole I've fallen into."

"I'm gonna need a whole wagonload of voodoo priestesses to get rid of this curse," Etienne said, shaking his head.

"Perhaps you should try some tongue humming," Abel suggested to Etienne. "You're lookin' mighty tense. Is it sexual deprivation?"

"Abel, you are a really dumb man with your continual sexual innuendoes. I've found that men who talk too much about sex are usually less than proficient in the sack," she observed. "For example, do you know the difference between a golf ball and a g-spot? What am I thinking? Of course, you don't."

"Another dumb-men joke!" the three dumb men complained.

"The answer is: A man will search forty-five minutes for a golf ball." She folded her arms with a self-satisfied "Hmpfh!"

"What's a golf ball?" Cain asked, puzzled.

"Damned if I know," Etienne answered. "What's a g-spot?"

"Is she questioning my abilities as a lover?" Abel wanted to know.

"Durn tootin' I am. You have this real fixation with sex, Abel. In fact, all men do."

Etienne, Cain and Abel all said at the same time, "Who? Me?"

She took a deep breath and threw out one last shot. "Most of all, I think it's really true what scientists say about men reaching their sexual prime at age eighteen. Everything is downhill from then on. So stop fighting nature, guys. There's nothing worse than an overaged studmuffin."

All three sets of jaws dropped in astonishment.

"I'm not downhill. Are you two downhill?" Abel asked.

"What's a studmuffin?" Etienne asked.

"I can't believe a lady would talk about such intimate matters," Cain said.

"I think I'll put her jokes to music," Abel announced.

"If you do, I'm going to stuff that trumpet down your throat," Etienne threatened.

Harriet plopped down to the ground and sighed, suddenly bone-weary. Like a slow-motion recap, all the horrible events of the past two days flicked through Harriet's mind. The train derailment. Her time-travel. Being locked in a coffin. Making love in a brothel. Her escape, then the kidnapping. And finally, a confrontation with an alligator. It was just too darn much for one woman to handle.

"*Chérie,* don't cry."

Harriet looked up to see Etienne hunkered at her side. He reached out a thumb and wiped a fat tear off her cheek. She hadn't even realized she'd been weeping. How sappy of her! But Harriet came to an even more alarming conclusion in that moment as she met Etienne's gentle gaze.

Oh, my God! I'm falling in love with a jerk. A ten.

Chapter Eleven

As dusk began to descend on the bayou, Etienne leaned his head back against an ancient cypress tree and folded his legs at the ankles, almost at the water's lapping edge. With an inner sigh, he took in the peace and beauty of the land he loved.

His family had moved from the remote southern Louisiana swamplands of Bayou Noir in Terrebonne Parish when he was six years old. Even though he'd been raised most of his life in California, had traveled the length and breadth of the United States before and after the war, had studied in Europe's most cosmopolitan cities, it was the bayou that felt like home to him.

There wasn't an animal or plant he didn't know in this semitropical paradise. And he held a special affection for all of them, whether they were deadly or beneficial to humankind. It was this landscape Etienne had dreamed of when life seemed most hopeless to him in prison. Here was simplicity. Every animal and plant had a purpose. This life he could understand.

He smiled as a spotted skunk waddled out of the bushes, and raccoons, opossums and moles scurried out of its path. *Poor thing!* Although it was smaller than a house cat, one squirt of this little fellow's musk could render the fiercest beast temporarily blind. And the stench had been known to carry for over a mile.

In the sky, thousands of squealing bats swept out *en masse* like black sheets floating on the wind. Flying squirrels glided through the dense trees, being careful to avoid the perched night owls. Across the stream a rare red wolf and her litter of four rangy cubs drank warily, watching him the entire time. Gators of every size and description— the undisputed royalty of this territory—glided by, surveying their domain.

If only his own life were so uncomplicated.

His gaze slid to his current complication, a few feet away near the fire. Harriet was prattling to Abel about his music and something akin to it, called *jazz*, in a faraway time. Words like *Dizzy, Jelly Roll, Louis, blues, ragtime* and *improvisation* rippled off her tongue and held Abel spellbound.

Cain was sleeping soundly on a mound of pine needles on the other side of the clearing. Earlier she'd kept him enthralled with her tales of modern medicine. The cures that were to come for such diseases as typhoid, smallpox and diphtheria. And the horrendous new diseases, like AIDS.

Cain was lying in his three-sided shebang—a crude temporary shelter comprised of brush and blankets. They'd decided to rotate guard duty during the night. The fire would keep most animals away, but it was best to be sure in this deadly environment.

"Oh, my goodness!" Harriet exclaimed to Abel, jarring Etienne to attention. She put a hand over her heart. "It just occurred to me. New Orleans was the birthplace of jazz after the Civil War."

"Jazz?" Abel laughed. "Is that what they'll call the new music?"

"Why is that so funny?"

"Honey, *jass* is a French word for . . . ah, fornicating. Same as that famous f-word. A jazzbow is a real Don Juan."

She smiled.

"Well, I guess the word's appropriate, though, because this kind of music is best when it's low-down and dirty, like sex."

"Leave it to you, Abel, to bring the subject back to sex. But, really, there's another reason I was so surprised before. What's your last name?"

"Lincoln," Abel said, perplexed at her question.

Harriet raised an eyebrow. "Abe-l Lincoln?"

"Yes," Abel chuckled. "White folks didn't give their slaves last names. So me and Cain decided Lincoln would do us fine."

"There was a man . . ." Harriet started to say, staring at Abel now as if he were some sort of God. "Oh, this is incredible, but there was a black man called A. B. Lincoln whom historians refer to as the godfather of jazz. A lot of early jazz wasn't written down; so it would have been easy to get the names mixed up, or mispronounced."

"Me? A godfather?" Abel scoffed, but he held his shoulders a little higher.

"And Abel, I just thought of something else." There were tears in her eyes. "One of the most famous jazz songs written by A. B. Lincoln was 'My Simone.' Experts say it is pure poetry."

Abel just gaped at her incredulously, and there were tears in his eyes, too.

"You and Cain were slaves?" she asked, referring back to Abel's earlier words.

Abel shook his head. "We were born at Bayou Noir, where our mother, Iris, was a slave. When Etienne's papa, James Baptiste, bought the sugar plantation, he gave the slaves a chance to earn their freedom. Our mother was freed soon after we were born.''

''How fascinating!''

Abel nodded. ''Mr. Baptiste hated slavery, just like Etienne did. That's why Etienne left college to fight in the war. That's why—''

''*Abel*,'' Etienne interrupted, not wanting him discussing his personal life. The witch knew too much about him already.

Harriet turned her head to look at him, and scowled. He understood. She feared the powerful feelings that had overcome them both the night before, and she wanted no repetition, especially after his ''dumping'' her, as she so aptly described his actions.

And he had the same fears. Sometimes she made him feel as helpless as a turtle on its back. So, for the past few hours, he'd avoided close contact with her, not even an accidental brush of flesh in passing. Mostly, he'd just watched and listened during the preparation and eating of their hastily gathered supper—a bayou hodgepodge of succulent frog legs and catfish cooked over the open fire, with tart wild cherries and crab apples for dessert. Like the rest of them, Harriet had eaten heartily. But then, all her appetites appeared to be hearty, he realized with a slow smile of remembrance.

''Are you laughing at me? Again?'' Harriet sniped, getting to her feet. Abel got up and, yawning widely, ambled off into the trees to relieve himself.

Harriet was wearing an old shirt of Etienne's with the sleeves rolled up numerous times to the elbow and the tails knotted at her midsection. His mortician trousers were much too big, but she'd managed to rope in the waist and roll up the pant legs so that they wouldn't slip down or trip her bare feet. And, blessed Lord, she had the sexiest feet in the world—narrow and high-arched with pink-painted toenails.

Maybe he was a pervert, after all. Getting all hot-blooded

over toes, of all things! And what he'd like to do with those slim appendages!

Using soapwort leaves for lather, they'd all bathed earlier in the stream, including Harriet, who insisted on privacy, even though he'd seen all she had to offer. But he hadn't objected. He didn't need that kind of temptation, or complication, in his life right now. Even fully covered in her mannish attire, she enticed him. Mightily.

"No, I'm not laughing at you, Harriet," he said finally, coming to his feet as well. They stood yards apart, but still too close. "I'm . . . I'm just surprised that you've bewitched Cain and Abel so quickly with your stories of the future."

"Bewitched? I don't know about that. They do seem to believe that I've time-traveled, even though I can hardly accept it myself."

He shrugged. "There just doesn't seem to be any other explanation. You have to understand that superstition and belief in unnatural events, like voodoo, are part of the Negro culture."

"And you?" she asked, tilting her head, which caused her hair to come undone from its loosely tied queue.

"Creoles are raised under the dictates of the Roman Catholic Church. Miracles are a big part of its dogma. Despite my absence from the church all these years, I believe in miracles."

She smiled.

And his traitorous heart skipped a beat.

"So you consider me a miracle?"

He had to smile back. "Hardly. Your method of coming here might be a miracle, but whoever sent you intended it as a curse on me. Perhaps for my misspent youth."

"Is that why you kidnapped me in New Orleans and forced me to come with you? And by the way, I don't appreciate your pinching the carotid artery in my neck; you could have done permanent nerve damage. Was it because you felt a responsibility for my being here?"

Sandra Hill

"No . . . well, perhaps. Mostly it was an impulse, engendered by your foolish escape and then selling the gold bar. You are in danger now, too, sweetheart. Don't for a second doubt that."

"Here I thought you were so overpowered with love for me that you couldn't help yourself."

He couldn't tell if she was being sarcastic or serious.

"I think of this as some kind of divine intervention, too," she added. "I doubt there's any logical scientific explanation. Yep, I was sent here for a purpose."

"And that is?"

"I haven't figured that out yet, but it's all tied in with you somehow."

He groaned.

"Changing the subject, there is something I want you to know. You treated me like a whore last night, leaving me the way you did, with no good-bye or explanation. But I—"

"No, you misunderstood what I—"

She raised a hand to stop his interruption. "I might give the impression of being promiscuous, but I'm not a slut. Casual sex never appealed to me, and one-night stands are a no-no. In fact, I haven't had a relationship for more than two years. Last night just . . . well, happened."

That was what she'd told him earlier, but he had hardly been able to credit it. "Two years! But those pills of yours? The ones you braved an alligator to retrieve, the ones you told Cain prevent conception?"

She waved a hand dismissively. "Women of my time take them for lots of reasons, even when they're not active sexually."

He shook his head at her bluntness. "So you're saying last night happened because we'd both been deprived for a long time?"

"Not at all. What I'm saying is that, at least for me, I behaved in a totally out-of-character manner. I think, however, that our lovemaking was meant to be."

188

He laughed. "God promoting illicit fornication? You've been reading a different Bible than I have."

"You know what they say? God moves in mysterious ways." She smiled again, and he decided this was a dangerous path they were treading. They were conversing almost like friends. Or lovers.

"Get some sleep now," he said gruffly. "We'd best start early tomorrow, at dawn. The heat won't be so bad then."

"I'm not sleeping with you," she snapped with fierce resolution. Her eyes glittered green fire at him, daring him to disagree, as she reached up to draw her clean hair back off her face. While he watched with undue interest, she retied the loose strands at the nape with a strip of cloth torn off her ruined lavender gown.

"I don't recall inviting you," he countered. *But I'd like to.* Her posture—arms upraised—inadvertently caused his shirt to pull across her chest. In the fading daylight, he could see her high breasts. Or perhaps he was imagining and remembering.

I want her.

Their eyes held in an extended moment of awareness.

She wants me. He could tell she shared the powerful yearning.

"You'll sleep there," he said, pointing to a nearby pile of pine needles covered with her discarded gown under a shebang similar to Cain's. "I'll sleep here." He indicated his own neat pile and shelter several yards away. It wasn't nearly distant enough. The next parish would be better. Or the next state.

She nodded and licked her bottom lip nervously.

Without thinking, he did the same, mirroring her action.

She gasped, a small sound that he heard only because his senses were so attuned to her.

How was he going to manage being around this woman for the next few days without making love to her?

Her eyes couldn't seem to move away—those odd cat eyes, whose darker, elliptical centers were dilated now to three times their normal size. A clear sign of arousal.

"Don't look at me like that," she whispered, folding her arms across her chest.

"How?"

"Like you're making love to me with your eyes."

His lips twitched, then broke into a grin. "Body language?"

She nodded.

"You're doing the same to me, darlin'. If you only knew what your eyes were saying to me!"

She blinked rapidly as if to hide her response.

He couldn't believe what was happening between them. Loveplay without touching. *Amazing!*

"You're going to try to abandon me at Bayou Noir, aren't you, Etienne? For a second time. I won't stay, you know."

"Oh, you will stay. Never doubt it. Don't cross wills with me on this, *chérie*. You won't win."

"Wanna bet?" Her hands were on her hips now. Another too-revealing pose, conjuring way too many images.

Luckily, Abel reappeared out of the bushes.

He took one look at the two of them and slapped his thigh with glee. "Lordy, Lordy, you two are like a mad hen and a randy ol' rooster. The air sizzles around you."

Harriet made a clucking sound of disagreement.

Etienne glowered. "That's enough, Abel."

But Abel got the last word in. "Well, look at that. I do believe, my rooster friend, that your comb is red. And, for a certainty, I just heard Harriet cluck at you." He referred to the old folk tale that the fleshy crest on a rooster's head turned bright red when sexually aroused, and that the hen demonstrated her willingness by clucking at the old bird.

It was true. Harriet was making a clucking sound, and Etienne didn't have to put a hand to his hot face to know that he was flushed bright red.

Stomping over to her "bed," Harriet muttered something about Abel getting a seven on her MCP scale for another crude innuendo. And Abel ambled over to his bed, laughing under his breath.

"Damn!" Etienne swore, but what he really wanted to say was, "Here, chickee. Here, chickee."

Chapter Twelve

A stark male scream ripped through the bayou. One cry of terror, that was all.

Harriet came instantly awake.

Birds and wild animals echoed the alarm and took flight from their nighttime hiding places. Only silence remained in the small clearing by the stream.

Rubbing her eyes, she tried to orient herself. A whimpering sound, followed by murmuring, came from the other side of the fire.

Harriet stood and made her way uneasily to the spot where Cain and Abel were ministering to a flailing, sleeping Etienne in the midst of one of his night terrors.

Etienne's head and shoulders were cradled on Abel's lap. The musician was softly crooning the words of a Negro spiritual—something about God easing man's misery. Big tears slid down the black man's face as he sang in a mournful cadence—a rhythm of soulful pain that would one day be called the blues.

A bare-chested Cain hunkered down at Etienne's side.

He repeatedly dipped a cloth—his own shirt—into a basin improvised from a naturally hollowed-out piece of driftwood. "Shush, now, Etienne, you're dreaming. It's all over. It's all over," Cain said over and over as he ran the cool cloth over Etienne's face, brushing his hair off his brow until he calmed and slipped back into a normal sleep.

Cain's anguish-filled eyes lifted and he saw her for the first time, standing a few feet away with a palm held against her lips to hold back a sob. He stiffened as if she were the enemy, a threat to the emotionally scarred man on the ground. Then Cain made a small motion of his hand. The silent message his gesture conveyed was that they had the situation under control, and Etienne would not want her to see him like this.

Back on her "bed," Harriet couldn't sleep. She listened and watched as Abel took over guard duty. Cain disdained Abel's empty pine pallet, and instead lay down next to Etienne in his makeshift shelter on the bare ground, as he must have done numerous times over the past years.

And Harriet understood. A small part of the puzzle was clear now. Why a serious doctor participated in a madcap gold heist. Why a talented musician traipsed off to the bayou, instead of practicing his craft and staying with the woman he loved. Etienne would do the same for them in a heartbeat if they needed him.

The love shared by these three friends was soul-wrenching in its purity. They joked and teased each other, as they had since childhood. Perhaps even because, in some ways, they yearned to return to that more innocent time before the war. Perhaps because, if they didn't laugh, they would cry.

Harriet realized something else in that moment, too. She now knew the reason for her time odyssey. *Etienne.* Oh, she'd known for some time that he was the link to her travel back in time. But her purpose was more clear now. He needed her psychotherapy skills.

She didn't doubt for one moment that she'd be able to

help him recover. The bigger question, though, was whether she would ever be able to return to her own time when she finished. Or whether she would want to. In healing Etienne, would she cripple herself? In making him strong, would she become weak?

As long as she protected herself, she should be all right, Harriet decided. The most important thing was not to fall in love with the man. That would spell sheer disaster for her when the time came to leave. Harriet would have to work closely with him, but touch was taboo. Touching led to other tempting activities. Like sex. And she couldn't, under any circumstances, make love with him again.

So that was the plan. Cure the man, and then, somehow, go home. Harriet only wished that niggling inner voice would stop laughing.

Three days later, they were moving slowly through the narrow bayou streams, one leading into another, sometimes so narrow they could reach out and touch both banks.

They should arrive at Bayou Noir by tomorrow morning. It had been a grueling trip, but Harriet didn't really mind. She adored the bayou, and she could see that Etienne did, too. The deeper they ventured into the swampland's mysterious depths, the more relaxed he became.

His head tilted with wonder at the fleeting beauty of a dragonfly dancing on an iridescent sunbeam. He reached out a hand as if to grasp the magic in his palm, but then he pulled back swiftly, glancing around sheepishly to see if he'd been observed.

A hawk circled majestically overhead, and Etienne shaded his eyes with a raised palm, watching for a long time, even after the bird flew away into the distance. He must have witnessed such a scene innumerable times over the years.

When they came upon a wild jaguar perched on an overhanging branch, Etienne stilled Cain's raised pistol. Some other animal would be its unwary prey.

He pointed to an alligator's nest—a raised mudflat—where the proud mama tended her large, elongated eggs. With a chuckle, he said to Harriet, "Remind me someday to tell you how a five-year-old bayou boy took his stepmother to visit a gator nest."

"It took half the plantation to get you and Selene down from that tree," Cain recalled.

"That would be your stepmother?" Harriet asked.

Etienne nodded. He'd already admitted that the woman in the photograph she'd seen was the former Sandra Selente, or Selene, although now her name was Selene Baptiste. He'd even listened uneasily as she told him of a famous fashion model by the same name who had disappeared mysteriously in New Orleans in 1996. None of them wanted to delve too deeply into the conundrum of her time-travel; so they all skirted around the issue, even as more and more pieces of information were added to the puzzle each day.

"Remember the first time you met Miz Selene, Etienne?" Abel reminisced. "You dropped your trousers and flashed your bare rear at her."

Now that image Harriet could picture—an adorable brat of a boy mooning his new stepmother. "So you were an MCP even as a child," she teased.

"I was a terror," Etienne admitted.

That simple statement caused Harriet's heart to swell. She was losing her fight to resist this guy.

"You escaped a whuppin' for the gator prank," Abel elaborated, "but Blossom got you good with her cane for showing disrespect to your new stepmother."

"Blossom?" Harriet inquired, fanning away a cloud of mosquitoes with her straw hat. They'd bought it days ago from a passing *caboteur*, a merchant boat that sold goods along the bayous. They'd also seen a grocery boat, and even a boat manned by a priest, complete with altar. All these to serve the needs of the remote bayou inhabitants.

"The cook. You'll meet her at Bayou Noir," Etienne

explained with a smile. "Blossom is a tiny little thing. Ancient. But she will, no doubt, flail me with her tongue for every little fault she's noted since she saw me last. I think she keeps a list. The Rascal List."

She loved the woman already—a fellow list-maker. Grinning, she asked, "And how long has it been since she's seen you?"

"A year." The flatness of his tone spoke volumes.

As they all succumbed to their inner thoughts, she leaned back in the pirogue and studied Etienne against the backdrop of his beloved bayou. They were both a marvel of contradictions.

The old and new vied continually in this biological throwback to ancient times. Thousand-year-old cypress trees stood in stately contrast to watermeal, the tiny green dots that floated on the sluggish water, a tasty treat for myriad ducks and birds. Ever-generating animal life replaced those creatures that grew old or couldn't survive. Old and new struggled within Etienne, too. Although he was older now—thirty-one—a younger version of Etienne fought to emerge as they neared his home.

Harriet welcomed the calming silence of the bayou, but it was a deceptive peace. Like Etienne's deceptive silence. Even when he stared quietly off into the distance, emotion churned just beneath the surface, waiting to break loose. As a psychotherapist, Harriet knew her greatest work lay in freeing him from those self-destructive energies.

The putrid odor of decay, even evil, permeated the air, but Harriet had a sense that goodness and purity would always prevail in the bayou. It was God's handiwork—a veritable Garden of Eden. How symbolic that the arched branches that met over the meandering creeks should resemble praying hands! Etienne was being eaten alive by some mistaken notion that he had failed, or was flawed, perhaps even rotten at the core. But Harriet knew he was basically a good man, albeit a jerk. She had only to see the friendship he shared with Cain and Abel to know that.

Mostly, though, Harriet felt a sense of danger underlying the illusive safety of the bayou. A man could hide forever here and never be found. But one never knew what peril loomed around the next bend in the river. And, without a doubt, Etienne was a dangerous man. To her, to himself, to those who crossed his path with ill intent.

The farther they delved into the swamplands, the fewer people and homes they saw. The ravages of war—destroyed plantations, fallow fields of cotton and cane—were less evident here than in the lands immediately surrounding New Orleans. But the inhabitants of the bayou had felt the effects of the Civil War, too.

"Too poor to paint and too proud to whitewash," Etienne had declared sadly on more than one occasion when viewing the downtrodden mansions of his neighbors.

Despite the poverty, even the meanest of homes had a quaint appeal. In many cases, Harriet had noted clapboard Cajun homesteads where the gate and chimney were whitewashed. Etienne had explained that it was Cajun tradition for a father to proclaim to all passersby in this manner that he had a marriageable daughter.

Harriet's musing was broken by a shout.

"Help! Help!" a young boy yelled from the stream bank as they cleared a bend. He stood down an incline from a raised Acadian-style home that resembled a lopsided box on stilts. A barefoot girl, no more than five, stood on the porch. "Help, m'sieurs! Help!"

Paddling swiftly toward shore, the three men jumped from the pirogue to the muddy bank. Harriet followed soon after, with Abel staying behind to tie the pirogue to a stump mooring.

"My papa, he went this morning for the midwife," the slim youth of about ten explained quickly, "but the *bébé*, she is coming, quick-quick."

"What's your name, son?" Etienne asked.

"Arman Venee."

"Is your father Henri Venee?"

"Oui."

Etienne muttered something unpleasant in French.

The boy's anxious eyes kept darting toward his ramshackle home. His sibling stood on the porch wide-eyed with terror.

"Are you two here alone with your mother?"

The boy nodded. "Geoffrey and Robert, they be trapping down the bayou a ways till tomorrow."

Cain went back for his medical bag, and they all headed for the house, where a woman's high-pitched screams were rolling out in patterns that probably followed her contractions.

"How long has she been in labor, Arman?" Cain asked as he dipped his hands in a washbasin on a bench beside the front door. He listened carefully while he soaped himself up to the elbows with a square of yellow soap. With no clean towel in sight, he shook his hands in the air to dry.

Shrugging, the boy who smelled to high heaven and whose tobacco-stained teeth looked as if they hadn't ever been brushed, finally replied, "Me, I am not sure. Mebbe since las' night."

Etienne swore under his breath.

Cain was about to enter the house.

"No!" Arman shouted, putting a halting hand on Cain's arm. "My papa, he don't want no niggers hereabouts, no. Best you and the mam'zelle go in." He pointed at Etienne and Harriet. "Lazy, no-'count niggers gots to stay outside, for certain."

Etienne's eyes flashed angrily as he picked Arman up by the scruff of his grimy collar and tossed him off the porch. "You ignorant little pissant! That man is a doctor. Best you show respect to your betters, boy, or you're gonna be sucking on that bar of lye soap."

The woman screamed again—a long, drawn-out wail of agony.

Dusting off his behind, the boy hitched up his trousers

and made a rude gesture. But Etienne and Cain were already inside. Harriet saw Abel pull a switch off a willow tree. He stalked purposefully toward Arman, who had the good sense to make a mad dash for the small, enclosed barnyard, where a lowing cow regarded his dust-raising passage benignly and chickens clucked their disapproval.

Harriet walked over to the little girl and introduced herself. "Hello. My name is Harriet Ginoza. And who are you?"

The child turned her filthy, tearstained face up to her. "Amelie."

"What a pretty name!" Harriet extended her arms, but Amelie backed away, her dark eyes going wide with distress. "Don't be afraid, honey. Why don't we go inside and get some clean clothing for you?"

Amelie shook her head. "*Non.* Me, I ain't goin' inside, me. Armon say all chilluns haf to stay away till the new *bébé* come." Clearly frightened, she added, "Will *bébé* die, like other one?"

"Your mother lost a baby before?" Harriet asked Amelie. That could be important information that Cain should know.

"Many time." Amelie's eyes blinked back tears.

Hunkering down to eye-level, Harriet brushed a strand of dirty hair off Amelie's equally dirty face. "Oh, honey! When was the last time?"

"Las' Christmas."

Less than a year ago. Oh, damn!

Harriet ruffled the girl's hair, which stood out in spikes, hoping she wouldn't come away with lice.

Then, taking the girl forcibly into her arms, Harriet went inside to get the clean garments and tell Cain about the mother's other pregnancies. A moment later she was back outside, washing the surprisingly docile girl on the porch bench. As she worked, Harriet pondered the fact that the wretched, screaming woman inside already had four children and "many" miscarriages.

Boy, would Harriet like to give her some advice!

A short time later, Harriet sat in a rocking chair with the clean girl on her lap, trying to ignore the screams and curses—male and female—that came from the interior of the house. She couldn't imagine what role Etienne was playing in the birthing.

Abel still held the switch in one hand and a pail of milk in the other as he approached from the barnyard area.

"*You* milked a cow?" she asked incredulously. Somehow the chore didn't quite fit the image of the womanizing charmer.

He raised an eyebrow at her. "The nasty beast sure as hell didn't milk itself." Then he surprised her further by advising, "Maybe you should give the girl some milk, and I'll see if I can forage some food. By the sounds of those screams, the mother isn't going to be up to cooking a meal anytime soon."

Harriet frowned. She hadn't even thought about that. Abel went off then to tend to the two horses and three pigs he said were in the barn.

"Harriet, can you go help Cain?" Etienne stood in the open doorway. There was blood on his hands and a distraught expression on his face. Washing up with quick efficiency, he gazed at her imploringly. "I think you would do a better job in there than me."

Harriet wasn't so sure about that, never having been present at a delivery and having no medical background. But she stood and handed the little girl to Etienne, who gawked at her as if she'd handed him a bomb.

"Have fun," she said, pushing him down into the rocker.

He frowned down at the child, who'd latched onto his middle finger, and was already closing her eyes sleepily.

The rogue master was staring down with amazement at the girl's easy acceptance of him. And Harriet's heart swelled at the sweet picture.

"Etienne . . ." she said softly, still leaning over him.

He glanced up.

"You look wonderful with a child."

His face went flat, and his eyes revealed a bleakness that obviously stemmed from events far removed from her carelessly made comment. He immediately shuttered his eyes and shrugged. "I was sixteen when my sister Melanie was born. I used to hold her like this."

"So you're an experienced 'father'?" she teased.

"Hardly. And don't get any silly female notion that I'm going to father a few brats on you. Not even if you beg me."

"Why you . . . you . . ." Harriet sputtered. "So, you have a lot of women dying to have your babies, huh?"

"You'd be surprised."

"You're delusional. In fact, I think you have a real problem facing reality."

"No, I'll tell you who's afraid to face reality," he said, reaching out an arm to her nape and pulling her closer. "It's you. You can't stop thinking about the way we made love. You hate the fact that I made you lose your precious control. And, even worse, you want it again. And again."

Harriet's heart was beating so fast she could barely breathe. Not just because of the words. Etienne's face was so close she could feel his body heat, or was it his sexual energy?

"Lost for words, sweetheart?" Etienne chuckled. "Well, isn't that just a 'Miracle in the Bayou.' Sounds like a great title for a book, if you ask me. Women who discover the secret of seduction—silence. Say that to your black box, honey."

Harriet did, in fact, pull her tape recorder from her pocket and say, "MCP File, October 15. Subject A thinks women should be seen and not heard."

"Flat on their back, naked, would be nice, too," Etienne added.

"A nine," Harriet declared.

"Is that all?"

Harriet clamped her mouth shut, forcing herself not to

react. "Did you hear about the dumb man who went to a mind reader? No? Well, she only charged him half price."

His laughter followed after her into the oppressive, pain-ridden hovel.

It was the last laughter a horrified Harriet heard for some time to come.

Chapter Thirteen

"Honey, you have to stop fighting this birth," Harriet told Solange Venee an hour later.

"*Non, non, non!* Me, I doan want this here chile," the frail woman shrieked in vivid Cajun patois. "No more chillun, by God, no more!"

Hmpfh! A fine time to be coming to that conclusion! You play, you pay, sweetheart! You don't need a PhD to learn that fact of life.

"Many women feel that way in the midst of labor," Cain told her gently from his position at the foot of the bed, kneeling between Solange's upraised knees. "After the birth, mothers forget the pain."

Oh, damn! You'd think a doctor would know when to choose his words with more sensitivity. Even a male doctor.

Solange raised her head and glared at Cain through huge, dark brown eyes that appeared sunken in her stark-thin face. She spat out a venomous stream of French words. "What you said, Dr. Cain, that is not true, no. Women never forget the pain. It is only a say-so, a man say-so."

A short time later, Cain's shoulder's slumped in despair. The only thing delaying the delivery, according to Cain, was the woman's stubborn resistance. She'd had other babies. Surely this one should just pop out, even though she was rather slim hipped. And young.

"How old are you?" Harriet asked as she wiped Solange's brow with tepid water, pushing strands of lank dark hair off her red face.

"Twenty," Solange answered with a sigh.

"Twenty! That's not possible."

"I married up when I was thirteen."

Harriet gasped, blinking back sudden tears of compassion.

Solange shrugged. "My Henri, he had a powerful lust for me then. He still does, yes-yes." Her tone of voice didn't reflect a reciprocal lust, or affection. But maybe that was a childbirth phenomenon. Often, in the midst of delivery, women exhibited a temporary hatred for the man responsible for their pain.

Solange added with fierce resentment, "Four children I have birthed, yes-yes, but ten times I swole up with my man's seed. Ten times! May the Blessed Virgin weep for me!"

Ten pregnancies in twelve years?

"What *plaisir* is there for a woman in that, you think, *chérie*?" The whole time, Solange held Harriet's eyes with an intensity bespeaking an age-old feminine need for understanding.

And Harriet did understand. If ever a person needed psychological help, this nineteenth-century baby machine did. But not now. Time was of the essence.

Harriet had changed the bed linens and bathed the poor woman's pain-racked body, but already her naked, flushed body was soaked with perspiration again. The muggy room reeked of earthy, fetid odors . . . the primal animal scent of creation at its rawest.

"Here comes another one," Cain warned. "I can see the baby's head."

With one arm under Solange's shoulders, Harriet lifted her slightly. Solange had a death grip on Harriet's other hand that would probably leave black-and-blue marks. The contraction rippled down the huge, hard mound of the woman's stomach, where blue veins stuck out like fine Italian marble. Solange tensed once again, bracing, instead of bearing down as nature demanded. At what point would Solange's body win in this tug-of-war with her overwrought mind? And would it be too late?

"Solange, you're not panting, like Dr. Cain told you to do. And you have to push."

"Help us, Solange. You have to help us," Cain urged as another contraction began. They were almost continuous now, without break.

Solange shook her head vehemently. "I'm too weakified."

"Let me catch the babe for you. Then you can rest and get your strength back."

"Foolish man!" Solange clucked. "I was wore out afore I ever got *enceinte* again."

"What if I could tell you how to prevent having more children?" Harriet asked tentatively.

Cain's head shot up like a bullet.

Solange regarded her as if she were the Madonna granting her a heavenly gift. The hand that had been clutching hers relaxed and turned over, palm upward, in a beseeching fashion. A small, hopeful smile tugged at her bruised lips. "Is there a way? But, *non*, I am Catholic. The church would not approve." Her smile collapsed before it even blossomed.

"I'm a Catholic, too. A pick-and-choose Catholic, to be sure, but there's a birth control technique that even the pope approves of, honey. It's called the rhythm method."

Solange began to sob, big tears of relief. The squeeze she gave Harriet's hand now was one of profound thanks.

Cain appeared thankful, too, and very interested in Harriet's words. He would surely grill her later, but for now a panting Solange Venee had decided to have a baby, and it was coming fast and furious.

Five minutes later, Paul-Joseph Venee was born. A long, dark-hued Cajun boy with strong lungs and healthy, flailing limbs. When Cain placed the wailing baby in Solange's exhausted arms, she embraced him gladly. Nuzzling the newborn close to her breasts, the young woman whispered, "Welcome, my little Paul, the sure-God last of the Venee children." At the same time, she glanced over to Harriet, who was bundling up the dirty linens. Despite her bone-weary exhaustion, Solange demanded, "Tell me now before Henri returns."

As Harriet sat down beside her on the edge of the bed, Solange noticed Cain packing up his medical bag and preparing to leave the room. "You're colored!" Solange exclaimed, her eyes wide with shock.

Harriet and Cain both grinned and shook their heads. In all her pain and misery, Solange had apparently missed an important fact—Cain's black skin.

"Henri, he is going to have a fit . . . that a colored man midwifed his *bébé*," Solange pronounced with a surprising whoop. Then she burst out laughing.

"And in the end, E.T. returned to his home on that far-away star." Etienne concluded his story as Amelie gazed up at him adoringly from her perch on his lap. Etienne was sitting with his back braced against a tree near the bayou stream.

It was the oddest sensation in the world, holding a little child. He pressed his lips down to Amelie's downy head and inhaled deeply of her baby-skin scent. The two of them had bathed in the bayou stream a short time ago.

A deep yearning ballooned in Etienne's heart, which he immediately deflated. There would be no children of his seed, if he could help it. Not with the possibility that the taint of his dead mother's madness might run in his blood. No, he'd never hold his own child thus, or watch it grow to adulthood.

Although . . .

There was that one mistake. No, no, he wouldn't think about that horrific possibility. The child was not his. It wasn't!

"I think we've had enough of E.T. and aliens and planets for today, *mon petit chou,*" Etienne commented to the squirming girl. "Why don't we go help Abel?"

Abel stood a few feet away catching crawfish for the evening meal. He was dragging a leafy branch under the water. When he pulled the branch up, the small, crablike creatures clung to the stems with their claws, and Abel shook them off into a basket. Etienne's mouth watered in anticipation of the bayou delight. It was the one food he'd missed most when he'd studied at Oxford. In Andersonville, years later, he'd dreamed not of exotic women or great wealth. Bayou Noir and piles of succulent crawfish fulfilled his nighttime fantasies.

"Tell me the story about Casper again," Amelie urged Etienne instead. "Casper the Bayou Ghost."

Etienne exhaled loudly. Playing with children was fine . . . for short periods of time. Perhaps he should go find Harriet, now that the baby had been born. They'd heard a loud wail a short time ago.

With perfect timing, Etienne heard another loud wail come from the cabin. He, Abel and Amelie turned as one. And for the first time, Etienne saw Harriet standing in a secluded thicket of dense trees behind him. She was leaning against a live oak tree, weeping huge, silent tears.

Handing Amelie to Abel, he went to Harriet.

"*Q'est-ce que c'est, chérie?*" he asked, taking her by the forearms and bending his knees so he was face-to-face with her. "Is something wrong with the infant?"

She shook her head. "Nooo," she blubbered. "The baby is a perfect little boy. Paul-Joseph Venee." Seeing the concern on Amelie's face, she added, "Dr. Cain said you can go see your mother and the baby for a minute."

In a rush, Amelie ran screeching toward the house, Abel following in her wake.

"If not for the mother and baby, why do you weep so?" he inquired now that they were alone. With the pad of one thumb, he wiped the tears off her cheek, leaving white streaks on her dirty face. She was filthy and perspiration-damp from the humidity, as well as her various exertions that day. He knew of a lagoon not far from Bayou Noir that provided a private bathing place. Maybe tomorrow, after they'd finally arrived, he and Harriet could—

How could I ever imagine such a possibility? No, no, no!

"E.T.," Harriet declared.

"What?"

"I'm crying because you were telling the story of E.T." He tilted his head with confusion.

"Oh, don't you see? The character E.T. wasn't created until the 1980s. There's no way your stepmother could have told you that story unless . . . unless she really is Selene. And Casper the Bayou Ghost? Really! It has to be based on Casper the Friendly Ghost, a modern, twentieth-century children's story."

"And?"

"Your stepmother must have come from my time. And that means I really did time-travel."

"But, *chérie*, this is nothing new. For days, you've been telling us that you must have time-traveled . . . somehow."

"I know what I said, but I didn't want to believe it," she cried, leaning into his hand, which was brushing strands of her damp ebony hair back behind her ears.

Why did she have to do that? He felt the tingle of her breath all the way from his palm to his toes.

He would be very sorry tomorrow if he didn't stop right now. Hell, he would be sorry five minutes from now. He must strengthen his defenses. He must.

Her clear green cat eyes gazed at him imploringly.

Etienne's defenses shook with that mere visual assault.

"In the back of my mind, I hoped that this was all a dream. That I'd wake up on a modern Amtrak train headed for the Big Easy. The worst problem I would have then would be a disgusting rogue who was forcefully seducing me every night in my sleep."

He chucked her under the chin playfully. "Now you have the disgusting rogue in person. Would you like me to forcefully seduce you, sweetheart?" *Now, why did I ask her such a question? I'm worse than those dumb men in her jokes.*

"No! I'm too tired to resist your tempting hands now."

He smiled. He couldn't help himself. It must be a dumb-man reflex. "Do I tempt you, darlin'?"

She flashed him one of those "dumb men" looks she did so well. "Tremendously."

He shouldn't care. From a young age, Etienne had sensed his appeal to women, and used the knowledge blithely, to his advantage, along with an innate Creole charm. But for some reason, it pleased him inordinately that Harriet was drawn to him. And he didn't feel at all blithe, either.

"Stop grinning. And do you have to keep using that lazy, Southern drawl? It's so . . . so . . ."

"Sexy?" he guessed.

". . . revolting," she finished.

Etienne knew she lied, and his male pride preened. *So, she likes the way I talk and the way I ply my hands on her.*

Harriet hiccoughed as she tried to stifle her continuing sobs. Wiping the remaining moisture off her cheeks with widespread fingertips, she looked down with distaste at the dirt. "I must look awful."

"Unfortunately, you look too damn good."

Her black hair, which had started the day in a neat plait down her back, now lay in tangles of damp waves. Her intelligent green eyes fringed with long, feathery lashes stared at him with honest question. Her lips, full and ripe and naturally pink, brought to mind all the things a man could do with a woman's mouth. His sun-bleached home-spun shirt clung damply to her womanly curves—curves he remembered with explicit detail.

Not that he was paying particular attention to her appearance.

"Why 'unfortunately'?"

"Because unfortunately I'm about to give in to my own temptations." Moaning, he succumbed to the arousal that had been pounding at his loins for days.

Putting his hands to her waist, he lifted her against the tree so her grimy feet dangled off the ground. Then, with exquisite finesse, he pressed his hardening need against her center and held her in place. There was something to be said for a woman in trousers, he thought as he cupped her buttocks. The woman did have a wonderfully full behind.

She blinked at him with surprise, probably preparing to wallop him between the eyes. But no, she put her hands on his shoulders.

He groaned and saw stars exploding behind his closed lids.

She sighed, "Oh, Etienne."

Oh, Etienne, indeed! "We shouldn't," he breathed against her mouth.

"We shouldn't," she agreed and parted her lips for him.

It was just a kiss. A light, teasing excursion of flesh against flesh. That was all.

"Ummmmm," she purred.

Etienne's knees wobbled. Only *le bon Dieu* knew how he managed to remain standing with Harriet still pressed against him in all the important places. Chest to breast. Hip to hip. Thigh to thigh. And more. Much more.

"Oh, *merde!*" He forgot for the moment that Harriet was the talkingest, sassiest, naggingest, orneriest woman that God ever created to plague a man. He forgot all the good reasons why he'd vowed never to touch her again. In fact, he forgot why he'd wanted to forget anything. "Oh, damn, that feels good," he admitted.

Sweeter Savage Love

Harriet tried to fight the seductive pull of the raunchiest, stubbornest, sexiest, slickest, love-'em-and-leave-'em rogue God had ever created to plague a woman. Really, her intentions had been ironclad four days ago when she'd sworn never to let the louse touch her again. Now, the least little sign of affection, and she practically melted in his arms.

She was going to put a stop to this foolishness right now.

Well, in a minute.

With the expertise of a born womanizer, Etienne was doing a really neat trick with his hips that just about amounted to having sex with your clothes on. At the same time, he blew softly into her ear, where he was doing incredible things with his teeth and tongue.

She ground her teeth and prayed he would never stop.

"Tell me what you want, *chérie*," he whispered. "Whatever you want, I'll give you. I'll fulfill all your needs."

"Just you. That's all," she responded, arching her neck in invitation. "I . . . need you."

Suddenly, like a bullet, the word penetrated through the blinding haze of her passion. Neon signs went off in her head, flashing, NEED . . . NEED . . . NEED . . . Sirens exploded in her ears, *Danger . . . Danger . . . Danger . . .*

"*No!*" She couldn't *need* a man. That was the one thing in the world she'd always avoided. Want, yes. Need, never.

"Don't go stiff on me now, sweetheart," Etienne implored as he slipped a hand inside her shirt. "We're halfway home to Dixie, and it's time to surrender the flag."

Surrender? Oh, Lord! First need. Now surrender. She swatted his hand away, but not before his knuckles grazed a nipple and ignited a wildfire of sensual magic. She whimpered. *Is this how my mother felt? All those times? All those men? Needy and vulnerable and weak? Who knew it could feel so good?*

"Stop it! Stop right now!" She shoved against Etienne's chest and he moved back, at last.

Stunned at her about-face, he stared at her, disbelieving. Then a cold, icy glower of contempt replaced the flush of passion on his sharp features. "I never took you for a tease."

"I'm not a tease," she protested. "I'm not."

She placed a hand on his shoulder, wanting desperately for him to understand her sudden change of mind.

He shrugged her hand away and said through gritted teeth, "Consider this fair warning. If you touch me again, I'm either going to throttle you or make love to you till neither one of us can walk."

Harriet opened her mouth to say something, but no words came out. Which was probably a good thing.

Etienne began to stomp toward the house. He had a really nice behind, she observed idly, and could only imagine how he'd look in a pair of tight button-fly jeans. *Oh, my, my, my!* His neck was way too stiff, though, and she didn't like his turning his back on her at all.

"I pick choice number two," she called after him.

Etienne stumbled, then pivoted slowly. "Wh-what?"

"Hey, if I get to choose between being strangled and a nonstop sexual satisfaction marathon . . . I guess I'll take the latter." She was just kidding, of course.

Etienne's jaw dropped. Then the anger peeled away from his features like a mask. He burst out laughing. "Truly I inherited my mother's madness if I can stand here laughing like a hyena . . . considering my condition." He peered down at his crotch.

"You have a beautiful smile, Etienne. You should use it more often," she said, coming up to his side. "In fact, did you know that laughter creates endorphins—the body's natural painkillers? It could be the best cure for your migraines."

"I should walk around laughing all the time so I don't get a headache?" He rolled his eyes and continued walking. At least he wasn't so angry anymore.

She skipped to keep up with his long strides. "Furthermore, you wouldn't make so many enemies if you'd stop glaring and snapping. You know what they say? 'A smile always comes back at you.' "

A gurgling sound erupted from deep in Etienne's chest and he halted. He wasn't smiling now.

Before she could defend herself, he picked her up, tossed her over his shoulder, stalked the short distance to the stream, and tried to toss her in with an exaggerated heave-ho.

She clung fiercely to his neck, refusing to let go. "Yikes! Don't you dare!"

So he walked into the water, boots and clothes and all, up to his waist. Without hesitation, he dunked them both under the water. The last words she heard were, "I should have done this fifteen erections ago."

When she came up sputtering through the murky green water, he stood on the bank, sopping wet but smiling from ear to ear. With a grimace of disgust, she pulled a clump of slimy moss off the top of her head and spat out a mouthful of water.

"You were right, darlin'," he cooed. "My end-whore-fins are feelin' mighty fine now."

Etienne didn't laugh for long.

While he'd been dumping the wench in the creek, Henri Venec had returned home with the midwife. And he was not a happy camper, as Harriet would say.

Etienne helped Harriet from the water and warned her with a tilt of his head to stand behind him. Reaching down to the ground, he grabbed his gun belt and buckled it on.

Arman was downstream from them, squawking like a jaybird to his father with wide gesticulations toward them and the cabin. Among the words Etienne caught were *nigger, nigger lover, slut* and *willow switch*. In the background could be heard the wailing of an infant.

The midwife, a short, hammer-jawed Cajun woman with no teeth and a chin that about met her nose, scurried up toward the house, casting suspicious glances at him and

Harriet along the way. Shortly after she entered the door-way, Amelie came out. But there was no joyous rush of welcome toward her returning father. Instead, the girl cowered silently on the porch. Cajun families were close-knit and suspicious of strangers. Arman and Amelie would, no doubt, be in trouble for seeking or accepting help from outsiders.

Henri nodded his dismissal to Arman, and the boy cast a gloating smirk their way.

Henri was about the same age as Etienne but a little shorter and heavier. He would have been a handsome man if cleaned up and not frowning, and without a huge wad of tobacco in his cheek. Dragging his right leg, he walked grimly toward them in his *cantiers*, knee-high leather moccasins—apparel still preferred by the Cajun trappers. He held his rifle prominently.

"Why is he so harsh-looking? And angry?" Harriet murmured.

"He took a round at Shiloh," Etienne whispered.

"What are you doin' on my property, Baptiste?" Henri growled.

He'd known Henri Venee as a friendly boy; he suspected that Henri, the man, would have been changed, like he had in the war. Henri was no different from all the other men Etienne ran into these days . . . all angry men, North and South. While many of Henri's Cajun fellows had turned mossyback during the war, hiding in the forest to avoid fighting, Henri had been a regular fire-eater, joining up right from the start. Even now he was a violent, uncompromising Southern partisan.

"Put the gun down, Henri," Etienne urged. "We just stopped to help. Your wife needed—"

"We don't need help from no home-grown Yankee," Henri snarled, spitting a stream of tobacco juice near Etienne's feet. "Nor those two smoked Yankees, neither," he added in reference to Cain and Abel, whom Arman must have mentioned since they were nowhere in sight. "Why don't you go back North where you're welcome? Ain't no place for you in the bayous no more."

Etienne wasn't surprised by Henri's reaction. It was only five years since the war had ended and many Southerners still carried a deep resentment against the North, but especially against those of their own kind who'd chosen the "wrong" side.

"Don't you even want to know how your wife's doing? Or the baby?" Harriet interjected shrilly, hands on hips.

Henri stepped back as if slapped. And raised his gun.

Etienne tried to shush her imprudent mouth and push her behind him, but she dug in her heels with her usual stubbornness.

"Really, Mr. Venee, you're just like a . . . a man. More concerned about violence and zones of privacy and all that masculine nonsense, when your first priority should be the woman you love and the mother of your children." She tossed her wet hair over her shoulder with dramatic contempt.

Henri gave Harriet's male attire, which clung to her body in an unseemly display, a sweeping assessment. Then he addressed Etienne, "Is she a whore or a half-wit?"

"Neither," Harriet stormed, bristling with indignation. "And don't talk over me, mister. I'm not invisible."

"Well, I'll be!" Henri almost began to grin, casting a commiserating look at Etienne. The silent communication said, *Where did you find this one? And how did you get so unlucky?*

But then Henri noticed Cain and Abel coming out of the cabin. He stiffened and his face appeared almost purple with rage. "What are those two niggers doin' in my house? Solange!" he yelled, rushing forward.

"Oh, for heaven's sake!" Harriet shouted to Henri's back. "One of those men is Dr. Cain Lincoln. If it wasn't for his medical skills, your child still wouldn't be born."

Henri slowed, then halted. Raising his rifle, he cocked

the trigger and aimed directly at Cain. "Are you sayin' that black bastard put a hand on my wife?"

Etienne's pistol was out in a flash, but not before Harriet had lunged at Henri. She wasn't able to tackle him to the ground, but she managed to deflect the course of the bullet when the rifle accidentally discharged.

Instead of hitting Cain, which Henri probably never intended to do anyway—he'd been bluffing, Etienne was sure—the bullet hit another object. Him.

Etienne glanced down with horror to see a wide red spot blooming rapidly across his right shoulder. He and Harriet would have matching scars, he thought with hysterical irrelevance.

At first, everyone's mouth just dropped open as Harriet flew into action. She was now pounding Henri on the chest, trying to grab the offending rifle.

After the initial instant of shock, Amelie began to cry. Cain and Abel rushed forward to help Etienne, but Etienne was tying to peel Harriet off Henri. The Cajun was now laughing as he fended off her assault. The Cajuns did appreciate good humor.

"You ignoramus! You terrorist! Who the hell do you think you are, Rambo?" Harriet was shrieking at Henri. "You shot Etienne." She got one good punch in to his jaw, which surprised everyone, especially Henri.

"*Merde!* Somebody get this harridan off me," Henri pleaded.

"Harridan? I'll give you harridan. If Etienne dies, I'm going to kill you, buster. Put that in your mouth along with that repulsive wad of nicotine and chew on it, buddy, 'cause your clock is ticking. If cancer doesn't get you, I will."

"Harriet, I'm all right," Etienne said, finally pulling her off Henri. He had scratch marks all over his face and neck and the beginnings of a bruise on his chin.

Blinking up at him, Harriet came back to sanity. "You're really all right?" she asked in a small voice.

He nodded.

With that, she slumped into a dead faint.

Cain ordered Abel to get a basin of cool water and cloths, both to revive Harriet and cleanse Etienne's shoulder wound. Etienne sank to the ground with Harriet in his arms.

Gazing at her with wonder, he concluded that it really had been a long day for the woman, who was rather frail, after all. The grueling boat ride, then helping to deliver a baby, then being dunked by him.

Well, not so frail, Etienne amended as he cradled her in his lap. His heart constricted at the image of the small-boned warrior woman defending him. *Him.* It was a picture he'd carry with him forever.

Within minutes, Harriet awakened, and they all made a hasty retreat toward their pirogue. Henri was inside with his wife and baby. It was best to escape without another confrontation. And it was a good thing, too. Just as they pushed off, Henri came storming outside, rushing after them, rifle raised once again.

"Where's the slut? I'm going to blow her head off. She tol' my wife to stop havin' my *bébés.*"

They paddled quickly and were soon out of sight. Only then did Etienne turn from his spot in front of Harriet in the pirogue and raise an eyebrow. "Birth control?"

She shrugged. "I couldn't help myself. It's my mission here, I guess."

"I thought I was your mission."

She smiled at him, and his blasted heart flipped over.

"You *and* the downtrodden women of the South."

"Oh, Lord!"

"Etienne, we should be at Bayou Noir by morning," Cain interrupted, glancing back at him over his shoulder. A worried frown clouded his face.

Etienne craned his neck to look at Cain. Why did he appear so apprehensive? And why would he think he'd need a reminder of their proximity to home?

They'd entered his home region of Terrebonne Parish that morning, skirting around Houma. Terrebonne was bounded by the parishes of Assumption, St. Mary and Lafourche, as well as Atchafalaya Bay and the Gulf of Mexico. Although one of the largest parishes in Louisiana, Terrebonne was wild, riddled with bayous and untillable land, but that was what Etienne loved most about it. Smaller farmsteads predominated here, rather than big plantations, although there had been a few showplaces before the war—Belle Grove, Greenwood, White Hall, Powhatan, Colomb House, Melrose. Etienne's home was in the northwest sector of this vast county and they would soon connect with its main artery—Bayou Noir.

"Etienne, there's something I need to tell you," Cain began again, "before we arrive at Bayou Noir plantation. I don't know how to say this, but, well, you should be aware . . ."

A tingly sensation of foreboding passed over the back of Etienne's neck. "What now? What's got you all fidgety?"

Cain took a deep breath, then informed him in a nervous rush, "Some of the old slaves have returned to Bayou Noir."

"Why?" A cold sweat turned Etienne's flesh clammy.

"Because they have no place else to go," Cain answered. "No work. No way to support their families. It's their home."

Etienne groaned. "There hasn't been a sugar crop planted there in years."

"Well, actually, some of them have started working on the fields, just in case. . . ."

"Just in case *what*?" Etienne snapped. "You haven't been encouraging them that I'll be coming back, have you?"

Cain's shoulders slumped guiltily.

Etienne swore under his breath. "How many have returned?"

Cain hesitated. "Do you mean in addition to the twenty-five or fifty who were already there?"

"Twenty-five or fifty?" Etienne sputtered. Then he drew himself up stiffly. "Exactly how many are there, total?"

Cain mumbled something.

"What did you say?" Etienne asked incredulously, his eyes wide with shock.

"One hundred and fifty!" Cain said.

"Oh, my God!"

"Since he's already fumin', you might as well tell him the rest," Abel advised Cain.

Cain grimaced.

Etienne said, "I'm getting a headache."

"Well, Etienne, the plain truth is . . . I know you're not gonna like this . . . but, well, Saralee is still there."

Etienne closed his eyes with a silent moan. He wasn't sure how much more shock he could take today. "My head is hurting."

"Who is Saralee?" Harriet asked in an icy tone.

Etienne didn't have to see her face to know she suspected he was keeping a mistress tucked away at his remote plantation. *If only that were the case!*

With a deep sigh of resignation, he turned.

Before he could speak, Cain answered for him. "Saralee is Etienne's daughter."

"She is *not* my—"

"A child? You slimeball!"

Etienne should have been prepared. But he wasn't.

Harriet picked up a paddle and knocked him overboard. Again.

Good thing she hit his good shoulder. Good thing she didn't hit his aching head. Good thing she didn't hit his ever-burgeoning manhood. Good thing he was still alive.

Really, it was a perfect ending to a perfect day.

"Do you two get some type of thrill out of dunking each other in the bayou?" Abel inquired a short time after Etienne had crawled back in the pirogue. "I mean, you do it to each other so often."

Etienne's shoulder ached to high heaven. He still had a goose egg on his forehead and a big lump on the top of his head. He was exhausted from lack of sleep. His ears rang from constant feminine nagging. He hadn't eaten since that morning, and he'd swallowed a bucket of swamp water.

Raking his fingers through his wet hair, he took a long look at Harriet. The witch was leaning back in a reclining position with her eyes closed, getting what she called a *suntan*. A small smile of satisfaction teased her full lips, although he could tell by the ramrod tenseness of her body that she was furious with him.

"Yeah, I'm thrilled."

Chapter Fourteen

The ancient black woman sat rocking on the ground level gallery of the mansion at Bayou Noir. In all of Terrebonne Parish, this was her favorite spot.

It didn't matter that she could barely see the stream at the bottom of the oak alley. Or that the overgrown swamp vegetation, redolent with the pungent scents of cypress, pine and myriad flowers, reached almost to the house. Her rheumy eyes knew the scene blindfolded. She preferred to picture Bayou Noir plantation the way it had been in the old days, before the war.

Not that Blossom fretted over change. Lordy, no! Just the opposite. In fact, she relished the sense of expectancy in the air. Finally, the circle would be completed.

Glancing down at the curly haired girl-child at her feet playing with three rag babies, Blossom felt a contentment she hadn't enjoyed in years.

Oh, it nigh broke her heart to see the neglect and decay surrounding her, but that would soon change. She hoped.

The kitchen and her bedchamber on the lower level were

the only rooms being used now in the four-story master house. The main flanks of the Union army hadn't come this far into the bayous, but marauding soldiers, from both sides, had broken windows and stolen whatever small items of value they could cart off. Blossom and the few former slaves who had remained hid what they could, waiting for the master to come home.

For nearly ten long years, they'd been waiting for the master to come home. And stay.

Blossom's time on earth was drawing to a close. She knew that and was unafraid. The Almighty had been calling her to the Promised Land for years, but she'd held on here. For the child's sake. And for that other needful child, though he was a man now.

"Will my papa be comin' home soon?" Saralee asked, tugging on Blossom's gown to get her attention.

"Yes, sweet girl. Soon."

Blossom patted the wild ebony waves of her seven-year-old darling's hair, which were topped today by a crown made of old newspapers intertwined with violets. Although there were a number of colored children about the plantation, the lonely child often played pretend games, off by herself. One day she played a princess, the next a cowboy. Saralee was as neglected and damaged as Bayou Noir itself.

"And will we live happily ever after? Like the fables Miz Ellen tells us in the schoolroom?"

"I surely hope so, chile. I surely do."

"Tell me about my papa again, Blossom. Please."

With a deep sigh, Blossom began, "When Etienne Baptiste was a li'l no-count boy, no higher than a tree stump . . ."

Harriet felt like sobbing the next morning when they arrived at Bayou Noir plantation.

The "grand old lady," a once noble mansion, was a wreck. Broken windows. Shutters off or hanging by a hinge. Honeysuckle vines covering almost all of the exterior. Roof caving in on one porch. The *garçonnière* half burned down. Even worse, the ever-encroaching bayou had turned the grounds into a veritable jungle.

And Etienne didn't help matters at all. He'd been complaining ever since they'd entered the outer perimeters of his property fifteen minutes ago.

"There's a damn crevasse in the levee.

"What're all those workers doin' in that sugar field?

"That sugar cane looks stunted.

"Who's makin' rum in that still behind the boiler sheds?

"The bayou has crept all the way up to the house.

"Who told Ellen she could start a school in the warehouse?

"Is that a three-legged chicken I see comin' out of that chicken coop?"

They all ignored his ranting, even when they emerged from the pirogue . . . until Harriet finally snapped. "Yeah, yeah, yeah. Why don't you direct some of that negative energy in a positive direction?"

"Like what?" he fumed, hands on hips.

Cain and Abel had scurried off toward the fields once they'd tied up the pirogue, no doubt wanting to escape Etienne's wrath.

She and Etienne were standing at the bottom of an incline that at one time would have led under a wide archway of two parallel lines of massive oak trees dripping Spanish moss all the way up to the colonnaded mansion. Now it would take a machete to get through the dense overgrowth.

"Well? Like what?" he repeated.

"Like stay home and take care of business. Like stop playing silly spy games and work where you're obviously needed. Like stop feeling sorry for yourself and count your blessings. Like get a life."

He clenched his fists and closed his eyes, probably counting to ten. She didn't care. Someone had to set the fool straight.

Sandra Hill

In the distance, she heard the field workers break out into a poignant work song:

> *"Bring me a little water, Silvie,*
> *Bring me a little water now.*
> *Bring me a little water, Silvie,*
> *Every little once in a while."*

Etienne tilted his head, listening. Harriet could tell that the song provoked strong memories for him.

"Listen, Etienne," she said more calmly. "You have this beautiful, wonderful paradise here. How can you neglect it so? How can you let it . . . die?" Her voice cracked with emotion.

Etienne tilted his head in puzzlement. "You consider this beautiful?" His voice also seemed choked. He obviously loved his home. Why did he stay away?

"Of course it's beautiful. Oh, not the way it is right now," she said, waving her hand to encompass the whole sorry mess. "But when I saw your photograph of Bayou Noir . . . the one you carry with you all the time . . . I felt such a deep pull in my heart." Harriet put both hands over her chest to demonstrate. And to her distress, she realized that she was weeping.

"I don't understand you at all," Etienne said. "You're crying over a broken-down house and worthless land."

She shook her head fiercely. "Not worthless. Never. And you're crying, too, Etienne. Yes, you are. Inside."

She could see the visible effort it took for him to swallow. When he finally spoke, she could barely hear his words. "It's hopeless." Then louder, "It would take a fortune to bring this plantation back. Too much work." His blue eyes were bleak with misery. "There were more than twelve hundred sugar plantations in Louisiana before the war. Now there are less than two hundred."

"Excuses!"

He grimaced with disgust at her obstinacy. "What the

Yankee blockade and Southern railroad takeovers didn't do to destroy the sugar empire is being finished off by foreclosures and lack of funds to replace expensive machinery. Not to mention hiring hands in place of slaves." He sighed deeply. "It's impossible."

"You could do it if you wanted. It would be expensive, yes, but it would be a labor of love. If I had a home like this"—she paused wistfully—"I'd never leave."

He regarded her with an odd intensity, but didn't speak.

At first, she thought Etienne was going to take her into his arms. If he did, Harriet feared she would never be the same again. It would mark a turning point of monumental importance.

Fortunately, he only took her hand and drew her toward a path through the thick foliage. His palm pressing against hers felt warm and comforting and sexual. And, oh, so right.

She was so confused.

"Harriet, prepare yourself," Etienne warned as they neared the house. His mouth turned up with a small, self-deprecating grin. "I'm about to introduce you to Blossom. The Holy Terror of the South. You're gonna love her."

A black woman of about ninety stood leaning on a cane. She watched their approach with patient dignity.

Under his breath, she thought Etienne added, "The bane of my old life meets the bane of my new life. *Sacrebleu!*"

Etienne glanced at the woman at his side and laced his fingers more tightly with hers. Somehow Harriet's clasp gave him strength to face all the haunting memories. With Harriet at his side, the demons stayed at bay. *Hah!* The demons probably feared she'd start lecturing. Her nagging could rub even the devil's tough hide raw, Etienne thought with a grin.

"Don't you be turnin' that wicked smile on me, Etienne Baptiste." Blossom stood imperiously at the edge of the lower gallery in a crisp red calico gown with a matching kerchief around her head.

Etienne expelled a long breath, then braced himself. *I sure hope there's some rum left in that still.*

"Where you been the past year, boy?" Blossom demanded. "I oughta take my cane to your backside, you rascal." She glared at him, the way she'd been doing the past thirty-one years, since his first misdeed . . . coming out of the womb, no doubt. It was the "evil eye," known to reduce little boys and grown men to mush.

Then, unable to suppress a whimpering cry, Blossom opened her arms wide. She never could stay angry with him for long.

Etienne hesitated only a moment before picking her up by the waist and dragging her into a tight embrace. Her feet dangled high off the floor. Had she shrunk even more the past year? Was she as ill as she appeared? No, no, Blossom would live forever. She would always be here for him. Always.

"Lord-a-mercy, how I missed you!" Blossom wailed, patting his shoulders. Her face was pressed into his neck, where tears streamed wetly under his open collar.

"I missed you, too, Blossom," he admitted and held the old woman much too long.

Deeply touched, Harriet watched the reunion between Etienne and Blossom. And she noticed what they didn't . . . the little girl, about seven years old, who stood in the deep recesses of the gallery. *Saralee. Etienne's daughter.*

But where is her mother? And was Etienne telling the truth when he said he'd never married? Is the child illegitimate? Hmmm. Etienne has a lot of explaining to do.

The precious girl with an unmanageable mop of long black curls gazed at her father with yearning in her blue eyes. She wore a homemade crown of newspapers and limp violets. Her cape, worn over a plain blue homespun gown that reached her ankles, was a much-darned lace tablecloth, and her scepter was a rolling pin. Three rag dolls were lined up at her feet—her royal subjects.

Etienne gave Blossom one full spin before placing her

firmly on her feet and handing her the cane that had fallen to the ground. "Blossom, I want you to meet Dr. Harriet Ginoza." He stretched out a hand and pulled Harriet closer. "She's my prisoner," he added, wiggling his eyebrows.

But Blossom's eyes were fixed on the clasp of Etienne's hand with hers. She raised her eyes in question, meeting Harriet's head-on. "Is she your intended, Etienne? You finally settlin' down?"

"Good God, no! Harriet is a . . . ah . . . *une vielle fille.*"

"What's that?" Harriet asked suspiciously. Knowing Etienne, it probably meant something like "a horse's ass."

"An old maid," Blossom translated.

"I am not!" He was probably using this tactic to divert Blossom's attention away from him and his errant ways.

"You two been nekkid together?" Blossom's voice was strangely hopeful.

Harriet rolled her eyes at Blossom in a feminine version of "In spades!" Then she narrowed her eyes at Etienne. "Did you hear about the dumb man who had a growth on his neck?"

Etienne buried his face in his hands, and Blossom put a thoughtful forefinger to her chin, waiting.

"His head."

Etienne groaned, and Blossom asked, "Is that one of those riddles? Like Miz Selene used to tell about blond women?"

"Precisely." Harriet smiled. "Then there was the dumb man who crossed a cow with a mule. He wanted to get milk with a kick in it."

Blossom giggled.

"That's enough, Harriet. You've made your point."

"If that don't beat all!" Blossom exclaimed. "The rascal done met up with his match." Then she gave Harriet a welcoming hug. Harriet had to bend down into the embrace and, in that split second, Blossom whispered, "You take care of my boy, you heah? Doan go hurtin' him none. He's seen too much misery."

Harriet nodded, though why Blossom would think she had the power to hurt Etienne, Harriet couldn't imagine.

"I gots your favorite jambalaya and corn bread warmin' in the kitchen," she told Etienne. "An' some dirty rice and fandaddies, too. I been expectin' you all week. You allus was a slowpoke."

His eyes crinkled with mirth. "And tipsy cake?"

Blossom nodded, slapping away his hand when he tried to pinch her cheek. Then a shuffling noise turned Blossom immediately serious as she remembered Saralee. Motioning to the little girl who still cowered in the background, Blossom coaxed, "Come here, sweet girl. Say hello to your papa."

Etienne flinched as if Blossom had struck him. "No," he protested, took one look at Saralee, whose eyes were huge with adoration, and walked right past her and into the house. Without a word of acknowledgment or greeting.

How could he?

Harriet and Blossom gasped.

Saralee's hopeful expression crumpled and she became as lifeless as the rag dolls surrounding her. The wounded look on her face would touch the most hardened heart. But apparently not Etienne's. Spinning on her heel, the little girl ran in the opposite direction, away from the house.

"That boy's got a head thicker'n a Loo-zee-anna cypress."

"You won't get any argument from me there."

"Someone oughta thump his gourd and see iffen he's got a lick of sense left."

"Yep." Harriet realized then that Blossom was staring at her. "Me?" she squeaked. "He never listens to me."

"Ain't nobody else here I'm jawin' at, missie. Besides, a woman in love can do anythin'."

"In love?" she shrieked. "Ha, ha, ha! No way, uh-uh!"

"Girl, you eye-eats that man even when he's spoutin' nonsense 'bout you bein' on the shelf. And he gives you the man-look right back."

The man-look? Oh, boy!

"Saralee needs her daddy. Etienne needs her, too. Yes, he does."

"Where's her mother?" Harriet was grasping for straws. *The man-look?*

"Dead. The las' thing Vera done afore she died was bring the baby back here, but Etienne was already in prison by then. He doan wanna believe that the woman what put him there birthed his baby. He reckons it was jus' another passel of her lies." Her face went stone-hard with anger.

Harriet's mind reeled with all the information being thrown at her. A woman had betrayed Etienne, resulting in his being sent to Andersonville Prison. Then Vera had given birth to his baby, which she'd brought to Bayou Noir before her death. "I don't understand. Why did Saralee's mother give her to her father if she hated him enough to put him in prison?"

"I doubts that Vera ever hated Etienne. In truth, I 'spect she loved him, in her own way. But she were a mighty ambitious girl, and . . ." Blossom's words trailed off, and she shrugged.

"But to turn traitor on a man you love, or loved. It's hard to believe," Harriet protested.

"Folks makes mistakes. Then they tries to make up fer their mistakes. Vera was dyin' of the wastin' disease when she come here. . . . I could see that plain as day. She wanted to make sure Saralee had a home. And she wanted to make her peace with Etienne afore she met her maker. Leastways, that's what I be thinkin'. 'Ceptin Etienne doan see it that way . . . yet."

That was an understatement.

"You believe that Saralee is Etienne's chile, don'tcha?"

"Of course. She's a mirror image of Etienne as a boy."

"How you recollectin' what Etienne looked like as a boy?"

"I saw a photograph."

Blossom nodded. "You gonna help?"

229

Harriet thought about the hurt on Saralee's face when Etienne had denied her. "Yes."

"Good. I been prayin' and prayin' on how to get them two together afore I pass on. And God sent you. Praise the Lord!"

Me? God sent me in answer to Blossom's prayer? Harriet sputtered, but no words came out. And she was still thinking about *the man-look*.

The old cook hobbled after Etienne, presumably toward the kitchen, muttering, "He best not be touchin' my jambalaya. That boy needs a good whuppin'. This is worse'n the time he fed Dreadful grapes and we had purple dog business ever'where. And where's Cain and Abel? They be needin' a whuppin', too, I reckon. 'Specially iffen they's drinkin' my rum."

Harriet stood alone on the gallery. Stunned.

There was a lot of work facing her here. And she wasn't sure who needed her help the most, Saralee or Etienne. The little child, or the big child.

She decided to tackle the big lug first.

Later, back in the kitchen, there was no sign of Etienne. A grumbling Blossom quickly informed her that he'd already scarfed down a bowl of jambalaya with corn bread and a half dozen fandaddies, a southern version of fried clams, before taking off with a huge chunk of cake in hand. Cain and Abel had also made an enormous dent in the feast that had been prepared for them.

"Sit down, girl. You gots to eat, too," Blossom said, setting a plate for her on the scarred oak table.

"This is delicious," Harriet said enthusiastically after her first bite of the stew, which was rich with smoked ham, shrimp, crab, onions, rice and red peppers. The corn bread melted in her mouth.

Blossom eased herself onto the opposite bench. "Thank you, but Saralee does most of the cooking now. All I gots to do is watch that she doan burn herself."

"Saralee?" Harriet asked with surprise. "She's too little to cook, isn't she?" Harriet hadn't spent much time with kids, except for some of her clients and her sister Sheila's brat, Hank the Horrid. But she knew lots of modern children, even as young as seven, were forced by the nature of their latch-key lifestyles to become proficient in cooking, at least of the microwave variety. So maybe Saralee wasn't so unusual, after all.

Blossom sipped at a cup of ultrastrong Creole coffee before speaking. "My laigs are too weakified to hold this ol' body for long. I jist cain't get 'round the way I used to. So I teached Saralee to cook. She makes the bestest cream cakes this side of Nawleans. And her biscuits are so light they pract'ly fly."

"Gee, I wonder if she might have a descendant someday who'll open a bakery," Harriet said with a chuckle.

"What?"

"Never mind." It was an interesting thought, though. "Cain mentioned that a lot of the former slaves have returned here. Aren't there women who could help you with the cooking?"

"Some of them does, but me and Saralee are the only ones livin' here in the big house. Too many rooms to clean and repairs to make when there ain't no white folks about to use 'em anyhows. Teachin' Saralee how to cook . . . well, it helps pass the time. Besides, every girl should know her way 'round a kitchen, I allus say." She eyed Harriet. "You knows how to cook?"

Harriet laughed. "A little. I don't have much time for it, though. I work so many hours."

"Are you a doctor, for true, like Etienne said?"

"Well, yes, but not a medical doctor. I'm a psychologist. That's sort of a mind doctor."

"Well, glory be!" Blossom hooted. "I reckon we both be knowin' someone 'round here in need of a mind healin'."

They smiled companionably at each other.

"Where's Saralee now?" Harriet asked, resuming her meal.

"Upstairs takin' a bath."

Harriet stopped eating. "A bath?" She sighed. "Upstairs?"

"Ain't much in this house that the mildew and mice and wood worms doan call home, but that big old marble tub upstairs survived it all. And I makes sure those field workers come by once a month to clean the cistern."

"Blossom, I'll make a deal with you. If I can have a bath and a change of clothes . . . I don't care what kind of clothes, a feedsack will do . . . if I can just have a half hour in a real tub with clean water and soap . . . well, I think I would do anything for you. Even help you thump some sense into Etienne's gourd."

Blossom beamed. "Sometimes the Lord does make a body's work easy. A bath? Thass all? And here I was plannin' on diggin' up all the silver to offer you a bribe."

Harriet gave the wily black woman a double take. Blossom played the part of a frail old lady, but Harriet suspected she was a lot stronger than she appeared. Yep, Blossom had more aces up her sleeve than a cardsharp.

Etienne had better beware.

In fact, the way Blossom was studying her, Harriet decided she'd better beware, too.

Toward evening, a clean, sweet-scented Harriet had still not found Etienne. She'd had a long soak in the fabulous marble tub on the third floor, having soaped and shampooed three times with Blossom's gardenia soap. Now she wore an old gown Selene had left behind more than twenty years before. The fact that it dragged on the ground and bagged in the chest and was pink calico didn't matter a bit to Harriet. It was clean, and that was the most important thing.

Harriet approached the back of the mansion from the "street" where the slave quarters used to be. Though ecstatic over their freedom, the blacks had apparently found that freedom didn't pay the rent. Nor did it bring the expected "forty acres and a mule." The war had been won, but it was an empty victory when empty bellies growled.

There were about forty of the unpainted cottages, many with little fenced-in gardens flourishing with fresh vegetables—pole beans, corn, beets, potatoes, squash, cucumbers, pumpkins and that Louisiana favorite, okra, which was a preferred ingredient for thickening the Creole gumbo, along with sassafras. The surprisingly well kept area housed about a hundred and fifty former slaves, who'd come back seeking work and living places for their families.

These people were dirt-poor, but self-sufficient. Too bad Etienne didn't see the value in that. Sure, it would take a long time to get the plantation back on its feet again, but he had all the time in the world . . . as long as he and the workers were able to survive physically. One step at a time was all it would take.

But Etienne would have to take the first step.

Whoa! Hold on a minute! Wasn't it odd that she, who had always held such ambitious goals, now considered day-to-day survival a noble ideal. Her much-valued independence didn't seem all that important when placed in the microcosm of a plantation on which all of the people comprised an interdependent unit, each needing one another to make the whole work. Fame and fortune waned in importance compared with the satisfaction there would surely be in bringing this land and home back to life. Not that Harriet would be around long enough to see all those things happen.

It was late afternoon by the time Harriet finally found Etienne in his old schoolroom on the fourth floor of the mansion. By then she was wild with worry.

"I've been searching for you. Where have—"

"Don't talk." Etienne pulled Harriet through the doorway and into his arms. If the foolish wench insisted on venturing into secluded spots, seeking him out, she would pay the consequences.

"But, Etienne . . ." she protested.

He wrapped his arms around her waist, lifted her off the floor and walked her the few steps to the wall.

"Oomph!"

He hadn't meant to slam against her. "I'm sorry, *chérie*. My body seems to have a mind of its own," he murmured.

"You know what they say about men's mighty minds?" she gasped out as he adjusted himself to her curves. She had delicious curves. "They're mighty empty."

He buried his face in the curve of her neck and nipped the soft flesh with his teeth. She smelled of gardenias and fresh woman skin. Suddenly his headache didn't pound quite so badly. "No talking," he said through gritted teeth. "And most definitely, no dumb-men jokes."

He'd ridden over the plantation most of the day. The swamplands had reclaimed Bayou Noir. The bayou and the sugar lands were demanding mistresses. Unless pampered and given attention on a regular basis, they lost their veneer of civilization and quickly reverted back to jungle.

After his tour, Etienne had bathed in his childhood swimming hole, hoping to restore his spirits. Harriet had warned him about being negative. She'd said he could bring Bayou Noir back if he really wanted to.

Did he want to?

Yes! Etienne realized that was exactly what he wanted, and needed. Although he'd spent only his first six years here, Etienne's love of the bayou was anchored firmly in his soul. When he thought of home, he didn't envision California. He conjured images of shimmering sunlight on slow-moving streams through age-old cypress forests. Bayou Noir. His father had hated the South and couldn't wait to leave; Etienne couldn't wait to return.

But could he restore Bayou Noir?

Maybe. If he completed this mission for President Grant, he'd get twenty thousand dollars in commissions and back pay. That would surely give him a firm foundation . . . a start.

He drew back a bit and studied Harriet. Then he smiled.

"Well, well, aren't you the picture of . . . pink," he drawled.

She looped her arms around his neck and smiled back. Etienne's heart constricted with breath-stopping yearning.

"I look like a big pink flower," she said with a grimace.

"A gardenia?" He sniffed deeply. "Perhaps," he said, running his fingertips down her sides from her armpits, over the indentation of her waist, then the flare of her hips, and back up again, "or a fluffy raspberry syllabub. Good enough to eat."

"No," she demurred weakly as he began to lower his mouth toward her parted lips. "That's not why I came here."

"I just want to kiss you, *chérie*. That's all."

He brushed his lips across hers. Once. Twice. Coaxing.

She moaned. "That's what men have been saying throughout the ages. That's the second biggest MCP lie on record; the first is 'I love you, baby.' "

"Just a kiss," he breathed against her mouth. *Who cares what men say in other times? The trick here is to keep Harriet's mouth busy so that she can't talk, or think.*

"No," she breathed back. "I can't resist your kisses."

"You can't?" he said and grinned. *Thank you, God!* Then he allowed himself the slow, exquisite pleasure of fitting his lips into the shape of hers. They were a perfect fit. Soft and hard. Teasing and punishing. Tempting and demanding.

"You are such a jerk, Etienne. But you sure can kiss, I'll give you that," she choked out.

He grinned and brushed aside a strand of hair that had loosened from the knot atop her head. Then he trailed his lips from her too-enticing mouth to the small shell of her exposed ear. "A good kisser, huh?"

"Don't act so surprised," she said, struggling to escape his hands, which were locked on her sinfully sweet buttocks. He noticed that she didn't struggle very hard, which

Sandra Hill

was convenient because he didn't think he could stop touching her if his life depended on it. "Women probably tell you that all the time."

"Tell me what?" he asked, having lost his concentration. Her meager struggle had caused her breasts to whisk across his shirt and peak. "Oh, that I'm a good kisser? No, women have told me that I do other things well, but I can't recall kissing being mentioned. Would you like me to demonstrate those *other* talents?"

"You are such a pig, Etienne. I've been looking for you all day to tell you that," she informed him hotly. Or was she just hot? His brain was too fuzzy with want to distinguish. "But all I can think about now is how much I want to kiss you. Endlessly."

It was Harriet then who took his face in both hands and pulled it down to hers. It was Harriet who pressed her lips against his and forced his mouth to open for her tongue. Well, not really *forced*. Etienne was just a mite surprised, that was all. "Endlessly," he echoed on a prayerful sigh of appreciation when he came up for air . . . the first time.

"Endlessly," she promised when she came up for air . . . the second time. Or was it the third? Etienne had lost count.

In the distance Etienne heard the sound of the dinner bell calling the sugar workers from the fields, but he was beyond caring about such bodily appetites as food. The only appetite his body had now was for the woman cradling his arousal against her parted thighs.

He drew the scooped neckline of her ridiculous pink gown as far as her elbows, trapping her arms at her sides and exposing her beautiful pink-tipped breasts. A rush of such exquisite pleasure-pain washed over him that his vision blurred.

"What are you doing to me?" he groaned, taking first one, then the other hardened pebble into his mouth and suckling wetly. He felt like a newborn child, needful and way too vulnerable, but he couldn't help himself.

She let out a keen, drawn-out wail of pleasure. The kind

236

that could make a man's ego bloom to outlandish proportions. "What are you doing to me?" she cried. "This isn't supposed to happen, you wretch. You weren't supposed to touch me."

"Did I touch you first?" he asked, his voice almost unrecognizable in its raspiness. "I don't remember."

He began to bunch her gown in his fists, gathering it higher and higher, exposing long legs and finally that little wispy undergarment Harriet called *panties.*

"You have been taking those birth-control pills, haven't you, Harriet?" he said against her neck as he undid the waistband of his trousers and let them drop to his ankles.

She nodded, as speechless with excitement as he was.

"This will be so good, darlin'," he promised as he began to slip the sides of her panties down her hips. "No worry. No babies. Just us, sweetheart. That's all."

Harriet went still and put halting hands on his. "No," she said on a whimper, then more loudly, *"No!"*

Etienne couldn't believe she was going to stop now. Just like before. But he couldn't be angry with the woman who crumpled to the floor and sobbed loudly into her widespread fingers. What was wrong with her?

Tucking his painfully hard erection back into his pants, he sank down beside her, taking her into his arms. She laid her face against his chest and sobbed even louder.

"What is it, *chérie?" Is that me, talking so calmly? When her bare breasts are moving against me with every sob? When her lips are swollen from my kisses, and begging for more? When I am so hard and hot for her I just might burst?*

I must be a saint.

"Babies," she blubbered.

"Babies?"

"You said, 'No babies.' "

Suddenly, Etienne didn't feel quite so aroused. "That's right. You know I don't want children. I've mentioned my

Sandra Hill

mother's madness. Dammit, why do you bring this up now? Why?''

"Because you already have a baby ... a child." She sniffled, wiping a hand across her nose. "That's why I've been looking for you all day. To talk to you about Saralee."

Etienne stiffened and then stood abruptly. Harriet scrambled to regain her balance.

"I have no children."

"Yes, you do," Harriet stormed. She stood, too, then belatedly remembered to pull up the bodice of her gown.

Etienne stifled a moan at the sight.

"Saralee is not my child. I will explain this to you one time, and one time only, Harriet. Then I never want to discuss it again. I have always been concerned about the possibility of passing on my mother's madness. I have always used precautions, even with prostitutes. Do I make myself clear?''

Walking over to the window, he stared blindly out at the fields. He inhaled and exhaled deeply to regain his composure.

"Now, let me make myself clear, Mr. Know-It-All Baptiste. You're always accusing me of giving lectures. Well, I'm giving you a lecture now. In my time we have the most advanced forms of birth control imaginable. When you refer to taking precautions, I'm assuming you mean those French Letter things. Well, listen up, babe ... condoms aren't infallible in the twentieth century, and they sure as hell aren't infallible in the nineteenth century." She took a deep breath and continued, "Furthermore, Cain says your mother wasn't insane, just addicted to laudanum. So forget that bad blood business.''

He turned slowly and gazed at her. She stood, hands on hips, glaring at him. Her hair spilled out over her shoulders, having lost its fastenings. Her face and shoulders were flushed from his caresses. Her green cat eyes flashed fire at him.

"Saralee is not my child," he repeated, more softly this

238

time. And his headache returned with a vengeance, exploding behind his eyeballs.

Tears welled in her eyes. She lifted one hand beseechingly, then dropped it. "You're not a cruel man. I know you're not. How can you hurt your own daughter so? She needs you."

He tightened his jaw and lifted his chin.

"You stubborn fool. Take that blasted picture you carry around . . . the one of you as a boy with your brothers and sisters . . . take that damn picture and hold it up next to Saralee. She looks just like you." Her voice broke. "She really does."

Etienne's shoulders slumped. Could Harriet be right? No, no, it was impossible. But what if she was right?

"Will you at least consider the possibility?"

He hesitated for several long moments, then nodded.

She nodded back and in a swirl of skirts headed for the doorway, then froze. "Oh, no! It can't be." She slapped a hand over her chest in alarm, then scowled at him accusingly over her shoulder. "How could you do this to me?"

"Do what?" Etienne snapped. His body and soul had been battered by this infuriating woman. *What next?*

"This is the worst thing that could happen to me." She shivered with distaste.

"Well, don't be afraid to speak up, darlin'." *Why stop now?*

"I love you, stupid."

Chapter Fifteen

Harriet didn't see Etienne again for another hour. She was sitting on a bench at the kitchen table waiting for dinner when he slipped in beside her.

By then her temper had settled down. But not her emotions. She abhorred Etienne's effect on her. All he had to do was flash her one of his roguish once-overs, and her passions were inflamed.

"I love you, stupid." Did I really say that?

She stole a glance at Etienne.

He winked.

Aaarrgh! I did.

The feminist and the rogue. A match made in hell.

God, I'm turning into my mother. I can't love him. I can't love any man. No, no, no. I will not stand for this.

Red faced, she scooted over, making room, but couldn't look at him directly. When she finally sneaked a sidelong glance, she noticed a flush underlying the dark skin of his cheeks. The fingertips of one hand tapped nervously on the table.

Okay, so he wasn't so calm either. *Good.*

No, that was bad. He should do something jerky so that I can say, "Blech! Sorry, Charlie, I don't love you after all."

His clean-shaven face smelled of soap lather. *Why couldn't he have a beard and b.o.?* He'd put on dark trousers and a faded blue cotton shirt, with several buttons open at the neck. *A few gold chains would help.* His black hair was combed wetly off his face, the bump on his forehead barely noticeable now.

Across from her sat Saralee, flanked by Cain and Abel, who were trying their best to get the little girl to loosen up.

"Will you play princess with me tomorrow, Sarie?" Abel implored. "I'll even be the frog this time. Ribet, ribet!"

Saralee was a shy thing who had burst out with an occasional giggle or given reluctant monosyllabic answers to their questions . . . before Etienne's arrival. At first sight of her father, she went rigid with fright and her skin paled to a ghostly white. If she hadn't been trapped on the bench, she would have fled like a scared bird.

"No, Sarie is going to be my nurse tomorrow," Cain insisted.

The adorable girl had a miniature cap perched on her head similar to those worn by women nurses during the Civil War. Cain had brought it for her as a coming-home gift. In the pocket of her long apron was the mouth organ Abel had presented to her moments ago, promising to give her lessons before his departure.

Saralee beamed at the two brothers who vied for her favors, but she remained silent, casting wary peeks at Etienne. Did she fear he would chastise her for speaking, or smiling?

Of course.

And where was Etienne's gift for his daughter? Harriet scowled at the louse. *Good idea . . . think about all his bad qualities.*

The louse squeezed her thigh under the table.

"Don't you dare touch me," she hissed. Luckily, Cain and Abel were playing a guessing game with Saralee that distracted them momentarily.

He squeezed tighter and moved his fingers higher. "You don't tell a man that you ... what you said ... then turn cold again. Uh-uh. Those words give a man rights."

He didn't have to say the words for her to know what he meant. Her face blazed even hotter.

"And what do you mean by 'I love you, *stupid*'? What kind of declaration is that?"

"It's the truth. You are stupid, *stupid*. And I lied about the other part." Then she gasped, "Ooooh!" His clever fingers had entered new territory. She tried discreetly to shove them away but he leaned close to whisper in her ear, thus dividing her attention between two equally sensitive zones.

"I want you," he breathed into her ear. "Desperately."

Oh, he is good. She closed her eyes and prayed for strength. An image of her mother crying flitted through her mind. *Thank you, God!* When she opened her eyes, three sets of eyes stared at her; actually, it was probably four sets, but she wasn't about to look at the rogue with the magic fingers.

"Wh-what?" she stammered, realizing that someone must have asked a question and was waiting for an answer.

"I asked you what's wrong?" Cain said, a grin twitching at his lips. "You look like you're in pain."

"What I want to know is, where is Etienne's hand?" Abel asked.

Etienne's hand whisked upward, holding a linen cloth. "Just retrieving my napkin," he said, smiling broadly.

Yep, the man did have clever hands, and a clever tongue. In fact, he had lots of clever body parts. Too bad he'd never get to use them on her now.

Everyone laughed, except Saralee, who didn't understand.

Verbena, a middle-aged black woman, was helping Blossom in the kitchen tonight. She waddled over now to hand Blossom the platter of ham and red-eye gravy, made from pan drippings and leftover coffee. Harriet had watched Saralee prepare much of the meal earlier, under Blossom's direction. They'd worked over a potager, a tile counter with built in "stew holes" heated by charcoal burners—a forerunner of stove-top ranges. On the sideboard had already been placed small Irish potatoes and fresh vegetables, not to mention warm bread and sweet butter. A glass of lemonade or coffee was at each setting.

Each person passed an empty plate to Blossom, who stood serving at the end of the table. When it came Etienne's turn, she gave him a pitifully small slice of meat, even smaller than Saralee's portion. He just raised an amused brow.

When it was Harriet's turn, Blossom pierced her with a withering appraisal. "I thought you was gonna help me turn this scamp around? He's still actin' scampy, far as I kin see."

"Huh?" Etienne glowered alternately at Blossom and her.

Scampy? Yep, that about says it. But did Blossom have to announce their stupid plans to everyone?

Saralee continued to blink with confusion.

Cain and Abel slapped their knees and went into hysterics.

"What you two cacklin' about?" Blossom said as she poured out more beverages. "I declare, you two was born tired and raised lazy. When you boys gonna give me some babies to play with? Ain't it time you stopped plowin' every field in the parish and married up with a nice, decent wife?" Her eyes shifted craftily. "Did I tell you 'bout the new schoolmistress, Miz Ellen?"

Cain and Abel rolled their eyes at each other.

"She come from California to visit her auntie Verbena. She be book-smart, too. Thass why she set up the school."

Etienne smiled, relieved that he was no longer the object of Blossom's attention. Then his brow creased with a frown. He was probably remembering his earlier question about who'd given permission to start up a school on his lands.

"Doan you be givin' me that 'I-am-the-master' eye, Mistuh Baptiste. Iffen you neglect yo' duties, others got to take up the slack. By the by, Ellen be needin' money for the school. Ain't nearly enough books and papers fer thirty young'uns."

"Thirty?" he choked out.

"She couldn't hardly turn away those other chilluns from down the bayou what needs book-learnin', too. Now could she?"

Cain and Abel gave each other congratulatory grins now that the ball of Blossom's sharp tongue had bounced to another court.

And Saralee's puzzled frown deepened.

"Yessirree, Miz Ellen be in Houma today . . ."

And the ball was back in the black men's laps. Abel's eyes crossed and Cain looked as if he'd swallowed a whole lemon, not a sip of lemonade.

". . . but she be back tomorrow. You boys stay put and ol' Blossom gonna find you a lady for a wife, not one of them fanfoots with big bosoms and city ways."

"What's wrong with big bosoms?" Cain asked innocently as he wiped his plate clean with a second slice of bread.

"I like the city," Abel added. "So don't be pushin' any country maid in my face. Besides, I got my standards."

Blossom harrumphed and focused her attention on Cain. "And what you mean by neglectin' all these sick people hereabouts? Lordy, we gots ailin' black folks comin' here from every plantation in the lowlands lookin' for the swamp doctor. You gots responsibilities, boy."

Abel put his face in his hands, sensing he was next.

"And Abel . . . Lord-a-mercy! . . . you still playin' that

low-down devil music? I never did hear of a grown man what wanted to devote his life to such lust-provokin' trash."

"Can I have another helping, Blossom?" Etienne held out his empty plate, batting his puppy dog eyes at the old cook. Cain and Abel exhaled thankfully at his interruption.

Blossom couldn't resist Etienne, and this time the plate was piled high, with a slice of tipsy cake added for good measure.

He winked at Blossom, and she harrumphed again, walking away pleased.

When the meal was finally over, with intermittent casual conversation about the plantation and work to be done during the few days they'd be here, Saralee squirmed. "Can ... can I ... be ... be ex-ex-excused?" she stuttered in a shaky voice.

"No," Etienne said firmly.

Saralee's blue eyes shot wide and a visible shiver passed over her thin body.

"Etienne!" Harriet and Cain and Abel turned on the brute with indignation.

He ignored their scorn. Pulling a worn photograph out of his pocket, Etienne laid it on the table.

Harriet's heart started beating so fast she could barely breathe. Cain and Abel tensed.

Etienne studied the photograph, then glanced over at Saralee, then back to the sepia-toned picture. Gulping, he fought for words. "Saralee, someone gave me hell ... I mean, a lecture today. She said I was blind. That I couldn't see what stared me in the face."

The little girl made a squeaking sound and put the fingertips of one hand to her quivering mouth. Abel patted her on the shoulder, murmuring, "It's gonna be all right, baby."

"Well, Saralee, I'm stubborn, but I'm not stupid." He gave Harriet a look at that last word, then went on, addressing Saralee. "I'm your father. You're my daughter."

"Hallelujah!" Blossom exclaimed in the background. Cain and Abel glowed with happiness. Saralee looked as if Etienne had just handed her the moon. Harriet was weeping.

I'm a goner, Harriet thought as *I love you, stupid* echoed through her mind.

"I don't know that it makes any difference," he went on, "but . . . that's all I wanted to say." Etienne shocked everyone by standing abruptly then and walking stiffly toward the back door.

Wasn't he going to hug his daughter? Or talk to her? Make up for lost years? Plan their future? The jerk! Where was her tape recorder? She saw a new chapter brewing: "Dumb Things Men Do to Their Children."

Boy, oh boy, did Etienne need one of her therapy sessions.

Boy, oh boy, did she need one of her therapy sessions.

At the last minute, Etienne turned and sent Harriet a smoldering "man-look."

Uh-oh!

He pointed a finger at her and smiled grimly. "You and I have unfinished business, darlin'."

They probably heard the thumping of her heart all the way to New Orleans.

And Harriet decided on the title for the last chapter of her book: "I Love You, Stupid."

Harriet caught up with Etienne a short time later as he stomped down a narrow path to the bayou stream. More than once, a branch or prickly bush hit her in the face. She didn't know if it was an accident, or if Etienne had heard her coming and was deliberately impeding her progress.

Talk about going back to nature. This whole area could use a good industrial-size weed-zapper, or a bulldozer. "Where's a machete when a girl needs one?" Harriet mumbled.

Etienne halted and she almost ran into his back. "A machete?" He propped his hands on his hips. "I've tolerated way too much abuse from you, sweetheart. Whacks over the head with a satchel and an oar. Dunking in a stream. But I draw the line at being a chopping block for your machete."

"Don't be silly—"

"I warned you about calling me silly."

"Don't be irrational then. I merely wanted a machete to cut down some of this jungle."

"Lady, I do not need you to raze my jungle. And I most definitely do not want to see a sharp weapon in your hands. When, or if, this land gets cleared, it will be by me and no one else." He jabbed a forefinger at her. "Do you understand?"

She nodded.

"And stop following me." He walked away.

"Then stand still."

"No. If I stand still, I'll remember that I'm harder than a poker," he said over his shoulder. "And it's not my own fire I've a mind to stoke."

She gasped. Damn, but this guy had a knack for making her feel like a quivering virgin, over and over. *Hey, that might make a good title for a book. Rediscovering Your Virginity.*

"Why do dumb men think sex is like air?" she twittered nervously, trying for a counterdefensive.

A small twitch near his right eye was his only reaction. "It's no big thing till they aren't getting any."

"*Merde!*" he muttered under his breath.

Harriet couldn't see Etienne's face as she stumbled to keep up with his wide strides, but she was pretty sure he was angry. And he had a right to be. He'd been through a lot today. And most of his pain and confusion had been brought on by her. He had to be confused by his relationship with Saralee. "Seriously, I need to talk to you," she tried again.

"Seriously, you've talked enough."

"Etienne, it's about Saralee. You can't just—"

"Aaarrgh!" He stopped and pressed his forehead against a tree, breathing deeply. When he finally looked at her again, his eyes were dark and stormy. "Are you still here? *Sacrebleu!* Don't push me any further, Harriet. I acknowledged my daughter. Isn't that sufficient for you?"

"No," she said weakly. Her first inclination was to back down. Accepting paternity for Saralee *was* a major breakthrough for Etienne, especially after all these years. She would like to leave him alone to digest all the new feelings that must be assailing him. But she had Saralee to consider, as well. And the little girl needed her father now. "You can't just tell a child that you're her father. You need to *be* a father, as well."

"Stop meddling in my life."

Etienne was walking again, and she skipped to keep pace with him. The path had widened and veered off to the right, following the natural contours of the stream.

"I only want to help. And I'm qualified to assist in a crisis like this. Are you listening to me, Etienne? This is my life work—counseling dysfunctional families. Today you had a breakthrough, but now the real work begins. Any man can father a child, but it takes a real man to be a father."

Etienne's shoulders slumped. "I have no idea in the world how to be a father."

Harriet brightened. "See, I can help you there."

Etienne shook his head as if he couldn't believe he'd actually confided in her.

"First off, you have to be there *physically* for Saralee. That means staying in one place, or taking her with you. No more abandoning her to other people, like Blossom."

He let out a sigh of exasperation. "I'm leaving in a few days."

"I know, I know, but there's got to be a way around that. How about taking Saralee with us?"

"*Us?* No, no, no! *You* are not going anywhere. And I

certainly wouldn't endanger a child on a mission such as this."

She tapped her chin thoughtfully with a forefinger. "Well, maybe you could send her to California to stay with her grandparents—your father and stepmother—until . . ." Her voice trailed off when she saw the rigid set of his jaw and the red fury flushing his cheeks. "Then again, maybe not."

"Don't you ever . . . *ever* . . . mention my father again. If you do, I swear, I really will strangle you."

"I just want you to form a plan for dealing with a difficult situation."

"I don't like plans," he grumbled. "Day by day is as much as I can handle right now."

Harriet wept silent tears at the bleakness of his tone. "Etienne, you were in prison for several years. Incarceration forces a man to change his normal habits in order to survive. You conditioned yourself to live only for the moment, to give up your dreams."

"What do you know about prison life?" he said with a snarl.

"I've read plenty. Oh, don't get your hackles up. There are some things a person can learn without the actual experience."

"Please, God, not another lecture."

"For example, it's a standard characteristic of prison inmates to hide their feelings and wants because exposure could bring out more cruelty from the guards. In essence, the prisoner deadens a part of himself in order to survive." She could see that Etienne's interest was caught, even if he wouldn't admit it. "I don't have to have been there to know that you've been hiding your emotions for so long you can't let loose. Now . . . well, now you have to let down your guard. Give yourself the freedom to map out a future."

"Harriet, do you have an opinion on everything?" He smiled when he asked the question, which meant he wasn't totally upset at her advice.

Sandra Hill

She shrugged. "Probably."

"And where do you fit into all these plans?" he asked, giving her a measuring assessment.

"Well, I don't," she stammered. *Okay, so we're back to the "I love you, stupid" bit again. He must think I have big plans for him myself. Marriage, and all that. Hah!* "I expect to be around here . . . in the past, I mean . . . two months max. But in the meantime, I'm at your disposal."

He arched a brow.

"Not in that way. Listen, can we just forget what I, uh, said up there earlier?"

"No."

"No?"

He grinned, obviously aware of her discomfort. "No woman has ever told me 'I love you, *stupid*.' I think the words will be emblazoned in my memory forever."

Great! "Back to the subject at hand. While I'm here, I can give you and Saralee my undivided *professional* attention. And I won't charge a cent." She beamed at him.

"Hah! That's probably because we'll end up playing leading roles in one of your upcoming books."

She blushed guiltily.

Raking the fingers of both hands through his hair, he glared at her. "Putting money into this plantation would be like spitting in the wind."

"Only if you spit in the wrong direction."

"You have an answer for everything."

"You have a roadblock for everything. Oh, Etienne, this isn't about money and you know it."

"Yes, it most definitely is. I might as well tell you . . . one of my reasons for being involved in this assignment for President Grant is that I'll finally get a large sum in back pay and commissions. *If* I decide to come back to Bayou Noir, I would need all those funds, and more, just to get the sugar operation restarted. Without those funds, it would be impossible."

"Well, perhaps the separation would be okay as long as

250

you promise Saralee that you'll be coming back soon. To stay.''

He scowled at her. "Don't try to back me into a corner, Harriet. I'm not making any promises to anyone.''

Harriet sighed. Lord, he was a hard nut to crack. And she'd never expected him to make her any promises. That was a misunderstanding she'd have to clear up later. "The most important thing is to show Saralee how much you love her.''

"Love her? I don't even know her." He was gritting his teeth and clenching his fists.

"This is good, this is good. Verbalize your feelings. Release the rage. Once you get all your emotions out in the open, we can come up with some solutions. Mirroring sessions, hypnotherapy, Rorschach tests, subliminal conditioning, age regression." Harriet couldn't wait to begin.

Etienne gaped at her with horror. "Harriet, I have a powerful headache. I've listened to more of your prattling today than any man deserves. Have mercy." He picked up a dead limb, only an inch or two in diameter and six feet long. Using it to rake an arc in front of him, he plodded into the underbrush.

"Why are you waving that stick around?"

"To ward off snakes.''

Yech!

"Don't ever go outside the house without wearing shoes," he warned conversationally, as if they hadn't just been having a serious discussion, "and I'd suggest you ask Blossom to find you some leather brogues. A cottonmouth could slip its fangs into those slippers of yours quicker'n a blink.''

Great! I needed to know that my feet are snake bait. "Where are we going? Wouldn't we be more comfy discussing this back at the house?" She watched where she placed her slippers more carefully now and, as a result, got another branch in her face. Probably poison oak.

"*We* aren't going anywhere. And *we* aren't discussing

251

anything more tonight.'' He hesitated for a moment, then added, ''*I'm* going on a snake hunt. Betcha I catch at least . . . fifty.''

Harriet stopped in her tracks. ''A snake hunt?'' she squeaked. ''Whatever for?''

Etienne chuckled as he continued strolling on ahead. *The creep!*

She scurried to catch up. ''That wasn't very funny.''

''Actually, I'm meeting a friend. And if you keep chattering away, my friend will be frightened off.''

''A friend? Why would a friend be frightened off?'' Oh, it must be one of the agents in the Secret Service making a covert contact with him. Or could it be . . . oh, no . . . could it be a woman?

Her heart constricted. *I don't care. I don't care.*

Hah!

I do care. I do care. Darn it, but I do care.

''Shhh,'' he warned in a hushed voice as he came to a bend in the stream. ''There's my friend.''

''Where?'' she whispered, her head swinging back and forth as she scanned the area. The whole time, she kept an eye on her slippers, as well. Now that Etienne had mentioned snakes and her vulnerable feet, she couldn't stop hearing little slithering noises. ''I don't see anything except that big boulder in the water over—Oh, my God!'' The boulder was moving toward them. *Kerplop, kerplop, kerplop . . .*

What she'd thought a green algae–covered rock was actually a hulking monster of a turtle—at least two hundred pounds and three feet across. It was the ugliest animal she'd ever seen.

''Meet Maurice.''

''Maurice?'' she squealed, jumping behind Etienne for protection as the lumbering beast poked a parrot-beaked head from its armor-plated shell and stared at them through beady eyes. Black leeches and other slimy critters clung to its exposed body joints. ''Your friend?''

He nodded. "An alligator snapping turtle. Isn't he a beauty?"

Harriet peeked up at Etienne to see if he was kidding, then back at the hissing reptile, which had high ridges and a long tail that were, indeed, similar to an alligator's. Then Harriet danced around from foot to foot. She'd forgotten to check for snakes in the last second or two.

Etienne smirked at her. "Maurice was born when I was five years old. See that knife blade sticking out of the shell near his neck? I put that there when Maurice was a few months old. We were having a wrestling match over a warmouth bass I caught."

Etienne grinned like a young boy, and she could just picture the scamp going one-on-one with a baby turtle. "Who won?"

"Maurice," Etienne admitted with a grimace, "but he'll carry my mark for the rest of his life. How you doin', Maurice? Have a wife yet? No? Me, neither. Too much trouble? I agree. Wenches tease you, then refuse to please you. Is it the same down there on the bottom? Bloodsuckers, you say? Yep!"

Maurice's only contribution to the one-way conversation was an occasional soughing hiss as he sucked in drafts of air. Then, as quickly as he'd emerged from the water, Maurice sashayed over to the edge of the stream and submerged himself. While he propelled his ponderous body along the bottom, the only evidence of his path was a trail of silt that rose to the surface.

Etienne smiled at her, and she smiled back.

The shared moment was precious, and Harriet wished she could hold it in her hands and never let go. *I love you*, she thought, and for some reason forgot to add *stupid*.

"You reckoned I was meeting a woman, didn't you?" he drawled, breaking the thread of intimate camaraderie.

"No, I thought you were adding animal sex to your necrophilia."

He laughed and chucked her under the chin. "You were

jealous when I mentioned a friend,'' he gloated with amusement. Then he tensed suddenly, frowning with concern. ''Why do you keep fidgeting from foot to foot?'' He contemplated her for a moment before a lazy smile spread across his lips. ''Do you have some of those pesky red ants on you? Perhaps in your drawers? Maybe I should check.''

Harriet shook her head at him and laughed, despite herself.

''They like to nestle in hot, moist places. Yep, you'd better drop your drawers.''

''Talk about lack of subtlety!'' But she could deliver tit for tat any day. ''I'm not wearing any underwear.''

''Neither am I,'' Etienne came right back, flashing a one-upmanship grin at her.

She chalked an imaginary one in the air for his side. ''You certainly recover quickly from your fits of frustration.'' His roller-coaster moods were enough to drive a poor girl batty. One minute he scorched her with one of those man-looks, and the next he laughed at her.

He shrugged. ''If I don't laugh, I might cry.''

''It's not that bad.''

''It's that bad.''

Twang, Twang, Twang!

''What is *that*?'' Harriet exclaimed. ''Oh, I see. It's just a frog, but what an ungodly noise it's making. I thought frogs were supposed to ribet.''

''It's a toad, not a frog. And that one's a male spadefoot toad,'' Etienne corrected, peering through the bushes at a stout little varmint about three inches long. The toad was sitting on a lily pad near a half-submerged gum tree log.

''We're in luck. They rarely come out in daylight.''

Harriet squinted to see what was so special about this animal. Its unwarted, smooth skin was brownish black with an olive hue, highlighted by two stripes down the back. Ted the Toad was bellowing out what she presumed must be a mating call, his entire body vibrating with the intensity of his resonation.

The wartless stud was doing something else interesting while beckoning his significant other. With his nostrils and mouth tightly closed, he expelled air from his lungs into a throat sac under his chin, causing it to balloon up into an enormous, almost transparent bubble. The female species in toad-dom probably considered it very sexy, comparable to big pecs or six-pack abs.

Oh, yeah, here came Tootsie Toad, bee-bop-hopping over to Ted's pad. With almost no foreplay—a six on the MCP scale—Ted jumped on Tootsie's back and locked his forelegs around hers.

When Harriet's eyes, as well as Tootsie's, grew wide at Ted's endurance, Etienne explained, "The thumb and inner fingers of the male's front hands have horny growths on them called nuptial pads. That's so he can hold on to her if she changes her mind."

"Oh, you!"

"Really, it's true. Look closer."

"I am not going to stand here and watch two toads have sex. You really are a pervert." She laughed and started to walk back toward the house.

"I think God missed a step in the evolutionary process," Etienne concluded as he followed her. "He forgot to give those horny spurs to men. If he had, women wouldn't be able to stop in the middle of the act."

"You are outrageous," Harriet said, turning and walking backward while she talked. She was still scanning the path warily for snakes. "But you see, God didn't make a mistake. He gave men something even better, something he didn't give to the lower animal classes."

"And that would be?" Etienne made a great show of closing the distance between them with a big toadlike hop.

"A heartbreaker smile and a talent for slick sweet-talk, both geared to wear a woman's defenses down."

Etienne favored her with one of his heartbreaker smiles. And the butterflies in her stomach went wild. But then Etienne froze, glancing upward.

Sandra Hill

What now? Uh-uh! She wasn't going to fall for that trick. He was pretending there was some danger, like the snake hunt, hoping she'd leapfrog into his arms, dropping her drawers in the process. She cut him one of her I'm-no-fool scowls.

"Harriet, remember when I told you to be careful of snakes?" he said cautiously.

"Yes." What if he wasn't teasing? She looked down in panic. Not a reptile in sight. *The stinker!*

"Well, try to remain calm, honey. I have something to tell you, and I want you to remember that not all snakes in the bayou are poisonous. In fact, most of them are completely harmless."

"What's your point?"

"Do you promise not to scream?"

"I'll scream my head off if you don't stop razzing me. I'm not afraid of snakes, by the way. Just cautious."

"You're not afraid of anything, are you, darlin'?" He came up close to her and held his arms wide open.

"As if!" she snickered.

"The most harmless of all the bayou snakes aren't even on the ground," he continued in a patient monotone, as if he didn't want to alarm her. He continued to hold his arms wide open. "They're . . . tree snakes."

Tree snakes? The fine hairs on the back of Harriet's neck and all over her arms came to attention in a slow-motion wave, just before she forced herself to look upward. Dozens of slender, slimy black snakes hung from the tree limbs, just waiting to fall into her hair, or slither down the neckline of her gown.

"Yikes!" Harriet screamed so loud the earth seemed to shake; then she launched herself into Etienne's waiting arms with such force that she knocked him over. The snakes probably fell from their perches with all her flailing about, but Harriet wouldn't know. Scrunching her eyes closed, she was still screaming into Etienne's ear. He was

256

sprawled on his back on the path with her plastered on top of him.

The brute was laughing so hard tears streamed down his face. "They're just . . . they're just vines," he finally sputtered out.

Harriet stilled. *The man is sick. Sick, sick, sick!* "Are you saying those aren't really snakes?"

"I never said those were snakes. I merely gave you a short lecture on the types of snakes in the bayou. You know what a lecture is, don't you, honey?"

"You are such a toad," she stormed, pounding his chest.

"There's one other thing we men have that toads don't." Etienne chortled, wrapping his arms tightly around her waist with his horny hands. His "other thing" was prodding her with intimate insinuation.

She snorted with disgust and tried to peel herself off of him. "I would imagine that toads have that appendage, too."

"Not that, sweetheart. What we men have that toads don't is a brain to outmaneuver the ever-devious, reluctant female." He ran both palms from her shoulders to her rear in emphasis of their positions. The lech had her right where he'd wanted her. "Dumb-men jokes aside, you were just outsmarted, Dr. Ginoza."

And Harriet realized that she was.

Chapter Sixteen

"You're playin' in my orchard,
Now don't you see.
If you don't like my peaches,
Stop shakin' my tree . . ."

Etienne heard Abel's strong baritone voice ripple out into the evening air, accompanied by the raucous squawk of a mouth organ, as he and Harriet neared the house. Laughter and talking followed, coming from the kitchen. Then the lyrics and music started over again.

Abel must be teaching Saralee to play her new gift. It was just like him to pick a bawdy song.

In the distance, he saw Cain striding toward the bayou stream and a waiting pirogue, his medical satchel in hand. One of the black families from a neighboring area must have requested the services of the swamp doctor, as Cain was sometimes called, although there were probably other physicians, black and white, given that appellation, too. All day long, former black slaves had been lined up outside the large cabin Cain used as a clinic.

Cain had been absent from Bayou Noir and his practice way too long. Cain, too, had demons to exorcise.

They'd both fought in the war for what they'd considered noble ends. But neither of them saw much fruit for those efforts. More than six hundred thousand men from both sides had died, and what had been gained? Slavery had been abolished, but the Negroes were still in bondage. In fact, for many of them, conditions were worse than before.

And Cain, a doctor, had to live with the fact that only one out of three wartime deaths resulted from actual battle. Most soldiers had died from disease.

Now a new sound drifted on the wind . . . sweet and poignant, pulling Etienne from his dismal musings. It was the mouth organ again, but this time an intricate trill of notes wailed of profound heartache and yearning. Of the three of them, Abel was the only one able to express his inner pain and rage . . . through his music.

Saralee's reedy, childlike voice sang the same lyrics to Abel's accompaniment, adding innocence and hope to an age-old message of despair. Oh, the words were light, but Abel's rendering was dramatic and full of anguish.

Etienne looped an arm over Harriet's shoulder and put a fingertip to her lips, cautioning silence. She tried to swat him away, having proclaimed there would be no more touching, but he held tight. Too bad he didn't have a set of those frog spurs.

"Listen to this," he whispered. "There isn't an instrument in the world Abel can't pick up and play." A complicated melody of improvised, syncopated rhythms and drawn-out notes followed with an underlying layer of the low-down blues music that Abel favored. Devil music, as Blossom would say.

Harriet tilted her head in appreciation. He could tell she was still mad at him for his trickery, but her insatiable curiosity won out.

"Was he always gifted?"

"Even as a child. I can remember him making music by

259

blowing on a blade of grass or banging on a gourd with a stick when nothing else was available.''

"It's too bad he never got to study music."

"Oh, he did. Abel studied classical music in Paris under the best of teachers . . . piano, violin, all the highbrow instruments. And composition. But once he discovered the trumpet, he never looked back."

"Can he make a living with his music? I mean, it's hard even in modern times unless the artist is really famous."

Shrugging, he took her hand, lacing their fingers, and drew her toward the house. Closing his eyes for a moment, he relished the contact of his skin against hers, restraining himself from raising her hand and brushing her knuckles against his lips.

The effect this strange woman had on him was alarming. Oh, the knee-buckling ecstasy of their numerous couplings back at Simone's, that he could understand. But she affected him in so many ways. A passing glance, an accidental brushing, her kisses—oh, Lord, her kisses! He had to pace himself with her, allow himself only small doses of physical contact, or he'd be overwhelmed. As helpless as a bird without wings. Or a frog without spurs, he thought with a grin.

He didn't love her. *Hell, no! And thank God!* He didn't doubt the existence of love. He just wasn't capable of it himself anymore . . . there were too many empty holes in his soul. He certainly didn't think she loved him, either—with or without the ''stupid'' tag. She was feeling the same lustful impulses that he was.

"Did you hear me, Etienne? Can Abel subsist on his music?"

"Huh?" He shook his head to clear it of all the unwanted questions. "Oh, I suppose. There's a demand for musicians in all the sporting houses and music halls, especially in New Orleans. Abel could play with any band he wanted, or start his own. And composers, like that Stephen Foster, seem to be able to make a good living from the sale of their sheet music. Besides, his stepfather and mother hit a bonanza during the Gold Rush in California. Abel has a generous income without ever working.'' He hesitated, then added, ''But what Abel should really do is return to Europe, and take Simone with him.''

''Because there's more tolerance there for mixed couples?''

He nodded.

''But he won't go, will he?''

''Probably not. There's bayou mud in his blood, same as mine.''

''I must have bayou mud in my veins, too. I feel such a harmony here. I can't explain it . . . it just seems like home.''

Etienne felt a warm flush of pleasure at her words.

''When I get back to the future, I'm thinking of moving from L.A. to Louisiana. Wouldn't it be funny if your house was still here? And I bought it and lived here? Ha, ha, ha! Now that would be true synchronicity.''

''Yes, that would be very funny. Ha, ha, ha,'' he responded sarcastically. His warm flush turned to a cold pall.

''Maybe I could haunt you.''

Etienne knew she would be going away, and he eagerly awaited that day. But, perversely, he didn't like hearing her talk about it. Or being so enthusiastic. And the fact that he cared one way or the other really annoyed him.

> *''You're playin' in my orchard,*
> *Now don't you see.*
> *If you don't like my peaches,*
> *Stop shakin' my tree . . .''*

Abel's voice belted out the song once again in a solo rendition different from the previous ones, complete with rumbling insinuation and sultry double entendres. That was how all his music was—changing, improvising, embellishing. Each version different from the last. Then, too, he'd probably had a cup or two of Blossom's home brew.

Etienne laughed. "That should be our song, Harriet."

She gave him one of her disapproving glares, but surprisingly she didn't pull her hand from his clasp. He squeezed his palm tighter against hers and watched with satisfaction as her color went high.

"Really, you harp on everything that's wrong with me, but you won't stay out of my orchard. And you damn well keep shakin' my tree."

"Well, just keep your tree in your orchard and everyone will be fine." She did try to pull her hand away now, but too late. "Know this, honey: I'm not plucking any more peaches. Harvest time is over."

He couldn't resist then. Raising her hand to his lips, he kissed each of the separate knuckles. With his thumb pressed against her wrist, he felt her pulse jump, then race with excitement. *Aaah! So, the merest caress from me affects her.* "Why such vehement protests, *chérie?* You professed to love me just a short time ago. I thought—"

"You thought a woman in love would be an easy lay?" she finished for him and managed to pull her hand away. With both hands on her hips, she glowered at him.

He bit his bottom lip to stifle a grin. "I wouldn't have said it in quite that way. But, yes, I'd like to lie with you—easy, hard, all ways. Is that what you meant by 'easy lay'?" Meantime, he'd backed her up against the wall of the veranda.

She shook her head and made a small whimpering sound. It was almost his undoing.

"That had better not be a limb from a peach tree poking my belly," she said with a nervous twitter.

He ran the pad of his thumb over her parted lips, and she hissed in pleasure.

"Why do you fight the inevitable? You asked me on the train to make love to you over and over till you wiped out your pesky dreams," he reminded her. Then a sudden thought occurred to him. "I'm not still satisfying you in those dream fantasies, am I? Because if I am, stop them. For me, it's most . . . unsatisfying.''

She laughed softly and traced his jaw with her fingertips in a loving fashion. It was his turn to hiss with an indrawn breath of pure ecstasy. How could such a slight touch affect him so?

"No, the forceful seduction fantasies have stopped. But I wonder if they'll return when I go home. Somehow I doubt it.''

"I refuse to make love to you in dreams," he asserted.

She shrugged. "Sometimes we can't control our minds.''

How true! "But that doesn't answer my question. If you were willing before, why not now? Don't tell me that you don't desire me. I know that you do.''

"It's Saralee.''

"Saralee?" he sputtered. "What has she to do with this . . . this thing between us?''

"Etienne, this 'thing between us' is more than a momentary lust, no matter what you say—''

"Who said momentary? I'm thinking much longer. Days. Till I leave." He smiled at her, but she didn't smile back.

"I'm not going to let you rile me now. What I'm trying to say is that I've never been into casual sex, despite that impulsive . . . uh . . . encounter back in New Orleans.''

"Encounter?" He hooted. "It was more like an assault, the way I remember it. And, honey, I remember it a lot.''

Her lashes lowered with unaccustomed modesty. Then she opened her eyes, leveling an honest gaze at him. "Okay, it was an assault . . . a mutual assault. But my point, which you keep interrupting, is that any relationship between you and me is going to be powerful. And then it's going to end. Oh, not when you leave, mister. When *I* leave to go back to the future.''

"So?" There she went again, recalling a reality he didn't like facing. "All the more reason to enjoy the moment.''

"You and I aren't the only ones involved. Now that

you've acknowledged Saralee as your daughter, I can't present myself as your potential spouse."

"Spouse?" he roared. "Who said anything about marriage?"

"Now, settle down. I'm not ringing the wedding bells. But Saralee is a child, and she will naturally think that the woman who sleeps with her father is going to become his wife, and her mother. I can't mislead her that way. It would be too cruel."

"We could be subtle," he argued.

"Hah! You're about as subtle with those man-looks of yours as . . . as a peach tree in full bloom."

He grinned. "There must be a way."

"No," she said, putting two halting hands on his chest. "There's another really important reason why you and I can't make love. Professional ethics."

"I beg your pardon?"

"A psychologist can't have intimate relations with a client."

Huh? A client? Does she mean me? "I never hired you. No, no, no. If that's all that's keeping you from my bed, then I'm dismissing you. Right now."

"I volunteered my services. Remember?"

"Unvolunteer."

She laughed. "Etienne, it's not going to work with us. We come from two different worlds."

"So did my father and Selene." He immediately regretted that comparison.

"Yes, but they loved each other. And one of them had to make a sacrifice and give up a former life." She stared at him pensively. "I don't suppose you'd consider coming to the future with me . . . if it were possible? With Saralee, of course."

His eyes went wide with horror at the prospect. Riding through time to a foreign existence? Starting over? Leaving behind Cain and Abel, Blossom and . . . well, others?

She watched him expectantly.

"I don't want you that badly, Harriet."

"I know," she replied, her shoulders slumping. "I know."

And Etienne suspected he'd lost something precious in that moment of truth.

Later that evening, Harriet sat with Saralee on a bed in the former overseer's cottage located at the rear of the mansion. It was a spacious, one-story house with a sloping mansard roof that overhung a porch circling it on four sides. All of the rooms had tall windows that took advantage of the ventilating breezes that came up from the bayou. It was in better condition than the mansion because it was smaller and easier to keep up.

Saralee hummed softly as she played with her dolls. The peaches song melody, Harriet recognized with a grimace. *Like I need that reminder.*

Harriet was transcribing data from her tape recorder into her notebook, having realized that her two cassettes were about to overflow with MCP ideas. The three jerks of the Old South were providing her with an abundance of material for her new book. Especially the super jerk.

" 'Men Who Scare Women with Snakes.' A three.

" 'Men Who Smoke Cigars.' A four." Harriet had seen Etienne and Abel smoking thin cheroots this evening as they'd strolled down the street to find Cain. *Ugh!*

" 'Men Who Make a Woman Fall in Love with Them . . . and Don't Fall in Love Themselves.' " Harriet winced at that one. "A ten."

Saralee had exhibited an initial fascination with the solar-powered machine when Harriet first brought it out, but soon lost interest and resumed playing with her three rag dolls— Marilee, Jewel and Francois. In a charming Southern twang, Saralee spoke to the dolls as if they were human beings.

In fact, Harriet noted that the only time the girl was truly exuberant or stutter-free was when she addressed her pretend playmates. This was an important factor that Harriet would consider in her counseling sessions, along with Saralee's constant role-playing, which, of course, masked a deep-seated need for affection. One of the dolls, Marilee, had long, black hair made of hemp, and Harriet was sure the doll represented Saralee.

Blossom, who was already asleep in the other room, had given up her bedchamber behind the kitchen to Etienne, and would be staying here with Harriet and Saralee, along with the schoolteacher, Ellen, when she returned. Cain and Abel lodged in the large cabin that housed the clinic. The sleeping arrangement was a temporary one . . . until Etienne left Bayou Noir again.

Those last words sounded like a death knell to Harriet, and she wasn't sure why. First of all, she had no intention of letting Etienne abandon her at the plantation in three days. Second, she'd known all along that she and Etienne would have to part when she returned to the future.

So why did she feel as if her heart were breaking?

Because she loved the jerk, of course.

Besides, she hadn't had a chance to help Etienne yet. Although she'd set up a reconciliation between father and daughter, she hadn't begun to use her psychological skills to cure Etienne of his postprison syndrome. And she was sure she could alleviate his migraine headaches. Until he was healed both physically and mentally, her job here wouldn't be completed.

Well, goodness, she was one of the most competent professionals in her field. Therapy for Etienne should be a snap, given the seven-plus weeks she had left till the Illinois Central railroad bridge was completed.

With a plan in mind, Harriet felt better.

Setting her tape recorder and notebook aside, she scooted over to the middle of the bed. She was wearing only the leopard-print nightie and panties with one of Etienne's old shirts for a robe. The tails reached all the way to her knees.

She sat cross-legged, facing the little girl, who was also

cross-legged in her long, sleeveless chemise. "Saralee, honey, how about you and I play a game with your dolls?"

Saralee shimmied backward slightly and stammered out, "I doan . . . doan wanna play a game."

"Don't be frightened, sweetheart. I used to play with dolls all the time when I was your age. Barbie dolls."

"Ba-Barbie?"

"Yes. Barbie and Ken. They were horrible, gender-stereotyping dolls," Harriet started to say, but saw the confusion on the little girl's face. "But that's another story. My favorite of all my Barbie dolls was the princess one. Maybe this doll of yours could be Princess Maralee." She picked up the one with the long black hair. "And that one over there could be the King—Princess Maralee's father. King . . . uh, Toadienne." She pointed to the male rag doll.

Still unconvinced, Saralee clutched the remaining two dolls to her chest protectively, unsure of Harriet's intentions.

"And who could the other doll be?" Harriet pretended to be thinking hard, tapping her chin. "I know," she said brightly. "That could be the fairy queen who comes to visit from another land. Queen Merry-Hat."

Saralee giggled.

"The fairy queen would be Saralee's friend."

She turned big blue eyes—like Etienne's—on her with such open yearning that Harriet's maternal instincts went into overdrive. Saralee wouldn't be the only one hurt by the eventual separation.

"Do you want to play?" Harriet asked, reaching out slowly, so as not to alarm the child, and cupping her downy cheek.

Saralee leaned into her hand, obviously starving for tactile affection. Then she nodded her agreement.

"Once upon a time there was a magic kingdom," Harriet began, "but it was like no other place in the whole world. Because here the subjects were splendid creatures. Dainty butterflies and fierce alligators. Three-legged chickens—

Harriet had actually seen one of those today—and wild hawks. Kitty cats and scary wolves. Smelly skunks and snapping turtles.''

''Were thar puppy dawgs?'' Saralee asked tentatively, still not sure she wanted to play this game.

''Absolutely! Lots of puppies. All kinds.'' Then Harriet thought of something. ''Do you have a dog?''

Saralee shook her head.

''Why not?''

''Blossom says a dog is too much botheration.'' Then she had second thoughts about criticizing the old cook, who was no doubt very good to her. ''Blossom is old. She cain't hardly chase no puppies 'round. Spec'ly ones that makes puddles in the house.''

''Well, this princess had oodles of puppies.''

''Oodles?'' she sighed.

''And they never made puddles in her house because they were such good and loyal subjects.''

''Did the princess have jewels and crowns?''

''Well, of course. What kind of princess would she be without those? But in this land all the jewels grew on trees and bushes. And they were all colors and all sizes.''

''Flowers!'' Saralee guessed, hopping up and down on the mattress with excitement. ''And I know what her crown was, too. A May crown of blossoms.''

''Yes! How clever you are, Saralee. But let me tell you more. This very special princess lived in a splendid house in this magic kingdom called Noir in the land of Bayou. She had many friends and loyal subjects. She had everything a princess could have except one thing, which made her very unhappy. Do you know what that was, Saralee?''

The girl stuck a thumb in her mouth.

''Well, one day a royal visitor came to see Princess Maralee. Her name was Queen Merry-Hat because she wore a funny hat like a wizard. Queen Merry-Hat had special powers that came from the fairy dust she kept in her magic hat.''

"Could we . . . could we make a hat like that tomorrow?"

"Sure thing, honey. Now, back to the story. Queen Merry-Hat saw that Princess Maralee was sad and she told her that she could have a teensy pinch of her fairy dust. And that would entitle her to one wish, and one wish only."

"Ooooh! What did the princess wish for?"

"Well, at first, Princess Maralee couldn't make up her mind. Should she wish for real jewels? Or a boat? Or twenty wagons full of candy? Or a swing? Or a puppy? Or a million gowns?"

Saralee laughed merrily.

"The princess just couldn't decide. So Queen Merry-Hat told her that she knew a story that might help. It seems there once was a brave knight in the land of Noir . . . King Toadienne. He was called Toadienne because he liked to play with the slimy critters when he was a boy and because sometimes he even acted like one."

"I lak to play with toads sometimes," Saralee offered defensively.

It probably runs in the genes. "Yes, well, one day the brave Toadienne went off to war, and never came back. He became lost, you see. Worst of all, he never knew that his wife, Queen Vera, gave birth to his most precious little girl, Maralee." Harriet figured it would be only a little fib to imply that Etienne married Saralee's mother. "Even when he wandered back to his kingdom on occasion, he didn't know the little girl was his."

"Someone should ha' told 'im," Saralee cried.

"Well, they did, but Toadienne had lived among toads for so long that he got warts on his brain. He didn't believe them. Maybe he was afraid."

"Afraid? Of the princess?" Saralee looked horrified.

"Maybe he was afraid that she wouldn't like him."

"Maybe the princess was afraid he wouldn't lak her either."

Harriet could barely restrain herself from hugging the

sweet girl and assuring her that she was very likeable. "For days and days, then weeks and weeks, years and years, the princess couldn't make up her mind. What should her wish be?"

"I know, I know," Saralee exclaimed.

"Really? What do you think the little princess wished for?"

Saralee paused dramatically, then whooped, "Her papa."

Etienne pressed his forehead against the wall in the corridor outside the bedchamber. He'd come to talk to Saralee . . . perhaps to get to know his daughter a little better.

The only light in the dark hall came from a lantern he'd set on the stand next to him and from the oil lamps on either side of the tester bed that shone through the open doorway.

He felt so damn guilty.

Saralee feared that he wouldn't like her.

What did "like" have to do with it? Love should be unconditional. Wasn't that the biggest wall separating him and his father all these years?

When Etienne had defied his father back in 1861 and left Oxford to join in the fray that was to become the Civil War, his father had been upset. He'd claimed that one of the most important reasons he'd left the South was to spare himself and his son from participating in what was doomed to be a hopeless cause.

But Etienne had been twenty-two at the time, and thought he knew everything. While in California to inform his father of his decision, Etienne had run into Lafe Baker, who was starting up the National Detective Agency, soon to become the Secret Service. Lafe, "the Spymaster," had talked Etienne into working for the Union army through covert operations as a double agent.

The most effective spies had to be trained in the nuances of language, customs and manners of the enemy forces, right down to eating habits, dress and personality traits.

Etienne already had those assets, being a Southerner by birth, Creole by appearance, speaking with a Southern drawl, fluent in English, French and Spanish, having a knowledge of Confederate geography, not to mention being daring and highly intelligent. Most important, he had to be willing, at all costs, to keep his work secret.

The last time Etienne had seen his father, Etienne had been wearing the uniform of a Rebel captain. He would never, ever forget his father's last words. "You are not my son. From this day forth, you are not my son."

"Papa," he'd pleaded.

"Take off that uniform, Etienne. All your life, you've been a wild child. Stubborn, willful, careless. But this . . . this is too much. For God's sake, how could you? How could you?"

Shouldn't his father have had faith in him? Hadn't he known him well enough to believe in his integrity? Did he truly think he would fight on the side that wanted to put his best friends, Cain and Abel, in chains? Most important, regardless of what he did, shouldn't his father have loved him unconditionally?

But Etienne hadn't had the freedom then to say those things to his father. And the years had only driven the rift wider.

Now, he thought, bringing himself back to the present . . . now his own child forced him to realize he was no better than his father. Saralee feared he wouldn't like her, thought that was why he hadn't wanted her all these years.

Shouldn't a father love a child unconditionally, the way he'd wanted his father to love him?

Harriet had told him earlier that he needed to show Saralee that he loved her, and he'd responded that it was unreasonable to expect him to love her when he didn't even know her.

The love between a parent and child should be given freely. From the heart, with no strings attached.

Etienne pulled away from the wall and straightened in

determination. That, at least, was one wrong in this misdirected life of his that he could correct. And it wouldn't cost him anything . . . just a little love. He hoped he had some left.

Intending to go in to Saralee now, he hesitated when he heard Harriet moving about and saying, "Sweet dreams, princess." Apparently, she'd just tucked the girl in for the night. The bed linens rustled as Saralee presumably squirmed around to get comfortable. Well, perhaps his talk could wait until the morning. Yes, it would give him time to get his emotions in order, to handle the situation in a carefully planned manner.

Planned? Oh, merde! The witch has got me making plans.

"Can we make a wizard hat tomorrow?" Saralee asked Harriet.

"Oh, I think so. I'll be in the room next door if you need me, hon." Harriet blew out the lamps and, seconds later, she was sashaying out toward him, closing the door partially on the already sleeping child. In fact, she sashayed right into him.

"Ooomph!"

Feeling good about all the progress she'd made with Saralee, Harriet hadn't been paying attention when she barreled out into the hall—and slammed into the rock-hard wall of Etienne's chest. He grabbed her upper arms to hold her upright.

"What are you doing here?" she snapped. *Spying on me, I suppose.*

"I came to talk to my daughter, and to get some reading material since I couldn't sleep," he replied, loosening his grip on her, then immediately wrapping his arms around her waist and backing her up against the wall. "I thought I'd borrow one of your books to read." Before she could think, he had lifted her to tippy-toes, a position that seemed to be a favorite of his—chest to breast, hip to hip, groin to groin. It was fast becoming a favorite of hers, too.

"You came to talk to Saralee?" She was encouraged to know he was willing to make a first step.

"Um-hmm," he murmured, up close to her lips.

She could smell his breath, redolent of cigars along with whiskey and peaches. *Peaches?*

"Where did you get peaches?"

"The orchard," he said, smiling. Then he nipped at her lower lip, forcing her to open for his kiss. "You smell like gardenias. Been taking another bath, I assume."

When her lips parted with anticipation, he teased her with a flutter of a kiss. A butterfly kiss, softer than the fuzz on a peach. "You taste like peaches," she breathed. "Peach kisses."

"You should try them sometime." He chuckled. "The peaches, I mean."

"I thought we agreed not to do this anymore." She groaned as Etienne moved himself against her and whispered sinful things in her ear. Intimate, wicked words insinuating what he would like to do with her.

"Darlin', I don't recollect agreein' to anything. But then, I think my brain is melting from all this tree shakin' you been doin'."

"What tree shaking?"

"Harriet, I told you not to interfere in my life anymore. What were you doing in there with my daughter?"

"Therapy."

"Therapy," he repeated with disgust. "Another word for meddling."

"Now, Etienne, you have to realize that psychologists use many analytical tools."

He raised an eyebrow mockingly. "Like *Toadienne*?"

"Oh, well, that was just a role-playing game."

"Hah? And this?" he added, drawing back to study her. "If wearing this cat garment isn't tantamount to shakin' my tree, nothing is." He growled and drew the shirt off her shoulders so he could view her better.

She loved . . . she absolutely loved . . . the way Etienne's blue eyes turned dark and misty with passion when he gazed at her. She loved the feel of his heart thundering against hers with rising excitement.

When he kissed her this time, it was no peach-fuzz kiss. It was sweet and wet and sinfully delicious. Over and over he tasted her, and she tasted back.

"Oh, Etienne," she whispered, raking her fingers through his hair to hold him in place so she could see him. They were tempting fate by touching each other so.

"I try to stay away from you . . . I really do. But I keep circling back," he admitted.

She nodded in understanding. This magnetism that drew them together was powerful, beyond human resistance.

"Say the words, Harriet," he urged in a soft whisper. "Just one more time. Then I'll leave you and go off to my bed. Alone. With a book."

She didn't need to ask him which words he meant. She knew.

"I love you." She could hardly breathe over the intensity of emotion engendered by those three words.

He smiled grimly in satisfaction. "Why don't you say, 'I would love you if you would behave as I want.' Or, 'I would love you if you were more reliable.' Or, 'I would love you if you . . . ' You know what I mean."

She frowned with confusion. "Love and the qualifier 'if' are incompatible. Love comes. No provisos. If there are stipulations, then it isn't love."

He seemed to have trouble swallowing.

"Where did you get such a stupid idea?"

He shrugged. Then, "Say it again."

"I love you, *stupid*."

"Ah, that's better," he murmured against her lips. Then he kissed her and kissed her and kissed her till Harriet wondered who was the stupid one in this relationship. Probably both of them.

When Etienne looked at her again, Harriet could swear he was about to tell her that he loved her, too.

But he didn't.

Chapter Seventeen

A shrill scream ripped through the night air.

Harriet sat bolt upright in bed.

The room was pitch black except for a stream of light from the full moon filtering through the veranda windows. She had no idea what time it was.

Had Etienne screamed in the midst of one of his nightmares? Could the sound travel all the way from the main house?

The scream came again. Not Etienne. The high-pitched feminine wail of agony came from outside.

Blossom, Harriet realized immediately.

Grabbing Etienne's shirt for a cover-up and a pair of trousers she'd worn on her journey here, Harriet checked next door on Saralee, who snored softly. Then she rushed out onto the porch and down the steps toward the street, where a large group of people had clustered.

To her outrage, Harriet saw a burning cross planted in the ground in front of Cain's cabin-clinic. A short distance away, a group of about ten riders were galloping off, dressed in white robes and hooded masks. One of them spun in his saddle at the last minute, giving a rude gesture, and Harriet saw a green ribbon badge pinned on his chest. When the force of his prancing horse caused the hem of his robe to lift, Harriet also noticed that the rider wore a pair of the knee-high leather moccasins called *cantiers*. Just like those Henri Venee had worn.

Her skin turned clammy with alarm. "Who are they?" Harriet asked Verbena, who stood at the outer edge of the crowd wringing her hands. Large tears streamed down her black face.

"The Swamp Angels," Verbena spat out in a venomous voice. "Them low-down white trash what sneaks out at night. Terrorizin' good black folks. And white folks, too . . . them what fought fer the Yankees . . . or them what helps the coloreds. They's jist like them Knights of the White Camellia."

"You're next, Baptiste," one of the riders called out. "Ain't no room in the bayou fer bluebelly nigger-lovers." Although the man had a thick Cajun accent, Harriet couldn't be sure if it was Henri Venee or not. As they rode off at a full gallop, the cowardly bunch broke into song:

> *"I am a good old Rebel—*
> *Yes, thass just what I am—*
> *And for this land of freedom*
> *I do not give a damn.*
> *I'm glad I fit agin 'em,*
> *And I only wish we'd won;*
> *And I don't ax no pardon*
> *For anythin' I've done."*

"What happened?" Harriet asked.

"They did a cat-haulin' on Abel," Verbena informed her with a shiver.

"A what?"

"Cat-haulin'. Some of the mens held Abel down. Then

they took a mean ol' tomcat—a powerful big one—and hauled 'im by the tail down Abel's back. Over and over. Oh, Lordy, I thought them days of cat-haulin' was over with slavery. But they ain't.''

"Jesus!" Harriet whispered and pushed her way through the throng of people until she reached the source of all their concern. Then she gasped in horror.

Abel, fortunately unconscious, lay facedown in the dirt, his bare back completely covered with blood. Numerous gashes ran from his shoulders to the waistband of his trousers where the cat's claws had ripped open the flesh. Even the cloth covering his buttocks had been shredded.

Blossom was kneeling with Abel's face resting in her lap. Unmindful of the blood that soaked her muslin nightgown, the black woman rocked from side to side, crooning a sorrowful dirge: "Bad times are acomin', bad times are acomin' . . .''

Etienne and several of his workers were fashioning a makeshift litter out of a solid plank door covered with a thin mattress. No one took the time now to chase after the attackers; Abel's condition was of utmost priority.

Harriet forced Blossom to stand, taking her into her arms as Etienne and the men lifted Abel carefully onto the primitive stretcher. Abel moaned at what must be excruciating pain, but luckily remained unconscious while Etienne and his helpers hurried Abel into Cain's clinic.

"Where's Cain?" Harriet asked Blossom.

"He ain't come back since he went down to Petite Terrebonne this evenin' to doctor a man's broken laig," Blossom told her in between sobs." "He should be back soon, God willin'. Iffen them Swamp Debbils doan catch up with him, too."

Harriet directed Verbena, "You take Blossom back to the overseer's house and clean her up. Try to get her to lie down. And send some women with water and clean cloths. See if Blossom has any salve to put on open wounds, and something for pain."

Verbena's head bobbed up and down. She was calmer now that she'd been given a job. Blossom, too traumatized to protest, went off willingly with Verbena.

Hours later, Etienne released a long sigh of relief, finally satisfied that Abel would survive. He slept soundly.

Etienne glanced up at Harriet, who'd been working at his side the whole time, cleaning and bandaging the deep wounds. She'd even stitched one of the especially brutal gashes, though she had no more medical expertise than he did. Her only concession to fear had been the slight trembling of her fingers.

The woman could do anything. As she so often boasted, he thought with a grin.

"Well, the situation must be better if you can find some humor here," she commented as she wiped up the last of the blood on the floor.

Several of the colored workers, men and women, had helped them as well, but he'd finally sent them off to bed. They had to be up at dawn, fully rested, to work in the sugar fields. The demands of the land didn't lessen even in the midst of human crisis. Not that he'd given orders, or permission, for the plantation to resume operation. They'd just resumed the work they had performed as slaves. And hoped he'd approve.

Merde!

With a jerk of his head, he motioned for Harriet to follow him outside. They'd done enough here for tonight. When they emerged onto the porch, he asked Verbena, who sat rocking in a rickety chair, to go inside and watch Abel for a while. She eased her bulk out of the chair, then shuffled into the cabin.

Looping an arm over Harriet's shoulder, he sank down to the top step, taking her with him. For once, she didn't resist.

"Thank you," he said in a thickened voice.

"For what?"

"Helping with Abel."

"Of course I helped. Anyone would." She looked at him in surprise.

"Everyone wouldn't, Harriet. Some wouldn't care enough. Others, especially women, would faint at the sight of so much blood. A lot of people wouldn't consider tackling a job for which they have no training, but you . . . well, you just dive in without a second thought."

She narrowed her eyes. "Is that a criticism or a compliment?"

"A compliment." He smiled and ruffled her hair, which was still sleep-mussed from hours ago.

"I'm a mess," she said, putting a hand to her hair, as well.

"We both are," he said, but what he really thought was that she looked beautiful. Her black hair was a tangled bird's nest. Dark circles underlined her eyes, and her full mouth was pinched with worry. The color of the shirt she wore was unrecognizable from blood stains. Baggy trousers hid her curves.

She was a mess. And she was magnificent to him.

Dangerous, dangerous, dangerous thoughts.

He pulled her tighter against his side and kissed the top of her head lightly. All kinds of strange emotions welled up in him. Tears brimmed in his eyes—a delayed reaction to the peril his good friend had faced. He was beginning to see that this woman he was starting to care for was better off without him. Some of the remarks made by the Swamp Angels tonight had made that all too clear. Not only had they believed it was Cain they were brutalizing—"Let's kill the bastard that dared lay a black hand on a white woman"—but one of them had also mentioned, "And where's the wench that's preachin' ways to stop our women from havin' any more babes?"

Undoubtedly, the marauders were led by Henri Venee. Their targets had been the swamp doctor, as well as Harriet. Oh, they wouldn't really attack a woman. Instead the cowards would issue vile threats through the torture of others. Their warped code of ethics still spared women . . . at least, white women.

"As soon as I deliver the gold to President Grant's agent in Abilene, I'm going to come back and take you to your train," he told her abruptly.

She stiffened, no doubt preparing to object to his abandoning her at Bayou Noir.

He put a silencing finger to her lips. "I can see now that it's too dangerous for you to remain in this time and place. You'll be safer in your own home."

She drew back slightly to gaze at him. "Etienne, there's violence in my time, too. And prejudice."

"Don't tell me . . . more than a hundred years after the Emancipation Proclamation . . . the Negroes still aren't free."

"Well, of course they're free. And things are much better. Blacks have more equality in employment and education. But bigotry is by no means dead. For example, the Ku Klux Klan is still alive and thriving in modern-day America."

He shook his head sadly. Still, it was clear to Etienne now that Harriet would be safer in her own time. Without him. Not that he'd been considering asking her to stay. *Oh, no!* But he had been entertaining reckless thoughts about sating some sexual appetites with her in the interim till her departure. Especially since he'd been reading her book last night, which had generated so many tantalizing ideas for . . . innovation. Who would have ever thought women harbored so many sexual fantasies? Or that men would enjoy them, too?

But that was before Abel's attack. Now he recognized the dangers for him and Harriet in becoming involved in any way.

"Okay, Etienne, what's going on here?" Harriet shrugged off his arm and glared at him. "You're sending enough body signals to sink a ship. Or a poor girl's already wobbly defenses.''

Wobbly? "You certainly have a way with words." He laughed. "Actually, I was thinking about your book. I was reading it last night before . . . before all the commotion."

"And?"

"It was interesting. I'm impressed. Really, I am. And if times were different . . . and we were different . . . I wouldn't mind trying one or two of those fantasies."

She smiled. "You are so bad."

"I know." He smiled back.

"Tsk-tsk!" she chided him. Then, "Now you have my curiosity roused. Which ones appealed to you?"

"Well, I wouldn't mind trying the aural-sex fantasy . . . where the man, or woman, talks the other person into an orgasm. No touching, just words. I'm not sure it's possible, but it poses an interesting challenge."

To his surprise, and pleasure, Harriet blushed.

"Then, too, now that I understand forceful seduction a little better, I must say that has its attraction, too. In the right setting."

Her blush grew brighter.

He chucked her playfully under the chin. "So tell me, Harriet. Which are your favorite fantasies?"

She lowered her lashes and gave him a sideways glance that might have passed for shyness with any other woman. "Maybe someday I'll show you."

That brought Etienne and his banter to a quick, icy halt. He'd forgotten. There was going to be no someday for them.

Luckily, any further conversation in this tempting territory was cut short by the arrival of Cain, accompanied by a tall, big-boned quadroon who was giving him what-for. The attractive quadroon, about twenty-five years old, wore a prim, long-sleeved white shirtwaist and a black ankle-length skirt. Her straight hair was yanked into a knot at the base of her neck. It must be Ellen, the schoolteacher.

Etienne realized that he knew Ellen. She was Verbena's niece who'd studied for a few years at a Negro church college in Ohio, thanks to some help from James and Selene Baptiste. In fact, she'd taught at Selene's school in Sacramento until recently.

By their casual conversation and slow gait, Etienne assumed they hadn't heard of Abel's injuries yet.

"I still don't see what I've done wrong," Cain argued. But Etienne could see the sparkle of mischief in his dark eyes. He was baiting the unsuspecting Ellen.

"All that womanizing, that's what. You got all these people what needs your doctoring here at Bayou Noir, and you just go gallavantin' all over the countryside."

"Gallavantin'?" Cain sputtered.

"Yes, gallavantin'. The war's been over for five years now. What's a doctor doin' with all this spy business anyhow?" She added a harrumph for emphasis.

"Who says I've been womanizin'?" Cain laughed.

"Your mother, that's who. Every female under thirty from here to Tuscaloosa, that's who. And don't you be flashin' them rascal eyes at me. I'm not one of them mush-brained fanfoots that swoon just because one of the Lincoln twins smiles at me."

"I would never consider you a fanfoot," Cain said with a straight face.

Their dialogue trailed off as they noticed Etienne and Harriet sitting on the steps.

"Where the hell have you been?" Etienne snapped.

"Don't gnash your teeth at me. I stayed overnight after I cared for my patient," Cain retorted. "The levee broke and couldn't be fixed till this morning. Then I ran into Ellen coming down from Houma with the grocer boat. We just . . ." Cain's words trailed off. The somber expressions on their faces must have alerted him to a disaster. "It's Abel, isn't it?" Cain rushed up the steps. "I woke last night, sensing he was in trouble. My back felt like it was on fire, and . . ." He darted an anxious look at Etienne.

"Yes, it's Abel, but he's fine now."

Cain, still carrying his medical satchel, practically leaped inside, and Ellen followed more sedately, nodding a greeting at Etienne and Harriet on the way.

"Everything will be all right now," Etienne assured Harriet.

But he knew that it wouldn't be. Not for them.

Later that morning, Harriet gave up trying to take a nap to make up for her interrupted sleep. Her mind churned with too many disturbing thoughts.

She decided to check on Abel's condition and found he was still asleep. Cain assured her that sleep was the best thing for him now.

He informed her that Ellen had stopped by, too, before she went over to her schoolhouse. She'd decided to cancel classes for the day because so many of the children were distressed.

Harriet told Cain she'd come back later to relieve him. Then, standing on the porch of Cain's cabin, she watched as the cutting gangs began the first of the sugar harvest in the nearby fields. There was a beauty in the flow of their bodies as they followed a routine of four blade strokes to each cane stalk. Two sweeping vertical blows stripped it of leaves, a horizontal movement cut it to the ground and a final chop took off the top. The whole time, the men chanted out a work song:

Well, she ask me—whuk—in de parlor—whuk
An' she cooled me—whuk—wid her fan—whuk
An' she whispered—whuk—to her mother—whuk
Mama, I love that—whuk—dark-eyed man—whuk!"

Mule carts took the cut cane to the sugarhouse to be boiled down. The sweet smell of syrup already filled the air.

"I can see why you love this land," Harriet told Etienne

Sandra Hill

as she saw him approaching. He was shirtless and covered with perspiration, having been cutting alongside the workers. Like her, he must have come to check on Abel.

Harriet clenched her fists at the overwhelming yearning she felt to lean into his body. It was probably exhaustion.

He stared at her, and a slow, lazy smile danced on his lips.

"How's the sugar crop coming?" she asked, seeking some neutral subject. Etienne had been out with the workers since dawn.

He grinned at her obvious nervousness. "It's a bumble-bee crop . . . so stunted that all a bee has to do is lie on its back on the ground and let the juice fall into its mouth."

"Is it worth all the work?"

He shrugged. "What else can they do?"

Soon after that brief encounter, Harriet entered the main house. Blossom sat at the kitchen table peeling crawfish. Harriet poured a cup of coffee for the old cook, who looked like death warmed over after last night's shock. Sitting down on a bench next to her, Harriet took over the peeling. Surprisingly, Blossom relinquished the task without protest.

"Go lie down, Blossom," Saralee advised, sharing Harriet's concern.

"In a bit, in a bit," Blossom said. "Soon I be lying where the woodbine twineth and I be gettin' all the rest I need."

With a sigh, the child went back to her chores. Wearing a Mother Hubbard–style apron, the girl stood on a low stool before the potager. She was thickening a sauce with the Creole staple filé, powdered sassafras leaves, for the crawfish gumbo. On the back burner, a pot of hearty chicken rice soup simmered for the invalid when he awakened. On the other front burner, Saralee carefully fried blobs of dough in hot grease. These would be *les oreilles de cochon*, or "pig's ears," a favorite pastry of Etienne's. She declined Harriet's offer of help.

Harriet suspected Saralee had learned to make all of

284

Etienne's preferred foods in hopes of snaring his attention. Her mature behavior also indicated a belief that, if she was good, her father would want her. Even her role-playing reflected a search for a winning personality, one sure to gain a father's love. The little girl didn't yet know that the love of a parent for a child didn't have to be earned, or shouldn't have to be. Like the jingle went, Harriet quipped silently, "Nobody doesn't like Saralee."

Harriet put a hand to her forehead in dismay. So much work for her to do here as a psychologist, and so little time.

Blossom, with her uncanny perception, sniped, "You taken care of that scamp yet?"

Harriet straightened her shoulders defensively. "He's admitted paternity, hasn't he? Surely that's a first step."

Blossom snorted. "You gots a long road to go yet, girlie."

"Huh? I only agreed to start Etienne on the right path. I'm not going to be here that long."

Blossom arched an eyebrow with skepticism.

Harriet groaned. "Why me?"

"I already tol' you. I prayed. You came. Praise God!"

Harriet tried not to laugh. "I'm not staying, Blossom. There are things you don't understand about me."

"Oh, I understands, all right," Blossom said enigmatically as she stood creakily, leaning on her cane. "You the one what gots a heap to learn, honey chile." Then she patted Harriet on the shoulder before limping over to check on Saralee's progress.

After that, Harriet explored the house. According to Blossom, James and Selene Baptiste had left Bayou Noir in 1846. The overseer and his wife, Fergus and Reba Cameron, had purchased the plantation, but Fergus had died at Shiloh in 1861. Reba and her three children went to California, where she taught in Selene's school in the Sacramento Valley. She still lived there, never having remarried.

The plantation was left deserted for more than four years, except for those few former slaves and free workers who stayed, like Blossom. When Etienne heard of its condition, he purchased it for the price of back taxes. But he'd never indicated any interest in living here permanently or bringing it back.

The first floor contained food and household storage rooms in reasonably good condition. Three servants' bedrooms lined the other side of the corridor, only one of which was being used by Blossom. That was where Etienne slept now. She noticed with wry amusement that her two books, *Female Fantasies Never Die* and the Rosemary Rogers novel, lay open on a bedside table next to a cold lamp.

The second or main floor was bisected by a wide hallway that opened onto the front veranda and a central outdoor marble staircase leading to the oak alley. In its day, it would have been magnificent. Now the pungent odor of mildew and rodent waste permeated the closed rooms. Plastered ceiling medallions and period wallpapers were moldy with decay. Draperies hung in tatters. The scant pieces of furniture left had wormholes. The upholstery was chewed up by mice.

Such a waste!

With a sigh of regret at the neglect, Harriet plodded up the once magnificent, *Gone With the Wind*–style staircase, which was at least eight feet wide. Its sturdy cypress wood appeared untouched by the ravages of neglect and would probably only need thorough polishing. The deep recessed doors and windows indicated a four-brick thickness of the walls—a solidly built house missing only a little TLC.

What am I thinking? I'm not polishing anything. And I most definitely won't be around to see this place restored. Unless I find it back in the 20th century and research its history. But then a harsh, suffocating sensation settled in her chest. *Oh, no! What if I go back to my time and find a history of this area? Could I stand to read about Etienne and what he did after I left? And what if there will be a bride and other children?* It was ludicrous that Harriet would care so much. But she did.

The third floor housed six large bedrooms, flanking the central hallway. And, of course, there was the bath chamber here, too.

On the fourth floor, Harriet found what must have been additional servants' bedrooms, a nursery, a schoolroom, and a large bedchamber that she could only believe must have once belonged to Etienne. The Cameron children must have used it after Etienne and his family had moved to California, but there was evidence of a packing case having been opened recently and childish keepsakes spread around the room.

So this is where Etienne disappeared to yesterday when I couldn't find him. She'd found him in the schoolroom next door.

Harriet picked up several snakeskins and ominous sets of snake rattles, the kinds of mementos a boy would think "neat" and a girl would consider "gross." Beautiful pebbles and oddly shaped shells lay here and there.

In one box, she found some old schoolbooks with the inscription *Etienne Baptiste, 1845* on the flyleaf. He would have been only five years old then. Then there was a homemade book, hand-printed and colored. Harriet felt a chill as she read the title page: *The Story of E.T., for Etienne Baptiste, Happy Birthday, 1845, from Selene.* Flicking through the dried and yellowed pages of the modern story, Harriet got further confirmation that at least one other person had traveled back in time, just as she had.

Placing it carefully back in the box, she picked up a small notebook, which she soon realized had been Selene's lesson plan book. Apparently she'd come here as a governess. Harriet smiled when she read one hastily scrawled note in the margin of a page. *Etienne is a highly precocious boy with a ravenous appetite for learning. A MENSA, for sure. Even at his age, he can spout more bayou biology than some scientists. Today the little snot just about killed me on an alligator hunt. Two pages of arithmetic for tomorrow.* She'd underlined the *two.*

Harriet put the items back where she'd found them. At the bottom of the box she found a pile of letters addressed to Etienne—at least twenty-five of them, some yellowed by the years. The return address indicated they were from Selene Baptiste in Sacramento Valley, California. None of them had been opened.

Oh, Etienne!

Scanning the room, she felt a strange heaviness weigh her down . . . wistful and poignant. From the windows of this room, she could see the bayou stream in the front, the sugar fields to the right, the former slave quarters in the back.

This is Etienne's home, and he belongs here, Harriet thought. *I can almost feel his presence here, in this room, in the air, on the very land.*

Something else caught Harriet's eyes then and she gasped. It was a scrap of blue cloth sticking out of a half-opened armoire. Harriet opened the door and saw the uniform of an army captain. She touched the medal pinned to one side. A Congressional Medal of Honor. She hadn't known they even gave them during the Civil War.

What other horrors did Etienne endure, aside from Andersonville Prison, to have earned this medal for valor?

Harriet rocked from side to side, eyes closed, tears streaming down her face as she digested all these new facets of Etienne's character she'd discovered today. She'd come to love him when she thought him nothing more than an amoral scamp. Now her love grew with each new discovery.

She was lost, lost, lost. How would she ever return to the future intact? How would she ever forget Etienne? Could she ever live a normal life in her time again?

"It doesn't mean a thing," a scornful voice said behind her.

Harriet jumped and saw that Etienne had come upstairs without her hearing him. He leaned against the doorjamb, staring disdainfully at the uniform and medal.

"Don't go weepy-eyed over me," he said tiredly. "And don't be getting any strange ideas that I'm some kind of hero. I'm not."

"But—"

"They gave me that medal out of guilt . . . to make up for their mistakes. It doesn't mean a thing," he repeated.

Well, she wasn't convinced of that, but she wouldn't argue with him now. "Were you looking for me?"

A flush crept up his deeply tanned neck and face. "Yes, could you find Saralee and bring her to the orchard? There's something I want to show her."

"Etienne?" she said, worried that he would inadvertently hurt Saralee.

"I didn't bring her a gift, like Cain and Abel. So . . . I was thinking—" He gulped. "Just bring her, dammit."

A short time later, Harriet led a frightened Saralee by the hand to the orchard beyond the former slave quarters. They'd just turned the bend, bringing the orchard into view.

Harriet jerked to a stop with surprise.

Saralee cried out with pleasure, "My papa built me a swing!"

Etienne stood next to the biggest swing in the whole bayou, which hung from a high apple tree. He shifted from foot to foot, his blue eyes vulnerable with question, unsure if he'd done the right thing.

While Saralee rushed forward to examine the gift, Harriet stood in place, weeping.

"What? I did the wrong thing? Again?" Etienne snapped as he walked up to her.

Speechless, she shook her head. Finally, she blubbered out, "I'm crying be-because . . . I'm crying because I love you, stupid."

"Oh," he said and walked back to Saralee.

Then he turned and winked.

I am a dead duck.

Chapter Eighteen

That night, for the first time since her train ride into the past a week earlier, Harriet's fantasy dream returned. And Steve Morgan aka Etienne Baptiste was in rare form.

The deep sleep and subsequent dream were probably induced by the cup of Blossom's potent home brew that she'd drunk before bed. She wore only her leopard-print nightie, but still her skin burned with an intense heat. A storm brewing over the bayou caused the humidity to hover in the 100 percent range.

At a violent rumble of thunder, she opened her heavy eyes, thinking she should close the veranda doors before the rain came. She noticed the oil lamp still burning on the bedside table.

And then she saw Steve Morgan—or was it Etienne?—leaning against the door frame, silhouetted by the occasional shimmer of heat lightning. A lazy smile of sensuality teased his lips.

Harriet lay with her arms outspread above her head and her thighs parted, a wanton pose prompted by the temperature. She wasn't tied to the bed, but she couldn't move her wrists or ankles for the life of her.

His blatant body language disturbed Harriet, as it always did. His stance—the way he stood with thighs apart and hips thrust forward slightly—gave him an unconscious aura of intimidating sexuality. His hunter's eyes lingered with insolence on her throat, her breasts, and lower—a deliberate attempt to throw his quarry off balance. The silent message was both a threat and an invitation: "I'm dangerous, baby, and I . . . want . . . you."

He approached the bed slowly, with his usual easy grace, his spurs jangling a sexual rhythm against the hardwood floor. And Harriet's heartbeat picked up the tempo—point, counterpoint. The whole time his blue eyes held hers captive.

His black hair was slicked back wetly off his forehead from a recent bath—she could smell the scent of Blossom's homemade soap—but his face remained unshaven. He wore homespun trousers and a faded cream-colored shirt, already half-unbuttoned.

"I've missed you, darlin'."

She wasn't sure if he meant Ginny or her. She didn't care. Arching upward in welcome, she purred, catlike.

He smiled. "Will you fight me today, *mi querida*?"

So, it was the Steve Morgan persona tonight, with Mexican, not French, endearments.

"Probably," she said. "Will that deter you?"

He laughed. "Never."

Taking a sharp knife from the scabbard at his belt, he trailed a bold path with its tip from her collarbone, over the top of her nightie between her breasts, skimming her waist and navel, hesitating at her groin, then ending at her upper thighs.

"So beautiful," he whispered.

Abruptly, he used the blade to flip up the hem of her gown and rend it totally down the center. The wispy sides parted in the increasing breeze coming in through the open windows.

Harriet forgot to be self-conscious. She forgot that the number-one hang-up women had with sex was dislike for their own bodies. She forgot that hers wasn't a perfect form. This man's sultry, appreciative eyes told her in hard-core nonverbal communication that he liked what he saw.

He moved to the bottom of the bed and grasped her ankles, pulling them toward him, then outward so that he stood between her feet. She still couldn't move her upraised arms or her moderately spread thighs. If she didn't know better, Harriet would think the man had hypnotized her.

"Do you know what we're going to do tonight, *cara mia*?"

She shook her head hesitantly, feeling suddenly vulnerable in her near-nude condition with him fully clothed.

"The fantasy."

She frowned. "What fantasy?"

"From your book. Remember?"

In that instant, Harriet understood. This morning, Steve . . . rather, Etienne . . . had mentioned aural sex. *Oh, boy! Talk about being trapped with your own words!*

She wanted to tell him then that, though she wrote books about fantasies . . . sometimes outrageous ones, that didn't mean she approved of them all. Or that she was uninhibited enough to try them herself. But—*oh, gosh!*—he was already removing his clothes. Slowly.

"We'll use that technique you mentioned in your book . . . what did you call it? Ah, yes. Mirroring," he explained huskily.

Harriet groaned.

He groaned back, mirroring her action.

"You will do everything for me. Everything."

It wasn't a question.

"No rules," he added.

She blinked and thought about asking what he meant, but her heart lodged in her throat.

" 'No' will be a word your tongue cannot utter."

"What . . . what exactly do you want from me?" This would be the time to tell him not to expect too much of her. Not to judge her by her book.

"Surrender."

A ripple of fear washed over her. "That's the one thing I don't think I can give."

"You will."

Such self-confidence! Or was it arrogance? "I need control . . . at least a little."

"Not with me, *guerida*."

When he stood once more between her feet, gloriously naked, Harriet closed her eyes at the intensity of pleasure engendered by just gazing at his beautifully tanned and muscled body.

"No!" he demanded. "Eyes open."

She obeyed and stared, fascinated, as he wet his lips with his tongue. A slow, slow exercise in teasing foreplay. Then he waited.

She understood her role in this game. Parting her lips, she mimicked the actions of his tongue, repeating the routine several times till her lips were moist and aching for his kisses.

He sucked in his breath and his swelling erection gave proof that he already wanted her. "You make me tremble," he murmured.

Tremble? She shook.

He took a forefinger, wet it with his tongue and traced his lips, further moistening them. He waited till she followed suit.

She did, and to her surprise, found it highly stimulating.

Lowering his hand, he used the wet finger to circle one flat male nipple, then another.

"Oh, I'm not sure I like this game."

"Don't be afraid."

Easy for you to say, Mr. Cool-and-Collected. Harriet, who couldn't believe she was trusting a man so completely, continued to play his game, touching her own breasts while he watched. A thrumming ache swelled the points. Only belatedly did she realize her arms were now free of their invisible bonds, but not her legs.

He continued the motion, over and over. Wetting both forefingers now, then manipulating his own nipples in the ways he wanted her to mirror.

She saw that he wasn't really cool and collected.

"Please," she begged.

"Please?" His voice thickened with raw male excitement.

"I . . . I want you," she confessed.

"Where?"

She lifted her breasts from the undersides. "Here. I want your mouth on me *here*."

"Tell me more," he ordered hoarsely, reminding her this was aural sex, not the real thing.

"I want you to tongue me softly. At first. Then . . . oh, Lord . . . I can't believe I'm saying this . . . then nip me with your teeth. Flutter the tip with your tongue. Fast. Then suck."

He raised a brow. "How?"

"Hard. Nonstop. And deep." She arched her back off the bed, raising her breasts high, and felt a keening ecstasy, almost as if he actually did as she'd described.

He nodded. "And would you do the same for me?"

"Oh, yes!"

Resuming the game, he trailed the fingertips of one hand down his chest, over his flat abdomen and belly.

She did the same.

He undulated his hips slightly in imitation of the sex act.

She gasped, and realized she'd already been doing the same. *Is this me doing these wanton things? Am I really this uninhibited? Yes. With Etienne, I can be anything he wants.*

Taking his erection in hand, he challenged her with up-raised chin to touch her own wetness.

She balked, then acquiesced when she realized that more than anything she wanted to please this man she loved beyond all reason.

He stroked.

She followed suit.

He moaned.

She whimpered.

"Let go, Harriet."

"I can't. Not this way."

"Do you surrender?"

"I surrendered to you a long time ago, Etienne," she cried, no longer confused over his identity. "The first time that I said I loved you."

"Say the words," he urged in a husky rasp.

"I surrender," she whispered.

In one fluid motion then, he entered her. And to the rhythm of his pounding strokes, she kept repeating, "I love you, I love you, I love you. . . ."

She wasn't sure, but she thought . . . at the end, when he braced himself on rigid arms and threw his head back, crying out his release . . . she thought she heard him murmur, "God help me, but I love you, too."

But it was only a dream.

He kissed her awake the next morning.

It wasn't a dream.

Harriet could tell, even before she opened her eyes, that she'd overslept. The sun coming through the open veranda windows heated the linen sheet covering her bare body from chest to thigh. But, sated and love-sore, she didn't care if she'd slept the week away.

Etienne was wetting her lips with his tongue, just like last night.

It wasn't a dream.

She smiled, eyes still closed, savoring the delicious erotic play. Her head lolled half on and half off the bed, her body sprawled across the mattress.

"I surrender." She sighed against his teasing moist kisses.

And he growled.

He *growled.*

Harriet cracked open an eyelid and shot upright, barely able to keep herself from falling off the side of the bed.

It was a dream, after all.

The lover licking her mouth was the most pitiful hound she'd ever seen. *Yech!* The dog was old and fat, its brown mangy fur no longer lustrous and healthy. Its sad eyes, rheumy with too many years of living, gazed at her with a weary resignation, as if it knew she wouldn't like him. "Go ahead, kick me," it reproached silently. Worst of all, the mutt wore a garland of flowers looped around its head, which had slipped over one eye.

Harriet knew in that moment . . . before an ecstatic Saralee rushed in after her dog and handed her the note . . . that Etienne was gone. How could he abandon her? And why today? He was supposed to stay another two days. She'd thought she had time to convince him to take her along.

In fact, there were two notes. Saralee first showed off her own letter.

Princess:

I heard you've always wanted a puppy. I looked and looked, but this is the best I could do on such short notice. Let me introduce you to your newest royal subject. Lancelot.

Love,
Papa

The signature had first read *Etienne*, but he'd crossed it out and written *Papa.* Despite her anger, Harriet felt a rush of thanks for Etienne's sensitivity.

"Isn't he beautiful?" Saralee asked Harriet as she knelt on the floor to hug her new dog.

"Huh? Oh, yeah." The animal, who tolerated Saralee's fierce embrace with a "Woe is me" roll of the eyes, looked as if it might have cardiac arrest if forced to walk from here to the door. And, Lord, Harriet hoped it was housetrained. Blossom was going to have a fit over this gift of Etienne's.

While Saralee picked up the heavy dog with a grunt and carried it out, cooing the whole time, Harriet opened her own letter. A pile of paper money fell out . . . probably the bundle she'd gotten from the bank for the gold bar. Setting it aside, she began to read.

Harriet:

Cain and I will be leaving at dawn. We have to be in Houston by the end of the month. Don't be angry. Well, I know you will be angry anyhow. But this was the only way.

Blossom knows what to do for Abel. The head driver has instructions for the harvest.

You can use the money to get back to New Orleans and for the train fare to your home. The mail boat will be by in two weeks. Go then, not before. Provided you want to leave, that is.

If you are still at Bayou Noir when I return, we will talk.

Etienne

What? He expected her to stay here, risk giving up her career and security in the future? All based on those nebulous words, *We will talk. The jerk!* Harriet didn't realize till she put fingertips to her face that she was weeping.

No words of love. He hadn't even asked her to wait. Just a vague hint of something more if she was still here on his return. No promises whatsoever. *The rat!*

With a flash of comprehension, Harriet saw the correlation between her predicament and that of Ginny Brandon in *Sweet Savage Love*. Steve Morgan had loved her to pieces, too, in a wild night of loving. Then he'd left. And poor Ginny had waited and waited for Steve to come back to her. Pathetic, that was what Ginny had been. Handicapped by her love for a hardheaded, hard-hearted rogue.

Even worse, this was all taking on the characteristics of codependency. Like Harriet's mother.

He hadn't even bothered to tell her good-bye. Harriet put her head down and cried her eyes out, then braced herself. As usual, she had only herself to rely upon. She'd been foolish, letting her defenses down, but she'd always believed in learning from her mistakes. She would look on this as a painful learning experience.

Never fall in love.

Never trust a man.

Watch your back and guard your heart.

That was when Harriet got her second shock of the day. Standing, Harriet peered down and saw that her nightgown had been torn down the front from neckline to hem. Of course, the flimsy fabric could have ripped with her thrashing during the heated night. But she knew better. Harriet's heart leaped joyously.

It wasn't a dream.

Etienne had come to say to good-bye to her, after all. In his own sweet, savage way.

"Get that dawg out of mah kitchen," Blossom stormed a week later. "I declare, I'm gonna whup that boy next time I see him. That Remy Lejune down the bayou been tryin' to unload this no-good cur for years. Never did see such a sorry animal in all my born days. Got fleas and dawg bizness ever'where."

"Lance doesn't have fleas. Me and Mam'zelle Harrie gave him a bath. And he only did his bizness once and that's cause you scared 'im with your cane," Saralee asserted from the table where she was eating dinner tonigh with Blossom, Ellen and Abel, who'd made his way over from his sickbed for the first time.

Harriet had prepared and was serving dinner tonight, after much protest from Blossom. She wasn't much of a cook, but she could whip up a mean Spanish omelette filled with onions, green peppers, mushrooms, and oozing melted cheese. On the side was a dandelion salad with bacon-and-vinegar dressing, and Saralee's beaten biscuits. A feast fit for the best gourmet connoisseur. Not that anyone noticed. Everyone was still talking about the ongoing implications of Etienne and Cain's abrupt departure.

"How you gonna straighten out that boy now he's gone?" Blossom demanded of Harriet, as if it were all her fault. As if she hadn't asked the same question a zillion times.

"I tried, but he tricked me."

"Hah!" Blossom exclaimed, giving her a thorough study. "Mebbe you was too busy thinkin' of yer own pleasures the night he skedaddled off, 'stead of our plan."

Here we go again! Harried blushed.

That caught Abel's interest. "I've been reading your book," he started.

And Harriet put her face in her hands. She just knew what was coming.

"What book is that?" Ellen asked politely.

"Mam'zelle Harriet is a book-writer," Blossom explained proudly, to Harriet's surprise. Then Blossom spoiled the effect by adding, "But she ain't learned how to pull in a man with her book-learnin'. Leastways, not yet."

Harriet peeked at Abel, who was grinning with wicked anticipation. Luckily, all of this passed over Saralee, who was engrossed in surreptitiously feeding Lance bits of omelette.

"Harriet's book is *Female Fantasies Never Die*," Abel told Ellen with a straight face. "You should read it sometime."

When understanding dawned, Ellen sputtered at Abel,

"Oh, you are a sinful man! You and your brother always were the teasin'est scoundrels in the bayou. Fornication and devilry . . . that's all you ever thought about as boys."

And as men. Some things never change.

"Do you know what the dumb man said when asked to spell Mississippi?" Harriet asked sweetly as she passed beverages to the others at the table.

Ellen shook her head as if she didn't understand what was going on around her. Blossom clucked her disapproval. Abel smirked, waiting for the punch line. And Saralee, in her own little world, was trying to get Lance to eat dandelion.

"The man asked, 'The state or the river?' " Harriet whooped.

Since no one laughed, Harriet blundered on, checking first to make sure Saralee wasn't listening. "Okay, this woman came home from a visit to the doctor and boasted to her husband, 'The doctor says I have the breasts of an eighteen-year-old.'

"The dumb husband responded, 'What did he say about your thirty-year-old ass?'

"The woman paused and replied, 'I don't believe we discussed you, dear.' "

Blossom and Abel laughed. Ellen said, "Really, Harriet, do you think that is appropriate talk for a lady? And, besides, I don't understand the humor."

"Harriet is saying that all men are dumb," Abel explained.

"Oh, well, of course," Ellen agreed, as if that was a given.

Blossom narrowed her eyes at Harriet. "You knows all this man-woman stuff but you couldn't keep Etienne here. Tsk-tsk!"

"And I needed to talk to Etienne." Ellen sighed. "Now I don't know what to do with the school."

"Dint yer trip to Houma help?" Blossom asked, patting Ellen on the arm. Caught up in the frenzy of *roullaison,*

300

the sugar harvest season, not to mention Abel's injuries, followed by Etienne and Cain's hasty departure, no one had really had a chance to sit down and talk at length about anything.

"No," Ellen said, then explained to Harriet and Abel. "I taught in Mam'zelle Baptiste's school in California for five years after I graduated from Messiah Normal School in Ohio. But I came back here when Blossom wrote and told me about all the families returning to the plantation with no school."

"How many children are in your school now?" Harriet asked, sitting down on the bench next to Abel. She slapped his hand away distractedly when he tickled her thigh playfully.

"Twenty-five ... sometimes thirty," Ellen said, picking at her salad. "There are just no supplies."

Harriet frowned. "Who's been funding the school?"

"At first, M'sieur and Mam'zelle Baptiste set us up. Then, after the war, the Freedman's Bureau supplied some money. But half of the grants coming from Washington never made it to the schools once they filtered through every corrupt politician from the highest to the lowest level, North and South."

"And?" Harriet prodded.

"When the Freedman's Bureau closed, church organizations began to help. I've been getting my money through the Blessed Waters Free Church of Louisiana. But they're poor, too. I went to Houma this week, to plead for at least two hundred dollars to buy books, paper, pencils, desks...." She exhaled wearily. "We need everything. The preacher told me they are rock-bottom dry and that I have to go to the church headquarters in Houston if I want to get more help."

"Houston!" Harriet, Blossom and Abel all said at once. *Coincidence?* Harriet wondered. *Or fate?*

Ellen nodded. "I was hoping Etienne would be willing to help. I just can't continue to ask his father to pay. When

I saw that he'd returned unexpectedly, I thought that maybe God had answered my prayers. But now it looks as if I'll have to close down the school, or make my way to Houston.''

"Hmmm," Harriet said aloud.

"Now, Harriet," Abel warned.

A loud commotion outside interrupted their discussion, followed by a shrill female voice inquiring of someone in the backyard, "Where's Abel?"

Uh-oh!

Dressed in a formfitting, dark traveling costume, Simone made a grand entrance into the kitchen. Abel, his face awash with astonishment and pleasure, stood abruptly, then groaned at the anguish caused by that simple movement.

"Oh, *chérie,* I came as soon as Etienne and Cain told me of your injuries. I have brought a *bateau* to take you back to New Orleans with me. Already I have hired the best physicians to care for you there. *Non,* do not worry about the trip. You can lie on the flat bottom. We will put a mattress there. It is all arranged.'' The whole time Simone blurted out her greeting, she held Abel's face between her hands and kept kissing his cheeks and neck. Tears streamed down her face.

"Is she what I think she is?" Blossom whispered in an aside to Harriet.

"Yes," Harriet said.

But even Blossom could see the love these two shared and she clamped her mouth shut, although she couldn't help adding, "Is the boy plum crazy? Hankerin' after a white woman? Them Swamp Angels will skin 'im alive, or cut off his pecker.''

In the end, after everyone settled down, Simone ate some dinner and sent a meal out for the black man who'd accompanied her. Then she told them all the news. Etienne and Cain had arrived days ago, checked to make sure that the caskets were still in the warehouse, transferred the gold to a piano and musical instrument cases, and planned to board the steamboat *Southern Star* in a few days for Galveston, Texas.

"A piano?" Harriet asked.

"Music cases?" Abel asked.

Simone grimaced. "They've joined a minstrel show."

Abel hooted with laughter. "Blackface? Oh, I would love to see Etienne singin' a coon song."

"But there is another reason why I rushed to your side," Simone told Abel, biting her bottom lip indecisively.

"What?" he demanded. "Tell me, Simone."

"Pope's scurrilous gang knows Etienne is the agent hired by Grant. One of Charity's customers told her several days ago. But I couldn't get word to Etienne."

"Oh, hell!" Abel exclaimed and put a hand to his lower back, bracing himself against the pain that must be throbbing there since his afternoon dose of laudanum was wearing off.

"They don't know that the gold was hidden in New Orleans, or where it is now, but they've discovered that Etienne's assignation point is somewhere in eastern Texas," Simone continued. "Pope has dozens of hired guns covering the region from Beaumont to Corpus Christi. *Zut alors*, what a mean, lawless bunch!" She sighed deeply. "Etienne and Cain are heading for a trap."

Harriet took a deep breath. "I'm going."

"Harriet, you don't know your way to the privy, let alone all the way to Texas," Abel chided her softly.

"Well, I know the way," Ellen declared, fingertips pressed to her lips in pensive concentration. "Harriet and I will both go. We can travel by pirogue to Morgan City with one of the field hands. That's one of the stops for the steamboat Etienne and Cain are taking from New Orleans. I know some back ways that will save time. That way, Harriet can warn them and I can meet with the church officials in Houston." She beamed at everyone.

"No, it's too dangerous," Abel said. "Besides, Etienne knows what he's doing."

"It's my choice," Harriet asserted. "You can't stop me."

"Well, at least it's a plan," Blossom said. "Of course, you gotta take Saralee with you."

"Absolutely not," Harriet said. "She stays here."

"Nosirree. How'm I gonna protect her when these bad mens come searchin' fer Etienne's baby girl? Doan be tellin' me they wouldn't try to take her to use against 'im."

"She could go with Simone and Abel," Harriet offered.

"And live in a fancy house?" Simone asked, arching a brow cynically. "I may be a madam, but even I have standards."

"A fan-fancy house?" Ellen sputtered, realizing for the first time that Simone owned a brothel.

"Well, send her to California to be with her grandparents," Harriet advised.

"No time," Abel concluded.

"Oh, blessed Lord, I'm surrounded by harlots and fornicators, and a woman book-writer who publishes works about harlotry and fornication," Ellen continued, fixing on the most irrelevant parts of their conversation.

"Well, that settles it," Blossom said, whisking her hands together with satisfaction. "That's the plan then. You all goin' to Texas to bring that rogue back here, safe and sound."

"I'm not goin' anywhere without my dawg," Saralee said from the floor, where she was hugging the big lump of fur.

"Now, Saralee," Harriet began.

"Uh-uh," the little girl said, picking up the dog, which probably weighed as much as she did, its four legs hanging limply with resignation. She backed away from the table defensively.

"I ain't carin' for no dawgs," Blossom said. "No sirree."

"Besides," Saralee added, "Lance will be a good guard dog for us on the trip."

Everyone looked at Lance, who had escaped Saralee's grasp and now perked up one ear. It immediately fell back down.

"Bet he could chase gators away. And bad men."

Lance rolled his big, sad eyes and let loose with a measly "Woof!" which probably was short for, "People! They must have kibbles for brains."

"First things first," Harriet said. "I'm gonna need a gun."

Everybody, including Saralee, groaned, and Lance put his face between both front paws and tried to hide under the table.

For just one second, Harriet wondered if Etienne would appreciate their help when she and Ellen and Saralee and Lance came charging down on him like the calvary to the rescue.

He'll probably be really thankful, she told herself.

Yeah, right.

Chapter Nineteen

There was one important thing Harriet needed to do before she left Bayou Noir . . . perhaps never to return. Write a letter.

She followed Blossom out onto the front gallery after dinner that evening and badgered the old woman into disclosing a few family secrets. During the informative chat, Harriet learned about Etienne's relationship with his father, James Baptiste, a wealthy rancher in the Sacramento Valley in California.

Finally, some crucial missing pieces fell into place in the puzzle that was Etienne Baptiste. Finally, Harriet understood the pain that consumed the man she loved. Yep, her beloved blockhead was a chip off the old blockhead. Apparently they both carried the same stubborn-to-the-point-of-stupidity chromosome.

Etienne's father had repudiated him almost ten years before when he'd left Oxford to fight in the Civil War. Due to the nature of his work, Etienne had been unable to divulge the fact that he was a double agent or explain away the Rebel uniform he'd worn at the time. Since then, the misunderstandings had snowballed.

His father had eventually found out about his service to the Union and his horrible imprisonment. Stricken, he'd tried to make amends, but by then Etienne had dug in his heels and refused any contact with his father. Furthermore, Etienne had forbidden anyone to talk about his father with him . . . not Blossom, Cain or Abel. James, equally bull-headed, forbade anyone to talk to him about his son, as well . . . not Selene, Iris, Rufus, Reba, or Cain and Abel on their infrequent visits.

And, of course, since Etienne himself had only acknowledged Saralee's paternity recently, his father knew nothing of her existence. No one would have dared reveal the secret child's existence until Etienne accepted her himself.

"Yer gonna write a letter to Etienne's papa?" Blossom asked with horror, jolting Harriet from her contemplation.

"Either James or Selene."

"Oh, Lordy!" Blossom exclaimed, dropping down into her porch rocker with a whoosh. "Etienne's gonna explode. He won't even read all them letters up in his room what come from Mam'zelle Selene. He made me swear a Bible oath one time not to ever tell his papa about his miseries."

"Well, I didn't make any promises."

Blossom slanted her a sidelong grin. "Thass true. But, honey, the boy hardened his heart agin' his papa fer so long, I figger it's gonna take a hammer 'n chisel to break 'im down now."

"How about a pen and paper?"

"Mebbe so, mebbe so," Blossom said. As she shuffled off to get those supplies, she added, "I'm gonna pray to God to help you. Um-hm, thass what I'll do. Dear Lord, please doan let Etienne kill Mam'zelle Harriet fer meddlin' in his affairs."

Blossom had a really comforting manner about her.

Now Harriet sat tapping her fingers on the desk in the

overseer's cottage. Should she write to Selene or James? Finally, she began to write.

Dear Selene:

My name is Dr. Harriet Ginoza. We've never met, but perhaps you've heard of me. I know I've heard of you.

You and I have something in common. Let's just say that you will know what I mean when I mention Domino's Pizza, Kevin Costner, Wonderbras, Bloomingdale's, Brad Pitt, the O. J. Simpson trial, jogging, and dumb-men jokes.

Actually, we have two things in common. We share a love for a stubborn, male chauvinist pig of an adorable rogue . . . Etienne Baptiste. (I'll bet you were nervous there for a minute, thinking I meant your husband <grin>).

Selene, I'm writing to you woman-to-woman, rather than to your husband, because sometimes men make such a muddle of things. It takes a woman to clean up the mess. If only men would let women run the country, do you think we'd have so many wars, or budget deficits, or football games . . . ? Well, I'm getting off the track. They just need a little direction from us women.

(By the way, do you know why it takes 400 million sperm to fertilize one egg? None of them wants to stop and ask for directions.) Forgive me for being flip. Chalk it up to nervousness.

Back to the serious business at hand. Etienne needs his father. Oh, he hasn't said so in so many words. But his body language . . . (Did you know I wrote a book on body language? Oops, I'm digressing again.) . . . his body language is one jumble of repressed rage engendered by years of self-recriminations. All his life he's been trying to ''earn'' his father's love. In his mind, he's failed miserably. Over and over. Do you think his father has a perfection complex?

Perhaps you won't understand this, Selene. Having a perfect body and face in a society that treasures those assets, you've never felt inadequate. But believe me, as a psychologist, I see our whole nineties culture suffering from the perfection syndrome. I'm not sure where this idea came from. Perhaps the Christian idea of original sin. Teachers who emphasize pupils' faults. Parents who want their children to fulfill their own unrealized dreams. Movies and ads that hold up impossible expectations for the human form. Athletics that emphasize winning is everything.

Etienne tells me that I lecture too much. As you can see, he's probably right. <grin>

The bottom line here is that Etienne loves his father and misses him terribly. He's placed himself in a very dangerous situation in order to raise enough cash to restore Bayou Noir plantation. Even now, he's off on a mission that might spell his death . . . as well as Cain's, I might add. Tell that to his mother, Iris. It doesn't hurt to get another woman involved here. Oh, and tell her that Abel got a cat-hauling from some group called the Swamp Angels, but he's okay now. He went back to New Orleans with Simone, the woman he loves. You don't need to tell her what Simone does for a living; suffice it to say, she's in the same profession as Xaviera Hollander. <double grin>

There's one more thing, Selene. Are you sitting down? Etienne has a daughter. Her name is Saralee (yeah, like the bakery). She's the most adorable seven-year-old girl. A miniature blue-eyed version of Etienne.

Don't be mad at Etienne for not telling you about Saralee. He didn't acknowledge her himself until a few days ago. Did I mention before how stubborn he is?

I'm not sure what I hope to accomplish with this letter. A miracle, maybe. But then, I consider my trip to this time and place a miracle; so who knows?

The one thing I am sure of is that there are no "do-overs" in real life. So we need to give ourselves permission to make mistakes ... to be less than perfect ... and move on from there. After all these years as a psychologist I've learned a simple truth: Love, whether between parent and child, or man and woman, is nothing without forgiveness. Real love is seeing faults and loving the person unconditionally.

Unlike you, Selene, I will not be staying in the past. Once I "rescue" Etienne, God willing, I must go home. I'm hoping ... no, I'm praying ... that Etienne's father will be here for him when I'm gone.

> *With deepest regards,*
> *Harriet*

Harriet wept as she sealed the envelope and left it for Blossom to mail on the first mail packet headed west.

It was over then. Another goal reached. Another door closed.

Who would have thought that a dog could get seasick? In a rowboat? But poor Lance had been puking his guts out over the side of the *bateau* for two straight days.

When he wasn't hotdogging after every female hound in every homestead along the endless bayou streams, that was. It turned out that Lance was a lech, and that there were a few doggie testosterones still alive and kicking in his old body. Amazingly, the women dogs loved him.

Now, they were finally approaching Morgan City, having made good time. And Harriet had to admit to a thrill of excitement. Despite all the dangers and inconveniences of her time-travel odyssey, she'd discovered that she was enjoying the adventure. That could be dangerous.

She smoothed out the wrinkles in her pink gown and breathed deeply, in and out. She couldn't control the butterflies that danced in her stomach in anticipation. She'd be seeing Etienne again soon. She hoped he would be as happy as she over their reunion.

"There it is," Ellen said now, pointing to the small, bustling town they were approaching. The schoolteacher sat stiff-backed in front of Harriet in the boat, wearing her usual white, long-sleeved, high-necked blouse with a dark blue, ankle-length skirt and sensible leather boots. Her ebony hair was pulled into a neat bun at her nape. She, like all of them, wore a wide-brimmed straw hat as protection against the sun's rays. Ellen had been a godsend.

As they came in on Bayou Chene, they found themselves surrounded by a number of pirogues carrying Cajun families to town for visits and shopping. Two flatboats piled high with hogsheads of sugar from nearby plantations followed them, steered by workers wielding long poles in the sluggish water.

Saralee took great joy in waving shyly to the passing vessels. She looked precious in a green calico gown Blossom had miraculously whipped out for her just before their departure.

"How's Lance doing?" Harriet asked when the girl peeked under the lid of the large wicker carrying basket on the floor of their boat. Abel and Simone had told them, before leaving for New Orleans, that most steamboats wouldn't allow a pet in regular passenger areas. Thus, the doggie hotel.

"He's sleeping," Saralee whispered, replacing the cover.

"What else is new?" Harriet murmured. Lance was obviously all pooped out. Not that he didn't sleep 90 percent of the time anyhow. He led a real dog's life.

Daniel, the black field hand accompanying them, rowed their boat over to the shore and tied it to a mooring, along with dozens of other similar craft. Then, on Harriet's instructions, he went off to make inquiries about the steamship. There were at least five sitting out in the waters of the three channels that ran southward from the flat waterfront town toward the Gulf. With any luck, one of them would be the *Southern Star*, the one Etienne and Cain presumably still traveled on.

Some of the steamships that came in from the Gulf would continue west to Houma, or north to Baton Rouge and eventually connect with the Mississippi en route to Missouri. Still others, like the one they sought, would backtrack out into the Gulf and follow the coastline, hitting the harbor towns, including Port Fourchon and Cocodrie and Galveston, Texas.

"There it is, there it is!" Saralee cried. "Ooooh!"

Harriet sighed too when she saw that the largest of the steamboats was, indeed, the *Southern Star*.

"It looks like a frosted cake," Saralee exclaimed, jumping up and down with excitement. Lance growled his displeasure at being disturbed.

Saralee was right. The majestic four-story steamboat was a confection of glittering white with gingerbread trim. Each level and its encircling deck were stacked atop the other like progressively smaller layers on a cake. The crowning glory was the all-glass pilothouse on the top deck with its two candlelike chimneys.

There was a scrambling of people coming and going down the gangplank. Passengers already crowded the decks. They were too many and too far away for her to make out if Etienne and Cain were up there. Roustabouts called out, "Make way, make way," as they carried barrels up into the hold.

A loud whistle shrieked through the air.

"That's the last signal for boarding," Ellen said worriedly.

"I'll go get our tickets," Harriet said and rushed over to the shipping office where Daniel was just turning toward her with dejection.

"Ain't no more tickets left," he informed her. "They's a band and minstrel show on this trip, and most folks booked their passages weeks ago." As if to punctuate his words, the Josiah Gilbert Ethiopian Brass Band came marching by, high-stepping and strutting as they played an exuberant version of "Dixie." The guard near the gangplank allowed them to pass up onto the boat.

"We'll see about that," Harriet said and stormed up to the ticket agent. A few minutes later, a dejected Harriet returned. "No luck. He says we can get the next boat tomorrow, but of course that will do us no good."

"Mebbe I kin find a way," Daniel said. "I'll go talk to that deckhand over there." He pointed to a black man who was rolling up a long loop of rope, preparatory to lifting anchor.

"I'll go, too," Ellen offered.

Left alone, Harriet and Saralee exchanged a glance of sad resignation. How could they have come so far and then failed?

A group of gaudily dressed women brushed past them, chattering loudly. The one in the lead, a heavyset, blowsy woman with dyed red hair and big breasts practically falling out of a chartreuse bombazine gown, was exclaiming, "Where's that Maxine? She was supposed to be here an hour ago. I swear, I'll never take on another girl sight unseen."

"Who is she?" Harriet whispered to a young black woman, dressed more sedately, who trailed behind the group, carrying several satchels.

The girl rolled her eyes. "Madam Irene. She's openin' a new house in Corpus Christi."

Harriet didn't need to ask what kind of house she meant.

"The Palace of Pleasure," the girl added.

Yep!

The whistle blew a final warning and the hookers headed toward the gangplank in a swish of garish, jewel-toned satins and ruffles and flounces. The engine of the massive steamship revved up with a roar.

In a panic, Harriet sought frantically for some solution to her problem. And came up with only one.

"Madam Irene," Harriet called out.

The woman stopped midwaddle and turned waspishly, "What?"

"I'm . . . I'm Maxine."

"Huh?" Saralee said at her side.

Harriet nudged her with an elbow to remain quiet.

Madam Irene gave Harriet's horrid pink gown a quick once-over of disgust. "Well, what you waitin' for, girl? Get yer ass over here. You got a lot of explainin' to do, but it'll have to wait till we're on board."

"Uh . . . well, there's a problem," Harriet stammered, picking up her briefcase and grabbing Saralee by the upper arm, dragging her forward with her. "You see, the reason why I was late is that I had to bring my daughter with me."

"Daughter?" Saralee squeaked.

"Oh, no! You ain't bringin' no snot-nosed guttersnipe with you. I don't 'low no young'uns in my establishments."

"Oh, well, I'm sorry. I can't go then." Harriet sighed dramatically. "Hand me my feather collection, Saralee. I guess we'll just have to head on down to New Orleans where they value the *special* talents of a hooker with creativity."

"Feathers?" Madam Irene inquired, eyeing Lance's basket. Then she made a quick decision. "Oh, come on then."

Harriet had to restrain herself from doing a little victory dance.

When the guard at the gangplank protested the lack of an extra ticket for Saralee, Madam Irene slipped him a few bills, then shoved Harriet and Saralee ahead of her up the gangplank. Harriet realized, too late, that she probably should have tried the bribery routine herself. Muttering over the outlay of extra cash, Madam Irene glared at Harriet. "You better be worth it, honey, or you're gonna pay me back double-time on your back."

In your dreams, Irene.

Midway up the gangplank, Harriet pivoted and saw Ellen

and Daniel dashing forward. In the rush, she'd forgotten them.

"You can't leave without me," Ellen shouted.

Harriet shrugged in an attitude of *What could I do?* Then she yelled back, "I'll talk to Etienne about the school funds."

Soon Harriet and Saralee were on the main deck with Madam Irene's troupe, leaning over the rail along with all the other passengers as the *Southern Star* took off. The shoreline grew increasingly smaller as the big steamboat eased its way out of the harbor channel and glided out toward the Gulf.

Harriet was as excited as Saralee. *What an adventure!* She couldn't wait to find Etienne. They could be excited together.

She hoped.

"Well, girls, let's go find our rooms," Madam Irene said, adding ominously—at least, it was ominous to Harriet, "We got work to do."

Harriet smiled weakly.

Madam Irene smiled right back. It was a steely, teeth-baring smile of threat. "Don't lose that feather collection, honey. I'm thinkin' of a particular gambler on this riverboat who might pay handsomely for a good feather-ticklin'."

By that evening, Harriet was gritting her teeth with frustration. Madam Irene, sensing a windfall in Harriet, wouldn't let her out of her sight. Even the lunch meal was delivered to the two adjoining dorm-style rooms the woman had obtained, with bunks stacked three-high for the six girls and one maid who accompanied her, not including Harriet and Saralee. Ms. Hitler permitted none of them to stroll on the decks either. Apparently, Madam Irene planned a grand entrance.

The magic hour arrived at ten o'clock, when Madam Irene deemed the timing right for parading her new goods. With Saralee back in the compartment with the maid, Harriet followed the line of hookers up to the main saloon. The brass band had started entertaining the crowd more than an hour ago, following dinner.

This was not the way Harriet had hoped to meet Etienne for the first time. Assuming he was actually on the boat.

Putting her hands under her breasts, Harriet tried to push up the fabric under the skin-hugging bodice of her flame-red gown edged with black lace. The small capped sleeves started at the top of her arms, leaving her shoulders and neck completely bare. Long black gloves completed the ensemble. Pure Frederick's of Hollywood sleaze.

Harriet had tried to tell Madam Irene that red was not her color, and that there was something to be said for subtlety, but the profit-minded procuress resisted adamantly.

Madam Irene's maid, Arletta, who sidelined as a hairdresser and makeup artist, had piled Harriet's black tresses atop her head, with a few curly strands dangling down to all that bare skin. "To entice the customers," Madam Irene chuckled.

As an added touch, Madam Irene had slapped a black mole patch at the right corner of Harriet's roughed lips, despite her protests that she'd probably swallow it before the evening was over. And she'd handed Harriet a black feather fan, declaring it good advertising for a new whore.

Etienne was going to have a fit.

Or die laughing.

"You'd better appreciate what I'm doing for you, Etienne," Cain grumbled as he hunkered down in front of a mirror in their cramped quarters on the lower deck. He was applying the last of a little pot of burnt cork to his face. "Putting blackface on a black face is going above and beyond the call of friendship."

"I told you to stay at Bayou Noir and take care of your patients. I don't need you or Abel nursemaiding me every minute of my life," Etienne snapped back. Already in blackface, Etienne slipped on a pair of white gloves, adjusted his short buttoned jacket and opened the door to let a little fresh air into the stuffy chamber.

"You're still upset over leaving Harriet behind," Cain said, washing his hands in a bowl and drying them off before donning his own gloves.

"I am not upset over Harriet."

"Hah!"

Cain grinned at him as they walked toward the staircase leading up to the main hall.

"Stop grinning."

"I'm practicing my coon face, mastuh."

"Do you remember the lines of your song?"

"Remember? You and I have been hearin' Abel sing these lyrics all our lives. Too bad he's not here. He might fancy doing a routine or two."

Etienne nodded, then slowed. Putting a hand on his friend's shoulder, he cautioned, "Be careful, Cain. We didn't get to check the passengers who came on at Morgan City."

"All right," Cain agreed. "But next time let's be riverboat gamblers. This persona is beneath even my dignity."

Harriet and the other girls employed by Madam Irene sashayed along the soft carpet of the sumptuous grand saloon, practically the length of a football field. Their role was to flirt and let the men buy them drinks, the ultimate goal being assignations in the gentlemen's cabins. Harriet kept an eye peeled for Etienne and Cain, but had not spotted them yet.

Passengers of all classes crowded the plush hall, from fashionable gentlemen to farmers. At one end, cigar-smoking gamblers held reign at the green baize tables. At the other end was the small stage where musicians played, trying to make more noise than the rumble of conversation. Harriet recognized brassy versions of old Stephen Foster tunes, such as "Camptown Races" and "Swanee River."

In between were sitting areas with satin-covered furniture, brass cuspidors and prismed chandeliers.

Harriet didn't shock easily, but Madam Irene's recitation as they walked along of her rates for various services, from straight, to French, to graphic specialties, inflamed her cheeks. Even worse, Harriet noticed lots of men studying her with decided interest, and not just because of her low-cut gown. Evidently, Madam Irene had already spread word of Harriet's feather tricks.

"Hey, darlin', come over here," cajoled one short, balding gentleman who resembled Elmer Fudd. She was about to turn away, but Madam Irene gave her a harsh shove with an admonition to start earning her keep. "And don't forget, you owe me extra for bringing that damn dog along."

Elmer smirked up at her from the table where he was playing poker with several other equally seedy characters. "Why don'tcha sit down here on my lap, sweetheart, and give me a little sample of yer feather trick?" The other men chortled, all of them leering at her cleavage.

Harriet leaned down close to Elmer's ear, discreetly angling her bare bosom the other way. She whispered to him exactly where she would like to put one of her feathers . . . a long, pointed one.

Elmer blanched and shrank away from her.

Just then, Harriet heard the band stop playing and someone announce that the minstrel show was about to begin. Slipping away from Madam Irene, Harriet made her way toward the stage. She stood at the back of the gathering crowd.

The production began with a group of ten men in blackface and dress suits making a grand entrance, marching around the stage in imitation of old plantation cakewalks. The leader, called the Interlocutor, gave the order, "Gentlemen be seated." They dropped into chairs arranged on the stage in a semicircle.

Harriet's heart leaped with joy when she recognized Etienne and Cain at either end of the lineup. Then she giggled at their disguises. Etienne looked especially adorable . . . her very own Al Jolson.

The man in the center, the Interlocutor, acted as straight man and master of ceremonies. He introduced the players, including Etienne as Mr. Tambo, holding a tambourine, and Cain as Mr. Bones, playing the bones.

A lot of bantering and riddles followed, including, to Harriet's delight, some of her own jokes. Except that they were adapted to be derogatory stereotypes of blacks as lazy, stupid, superstitious, cheating, lying, thieving dandies with a tendency toward drunkenness.

"Mr. Bones," Etienne called out, "didja hear 'bout the coon who stopped a man from beatin' a donkey?"

"Cain't say that I have, Mr. Tambo," Cain replied.

"It were a case of brotherly love," Etienne replied to the whooping laughter of the audience.

After one of the other entertainers did a soft-shoe tap dance, Cain called out to Etienne, "Say, Brother Tambo, I 'spect you knows the hardest thing to teach a darkie."

"Cain't say I do," Etienne responded with a straight face.

"How to use the privy." Cain chuckled at his own joke. And the audience joined in.

It was the weirdest sort of self-deprecating humor Harriet had ever heard. Even the blacks in the audience seemed to enjoy the performance. Harriet suspected it was almost a reverse joke by the blacks, as if they were pulling a scam on the unknowing whites.

Next followed the "olio" portion of the program, in which each man got to display his particular talents. Everything from a farce, "The Three Coon Musketeers," in which everyone joined in, to slapstick pie-throwing, then songs and dancing. Cain did a fair rendition of "Dixie" on the banjo, while Etienne sang a horrible, shrilly falsetto version of "My Old Kentucky Home."

Finally came the grand finale, in which the performers formed a line, doing a "walk-around" skirting the clap-

319

ping, singing audience, passing hats for donations. They were circling for a second time when Etienne caught sight of Harriet, then did a double take. He tripped, causing Cain to hit his back. Cain noticed her now, as well. He smiled a big, toothy welcome, prompting Etienne to elbow him in the gut.

Etienne's eyes, exaggeratedly big with blackface makeup, went even wider as they homed in on her exposed cleavage. Stumbling along in the cakewalk, sort of a nineteen-hundreds' version of the stroll, he continued to hold eye contact. When the performers arrived back at the stage and were bowing before the applauding audience, Etienne mouthed some indistinguishable silent words at her.

Harriet hoped whimsically that the message was something like, "I love you, stupid."

What he'd probably said was, "I'm going to kill you, stupid."

Chapter Twenty

Etienne was so brain-boiling furious he felt as if his eyeballs were blistering.

"Well, shut my mouth!" Cain muttered to him for the third time since they'd noticed the outrageous woman who'd apparently decided to become his personal shadow.

"I'm gonna kill her. Slowly. And I'm gonna enjoy it."

"Do you suppose it's one of those mental connection things Harriet always yammers about—telepathy, I think she calls it? You know what I mean, Etienne? You were missing her so bad, and she received your heart message and came a-runnin'."

Etienne told Cain to do something to himself that was physically impossible.

As he pushed his way through the milling people, Harriet obviously sensed his displeasure. *Displeasure? Hah! I probably have smoke coming out of my ears.* She was backing up, trying to blend into the crowd. As if she could hide from him with her rouged lips and ridiculous black face patch, and wearing that scarlet dress with a neckline cut practically to her knocking knees. *Merde,* if she sneezed, every man in the room would get to view what he unreasonably considered his private property.

Private property? Oh, damn! I'm jealous, Etienne realized with a sorry shake of his head. *When did the witch bore herself so deeply into my feelings? How could I have allowed that to happen? And what can I do about it now?*

"What're you gonna do with your *soul mate* now that she's here?" Cain asked, tagging close to his heels. "Aside from the obvious, that is."

Etienne snorted with disgust and resumed stomping toward Harriet. "You've been in Abel's company too much of late; you're beginning to think like him. Low-down and dirty."

Cain blathered on, "That's another thing you should do with her. Get low-down and dirty. I was reading that book of Harriet's one day, and it says even ladies want to be treated like whores sometimes. Yep, you've been pussyfooting around with Harriet for too long, if you ask me. Time for some low-down-and-dirty tomcatting."

"Who asked you?" Etienne retorted, spotting Harriet again in the crowd.

She was backed up against the far wall, beyond the gaming tables. A red-haired, face-painted woman the size of a locomotive in a garish purple dress was wagging a finger in Harriet's face, to which Harriet was arguing vehemently. Meanwhile, a short, balding man with a bulbous nose and a leer in his eyes seemed to be making some kind of proposition.

It didn't take a scholar to figure out what kind of proposition, especially since the little worm was about to lay a pudgy finger on the upper curve of Harriet's right breast.

The temperature of Etienne's blood rose a notch higher.

Without thinking, he grabbed the weasel by the back of the jacket collar and held him up off the floor. "If you touch one hair on her head, I'm gonna turn you into fish bait."

The little man's eyes bulged out and he sputtered helplessly. "Do you understand?" Etienne grated out.

His victim nodded, still tongue-tied and scared witless.

Etienne dropped the man abruptly, and he scurried off and out through the open door to the deck, never once looking back.

Now it was Harriet's turn. He reached out a hand but found nothing to grab. Just all that skin. Her mouth still gaped open at the spectacle he'd put on. With each panting breath, her breasts heaved in. And out. And in. And out.

"Cover yourself," he snarled.

"Oh!" she said weakly with a moue of embarrassment as she glanced downward. Then she flicked the black feather fan open, spreading it over her décolletage. Some poor ostrich went to the grave to supply all the plumes for that frippery, he'd warrant.

A sudden thought nagged at Etienne. *A black feather fan! Oh, good Lord!* His gaze moved reluctantly to the slattern whose face was flushed a shade closely approximating her purple garment. She stammered with barely controlled rage over her interrupted transaction. *It must be Madam Irene. That would mean that Harriet was the whore everyone was talking about today . . . the one with a remarkable repertoire of feather tricks.*

To make matters worse, Harriet was gawking at him and Cain. And she was giggling.

"You think this situation is humorous?" He moved closer—invading her personal space, as Harriet would say. He hoped his body language threatened her. He hoped she knew that if she giggled one more time he was going to kiss her speechless, then throw her overboard.

"It's just that you and Cain look so ridiculous." She twittered nervously, meanwhile sidling toward the doorway.

He stepped into her path, blocking her exit.

"Etienne," Cain said softly at his side, "you'd best

move this show outside. You're gathering attention we don't need.''

Etienne inhaled and exhaled several times to calm himself. Cain was right. Dozens of people had turned their way. Without hesitation, he gripped Harriet by the upper arm, pulling her against his side. She smelled of gardenias and clean hair and pure Harriet. His traitorous heart constricted with suffocating, unwelcome emotion. "Let's get out of here," he murmured huskily.

"Oh, no, you don't," Madam Irene shrieked, finally having regained her voice. Her crafty eyes swept over him in appraisal and found him wanting. "Maxine has a whole night's work ahead of her. She ain't goin' off with the likes of you."

"Maxine?" Etienne arched a brow at Harriet, who still nestled against his side, scanning him in wonder. She was still giggling. He wasn't sure if it was his appearance, his overreaction to her suitor or Madam Irene's claim on her that sparked Harriet's mirth.

"Take yer hands off Maxine. The only gentlemen what goes off with my girls have got to have the coins to pay," Madam Irene asserted. "And I know how much you coon performers earn. Not enough fer one of my high-class whores, that's fer certain."

Etienne saw from the corner of his eye that the captain was approaching, no doubt upset over the unseemly confrontation taking place on his boat. Wasting no time, Etienne ignored Madam Irene's squeal of objection and drew Harriet outside and down the deck. Cain followed quickly behind them.

"Etienne, you're hurting me," Harriet protested. "And my gown is falling off."

He slowed down and loosened his grasp on her arm. Only God knew how he restrained himself from watching her while she adjusted her dress. They were at the far end of the deck where only an occasional passenger strolled by, getting the night air.

"Let's go wash this burnt cork off," Cain urged him, then winked at Harriet. "Nice to see you again so soon, my dear."

"Likewise," she said sweetly.

I'll give her "likewise." "You go ahead," Etienne told Cain. "We'll catch up with you. See if you can get a few extra buckets of water."

Then, turning on Harriet, he pressed her into a small alcove dimly lit by a lantern. Looming over her, he braced both white-gloved hands against the wall on either side of her head. "What the hell are you doing here, Harriet?"

"I came to warn you."

"Warn me? By disobeying orders to stay at Bayou Noir? By dressing as a prostitute selling her wares? By laughing at me?"

She waved a hand dismissively, explaining how Simone had come to Bayou Noir with a message that Pope's men now knew Etienne was headed for Texas. "I couldn't just let you walk into a trap. By the way, I didn't appreciate your non-good-bye to me. One of these times you're going to dump me, and I won't come after you."

"That's the point, Harriet. Besides, I think I said goodbye rather well."

She lowered her lashes with embarrassment, then immediately raised her chin, brazening out his scrutiny. "Oh, no! You don't get off that easy. I told you not to touch me anymore."

"I didn't touch you," he reminded her with a crooked smile.

"Oh, then that hard thing inside me was my imagination."

He let out a hoot of amusement. "Harriet, your bluntness is refreshing. And I didn't touch you until you begged me to."

"That's debatable . . . who begged whom, I mean."

"Let's get back to the subject at hand. Why are you with Madam Irene?"

"Well, you see, it's a long story. Oh, if you must know, she paid my fare."

Etienne crossed his eyes and ground his teeth. "Harriet, why did a sporting house madam pay your fare? Where's the money I left you? That was more than enough for a ticket and a suite of cabins."

She then related a rambling, bizarre, impossible-to-believe story about going to Morgan City with Ellen and Daniel. And somehow losing them there.

He frowned, trying to make sense of her confusing words. "Do you still have the money?"

"Of course. Right here," she said, patting her waist. "It's in my panty hose."

He must have looked as puzzled as he felt because she began to lift the hem of her gown to show him her panty hose. He recognized the silk garment he'd used to tie her hands back on the train, but he'd never imagined its full appeal. The hem of her dress crept higher and higher, exposing more and more of the sheer stockings that went all the way to her waist, where a flat, leather pouch was tied over her hip with a length of ribbon.

He groaned inwardly at the sight of all that transparent silk. "It's a good thing Madam Irene didn't know about these stockings. She would have been drumming up trade for you with them, as well as your feather tricks."

Harriet had the good sense to blush and dropped her gown back in place. "You're not mad at me anymore, are you, Etienne? I mean, you can understand why I had to come?"

"Oh, I'm still mad." He let out a loud whoosh of exasperation at the implications of Harriet's interference. "I knew Pope's men were setting up a trap. That was the goal of this entire escapade."

"It was?" She tilted her head in bafflement.

He nodded, disconcerted by a strand of ebony hair that was blowing in the slight breeze, back and forth across her smooth shoulder. She was so damn beautiful.

"Etienne?" she prodded.

Concentrate, Etienne. Concentrate. "Harriet, we think that Pope is an underling in this operation and that the real leader is operating out of Texas. For years, ever since Reconstruction began, corruption in government projects has been rampant. Half of the funds appropriated by Congress never make it to the local level. It's routine business for officials, North and South, to take their cut of any allocation, from railroads to Freedman's Bureau. But this is bigger than that, more systematic."

"And President Grant is afraid to trust even those in his own staff?" she guessed.

"That's right. It has to be an inside job, probably ex-agents like myself, disgruntled and out for themselves."

"Sounds like a post–Civil War mafia."

"Mafia?"

"Ummm . . . a crime syndicate."

"I suppose you could call it that."

She narrowed her eyes at him. "Are you saying that you're deliberately courting danger? That you and Cain are decoys?"

"Exactly. Why do you think we didn't just take the gold directly to Washington when we recovered it?"

"I guess I didn't think."

Now that's an admission that oughtta be chipped in stone. "We didn't want just Pope and his lower-level men. By having them follow us, we hope he'll lead us to the ringleader in Texas."

Tears welled in her eyes.

"What now?" His voice was harsh, but inside Etienne felt like a melting bowl of butter. Dammit, how could the sight of her tears affect him so?

"You're in danger, and you might get killed."

He smiled grimly at her concern for his safety. "Maybe, but you won't be here to witness my sad demise, darlin'. You'll be long gone, back to your own time. You're getting off at the next stop in the morning."

She shook her head vehemently. "No, I'm not, Etienne. I'm in this for the long haul. I can't leave till you're safe and sound, back at Bayou Noir."

"Harriet, don't you ever give a care for your own safety? Do you always jump before thinking? And who the hell named you my protector? I've been taking care of myself for a good many years without your help."

She winced at his cutting words. "Which one of those questions do you want me to answer?"

"None," he said with a laugh, pushing himself away from the wall. "Where's Madam Irene's room? Let's get your clothes."

"We're staying on the second level," she said as they moved out onto the walkway again.

"We?" Little alarm bells went off in his head, in part due to the sudden defensive hunching of her shoulders. He was becoming an expert at interpreting her nonverbal communication.

"Well, yes, did I forget to mention . . . oh, my . . . didn't you know that Saralee is with me?"

"I beg your pardon?" he choked out.

Sensing his renewed anger, she inched away from him, but he caught hold of her with a gloved palm latched onto the nape of her neck. Slowly, he drew her closer.

"Etienne, you really do look ridiculous in that makeup. And it's so politically incorrect. Why, in my time—"

"Shut up, Harriet, and tell me why you brought my daughter on such a dangerous, foolhardy trip." They were so close, he could feel her breath against his mouth.

"I had to. Blossom was worried, and rightly so. Pope's men could have come to Bayou Noir and kidnapped Saralee. To get to you."

"Why the hell didn't you bring everyone else, too? Even the damn dog?"

"Well, actually," she began, refusing to make eye contact.

She wouldn't! "You didn't!"

"What was I supposed to do? Blossom said she's too old to take care of a dog, and Saralee wouldn't come without Lance."

Lance?

"Besides, you're the one who gave her the mangy mutt," she reminded him, "which, incidentally, was the nicest thing you've ever done. Saralee adores him. . . . Why are you glowering again?"

"Harriet, ever since I've met you, I've been glowering. You have that effect on me." His hand was still wrapped around the back of her neck, and she stood only inches away from him, looking wounded and vulnerable.

"Etienne," she said softly, "I missed you."

Those three words, coming so unexpectedly, were his undoing. They blindsided him with their simple sincerity. He felt as if he'd been kicked in the gut.

"Hell!" he whispered and hauled her into his arms. Uncaring of his blackface, he buried his fingers, gloves and all, in her hair and kissed her with the madness that consumed him.

"Did you miss me?" she gasped out during the one moment when he let her up for air.

He didn't answer, but he showed her.

They couldn't make love. Not here in the open. Not even in the semiprivacy of the alcove where he backed her once again. Harriet would be shuffling off to her own time soon. She would leave him behind. But she would damn well take a few memories with her. He vowed in that instant to make certain she never forgot him, just as he would never forget her.

Sacramento, California

Selene Baptiste had been weeping for more than an hour when her husband James returned from the barns. He'd been helping to deliver a new foal.

"Selene, *chérie*," he called out from the front door. "Queen's Delight has a lovely new daughter."

"In here, darling," she answered, dabbing quickly at her eyes with a linen handkerchief. She heard the sharp click of his boots as he made his way down the tiled hall of the rambling Spanish-style ranch house.

Entering the library, he held out his arms for her in greeting, as he always did. Twenty-five years of marriage and he still showed his love for her every day, even in the smallest ways. Today, especially, she needed the comfort of his embrace.

Wrapping her arms around his wide shoulders, she hugged him tightly. James pulled back, observing her reddened eyes and nose for the first time. "Selene, sweetheart, what is it? Have you had another argument with Melanie?"

She shook her head mutely. From the back of the house, their youngest daughter could be heard pounding out her piano lessons in discordant rebellion. She was only fifteen years old, but yesterday she'd been suspended from her third boarding school. This time she'd been smoking a cigar.

"What is it then?" James asked, raking his fingers through black hair only lightly salted with gray. He was fifty-nine years old, but he could still make her tremble with a mere glance. Just then, her husband noticed letters on the desk, and the opened one that she'd obviously been reading.

She saw the alarm on James's face, which he immediately covered with a bullish scowl. "Not from Etienne, I hope. If it is, don't tell me. I don't want to know what the foolish miscreant is doing now." James stomped to the window, staring out blindly, and Selene's heart ached for his self-inflicted pain. His words meant nothing. She knew—and he knew—that he missed his first son desperately. Finally, James turned back to her. "Just one thing . . . Is he"—he gulped—"all right?"

"No, James, he's not all right. And the letter's not from Etienne. It's from a woman he met recently—"

"A woman? What's he done now?"

"A special woman, James. A woman who loves our boy, I think. Come. You have to read this."

James began to peruse the page reluctantly, standing up. Halfway through the letter, he plopped down into the desk chair and wiped at his eyes.

"Earn my love?" He peered up from the letter. "Do you think I was that judgmental with Etienne? Do you truly think he doubted that I loved him? Ever?"

Selene shrugged. "Did you tell him?"

He thought a moment. "He should have known, without the words."

"Oh, so you don't need to hear me say the words to you? They're understood?"

"That's different," he balked.

"Maybe so. And, of course, you feel his affection for you, as well, without those three precious words?"

"Stop manipulating me, Selene."

"I'm just trying to make you see what you've refused to face all these years."

"I do love him," he said, and his voice cracked. He swallowed hard several times to control himself. "That boy has done more things to make me furious, practically from the time he came flailing from the womb, but not once, *never,* did I stop loving him."

"Too bad he doesn't know that." Selene felt as if a heavy weight were being lifted from her shoulders. Finally, James appeared to be melting toward his son. "You'd better read the rest. And maybe you should have a drink first."

James gave her a measuring frown before resuming his reading. Selene walked over to the sideboard and poured not one, but two tumblers of bourbon.

James gasped. "She's from the future? Like you?"

Selene handed him his drink and began to sip hers. "It would seem so. And it's really ironic, too, because it was one of her books that prompted me to give up modeling."

He laughed then. "And dumb-men jokes! This is priceless. I wish I could have seen Etienne's face the first time he heard one of those riddles—'' He stopped himself, realizing what he'd just said. He'd actually voiced aloud what he'd been yearning for all these years: He would like to see his son's face.

"There's more, James," Selene said, pointing to the rest of the long letter.

James took a long swallow of the potent liquor before he continued. "I don't understand half of what this woman says. Body language. Psychologist.'' He inhaled sharply, and Selene knew he'd gotten to the part where Harriet mentioned Etienne's child. He put his head in his hands for a moment, trying to digest the monumental revelation. She'd felt the same way the first time she read the letter. "A granddaughter? A child of Etienne's and she's been staying alone at that decrepit old plantation? With only Blossom for company?"

She walked behind the desk and put a comforting hand on his shoulder. "He didn't know, James. Don't judge him too harshly.''

He raised his head and scrutinized her with sadness. "Even you, Selene . . . even you blame me for this separation? Even you think it's my narrow-minded pride that has kept this feud going?''

"Oh, no, honey! You and Etienne share the same stubbornness. And maybe I'm at fault, too, for not having acted. Why should it have taken a stranger to solve our family crisis?''

"I'm not sure I can take any more shocks today," James said, even as he picked up the letter again. His eyes flashed indignantly a moment later. "Is she saying I have a 'perfection syndrome'? Me?''

Selene smiled. "Hey, she accuses me of the same thing. But, you know something, James, I like this woman. She appears strong and opinionated and caring. I think she would be just the kind of woman Etienne needs.''

"She says she's going back to her time.''

Selene tapped her chin thoughtfully. "Who knows what will happen?"

James stared bleakly at her then. "Etienne is in grave danger. I can sense it most in what this woman leaves unsaid."

Selene nodded and sat down in her husband's lap.

"We're going back, aren't we?" he said as he drew her closer and nuzzled her neck.

"I've already started Iris packing. And you should hear the threats she's making against Abel."

"Because of this new woman that Harriet alluded to in the letter? Who is Xaviera Hollander, by the way?"

"A madam."

"Oh, good Lord!"

She and James exchanged a rueful glance. Cain and Abel were notorious for their women.

"What of the children?" James asked.

"They'll come, too. Rufus and Iris, as well. And Reba."

"All of them? And their families?" His blue eyes widened with incredulity. She and James had five grown children, including Etienne. Two spouses. And two grandchildren . . . no, three now.

"Ashley is on his way to Los Angeles now to make arrangements for a private railway car. You know the children have always wanted to see the bayou."

James's face turned solemn. "I can't believe it. After all these years, after all my threats never to return, we're going back to Bayou Noir."

"Yes," Selene said brightly. "Isn't it wonderful?"

A slow smile crept across James's lips. "Do you think the herons are still there?"

Franklin, Louisiana

Seven days after being reunited with Harriet on the steamboat, the blind minister, Rev. Hiram Frogash, was sitting on the high bench seat of a buckboard being driven by his servant, Hippocrates Jones.

They had headed out of Lafayette that morning, joining a group named the Good Faith of Babylon Church. The congregation intended to form a new settlement in West Texas that they'd already named Nineveh. The Babylons, as they called themselves, were led by Nebuchadnezzar Lezzer, who stemmed from Pittsburgh, Pennsylvania. He was the flakiest preacher in the universe. Flaky was a word Harriet had taught him. It meant driving with two bales short of a full load of cotton. Like Harriet.

In his role as the Reverend Frogash, Etienne wore dark spectacles, carried a cane and had his hair parted down the center. The last was a touch much favored by his primly gowned wife, Harriet Frogash, who drove the other wagon. She had an odd fascination with men who wore glasses, especially when they took them off—a weakness he intended to take advantage of soon.

"This is just like *Sweet Savage Love*. Steve and Ginny were on a wagon train going west, too," she called over to him.

"I have news for you, honey," he answered in a loud, carrying voice. None of the other wagons were close enough to overhear. "This sorry line of decrepit carts is a far cry from a wagon train. And the only west we're headed for is the other side of the border into Texas."

On the other hand, her allusion to that blasted book recalled to him an earlier conversation in which she'd mentioned that Steve Morgan had forcefully seduced Ginny Brandon under a wagon bed.

Now that held some appeal. Though he'd much prefer a soft mattress in a hotel, he thought as his rear slammed the wood with a thunk. That must be the hundredth rut Cain had hit today. He glared at his friend. "Did you do that deliberately?"

Cain grinned. "I could tell what you were thinking. You

needed a jolt before you forgot your blindness and leap-frogged over into Harriet's lap.''

He glanced at Harriet, barely visible through his dark lenses. Wearing a sedate calico gown and a poke bonnet he'd bought for her, she was seated next to his daughter Saralee Frogash and Lance Frogash, the newest additions to his happy family. Saralee was pretending to be an angel today, wearing an old nightgown, a halo made of golden-rods and wings improvised out of giant elephant-ear leaves.

Sacrebleu!

He was worried about Harriet and Saralee. They didn't know it, but once they hit Texas, the two of them, along with the cur that was trying its damnedest to impregnate every dog within barking distance, were boarding a steamboat from Galveston to New Orleans. He'd rather see Harriet and Saralee riding out this dangerous situation in a brothel than take a chance on their being hurt—or worse—in Texas.

The wagon hit another rut, this time a big one, and Etienne actually rose in the air before coming down hard. "Damn, I hope our cargo holds up better than my back-side." Both wagons carried a dozen crates of "Bibles" that had been transferred from the music cases in Franklin seven days ago when the captain of the *Southern Star* evicted the entire minstrel group, as well as Madam Irene's contingent of whores, for "disruption of the peace and respectability" of his passengers.

Actually, the last nail in their coffin, so to speak, had been pounded by the Interlocutor, who'd taken a fancy to the captain's wife, and vice versa. They'd been found "interlocking" in the captain's bed the night before.

Luckily—or perhaps not so luckily—he'd met the Babylons almost immediately. More than anything, the Babylons yearned to Christianize some wild savages. They would hear none of Hiram's preaching that most of the primitive redskins had smoked way too many peace pipes, or were long gone to reservations.

Sandra Hill

Of course, Harriet had spoiled the whole effect by telling the two dozen gullible men, women and children, "Don't worry. If we run into any wild Indians, my husband will take care of them. He used to live with the Comanches, you know. In fact, his first wife was the daughter of one of the chiefs."

That Steve Morgan sure had gotten around.

Neither Harriet nor the blithering Babylons had taken into account the fact that he was supposedly blind.

That night they all slept on the ground under the wagon. In the pouring rain. Steve Morgan apparently had had better luck than he did. Like peas in a pod, there were Cain, Saralee, him, Lance and Harriet. Lance had insisted on squirming between him and his "wife," resting his face on Etienne's chest. He'd been about to toss the mongrel out into the rain . . . till he saw Saralee's tearful eyes. His relationship with his daughter was still too tenuous to risk alienating her.

So now he had Lance snoring under his chin, blowing foul breath into his face. He suspected that Lance had dined on wild rabbit and wilder onion grass that evening. Which was a lot better than the fare served by Harriet over a sputtering fire. A good cook she was not, but then the same was true of the other wives in the congregation, as well. The whole lot were spoiled by modern conveniences, like stoves, Preacher Lezzer had declared with disgust. "But the Lord will provide," he'd added with his usual optimism. "Let us all pray for heavenly assistance. And better vittles."

God answered their prayers the following day when Saralee took over the cooking for the entire group. His daughter was a marvel. While Harriet and the other women helped gather the food around one communal cook fire, the seven-year-old girl put them all to shame with one after another of Blossom's recipes.

For breakfast, there were hoecakes thick with wild huckleberries, sorghum syrup and rich chicory coffee. At a quick midday stop, she'd served up a hastily prepared sweet potato soup with spoon bread and more coffee. Now, as evening approached, Etienne lay back against a rock and digested the two servings he'd had of her wonderful Hopping John—a thick stew of black-eyed peas, rice, ham hocks, peppers and seasonings she'd gathered from the nearby woods. The Reverend Lezzer had proclaimed her featherlight biscuits a gift from God, at which Saralee had beamed. Etienne had also complimented her profusely, but Saralee trembled every time he came near. He had a lot of work to do yet with his daughter.

Sipping a cup of coffee, Etienne watched—although he still wore his dark spectacles and pretended to be staring blankly—as Harriet was teaching Saralee, who was an Indian maiden today, and a half dozen of the Babylon children how to play a game called *hula hoop*. She'd asked Cain to cut down a number of thin saplings about a man's height, which she'd tied into circles. Now she was doing the most outrageous, erotic things with her hips. Over and over, she raised her elbows high and rotated her hips, trying to keep the circle aloft. She and the children laughed gaily as they practiced.

From his vantage point directly behind Harriet, Etienne thought there were some advantages to being blind. Like a full-blown view of the curve of her bottom every single damn time she twirled her hips. He was thinking about asking her to give him a demonstration later . . . wearing only her panty hose . . . and maybe the leopard-print chemise. Yep, that would be a sight to stir a man's blood. Not that his blood wasn't already boiling. In fact, it had been on a slow simmer since he'd entered a certain train compartment about two weeks ago.

Several of the other women came closer, and Harriet soon enticed them to try the hula hoops. Some of the younger men tried them also. Soon the small clearing rang with the giggles of young and old alike.

Reverend Lezzer squinted uncertainly at all the shenanigans. "I don't know if this is quite respectable."

"Oh, pooh, Nebbie," his wife responded. "The good Lord never said jolliment was a sin." So, *Nebbie* joined them, too.

Harriet came over and sank down beside him, smiling. "It's amazing how little it takes to entertain kids. In my time, parents buy children all kinds of expensive toys. And one of the all-time best inventions was the hula hoop. The man who thought it up first made a fortune."

That seemed hardly credible but he didn't argue. He was enjoying her close proximity too much. "I think we should go take a bath," he suggested suddenly. "Cain said there's a secluded spot downstream a bit."

She gave him a sidelong glance of disbelief. "Together?"

"Well, of course. Being blind and all, I could hardly make my way there alone."

She laughed. "You're incorrigible." While laughing, she knocked against his arm and a little of his coffee spilled into the dust. "That looks just like a Rorschach ink-blot design."

"A what?"

"Rorschach. It's a psychological test that determines certain intellectual and emotional factors."

All Etienne saw was a wet spot in the shape of a circle.

"For example, what do you see there? Say the first thing that comes into your mind."

"Breast."

She clucked her disapproval.

"How about this?" She took his cup and drizzled another spot on the ground, this time in the shape of a square.

"Buttocks."

"Etienne! Be serious."

"I am. What do I get if I pass this test? A bath?"

"There is no passing or failing of this test. Look at this one." Now she dribbled a wobbly triangle.

He grinned and stared meaningfully at her lap . . . more specifically, the joining of her thighs.

"You're teasing me. Let's try another test. This is called word association. I'll say a number of words, and you say the first thing that comes into your head. Do you understand?"

He didn't. "Sure."

"Bed."

"Nipple."

She frowned. "House."

"Bed."

The frown disappeared. "Wet."

"Kiss."

The frown was back. "Animal."

"Cock."

"Oh, you!"

"Keep going, this is fun. I think I would make a good psychologist."

"Cotton."

"Sex."

"Give me a break, Etienne. There's no way you could associate cotton with sex."

"Yes, there is. Cotton sheets on a bed where two naked bodies are —"

"I give up," she said, shaking her head at him.

"Guess that means I'm the winner." Making sure no one was watching, he lowered his spectacles a mite and peered up at her, wiggling his eyebrows. "Want to come to my blanket tonight and ogle me while I take off my spectacles?"

She *tsk-tsk*ed him. "Rascal to the end, aren't you?"

"Only for you, darlin'."

Saralee walked up hesitantly then, her three pitiful rag dolls clutched in her arms. The braids Harriet had plaited for her that morning were half undone, and there were dirt smudges on her cheeks. She was the spitting image of him at that age.

As an Indian maiden, Saralee wore a leather thong around her forehead with a bedraggled black feather, which he assumed came from Harriet's harlot fan. He hoped Harriet hadn't gotten rid of all her feathers; he had another fantasy in mind for the future. Saralee also wore a leather belt with a scabbard for a small knife, and around her neck was a strand of chinaberry beads. When they'd asked her days ago to play along with their "game" of pretending to be a blind man with his wife and child, Saralee had had no trouble falling into the role-playing.

"Sit down, Saralee," Etienne urged, making room for her on the ground between him and Harriet. The other children and adults began to move off to their own wagons and campfires.

Saralee's lower lip trembled, but she did as she was told. A brave little soul, he thought.

Harriet remained quiet during this interchange. Etienne impressed her with a surprising sensitivity and endearing clumsiness as he tried to draw his daughter out of her shell.

"Would you like me to tell you some tales my stepmother told me when I was your age? She was a great storyteller."

Saralee shook her head. "Tell me 'bout Selene. Is she my grandmother?"

Etienne took off his glasses and rubbed the bridge of his nose. He didn't talk about his family . . . *ever*. Harriet saw the effort it took for him to unstiffen and answer in a civil tone. "Yes, she's your grandmother."

"Where is she?"

Etienne's jaw worked. "California."

"Blossom says she's beautiful."

Etienne's lips turned up at the edges. "Very beautiful."

"And my grandfather? Does he live in California, too?"

Etienne nodded, the stiffness back in his jaw and a bleakness in his eyes. He hadn't put his glasses back on.

"Will I ever meet them?"

Etienne closed his eyes for a brief moment, then looked

directly at Saralee. "I don't know, sweetie. I don't know."

His honesty seemed to satisfy Saralee. But then the very perceptive little girl asked, "Do you ever miss your papa? You looked sad when I asked 'bout him. Sometimes I miss having a mama and papa so bad."

Staggered, Etienne glanced at Harriet for help, but before she could intervene, Saralee added the zinger. "Do you wanna hug one of my dolls? Sometimes, when I'm sad, it helps."

He groaned. "Saralee, I'd love to hug one of your dolls. But more than anything, I'd like a hug from my own little girl."

Saralee's eyes went big as saucers before she leaped into his arms, dolls flying. She held on tight around his neck as Etienne rocked her back and forth, eyes closed. "Shhh, now, Saralee. You don't have to be sad anymore. Shhh! Papa's here. Shhh!"

For a long time, Saralee clung fiercely to Etienne, afraid the magic moment would disappear if she didn't hang on for dear life. Little by little, she relaxed as Etienne whispered to her of all the things he would show her when they got home to Bayou Noir . . . a secret bayou glen, an alligator's nest, the best place to pick wild berries, the best method of fishing. On and on he went till Saralee fell asleep in his arms. And then it was Etienne who held on tight, not wanting to relinquish his precious daughter.

Finally, he lifted his lids, his eyes locking with Harriet's. She'd been weeping silently. He didn't question her tears. Instead, he put a free hand around the nape of her neck, pulling her closer.

Laying his lips softly against hers, he kissed her. A heart-and-soul kiss. A featherlight gesture that reached into her essence and with its gentleness shredded everything that was Harriet Ginoza. Nothing that came before this kiss mattered. Nothing. This kiss represented all that she, or any woman, could ever want from life.

Etienne was her soul mate, and she'd be a fool to let him go.

Chapter Twenty-one

The next day, they crossed the Texas border into Devil's Junction, where the Babylons prepared to part company with Reverend Frogash, heading in another direction. In a flurry of good-byes and promises to keep in touch, the Babylons rode off.

That was when they realized that Saralee was missing.

Frantically, they searched the town, asked every passerby they saw for news of the child. They even followed after the Babylons to see if she'd inadvertently gotten mixed in their group. Nothing. Lance whimpered at Harriet's feet, rubbing against her leg. And Harriet knew that Saralee would never have left without her dog.

With a speed born of years of experience, Etienne dropped his disguise and strapped on his gun belts. Cain did likewise. They walked briskly out of the livery stable, where they'd just boarded their wagons and horses. The two fresh riding horses Etienne and Cain had rented stood saddled and waiting.

"What is it?" Harriet asked Etienne. His eyes glittered

with fury. She wasn't sure if it was directed at himself or her for bringing Saralee into this danger.

"Briggs," Etienne clipped out. "I knew he was a snake, but I didn't think he'd strike so soon. Or in such an underhanded manner—kidnapping a child, for chrissake. He must be desperate."

"You should have killed him three years ago when you had the chance," Cain said. Both men were checking ammunition belts and adding rifles to their arsenal of weapons.

"We needed more evidence," Etienne responded. "The hell with evidence now! If he harms Saralee in any way, I'll kill him with my bare hands."

Harriet was thoroughly confused. "Who is Briggs?"

"Brandon Briggs. The honorable U.S. Senator from Texas," Etienne said with a sneer. "And the biggest thief in the country. He's the man President Grant wanted to snare in this whole entrapment scenario. He's the mastermind behind a network of government graft that covers every state. He got his start by working with us in the Secret Service in the early years of the war."

"Does he live here in Devil's Junction?"

Both men shook their heads.

"He has a ranch about three hours south of here, near Beaumont. The Double B," Cain explained as he swung up onto the saddle of his horse.

"But . . . but where are you going now? And where's my horse?" Harriet asked in alarm.

Etienne turned on her, jaw set stubbornly. "You're staying here. No, Harriet, don't argue. There's no time. I want you to register at the hotel over there." He pointed to the Empire, a three-story plank building fronting a board sidewalk that lined the entire main street. In fact, it was the only street.

"But—"

"No 'buts,' Harriet. I want your promise."

She nodded.

He held her gaze for a long moment, measuring her sincerity. When satisfied, he went on, "If we're not back by tomorrow evening, I want you to go to Galveston and board the steamboat for New Orleans. Go to Simone's. If you don't hear from me by the twenty-eighth, three weeks from now, I want you to hotfoot it to the train station and buy a ticket for that first train over the bridge to Chicago. And never look back.'' He added that last with a hitch in his voice.

Never look back? As if that were possible! "Are you crazy? I'm not leaving here till I know for sure that you're either safe . . . or . . . or not safe.''

"Yes, you are, Harriet. I want your promise on this or else I'm gonna tie you to a bedpost in that hotel with orders for the proprietor to do as I say. Is that clear?''

Once again, she nodded. But she wasn't happy about it. "What about Lance?''

Etienne blinked, obviously having forgotten the mutt. "Hold on to him for Saralee.''

"Shouldn't I go to the sheriff, or something?''

"*No!*'' they both exclaimed.

"Or wire Abel, or your father?''

"*No!*'' they responded in unison.

Seeing that Etienne was about to mount the horse, Harriet panicked. "Etienne,'' she pleaded.

This was it then. He was riding off and might never return. And he didn't even seem to care. How could he be so heartless? Oh, she knew he was preoccupied with worry over Saralee. She was, too. But they might never see each other again. Ever.

"You are a gold-plated jerk.''

He arched one brow. "So you've said before.''

"Be careful,'' she whispered. Tears were already welling in her eyes. She knew that he noticed and tried not to be touched.

He nodded.

"I love you, you know?''

He nodded again.

"Say something, dammit!"

He smiled. "If I come back . . ." he drawled.

If? That word more than anything washed over Harriet like a cold premonition of doom.

"If I come back," he started over again, forcing her chin up with a forefinger, "will you do me a favor?"

"Anything," she said softly.

He laughed. "Now that has possibilities. Would you consider putting it in writing? Actually, what I was wondering was . . . if I come back, would you mind giving me a personal demonstration with that hula hoop, wearing your leopard-print chemise and those sinful panty hose?"

She tried to smile. "On one condition."

He grinned at her . . . a lazy, rogue's grin, which never reached his grim eyes. And he repeated her quick retort of moments ago, "Anything."

"As long as you give me a demonstration wearing boots and a cowboy hat."

"And what else?"

"That's all. Oh, maybe spectacles, too."

He chuckled and the grin did reach his eyes for an instant. Leaning down, he brushed a quick kiss across her lips and murmured against her mouth, "It's a deal, sweetheart."

Then he was gone.

For once, Harriet obeyed Etienne's orders. She stayed at the hotel, wringing her hands with worry, straying from her room only to eat in the hotel dining room or take Lance for a stroll down the town's boardwalk. The exercise took about five minutes.

By the afternoon of the second day, she was a mass of jittery nerves, alternately weeping and praying. Lance slept through most of it. *The cad!*

That was when Cain arrived with a dirty, distraught Saralee on the horse in front of him. And no Etienne. Harriet saw them from her second-story window, where she'd been

345

sitting vigil. Townspeople scurried out of sight and shop-keepers pulled down their shades and locked their doors.

Six armed men surrounded them, all wearing kerchief masks over their faces. Two of them accompanied a limping Cain into the hotel lobby, spurs jangling and guns out. A tear in the cloth of Cain's trousers at thigh-level revealed a bloody bandage. He'd been shot.

Saralee rushed into her arms, sobbing profusely and burying her face in Harriet's neck. "They took Papa," Saralee whispered in a rush of words. "The bad men beat him . . . *bad.* . . . Papa was crying . . . and they took him away."

Crying? Etienne? Harriet studied Cain's demeanor, and she knew the situation was very grave.

One of Briggs's two armed men motioned her toward a little sitting room off the lobby. Apparently they weren't going to speak and provide any means of identification to any townspeople who might be eavesdropping. Within seconds, Harriet was informed by Cain of what had transpired.

Six of Briggs's men had been killed, including Brisk and Franklin, the two men from the train, and Pope. Etienne was beaten to a pulp to get information on the gold shipment and just how much President Grant knew of their operation. Now he was incarcerated in a jail of sorts on Briggs's property.

Etienne imprisoned again? Oh, Lord! After he'd said he'd never allow himself to be put in a prison ever again. But he'd done it for his daughter. He'd had no choice. Oh, Lord!

"What now?" Harriet asked, glaring at the two deliberately silent Rambos in cowboy boots who glared right back at her. Their dark eyes above the masks were cold and merciless.

"Saralee and I are going back to New Orleans by train with these men to hand over the gold. It should take two days."

Saralee whimpered at the prospect of having to go anywhere else with these men.

"I thought the gold was—" She started to say "here in the livery stable," then stopped herself.

Cain shook his head. "No, those really are Bibles in those crates. The real gold is back in New Orleans."

That was news to her. "Can't they get it themselves?"

Cain shook his head. "Gautier has instructions to turn the shipment over only to me or Etienne."

Harriet realized that M. Gautier must also be in the government service.

"You'll stay here at the hotel," Cain went on quickly, "under guard, of course."

"And when the gold is recovered?" Harriet asked with a shiver of foreboding.

"Saralee will be released," Cain said flatly.

The message was clear. Saralee would be free, or at least they'd promised to release her. But the rest of them . . . Etienne, Cain and Harriet . . . would be killed.

"Why don't they just kill us now?"

"Because if I alert the authorities at my end, they intend to take you to the Double B and torture you in front of Etienne. You and Saralee are their guarantees that neither I nor Etienne will try to escape or call for help."

Harriet concluded, as Cain must have already, that there was no way these men were going to release Saralee. Even though she was a child, she'd seen and heard too much.

Harriet nodded her agreement. After much soothing of Saralee and convincing the Rambos that Saralee would be more docile if allowed to take her dog with her, Harriet handed her and Lance up to Cain's arms. She shoved the dog's basket at one of the men. Finally her eyes locked with Cain's, and Harriet hoped that he understood that she wasn't going to sit still and let anyone die. *No way!*

Two men stayed behind to guard Harriet.

And guard her they did. She wasn't permitted to leave her room for any reason. They brought her food. They emptied her chamber pot and brought fresh water. One of them slept on the double bed beside her. The only privacy she was permitted—such as it was—was when she retreated behind a screen in her room.

By the end of the fourth day, Harriet was running out of ideas. She'd tried cajolery. And bribery. Even seduction. Nothing worked. Time to use some of her modern psychological skills, Harriet decided. For the first time in her life, she questioned whether her expertise would be sufficient.

"Frank," she said to her guard of the moment. She stood at the foot of the bed.

"What now?" he growled. The hardened, pockmarked man of about forty was lying on the bed, propped up by two pillows, watching her with lewd interest. Oh, he hadn't made a move on her, but his eyes did. Frank fancied himself a ladies' man. His graying hair and mustache were trimmed to perfection. His black jacket and trousers and white linen shirt were of better than average tailoring. "I'm not gonna release you for any reason, sweetheart. Not if you keep preachin' all that mind mumbo jumbo till your voice runs out. Not to save my soul. Not for your money, which I reckon I'll get soon anyways. And not for a quick poke, either, which I also reckon I'll get soon. And I 'spect you'll like it, too, honey. You look like a woman what enjoys a good poke from a real man."

Harriet forced herself not to grimace with revulsion.

Okay, so he was a vain man, Harriet thought. Work on the man's weakness. "Has anyone ever told you that you have beautiful eyes?" Harriet remarked, hoping that this brute would be susceptible to flattery.

"No," he snorted with disbelief, but she could see that he was pleased.

"Really?" she said sweetly. "Let me see. Are they blue or gray? No, I see hints of violet in there, too."

"Well, my mother did have right pretty eyes," he conceded, allowing her to come closer than he had thus far. He widened his eyes for her perusal.

"They're so pretty. The kind of eyes a lady could drown

348

in. Like mine. Lots of people say they could drown in my eyes. What do you think?''

Frank stared into her eyes. ''Now that you mention it, they are mighty strange. Green, like a cat. They make me feel kinda funny.''

''Tired,'' Harriet offered. ''Some men say when they stare into my eyes, they feel so relaxed. Sleepy . . . sleepy . . . sleepy . . .''

Within minutes, Frank was zonked out.

Thank you, God!

The posthypnotic suggestion she gave Frank was to keep singing ''Nobody Knows the Trouble I Seen'' once he was awakened, and to refuse to come after her. Furthermore, he was to restrain his partner from coming after her, too. The sound of a door slamming would be the cue to come out of the trance.

Lord, she could lose her license for all these unethical uses of her hypnotherapy skills. Or would this be considered unethical? Well, it was a moot point, really.

Harriet worked quickly, binding Frank with the ties from the draperies, gagging him with a linen towel, then shoving him under the high bed, where she further incapacitated him by fastening his bound feet and hands to the top and bottom legs of the bed.

That done, Harriet took a deep breath and tried to slow her thundering heart. Charlie Mendel, the other guard, should be back soon. He'd gone down to the dining room to get their midday meal. Harriet was afraid to risk hypnotism again. So she waited behind the locked door for Charlie's return, the wooden stock of an empty rifle raised high in the air.

''What the hell!'' Charlie barely got out before Harriet slammed the stock down hard on his head, knocking him unconscious. She bound and gagged him the same as Frank.

Now what?

A plan. I need a plan.

Soon after that, Harriet left the telegraph office, where

she'd sent wires to Abel in New Orleans, James Baptiste in California and Blossom at Bayou Noir. She was covering all her bases, hoping someone would respond.

An hour later, Harriet, whose riding skills left much to be desired, was riding astride a mare that the gape-mouthed livery stable owner had assured her was gentle. He was gape-mouthed because she wore her red harlot dress, covered only with a thin, black lace shawl. She'd tied her money in a pouch under her panty hose as she'd done before, but this time Harriet wore a gun belt on her hips, and she carried a rifle in the side scabbard of the saddle. Her briefcase was tied to the back. Harriet headed out of the city in the direction of the Double B, which the liveryman assured her she couldn't miss if she kept riding south.

She was going to rescue Etienne, or die trying.

Brandon Briggs was an oilier version of J. R. Ewing in a nineteenth-century leisure-style cowboy suit. His graying brown hair and goatee were too perfectly styled with too much Macassar oil. His fancy boots carried too high a shine. The gold onyx ring on his left hand was too gaudy for a rancher, or a senator.

"Have a drink, Scarlett," Briggs advised with exaggerated concern. His clammy hand rested a second too long on her shoulder as he steered her forward through the hallway of his rambling mansion in the middle of nowhere. "I think you need a spot of brandy to settle your nerves after that ride."

Harriet had decided to pretend to be Etienne's sister, Scarlett Baptiste, to give her story a note of authenticity, just in case Briggs had some background information on Etienne and his family.

"Thank you," Harriet said, sinking into a leather wingback chair in the plush library. The walls were lined floor to ceiling with leather-bound first editions whose pages had probably never been slit.

As Briggs leaned against the fireplace mantel, he studied

her through crafty, hard-as-steel eyes. "Tell me again why you made that long ride from Houston, my dear."

Harriet hadn't wanted Briggs to know she'd come from Devil's Junction; so she'd ridden slightly west and south of Beaumont, coming to his ranch from the southwest. She probably wasn't fooling him, but she'd thought it was worth a try.

"I have to admit," she said, batting her eyelashes at him, "that I ran away from home. Again. My Papa is such a tyrant and so . . . so rigid in his way."

Briggs made a clucking sound of commiseration, but the whole time his eyes were riveted on the expanse of bare shoulder she exposed when her shawl "accidentally" slipped. Harriet wasn't comfortable in this vamp role, and hoped she wasn't making a real muddle of things.

Licking her lips, which really were dry with nervousness, Harriet continued, "I always wanted to visit my brother, Etienne, in Louisiana. Papa said he was such a wild ruffian, and, well, I figured Etienne would be more understanding of a young woman's . . . uh . . . needs." She put special emphasis on that last word, and was pleased to see Briggs's florid complexion burn a shade brighter. "But then when I got to Bayou Noir, I learned that he'd gone off to Texas. I didn't know what else to do but follow after him."

Briggs looked skeptical.

"But I didn't know he was a thief," Harriet added, taking a good swig of brandy to bolster her flagging courage. "Truly I didn't know about his horrible character, or I never would have come. Please let me apologize on behalf of my entire family for his stealing your gold. Papa would be horrified."

Briggs's skeptical demeanor softened a bit. "There's always one black sheep in every family."

Briggs seemed to accept her story about being Scarlett, but she didn't doubt that he considered her a gift horse . . . another wedge to use against Etienne. She would have to be careful.

Sandra Hill

"Now I guess I'll have to go back to California." She sighed. "I don't suppose you could have one of your men drive me to Houston?" There were dozens of cowhands and what she assumed were armed guards all over the sprawling ranch and the house itself. "I'm sure I could arrange transportation from there to California, but I don't think I could face riding there myself. The trip here about did me in."

"Certainly, my dear, but you must stay overnight. It would be best to leave early in the morning after you've rested."

Uh-oh! "Oh, I couldn't intrude on your hospitality. Nor that of Mrs. Briggs." *Oh, please, God, let there be a Mrs. Briggs.*

"My wife is in Washington," he told her with a smarmy leer. "But you've no need to fear for your . . . ah, reputation. There are maids aplenty about the house." The way he said *reputation* made it clear he didn't think she had one worth saving.

"Well, if you insist." She smiled weakly at him and batted her eyelashes again. God, her eyelids were beginning to hurt. How did those Southern belles do it?

"I'll have Lillian take you up to a guest room," he said, ringing a little bell. "You can refresh yourself; then we'll talk some more before dinner."

"You are so kind."

"I suppose you'd like to see your brother?" he asked, as if reading her mind.

Harriet forced herself to remain calm. There was a calculating glimmer in Briggs's beady eyes. She couldn't appear too anxious. What would be the best reaction to his question?

Harriet fluttered her fan. "If you insist, although I have to admit I'd like to clobber the fool. I'm ashamed to claim he's my brother right now, I truly am. I don't think we've ever had a thief in our family before."

Briggs relaxed, obviously pleased with her answer.

"Perhaps you can tell me later how you built up such a big ranch. From what I could see, the Double B is very impressive. Why, it must be twice the size of my papa's ranch in California."

Preening at her compliment, Briggs said, "Yes, I can see that you are in no way like that villainous brother of yours. I look forward to our conversation. You will join me for dinner, of course. Perhaps we'll find other areas of common interest." His gaze was directed at her breasts as he spoke.

In your dreams, mister. In your dreams.

It was late evening before Harriet got to visit Etienne. Holding lanterns, Briggs and a guard led the way out the back door and about five hundred yards to a small stone building with iron bars on the windows. The two wagons sat beside the miniature fortress, with open crates and Bibles strewn about.

Only one guard sat in the little anteroom before the iron-barred cell that presumably held Etienne. The guard was reading a dime novel by the light of an oil lamp. Harriet was afraid to examine her surroundings, fearful of appearing too anxious, and fearful of what she would see.

"Are you sure I should be here, Mr. Briggs?" Harriet twittered. "I know you insisted, but the smell is atrocious."

"It'll only take a second," Briggs soothed, then banged on the cell bars with the butt of his pistol. "Wake up, Baptiste. You got a visitor."

There was a stirring in the pile of rags in one corner, which, to Harriet's horror, turned out to be Etienne. He stood slowly, painfully, and blinked in the dim light from the two lanterns. A bone protruded against the skin of his left forearm where the arm had been fractured and left unset. His once beautiful face was a mass of purple and yellow bruises.

Harriet steeled herself not to show her distress.

"I brought your sister Scarlett to see you, Baptiste," Briggs announced with jovial cruelty. "Don'tcha wanna

353

Sandra Hill

come over here and show her what a brave brother she has? Ha, ha, ha!''

If Etienne doesn't kill this man, I will, Harriet vowed.

Etienne inhaled sharply on recognizing her. "Scarlett?"

Harriet tried to signal him with her eyes, but she wasn't sure he could see with his almost swollen shut. "Etienne Baptiste, I am ashamed of you. Stealin' gold from decent folks. Runnin' from the law. Why, Papa would whup you good if he was here, just like Mr. Briggs's men did.''

Etienne shuffled closer.

"What the hell are you doin' here, *Scarlett?*" Etienne gritted out through his split lips. That little speech caused the cuts to start bleeding again.

"I ran away from home, if you must know. I went to Bayou Noir, but I shoulda known I wouldn't be able to depend on you. You no-good rascal.''

"Go away, Scarlett," Etienne said. Harriet could see that her presence angered him. "I don't want your help.''

"Well, I'm not here to help, you ungrateful lout. You deserve whatever you get, although''—she put a beseeching hand on Briggs's arm—"although I think it would be decent Christian charity to set Etienne's broken arm.''

Briggs muttered something about it not making sense when he was going to die anyway, but Harriet moved closer, brushing against his chest with her breasts, now almost totally exposed by the shawl, which she let fall to the floor.

"Please," she coaxed.

There was a sharp inhale of breath in the room. She wasn't sure if it came from Briggs or Etienne.

A short time later, the guard went into the cell with Harriet. Briggs stayed outside the locked cell door, coward that he was. The guard allowed her to pull on Etienne's arm until the bone popped back into place. It must have been extremely painful for Etienne but he just glared angrily at her through his unforgiving blue eyes. As she was wrapping the arm with a splint and some clean linen cloths that

Briggs had reluctantly sent for, Etienne rasped out, "I don't want your help."

"Big deal!" She gave him back an equal glare.

"So you ran away from home, did you?" he asked, trying a different approach. "You always were a selfish little bitch. Just how far are you willing to go to attain your ends this time?"

Harriet knew he was asking in his convoluted way just what she was willing to do to save him.

"As far as I have to," she said, giving him a level stare.

His eyes did a quick survey of her harlot gown. "Don't do it," he whispered.

"Don't tell me what to do," she snapped. "You have no rights over me."

"I don't deserve it."

"That's for damn sure."

"You know what he wants from you," Etienne said in a rushed undertone when the guard stood and turned for a moment.

"Yes."

"And you'd do that?"

"Etienne, I would do tricks for the devil to save you."

"Don't," he repeated. "I'll hate you for it. I'll hate myself."

She shrugged, but her heart was breaking. He was telling the truth. In doing whatever she had to in order to save him, even if she succeeded, she would lose him. A lose-lose situation all around, for her.

"What're you two whisperin' about in there?" Briggs snarled.

"Oh, he was just asking me if I had a knife," Harriet said flippantly. "As if I would do anything to save him!"

After the cell was locked behind her, Harriet proceeded to leave with Briggs who looped an arm over her shoulder, becoming increasingly bold. She spun around suddenly. Addressing Etienne, who stood with his white-knuckled fists encircling the bars, watching her, she said, "Oh,

Etienne, I just thought of something. Do you remember that book you gave me once, a long time ago . . . something about body language?''

He moved his head up and down hesitantly.

Then, holding his eyes, she made a quick fluid gesture before Briggs or the guard could understand what she was doing. The fingertips of her right hand pointed to herself, pressed briefly over her heart, pointed to him, then made a circular motion near her head.

I love you, stupid.

Etienne's jaw clenched with anguish, but he nodded.

Harriet knew by late evening that she would have to kill Briggs, or have sex with him. Neither prospect was attractive.

The slimy senator had the tentacles of an octopus and the wet mouth of a fish. She'd felt both on various parts of her anatomy throughout the lengthy dinner and after-dinner drinks, and she knew she wouldn't be able to put him off much longer.

Harriet had stashed her guns in a small cave before entering Briggs's property, knowing she would be disarmed as soon as she encountered any of his guards. As expected, she was searched immediately. But she'd hidden a small, lethal knife in her hair, which she'd French-twisted and anchored with a number of bone hairpins. It hardly seemed equal to the challenge of fighting off Briggs, but a gun wouldn't have worked, either. Its sharp report would have alerted every man on the ranch.

She was in her bedroom now, presumably preparing herself for Briggs's late-night visit. *Yech!* She'd tried the eye-hypnotism trick on Briggs earlier, but it hadn't worked And her instincts told her not to try standing behind the door and bashing him over the head. Briggs was a creep but a smart one. And though he pretended to be taken in by her pretense, Harriet was sure he would be on his guard

When Briggs rapped on her door, she called out, "Come in."

Not surprisingly, he kicked in the door and waited a few seconds before entering. He beamed with pleasure when he saw her on the other side of the room, wearing only her leopard-print nightie, which Blossom had mended, and panties.

Etienne would have a fit if he knew.

"Well, well, well, aren't you just the sweetest picture," Briggs said as he moved closer to her, already removing his jacket and unbuttoning his shirt.

Fifteen minutes later, the naked, bug-eyed, evil man was flat on his back on the bed, a knife blade sticking out of his jugular vein, which gushed blood onto the pure white counterpane.

Harriet retched the contents of her stomach into a chamber pot. *Oh, God, oh, God! I actually killed a man. Not that he didn't deserve it. Oh, I will never forget how his horrible hands felt on me. Never! But he didn't get inside me. At least I have that. Oh, God!*

Finally, Harriet washed herself all over and dressed again. It was after midnight by now, and Harriet knew she'd have to proceed carefully. With tonight's full moon, her red dress would be instantly visible to any of the many nighttime guards.

Amazingly, Harriet made it to the guardhouse with little trouble, having to wait twice while guards passed by on their rounds before slipping outside. The jailer was luckily the same one as before. He stood abruptly, knocking over a chair when she entered. "What the hell—"

Harriet also noticed that Etienne rose to a sitting position, watching alertly. She ignored him totally, knowing she needed all her concentration.

Dropping down into a second chair near the desk where the guard had probably been snoozing, Harriet hurried to explain her presence before he kicked her out. "I couldn't sleep, and the only book I have with me I've read a hundred times. I noticed you were reading one of those dime novels, and I was just wondering if we might trade for the night.''

She'd startled him with that one. Before he could react, she pulled up her briefcase, flicked open the locks and pulled out *Sweet Savage Love*. ''This is my favorite novel. I think you'd like it. It's about this rogue who seduces all the women and kills lots of bad guys. What's yours about?''

The guard was younger than she'd realized . . . probably no more than twenty-five, although it was hard to say with his scruffy whiskers and unkempt clothing. He smiled tentatively and picked up a slim, well-worn edition of *The Wild Times of the Texas Kid*. ''Mine's about a rogue who seduces all the women and kills lots of bad guys.''

They exchanged a glance and laughed.

''Do you read a lot? By the way, what's your name? Mine's Scarlett.'' She chatted companionably, meanwhile letting her shawl slip and pulling out her black feather fan.

''I'm Zeke . . . Zeke Taylor,'' he said with a gulp. His eyes were transfixed by the motion of the fan, which swept in a slow, rhythmic pattern, like a metronome, back and forth, the feathers brushing lightly over the tops of her breasts. ''Yeah, I like to read. It gets lonely out here.''

''Oh, I understand loneliness,'' Harriet said. She talked and talked to him about books and inconsequential things. The whole time her voice droned in a monotone, the mesmerizing motion of the fan continuing to hold his attention. By the time she said, ''You have beautiful eyes, Zeke,'' he was already in a trance.

Then Harriet gave Zeke the posthypnotic suggestion. He would scratch his armpits when asked a question and make a blubbering sound . . . until he heard a cow moo.

Then Harriet turned on Etienne, who was braced up against the bars by now. He stared at her coldly, his judgmental eyes focused on her bruised lips and finger-marked shoulders, but especially the brush-burn over one breast.

She raised her chin defiantly. "You would have done the same for me."

"Would I?" he said with a sneer.

"Maybe not." Maybe he really didn't care for her as much as she cared for him. "Do you want to get out of here or not? Would you rather wallow in there with your self-righteousness?"

"I want out," he said without hesitation.

She fumbled with the key, then watched as he tied and gagged the guard, a difficult task with his sling.

"Where's Briggs?" Etienne asked finally, not looking her way as he buckled on the guard's gun belt.

At first, she didn't answer.

"Where's Briggs, Harriet?" Etienne asked again, this time straightening and tilting his head with suspicion.

"Dead." She stared Etienne in the eye, refusing to cower.

For only a brief second, she thought she saw a flicker of compassion pass over Etienne's harsh features. His gaze lowered to her hands, which were laced together tightly to still their trembling. Then his eyes came back up to her exposed bosom and the evidence of what she'd done for him.

He deliberately blanked his face. "Let's go. We have a lot of traveling to do if you're going to make that train home."

So I really am going home. Not to Bayou Noir, which I've come to regard as home, but back to the future.

She should have been glad.

She was devastated.

"You know, Etienne," she remarked sadly as they walked toward the doorway and he made a concerted effort not to so much as brush shoulders with her, "there's such a thing as cutting off your nose to spite your face."

"Is this another dumb-men joke?"

"No, it's not a joke. It's the story of your life."

* * *

359

"I didn't have sex with Briggs, you know," Harriet told him more than two weeks later. She sat on a window seat in the saloon of a New Orleans–bound steamboat. Her remark came out of the throbbing silence that had enveloped them ever since they'd made their remarkable escape from Briggs's ranch.

Three men had died in the process. They'd had to hide out in a cave for another ten days while he'd succumbed to the pain and fever resulting from his injuries and the further aggravation caused by riding a horse in the escape.

He refused to ponder how Harriet had cared for him during those rough days . . . how she'd managed to maneuver his much heavier weight, how she'd kept him clean when he was soiled, how she'd found food. If he didn't think, he wouldn't have to face some harsh facts. She'd killed a man. For him.

How the hell was he going to live with that fact the rest of his miserable life? She'd been willing to sacrifice herself in the most intimate, degrading manner to save him. He felt like the dregs of humanity . . . less than a man.

Harriet would leave him soon. It was what he wanted, of course. It would be best for her to depart from this dangerous time and place. Still, he felt as if a bone-crushing weight pressed against his heart.

"Did you hear what I said, Etienne?" Harriet repeated, glancing at him with a resigned acceptance of his taciturn mood. "I didn't actually do anything with Briggs."

"*Actually?*" He couldn't keep the bitterness from his voice.

She blushed, and he forced himself not to reach out his good hand and touch her heated cheek. Her hair was swept up into a prim knot atop her head, and she wore a dark blue, high-necked gown she'd purchased in Houston. He knew she was going to extra pains to counteract his memory of her lewd conduct. He knew his behavior made her shrivel with shame. He knew he was being a jackass. But he couldn't stop himself. Every time he closed his eyes he saw Harriet and Briggs, naked together.

"What you don't understand, Harriet," he said wearily, "is that it doesn't matter if you consummated your encounter with Briggs. You would have."

She sighed. "You're right. I would have."

"How did you kill Briggs anyhow? Talk him to death?" Almost immediately, he wished he could take the words back. *God, I can't seem to control my tongue. Why am I doing this to her? Look at that wounded-doe look in her eyes. I'm turning into a monster.*

Her lips trembled as she answered, "No, with a knife."

A knife? Oh, God, no! Now I'll have that image to haunt me forever, too. "Harriet, I'm . . . I'm sorry for what I said. About Briggs, I mean."

"You're sorry, are you? But only for what you said about Briggs, right? Spare me your sympathy and forgive me if I don't believe you." Opening her briefcase, Harriet slammed a copy of *Sweet Savage Love* into his lap. "You ought to read this sometime. You'd be surprised at the similarities in our stories."

He arched a brow in disbelief.

"Really. Even your imprisonment parallels that of Steve Morgan. And he misjudged Ginny's actions on his behalf, too."

"Oh? And did it all end happily ever after?" he mocked.

She refused to answer. "Read the book and find out."

He started to shove the novel back into her hands, then changed his mind, slipping it into his jacket pocket. "You'll be happier when you're away from here," he told her with more civility than he'd shown in days.

"Don't salve your conscience with those hokey sentiments." Harriet sliced him one of her old glowers of condescension. "I'm going to write a book about you when I get back, Etienne."

He shook his head at her. She just never gave up.

"The Dumbest Man in the World."

He couldn't argue with that.

Chapter Twenty-two

Harriet was an open wound of suffering, and the man slouching on the window seat of the steamboat beside her twiddling his thumbs was the knife. *Twiddling his thumbs? Talk about body language! Where's a thumbscrew when a girl needs one?* The brute didn't have to say a word for the knife to turn and draw new blood. His silence and condemning stares did the job very well, indeed.

Worst of all, Etienne was hurting, too. And Harriet cared more for his anguish than her own.

Harriet was resigned to leaving the past and Etienne. He hadn't asked her to stay, and she told herself she didn't want to anyway. But she'd hoped to have healed Etienne before she left. Now he appeared more withdrawn and bitter than ever before. Her "meddling" had increased his problems, not solved them, according to Etienne.

"I'm not going to New Orleans," Etienne said abruptly.

Harriet jolted to alertness and almost banged her head on the window against which she'd been leaning. It was the first he'd spoken to her in more than an hour. He'd been sitting next to her, long legs stretched out and crossed at the ankles, reading *Sweet Savage Love,* to the accompaniment of an occasional snicker or raised eyebrow. When he wasn't twiddling his thumbs, that was.

She glanced sideways and saw him rubbing his left arm in its bandaged splint. A doctor in Galveston had examined him two days before and said the break should heal perfectly, thanks to her efforts. Etienne hadn't even bothered to thank her.

She homed in on his sudden comment. "What do you mean . . . you're not going to New Orleans?"

"We'll be in Morgan City tomorrow. I've decided to get off, and go up by pirogue to Bayou Noir. I want to check on Saralee."

Harriet nodded, but a wild hammering began in her head and resonated throughout her body.

Tomorrow? He's going to leave me tomorrow, and I'll never see him again. Will he kiss me good-bye, or just get off the boat and never look back? Oh, God! I'm shattering to pieces inside. I can't let him know. I can't. "Cain told you in that wire waiting in Galveston that Saralee was fine, that he'd taken her to Blossom after Abel and those government agents rescued them at the warehouse." *Is that me talking so calmly? Amazing!*

"I want to see for myself."

She could understand that. She felt the same. "Will you stay at Bayou Noir?"

"I doubt it. Now that the gold is lost . . ." The stubborn goat didn't need to say any more. That was another thing he no doubt blamed on her meddling. Because of her telegraphed message, Abel had managed to remove the gold-laden caskets from the warehouse and had attempted to take them by flatboat to Bayou Noir. In the midst of a violent storm, the glorified raft had tipped over, and the gold now rested in its eternal burial place—the mudflat of a bottomless bayou stream. It would seem that President Grant wouldn't be obliged to give Etienne his money without the goods.

"Your train to . . . well, your train back to Chicago won't be leaving New Orleans for another twelve days," Etienne said in a raspy voice. "If you want to come to Bayou Noir first, you can."

Harriet's eyes shot wide.

Etienne avoided her gaze as he spoke, and she couldn't tell what he meant. He'd resumed the blasted twiddling. Was he saying . . . ?

"I think Saralee will be distraught if she doesn't see you one more time, don't you?"

Oh, so it was concern for Saralee that prompted his offer. Harriet's spirits deflated, but not totally. The separation wouldn't come tomorrow then. She had a few more days to get accustomed to the concept of a life without Etienne.

Etienne put her book back into his jacket pocket and rubbed a hand over his forehead, closing his eyes. He still had bruises, but they were almost healed now. Even his arm didn't have to be in a sling all the time. With time and rest and Cain's medical attention, he would soon be as good as new. On the outside, at least.

"Do you have a migraine?" she asked when he continued to massage his brow.

"Harriet, I always have a headache lately." The implication was that she was the cause.

Harriet winced. She wanted to help, not hurt him. "Etienne, I can alleviate your migraine if only you'd let—"

"Like you did with the guard back at Briggs's ranch? Put me in a trance?" he snapped. Still no eye contact, just twiddle, twiddle, twiddle.

"Oh, that was so mean of you!" she cried and turned away from him, hiding her tears. Harriet couldn't be sure if she wept for the pain caused by his insults, or for the horrendous pain looming on the horizon when she left him for good.

Even if he was a randy, mean old billy goat, she was going to miss him terribly. Luckily, she'd have a few more days to prepare herself and perhaps accomplish the goals of this time-travel fiasco.

Okay, God, Harriet prayed, *I've got a reprieve here. How about some help? A little heavenly intervention could go a long way in shaking this jerk's boat. You sent me here. If you want success, you gotta give me some clues. What's the plan? Huh?*

Just then, the pilothouse whistle blew shrilly. The steamboat vibrated a bit as the captain slowed the engines for passage over a low sandbar. Etienne, off balance because of the sling, rocked forward and almost fell off his seat.

Rocked? Okay, so it was a steamboat, and not Etienne's emotional boat. Who was quibbling? Harriet smiled as Etienne straightened himself.

With a flash of insight she remembered a legend that a bell rang every time God performed a miracle. Or was that when an angel got its wings? *Whatever! Bell, whistle, miracle, angel, big difference!* She considered this a divine sign. God was about to perform a miracle.

The goat had better hold on to his boat.

By late that night, Harriet had given up on miracles.

She sat alone in her cabin, crying. What had happened to the old Harriet . . . the self-confident professional woman who never engaged in bouts of self-pity? The one who tackled any job with gusto? The one who never said never?

She'd fallen in love, that was what. And love had made her weak, exactly as she'd always feared. Just like her mother. Yep, love put a chink in the old armor, for sure. How was a lady knight to go off to battle with a hole in her metal suit?

Harriet smiled at her mental analogy. *Geez, I'm a woman of the nineties. I'm intelligent. Power suits, suits of armor . . . the same thing! A little chewing gum in the weak links and I should be as good as new.* Harriet sat up straighter on her narrow bed. That wasn't a bad idea, really. A battle plan.

The target? Etienne, of course. He'd been sleeping in a separate cabin next to hers, declining even to stay in the same room with her. *The coward!* He was gambling in the upper saloon right now, but it was after midnight. He should return soon.

Weapons? Harriet had a gun and a knife in her briefcase, but she needed different tools for Etienne. Where was a battering ram when a girl needed one?

Be creative, Harriet. Think like the smart woman you are, not the blind bimbo you've been the past few days.

She laughed suddenly, clicking open her briefcase. In one hand, she held up the silk leopard-print nightie, and in the other, a pair of remarkably intact panty hose. She planned to write a letter of commendation to Christian Dior's hosiery department when she returned home.

Wiping away her remaining tears, Harriet threw in a quick prayer. *Please, God, help me break through the defenses this hardheaded man has erected around his emotions. He's a prisoner in his own castle of bitterness and fear. Help me demonstrate that only love can free him, especially love for himself.*

One last thing, God. Please don't let me fall in the moat.

Etienne couldn't avoid his bed any longer. Or the dreams. Gambling didn't help. Reading that blasted novel didn't help. Drinking didn't help. Somehow, some way, Harriet had exorcised her dreaded sexual fantasy dreams. And passed them on to him.

He'd become Steve Morgan aka Etienne Baptiste and he was having a powerful good time every night with his nemesis, Ginny Brandon aka Harriet Ginoza. A very unsatisfying replica of the real thing. Not that he'd tell Harriet. Oh, no! She'd dive right in, psychoanalyzing him. Talk, talk, talk. Force him to think. Make his nonstop headaches even worse.

What had possessed him to suggest she accompany him to Bayou Noir one last time? Why hadn't he let her part from him tomorrow? A clean break? No loose ends?

He hated her for what she'd done with Briggs, or almost done. Perhaps there was a bit of the harlot in all women, even her . . . or especially her. But stronger, more frightening emotions fought to overcome that hate. Stupidity, that was what it must be. Only a thoroughly stupid man would willingly jump in the lion's den, waiting for the cat to strike. And Harriet would tear him to shreds before she left Bayou Noir, he just knew it.

Making his way along the corridor to his cabin, he hesitated before her door. Another dumb notion occurred to him. Maybe he should knock on the lion's door, walk right in and surrender without a fight.

No, he decided. *I'm not that dumb.*

Harriet had drunk a glass of bourbon from the bottle in Etienne's room to reinforce her courage before she finally heard his key turning in the lock. Taking a deep breath, she stepped back into the corner and waited.

At first, Etienne stumbled around in the dark. The only light came from a small window on the deckside wall where she braced herself woozily. She sensed, rather than saw, him remove his jacket, drop his gun belt onto a built-in cabinet, then sit down on a chair and take off his boots. *Thud! Thud!* With a loud yawn, he stood and padded over to a bedside table, lighting the oil lamp with a sulfur match. Instantly, a yellowish glow filled the room. Yawning again, he slipped his left arm out of its sling and rotated his shoulder socket. The broken arm was still splinted and bandaged from elbow to wrist, but he didn't need the sling all the time now. He unbuttoned his shirt and pulled it from the waistband of his trousers.

He was so damn handsome. Even clothed. Even from the back. Wide shoulders, well-defined muscles in his arms, slim waist and hips, long legs, and, of course, all that wonderful territory in between. Much of his skin, which she expected to see soon, was covered with bruises not yet healed from Briggs and his ruffians.

Then he turned.

"Holy hell!" Etienne exclaimed, seeing Harriet for the first time on the other side of the little chamber. He recoiled in surprise and hit the back of his head against a tall post on the narrow bed. But then, every time he was around Harriet, he sustained one kind of injury or another. As he straightened, he got his first good glimpse of her, and his jaw dropped practically to his kneecaps. "Holy hell!" he said again.

She wore her leopard-print chemise and waist-high, sheer hose, plus she'd added a gun belt slung low on her hips for an extra touch. In one hand she held a pistol and in the other a knife. *Sacrebleu! Guns and a chemise? Is it some kind of sporting house outfit? Like the jockey suit he'd seen a diminutive whore wear one time? But, no, that prostitute had wielded a whip, not a gun.* "What are you doin' here, Harriet?"

"Laying siege."

"Huh? On what?" *Really, I must give the woman credit. She always manages to shock me.*

"You."

Me? "Me? Trust me, Harriet, this is not a good idea." *Actually, it's looking more and more like a good idea, and that's the problem. I knew I should have left her back in Galveston. Maybe I can slip back to the gambling tables. If I can peel my eyes off her breasts, that is. Lord, does she know that garment is nearly transparent? And surely, surely, she didn't come out on the deck from her cabin attired in so little.* "Besides, I have a piercing headache," he added. *Merde! That was such a dumb excuse, even for a dumb man.*

"Maybe your head hurts so much because your halo's on too tight," she sniped.

Insults now? "Are you saying I'm self-righteous?"

"If the shoe fits, Mr. Holier-than-Thou . . ."

"Very good, Harriet. Ha, ha, ha! Now let me tell you one. Do you know the difference between a dumb woman and a brick?"

She raised her chin haughtily, refusing to answer.

"When you lay a brick, it doesn't follow you around forever."

Her nostrils flared on a quick intake of breath.

I am lower'n a pig's chin on market day. Since when do I get pleasure from hurting women? "You're not smiling, Harriet. I thought you appreciated a good joke." *Now I'm telling dumb-women jokes. I need a drink.* He spied his bottle of bourbon on the other side of the room; it was no longer full. *Wonderful! She's drunk on top of everything else.* "Maybe you didn't understand the joke. I don't want you."

Etienne couldn't believe the words that spewed from his mouth, like vomit. He tunneled the fingers of one hand through his hair and gripped his throbbing skull. *Beast, beast, beast, beast . . .* he berated himself to the agonizing pounding of his headache.

She flinched. "Etienne, don't," she said softly. But she didn't back down.

Etienne had gambled with the best, and he just knew that Harriet was betting all her cards on the hope that he really did want her. She was bluffing, pure and simple, but, damn, he had to admire her nerve. And, damn, he really did want her.

"I'm calling the shots here, buster. I'll decide on the battle plan, not you." Her bottom lip trembled as she threw out the brave challenge.

He shook his head in awe. If the South had engaged a few Harriets on its side, the war might have turned out differently. "Battle plan? Siege? Where's the battering ram, darlin'? Cause I'm not giving in without a fight." He sliced her a condescending smirk.

"Call me crazy, *darlin'*, but is that a battering ram I see between your legs?"

He gasped at her vulgarity, but inside he toasted her audacity. "Harriet, get out of here." He wearied of the contest and feared the cruel demons that had overtaken his tongue. He moved toward her purposefully, intending to toss her out the door.

"Stop right there," she said, raising the gun. "I'm freaking out here, and I can't predict what I might do."

I can, honey. And you're about to land flat on your rear, back in your own compartment. "That revolver isn't worth a pisshole in the snow if I decide to take it from you." *And it's probably not loaded.*

"I warned you." She raised the gun high, closing her eyes and pressing the trigger.

He ducked his head at the loud report. "Harriet!"

She'd been aiming for the ceiling, but what she hit was a pineapple spindle atop one of the bedposts behind him. He could tell she was as amazed as he was.

"You're crazy," he observed, halting his advance on her.

"Yep. Now, do as I say. First, take off your shirt."

Take off my shirt? he echoed silently. "Harriet," he protested with a whoosh of disbelief.

She raised the pistol again.

"Whatever you say, sweetheart." He did as ordered, wondering if Harriet suffered from strange mood swings before her monthly time. She probably wouldn't appreciate his asking. So he raised an eyebrow in question.

"Undo your trousers, slowly, then drop them to the floor."

He hesitated only a second, then complied. He was no longer weary of the contest. And he didn't give a damn about her mood.

"The socks, too."

When he stood there, naked as a plucked chicken, about

six feet from her, she wavered, as if not sure what to do next.

"What's the point of this . . . seige?" he asked thickly. His "drawbridge" was certainly rising to the occasion.

"Forceful seduction."

"I beg your pardon?"

"I'm going to forcefully seduce you. I don't like the "Happy Trails" tune you've been playing, ditching me in your dust. Now I'm calling the tune, and you're gonna dance, I promise you."

A grin tugged at his lips, but he managed to hold it at bay. "Do you have any idea the size of battle required to seduce me?"

He could tell she wasn't sure if he meant that he would be easy or hard. All she'd have to do was to drop her eyes a few feet and she'd see his "drawbridge." And she called men dumb!

"Now take one of those socks and tie your right arm to that post at the bottom of the bed."

He obeyed, intrigued now and wondering just how far she'd carry the game. He stood still while she helped him slide his broken arm back in its sling. Still not satisfied, she made him stand against the bed frame at its bottom, thighs parted, and she tied his left foot to the base of the other bedpost.

"Satisfied?" He tugged with his right arm and left foot to show he was secured.

"Hardly."

He grinned.

"Tell me what you'd like me to do," she urged, putting her gun aside and moving up close.

Oh, sweetheart, don't ever give a man an open invitation like that. "Untie me."

"Besides that." She ran the tip of her tongue over her lips—a nervous gesture.

You could start with your tongue. "This is your battle, not mine."

371

"Okay, then." She dropped her knife to the floor and raised herself on tiptoes. Fingering the edges of his hair, she cupped one side of his jawline tenderly. Gliding her tongue along the seam of his lips till he sighed, she molded her mouth against his with changing moist patterns.

"Harder," he rasped out. "Inside. Give me your tongue."

She smiled against his mouth and nipped his bottom lip in chastisement. "Easy, babe, easy. Not yet."

He rewarded her with a soft moan.

Taking all the time in the world, she kissed the curve of his neck, his inner elbow and the soft flesh of his wrist on the upraised arm. His eyes followed her every movement mesmerized. She whispered her admiration for all his various body parts. When she rubbed her silk-clad breasts against his chest, abrading his nipples, he moaned.

"I'm seduced," he said with a raspy laugh. "Untie me now."

"Oh, no, no, no! That's not the way forceful seduction works. You have to be brought to your knees, figuratively speaking, that is," she said, and did, in fact, drop to the floor on her own knees. "You have to be brought to the point of begging for release."

"I'm begging you to release me now."

"Tsk-tsk! Not that kind of release."

"Oh." Then, "Are you sure there are all these rigid rules for forceful seduction?"

"I'm sure," she purred, as she caressed his toes and the arches of his feet, then the backs of his knees. "Very rigid."

He sucked in a deep draft of air.

"Ah! The backs of your knees are extra sensitive, aren't they?" she murmured, and went back to those knees over and over as she kissed his navel, his hard abdomen, his inner thighs.

He couldn't speak.

Then, still kneeling, she peered up at him and back to

the source of all his pleasurable anguish, which stood out in rampant need from his body. She traced a forefinger lightly along the engorged veins and he jerked involuntarily. She did the same with the tip of her tongue and he said through gritted teeth, *"Mon Dieu!"* When she put her fingers to the backs of his knees, fluttering them like birds' wings, and took him into her mouth, all of him, his legs buckled and he sank to the edge of the bed.

"I'm calling a cease-fire here before you get caught in the reverse artillery." His body went stiff then as an unwelcome image flicked through his mind. "Did you do that for Briggs?"

Harriet recoiled, but she refused to answer. "What do you want me from me, Etienne? Blood? You got it. Do you enjoy torturing me with accusations? What I did with Briggs has nothing to do with us. Nothing. But punish me if it makes you feel better." She lifted her hands in a hopeless gesture.

"Were you aroused with Briggs?" *Oh, God, where did that question come from?*

A small cry escaped her parted lips.

The devil in his head replied, "I take that for a 'yes.' "

Her eyes went huge and filled with the diamond sparkle of tears. Shamed, she folded both arms over her chest and rocked from side to side. He could tell she was about to flee.

Reacting instinctively, he slipped his broken arm from its sling and grasped her wrist. Pain shot like a lance from his splinted forearm to his shoulder, but he wouldn't let go of her struggling body. With monumental effort, he drew her closer and ordered, "Reach down and pick up the knife."

She did, sobbing loudly now.

"Cut me loose," he grated out, "and stop squirming unless you want to reset a broken arm."

She immediately stilled, glancing at his splinted arm.

He was touched to the core that, even now, she cared more for his well-being than her own.

When he was free, he fell backward on the mattress, taking her with him. First he held her on top of his body; then he rolled over to the side. Huge tears streamed from her liquid eyes and she held a breath every few moments in an effort to stifle her sobs.

"Shhh," he soothed, shimmying up to the center of the mattress and compelling her to come with him. "I didn't mean what I said."

"Yes, you did. You'll never forget about me and Briggs, no matter what I say. You're a pig, but an honest pig. Don't stop now." She sniffled and once again tried to turn away from his embrace. "Let me go. You were right. I shouldn't have come."

"I changed my mind," he said, wiping her tears with the edge of the linen sheet.

"You did?" She hiccoughed.

He nodded. "Harriet, I'm not myself these days. I don't mean the filth that pours from my mouth. It's like the connection between my brain and my tongue has been severed."

She put fingertips over his mouth to halt further words. "I understand," she said softly.

He wished he did.

Then she grimaced. "Gawd, I can't even do a forceful seduction right."

"Oh, I don't know about that." He chuckled, rolling to his back and hauling her half onto his chest so that his injured arm could lie flat on the mattress while his right arm caressed her shoulders, her waist, her buttocks. "Seems to me the seige was more than a victory. You got the 'drawbridge' up, at least."

She blinked at him in confusion, then laughed, peeking with mock horror down below.

"Aren't you going to finish the seige? Take the castle?"

Narrowing her eyes at him, she asked, "What'd you have in mind?"

"Well, I'm a crippled man," he whined, raising his splint with exaggerated weakness. "I guess I'm at your mercy."

She brightened. "I take no hostages."

"Overconfidence has been the downfall of some of the greatest military commanders. Beware of ambushes." He wiggled his eyebrows for emphasis.

"One thing first, Etienne," she said, throwing one leg over his waist and straddling his stomach. "I want you to know why I came tonight."

Talk? She's going to talk. Now? "Harriet, honey, please. When we talk . . . when *I* talk . . . we always end in an argument."

She slid her bottom lower over that oversensitized evidence of his arousal and talked, ignoring his advice. "I came because I couldn't bear to have our relationship end with you hating me."

"I don't . . . hate . . . you," he said in a strangled moan. While she'd been speaking, she slid even lower, sitting on his thighs now. And she was examining his "drawbridge" with delicate, fingering strokes. He arched upward, trying desperately to withstand the oncoming waves of pleasure those mere strokes evoked.

"Yes, you do hate me. Your revulsion is evident," she insisted as she continued to fondle him. "But at the same time, you feel this guilt. There's no need for repression with me, though. Don't think I'm under the delusion that—"

He regarded her with amusement. "Harriet, I swear, you know must know every '-ion' word in the dictionary. Is that a prerequisite for being a mind doctor? But I know some even better ones."

She raised a brow at him.

"Stimulat-ion. Erect-ion. Fornicat-ion. Satisfact-ion."

She gave him a playful slap on the chest and then, unmercifully, prattled on. It was probably part of her assault plan. "Believe me, it hurts to admit that I love you and that my love will never be reciprocated."

Why, oh why do women have to talk at a time like this? With a rumbling growl, he spread his thighs wide and dragged her upward so she lay on top of him. "Would you like to see my sword, m'lady soldier?"

"Only if you want to see my sheath."

"Enough conversation, sweetheart," he pleaded. "It's time for the drawbridge and the moat to come together."

"Oh." She appeared dazed as he bucked upward, imbedding himself inside her to the hilt. Her tight folds clenched him spasmodically in welcome.

"Oh" just about says it all. "Harriet," he rasped out and silenced any further talk with his openmouthed kiss.

It was the shortest seige in history.

The battle wasn't over yet, though. Throughout the night she tried to talk, and he conducted an admirable campaign of keeping her too busy to think, let alone lecture him on all his admittedly numerous faults.

She must have told him that she loved him a hundred times.

He never said the words once, although he thought them. He would never tell her of his suspicions that he was falling in love with her because that would change the outcome of this entire bizarre drama he'd been thrown into with her.

Or was it that he feared that saying the words aloud would change nothing? Oh, that would be the cruelest blow of all to him. To tell a woman for the first time that he loved her, and have her leave him nonetheless.

Harriet was going away, to her time, of that there was no doubt. She had a life there. A successful career.

What if he asked her to stay? Would she?

No, no, no! He would never pressure her to make that kind of decision. All she wanted and valued was in another world. She said she loved him, but it was only that he was her anchor in this time-travel. She'd forget him soon enough.

How about him going back with her?

Etienne immediately discarded that possibility. What would he do there? Be a parasite, living off Harriet's fame and fortune? And what about Saralee?

He could picture the scenario. Harriet parading him around on her lecture tours as an example of an MCP. Dumb Man Extraordinaire.

All these thoughts went through Etienne's mind as Harriet dozed at his side. He smiled against her hair and whispered, "I love you, stupid." To his amazement, he felt a tear creep down his cheek.

He woke her up then. She'd have plenty of time to sleep when she left the past. And this was the only night he would have her with him. He knew that he couldn't risk making love with her again after this night or he'd never be able to let her go.

Three days later, Etienne's whole world rocked, then came crumbling apart as he got his first view of Bayou Noir plantation.

How could his home have changed so dramatically in the short time he'd been away? The oak alley had been cleared of all the encroaching swamp vegetation, leaving a clear lawn from the stream where he'd just tied his pirogue all the way to the main house. The mansion was still in a state of disrepair, but broken shutters had been reattached, the roof repaired, and a first coat of whitewash applied to the exterior. A bonfire blazed behind the house, where workers seemed to be throwing pieces of broken furniture and the remains of the *garçonniére*. Off in the distance, the sugarcane had been harvested and field hands were hard at work planting a winter crop. There was an air of renewal about the place.

He closed his eyes, then opened them again, to see if he might be dreaming. He wasn't.

Etienne tilted his head with puzzlement at the tall man who walked out onto the gallery from inside the house. He looked vaguely familiar, lean and muscular, with black hair mixed with strands of gray. When the man lifted his chin defiantly and stared right back at him, Etienne groaned.

My father.

Thoroughly confused, he turned to Harriet in question.

She struggled out of the pirogue with the help of a hired hand he'd employed from down the bayou to row the boat. She'd actually believed he would let her, a woman, paddle the pirogue since he was incapacitated by his sling. As if he would sit in a boat with her wielding a paddle!

She shifted nervously from foot to foot, glancing everywhere but at him.

"Harriet?" he prodded.

Her face was a guilty shade of pink, and not from the sun that she'd been complaining about all morning.

"You! You're responsible for this, aren't you? You brought my father here," he accused her savagely, taking her by the forearms and shaking her. When he saw that tears were brimming in her eyes, he dropped his hands and paced in front of her on the bank.

She'd been near tears for days, ever since she'd awakened in her own bed, alone, in the steamboat, where he'd deposited her sleeping form after their extraordinary night of lovemaking. She hadn't been able to understand his resistance to sleeping with her again, and he'd refused to explain. Sometimes the fewer words said the better. But now she'd forced a reaction from him.

"This time your meddling has gone beyond the limits of human decency. How could you do this to me?"

"Etienne, I sent a letter to your father when I feared for your safety. I thought it was best. Can't you see—"

"No! Can't you see that I don't want you meddling in my life? Can't you see that I don't want you in my life at all?" *I don't mean it, I don't mean it. I desperately want you in my life,* he said silently, but his tongue was too twisted with fury to let the sentiments escape.

She inhaled sharply and staggered backward, clutching her stomach.

There was no more time for words then. He would have to apologize later.

"Papa." Saralee came running forward and threw herself into his arms. "We was so worried about you. Me and Blossom made all your favorite foods, every day this week. Abel ran away to Nawleans 'cause his mama was comin'. And, oh, I'm so happy you came home safe." She gave him a big wet kiss on the mouth, then leaned over to give one to Harriet, too. Before he could blink, she skipped off with Lance trotting slowly behind. Was this the same shy daughter he'd first met less than a month ago?

"*Etienne!*" A young girl of about fifteen came barreling down the incline toward them, blond curls blowing askew, her green cambric gown billowing in her wake. Before he had a chance to digest that it was his sister Melanie, whom he hadn't seen since she was five, she was hugging him warmly, mindful of his one arm in a sling.

It was hard for him to understand all her jabbering about school and suspensions and piano lessons and what a brute he was for never writing, because by now his other brothers and sisters surrounded him. Scarlett, a stunning brunette with creamy skin, wore a riding outfit that showed off a form that must drive the young men of California mad. She was equally exuberant in her welcome, but she chastised him for never inviting her to come visit him at Bayou Noir. "I've waited all these years to marry because I've wanted to meet a Southern gentleman," she confessed. "Ah've even been practicin' a So'then drahl."

Then there was Rhett, twenty-four years old now and bearing a strong resemblance to his mother Selene, even with his dark mustache. Rhett shook his hand, then pulled Etienne into a bear hug from which he couldn't escape if he'd wanted to. "Where've you been hidin', you dumb son of a bitch?" He'd been fourteen when Etienne had left and was his closest friend, next to Cain and Abel. "It was real

Sandra Hill

nice of you to leave me at the ranch to help Papa while you went gallavantin' all these years.''

The familial assault continued. A more somber Ashley, who at twenty was studying law at Harvard, came up then. He wore a staid suit and sharply pressed shirt. Etienne made the first move, looping an arm over his brother's shoulders and squeezing him against his side. "You look as if you could use a little Loo-zee-anna sunshine to melt your starch, Ash,'' he teased.

His brother grinned at him. "And you look as if you could use a little starch to iron out your rough edges.''

Tara, at nineteen and already the mother of two sons, wagged her finger in his face. "You are the most despicable beast to have stayed away so long. Make sure you don't ever do it again.'' Then she kissed him and introduced him to her husband Harrison Beech, a farmer, who nodded and quickly ran off after his rambunctious two-year-old twins, who were heading for the stream.

There was nothing left to do then but go up to the house. With a heavy heart, Etienne moved slowly upward, dragging one reluctant foot after the other.

At first, his father merely glared at him. Lord, how he remembered that glare! When he was five and bared his bottom at Selene. When he was nine and showed his private parts to Ellie Mae Morgan. When he was twelve and . . .

His father stepped off the porch and began to move toward him. The glare disappeared, replaced with a strange, vulnerable softness. If he didn't know better, Etienne could swear there were tears in his father's eyes. Or were the tears in his own eyes?

Halfway up the oak alley they both stopped, although there were still a good three paces between them. His father had aged these past ten years. Wrinkles bracketed his eyes and mouth. Dark shadows etched his eyes.

"You look like hell,'' his father growled, taking in his cuts and bruises and broken arm.

"Likewise,'' he growled back.

The silence grew like a palpable presence between them. Finally, Etienne started, "You shouldn't have come—"

"I shouldn't have come," his father said at the same time.

More silence.

"Your . . . ah, friend . . . Harriet said I was too rigid in my ways," his father said, clearing his throat and wiping the back of his hand across his eyes in a surreptitious sweep. "She had the temerity to say that I have a perfection complex."

Etienne fought a grin. "She would say something like that."

"But she's wrong. Surely you never thought you had to earn my affection, as she suggested."

"Papa, don't do this," Etienne protested, fearing where this conversation was headed.

His father put up a hand as if his words had to be said. "Surely, Etienne, even when we were at each other's throats, you knew"—his voice broke—"you knew that I . . . that I loved you."

"Damn!" Etienne muttered and scraped the toe of one boot in the dirt, unable to look his father in the eye. He really, really couldn't handle this. *Damn you, Harriet! Damn you for your meddling! Damn you for backing me into a corner!*

His father's fingers dug into his upper arms, even the one in a sling, obliging him to make eye contact. "You didn't know, did you?" his father cried. "Harriet was right. You didn't know that I loved you unconditionally."

Then his father hauled him into his arms. "You silly boy, how could you have ever doubted my love?"

Etienne couldn't answer. *Because you doubted me,* he wanted to say, but it seemed, unbelievably, so unimportant now. Tears ran down his face, and he feared if he spoke, his words would come out as a sob. There was such a groundswell of emotion building and building inside him. One slip and the floodtide would come rushing out.

"Do you forgive me, Etienne?" his father asked finally, drawing back to study him.

"Me forgive you? Can you forgive me?" Moving backward, Etienne put a hand to his forehead and began to weep, loudly. His shoulders shook and he couldn't control the trembling of his lips. Embarrassed, he tried to pull away from his father's arms, which wrapped around him tightly. His father wouldn't budge.

"No, my son, I will never, ever let you go now that I've found you again. Never."

A short time later, they walked up to the house, arms hooked casually over each other's shoulders. Selene and Reba and Rufus and Iris waited on the gallery to greet him, as well.

"How could two men be so dumb?" his father wondered aloud just before they arrived at the house.

Etienne shrugged, then chuckled. "Harriet would probably have a dumb-men joke to make at this point."

"I already got one of her dumb-men jokes in her letter."

"Well, be prepared. She has dozens of them. Dozens."

Only then did he recall how furious he'd been with Harriet. And that he hadn't seen her since that moment when he'd shaken her and told her he didn't want her in his life. In a panic, he scanned the plantation grounds and the galleries of the house.

Harriet was gone.

Chapter Twenty-three

On October 28, 1870, Harriet Ginoza sat in a private compartment of a New Orleans train bound for Chicago. For the first time ever, a person would be able to travel by rail from Louisiana to Illinois without interrupting the journey to take a steamboat. The passenger list had been filled days before. Outside on the railway platform, a brass band played in celebration of the momentous event.

Numb and beyond crying—she'd done more than enough of that the past nine days—Harriet stared straight ahead. Filled with an overwhelming sense of loss, Harriet was oblivious to the pomp surrounding her. She just wished the train would get started so that she could begin to get her life back in order again.

I don't want you in my life at all. Etienne's words rang in her head and stabbed at her heart. She would never forget them.

There was absolutely no doubt in her mind that once the train passed onto the bridge . . . at the exact spot where her 1997 train had derailed . . . she'd be back in the future. Life

Sandra Hill

would go on for her in 1997, and for those she'd left behind in the past.

She felt only a slight twinge of guilt over her impromptu departure from Bayou Noir. After Etienne had issued his cruel declaration to her and been engulfed in the warmth of his reunited family, Harriet had exchanged a few quick words with Blossom, then asked the black man who'd rowed them from Morgan City to take her to New Orleans.

No one had even noticed her leaving.

And no one had come after her.

Harriet hadn't gone to Simone's when she reentered the Crescent City, although she knew that Abel was still there. Instead, she'd rented a room in a small hotel near the train depot, waiting for the days to pass in increasing misery.

She should be happy to have this nightmare end. She should be looking forward to all her modern conveniences. She should already be planning the new books that would practically write themselves.

If only he'd said he loved me. If only he'd asked me to stay. She obsessed endlessly with this "if only" game, but the bottom line was that she truly didn't know what she would have done in that circumstance. And it was a moot point because what he'd said, instead, was, *I don't want you in my life at all.*

She'd left a letter for him at her hotel, to be mailed after her departure. Over and over, she'd rewritten the words, wanting them to be just right. In the end, she'd settled for a lighthearted message:

Etienne:
By the time you get this note, I'll be gone. Good-bye, my love. I will never forget you. Never.
I'm going to visit Bayou Noir plantation someday, if it still exists. If your ghostly self is floating about, do something really dumb, and I'll know you're there. Like blow in my ear. Or dangle a snake in my face.
I suspect you'll be feeling bad about your parting

384

*shot at me. Don't. You never had to say the words. I
know you care. Just not enough. And that's okay.
There's no divine law that says love given has to be
returned in equal measure.*

*At one time, I thought I was sent back in time to
help heal your inner pain. How presumptuous of me!
You made me grow, Etienne. I'm a better person for
having known you. And I can only hope that I influ-
enced you in a positive way, too. But even if I didn't,
my journey was a success for all it taught me. And I
will never, ever regret the experience.*

This letter is starting to sound like a lecture.

I love you. That's all. I love you.

Harriet

"All Aboard!" the conductor yelled as the steam engine
blew clouds of black, sooty smoke all over the station area.

Harriet planned to lie down and sleep once the train was
on its way. When she awakened, she fully expected to be
back in her century. But first, she took one last look out
the window at 1870 New Orleans.

Then she did a double take.

Lined up along the platform, waving and sobbing, were
James and Selene Baptiste, all of Etienne's brothers and
sisters, Cain and Abel and Simone, even Blossom. Oh, my
God! How did Blossom get to New Orleans in her condition? Everyone was waving at her and yelling, "Good-
bye," the men with tears glistening in their eyes, the
women crying openly.

For me? Harriet questioned with confusion. Then she
began to cry, too. And once she let one whimper out, the
floodtide of sorrow broke loose.

"Well, Lordy, darlin', is that how you greet your hus-
band-to-be?"

Harriet jerked upright and saw Etienne leaning against
the frame of her open compartment door. He wore a dark

suit, crisp white linen shirt, and new spit-shined leather boots—"widow-bait" clothes, Abel would call an outfit like this. His dark hair had been recently trimmed and parted down the center. On his nose was perched a pair of wire-rimmed spectacles.

He grinned roguishly at her inspection.

At his side stood Saralee, equally dolled up in a blue calico gown with tons and tons of white lace ruffles, white stockings and black patent-leather shoes. A huge blue bow tied her hair back off her face. With one hand, Saralee held tightly to her father's hand, and with the other hand, a basket that undoubtedly contained Lance.

"Tsk-tsk, Harriet," Etienne clucked at her. "Were you really going to leave without saying good-bye?" There was an odd vulnerability in his clear gaze that Harriet didn't understand.

"I . . . I left a letter for you," she stammered.

"I got it." He patted his breast pocket. "The mail packet was just leaving when we arrived this morning." He leaned forward, and she thought he was going to whisper something to her. Instead, he blew in her ear and said, "Whoo-whoo!"

She arched a brow at him.

"I was fresh out of snakes."

"Etienne, what's going on?"

"Papa says we're takin' an adventure ride with you," Saralee blurted out, then glanced up at her father for approval.

He nodded.

Harriet's pulse quickened. She put her fingertips to her lips to stop their quivering.

"We're coming with you," he said simply.

With those words, Harriet realized why Etienne's family was crowded outside on the platform, weeping. He was leaving them, never to return.

"For me?" she choked out.

"For you."

She stared at him incredulously, her heart in her throat. "You would give up everything you know . . . family and friends . . . for me? Why?" The enormity of his sacrifice staggered her.

The slow smile that crept across Etienne's lips was glorious. Then he shrugged. "I love you, stupid."

Harriet put her face in her hands and began to wail. Rocking from side to side, she let out all the pent-up emotion she'd been bottling up for days . . . *no, years*, she amended.

"Shh, don't cry, *chérie*," Etienne soothed, dropping down onto the bench seat next to her. "We won't come with you if you'd rather we didn't. I just wanted you to know . . . I just wanted you to know that you mean more to me than anything else."

"You big dope!" she sputtered out between sobs as she threw herself into his arms and kissed his cheeks and mouth and forehead and hair. In between kisses, she kept berating him, "Dumb, dumb, dumb . . . he waits till I'm on the train . . . dumb, dumb, dumb . . ."

"Well, actually, honey, I did a dumb thing. I decided to go to Washington to demand my money from President Grant, and halfway there . . . well, I hit myself on the head and said something like, 'You big dope! You've got somethin' worth lots more than money about to slip through your fingers. So I hightailed it back here."

"Oh, Etienne," she said and began to sob and kiss him and sob and kiss him again.

"You're steamin' up my glasses, honey," he told her, then chuckled. "Do you want me to take them off?"

"Last call! All aboard who's comin' aboard! Last call fer Memphis, St. Loo-ie and Chi-ca-go!"

Harriet's heart thundered as she stood abruptly and grabbed Etienne's hand. "Hurry!" She took Saralee's hand as well.

"Wh-what?" Etienne asked as she ran down the corridor, pulling them with her.

Just before the conductor was about to draw up the fold-away steps at the end of the train, she said, "Etienne, let's go home . . . to Bayou Noir."

He blinked hard against the wetness that instantly filled his blue eyes. "Are you sure?"

"Etienne," she said softly, cupping his cheek with one hand, "if you're willing to give up everything for me, it's the least I can do for you. And do you know something, honey? It's no sacrifice at all."

Saralee let out a little whoop of joy.

Then, as Etienne hauled her against one side and Saralee against the other, they jumped off the train, which was already chugging into motion. They were immediately enfolded in the rejoicing embrace of Etienne's family, but not before Harriet murmured a silent prayer.

Thank you, God, for sending me this man to love. He's a savage, to be sure, but sweet, sweet, sweet. Then she smiled up at Etienne—her sweeter, savage love.

Sometimes fantasies, like prayers, did come true.

Epilogue

November 28, 1870

Everyone agreed it was the grandest party ever held at Bayou Noir plantation . . . the wedding of Dr. Harriet Ginoza and Etienne Baptiste.

The bride wore a gorgeous eggshell satin, off-the-shoulder wedding dress that her new stepmother-in-law had purchased for her before leaving California—*just in case*. The groom said the gown was so low-cut *he* could hardly breathe.

Cain Lincoln gave the bride away. James Baptiste gave his son away, although he'd balked, at first, until his wife had convinced him it was only a symbolic gesture.

Abel Lincoln played his own improvised trumpet version of "Ave Maria." The recessional proved a bit more nontraditional . . . the bride and groom's own special song dealing with peach orchards. Abel and Simone did a sensual duet of the peach lyrics that gave new meaning to *risqué* and *double entendre*.

The groom said he could see the bride's blush all the way to her peach pit, which caused Blossom to whack him with her cane.

Saralee, who was the flower girl, made the most spectacular six-tiered cake with cream filling. There was nobody who didn't like Saralee's cake. Even Lance. Saralee had been offered an opportunity to dress up as a fairy princess for her wedding party, but she'd declined, saying she'd rather just be her papa's little girl.

After the ceremony, since the weather was unseasonably warm, a reception was held outdoors in the oak alley. All the workers were invited, as well as a few neighbors, and, of course, Etienne's numerous family members. Colored lanterns hung from the limbs, giving the hanging Spanish moss the appearance of golden tresses.

A group of Abel's musician friends came from New Orleans to form a band for dancing. Blossom had already warned two of them that if she heard any more of their low-down devil lyrics she was going to soap out their mouths.

All the young people, black and white alike, were doing the macarena, which Harriet had taught them days before. Once Cain was seen macarenaing with sensual rhythm toward Ellen, who kept backing away from him in her usual prissy way. Finally, she relented, as everyone knew she would. Those Lincoln boys always did have a way with the women.

When the last of the peach punch was drunk, and not a speck of cake remained, and the dancers were all pooped out, Etienne Baptiste looked at his new wife and grinned.

"I've got the hula hoop, darlin'."

She responded with her own grin. "I've got the cowboy boots and the spectacles."

He winked. Harriet was known to have a thing about his winks. And spectacles.

"You are such a frog," she told him.

He chuckled. "Yeah, but if you rub my wart, I turn into a prince."

And then they both laughed as they walked up the grand staircase, arm in arm. Later, someone reported overhearing them remark, "*Vive la fantaisie!*"

Author's Note

Louisiana was an exciting place to live in the years after the Civil War. However, I have taken some literary license with dates to accommodate my story, which took place in 1870.

Without a doubt, New Orleans was the birthplace of jazz. Or at least, it was the spawning ground, pulling together all the different types of music that eventually became what would be called *jass* (sic)—Negro spirituals (sorrows and jubilations), work chants, Creole folk songs, water calls, African melodies. Even by 1870, the elements of the low-down blues essential to early jazz were being played by the street brass and scat bands, in the brothels, in funeral and wedding processions, and in minstrel shows. But it wasn't until about twenty years later that a historical record was set down of these early jazz musicians.

There was no direct railroad connection between Chicago and New Orleans until 1885. And the bridge at Cairo wasn't built until a number of years later, unlike my story. In 1870, a passenger would still have had to take a train from Chicago to Cairo, a steamboat across the river, then board another train for New Orleans, and vice versa—a three-day trip.

The Blue Book, an annual publication listing in graphic detail all the brothels in New Orleans's legally sanctioned red-light district, did exist, as mentioned on page 119. However, the first known edition was put out in 1895 and it was discontinued in 1902 when, as one famous madam said, "Business went downhill 'cause the country-club girls started giving it away."

Improvisation was the key to early Louisiana songs, many of which were just variations of older European ballads. Such is the case in the lyrics quoted on pages 22–24 from the Creole love song "*Celeste, mo bel Bijou*," which is similar to the eighteenth-century European ballad, "Oh, Sally, My Dear." (*Daily Life in Louisiana*, Liliane Crété, Louisiana University Press, 1978, pp. 140–141).

Water calls by the slave workers, or "hollers," such as the one shown on page 224, were among the lyrics and music that became the backbone of many jazz songs. This particular stanza eventually made its way into the repertoire of Huddie "Lead Belly" Ledbetter (*Negro Folk Music, U.S.A.*, Harold Courlander, Columbia University Press, 1963, p. 87.)

The peach-orchard lyrics quoted on page 258 come from an early Louisiana folk song (*Sportin' House* by Stephen Longstreet, Sherbourne Press, LA, 1965, p. 114).

The lyrics on page 276 are excerpted from "A Good Old Rebel (Unreconstructed)" by Innes Randolph (1837–87), as listed in most Civil War songbooks. *Unreconstructed rebel* was a term applied to a Southerner not reconciled to the results of the Civil War.

The lyrics on page 283 were collected (according to Giles Oakley, *Devil's Music*, Taplinger Publishing, New York, 1976, p. 38) by the folklorists Howard Odum and Guy Johnson. Blacks were singing the blues in work songs such as this long before jazz or the blues were born.

SANDRA HILL

The Very Virile Viking

Magnus Ericsson is a simple man. He loves the smell of fresh-turned dirt after springtime plowing. He loves the heft of a good sword in his fighting arm. But, Holy Thor, what he does not relish is the bothersome brood of children he's been saddled with. Or the mysterious happenstance that strands him and his longship full of maddening offspring in a strange new land—the kingdom of Holly Wood. Here is a place where the blazing sun seems to bake his already befuddled brain, where the folks think he is an act-whore (whatever that is), and the woman of his dreams fails to accept that he is her soul mate . . . a man of exceptional talents, not to mention a very virile Viking.

ISBN 13: 978-0-8439-5205-6

To order a book or to request a catalog call:
1-800-481-9191
This book is also available at your local bookstore, or you can check out our Web site **www.dorchesterpub.com** where you can look up your favorite authors, read excerpts, or glance at our discussion forum to see what people have to say about your favorite books.

SANDRA HILL

As Lieutenant Ian MacLean prepares for his special ops mission in Northern Iraq, he sees no reason the insertion should not go down as planned. He leads a team of highly trained Navy SEALS, the toughest, buffest fighting men in the world. As a 34-year-old bachelor he has nothing to lose. He has the brains, guts, and brawn to out-maneuver, out-gun and just plain run circles around any enemy.

Madrene Olgadottir comes from a time a thousand years before Ian was born, and she has no idea she's landed in the future. After giving him a tongue lashing that makes a drill sergeant sound like a kindergarten teacher, she lets him know she has her own special way of dealing with over-confident males...

HOT & HEAVY

ISBN 13: 978-0-8439-5160-8

SANDRA HILL

Toste and Vagn Ivarsson are identical Viking twins. They came squalling into this world together, rode their first horses at the age of seven, their first maids during their thir-teenth summer, and rode off on longships as untried four-teen-year-old warriors. And now they are about to face Valhalla together. Or maybe something even more tragic: being separated. For even the most virile Viking must eventually leave his best buddy behind and do battle with that most fearsome of all opponents—the love of his life.

A TALE OF
TWO VIKINGS

ISBN 13: 978-0-8439-5158-5

SANDRA HILL

What do you get when you cross a Viking with a Navy SEAL?

A warrior with the fierce instincts of the past and the rigorous training of America's most elite fighting corps?

A totally buff hero-in-the-making who hasn't had a woman in roughly a thousand years?

A wise guy with a time-warped sense of humor chanting grody jody calls?

A dyed-in-the-wool romantic with a hopeless crush on his hands-off superior officer?

Hoo-yah! Whatever you get, women everywhere can't wait to meet him, and his story is guaranteed to be...

WET & WILD

ISBN 13: 978-0-8439-5159-2

☐ **YES!**

Sign me up for the Love Spell Book Club and send my
REE BOOKS! If I choose to stay in the club, I will pay only
$8.50* each month, a savings of $6.48!

AME: _____

ODRESS: _____

ELEPHONE: _____

MAIL: _____

☐ I want to pay by credit card.

☐    ☐ MasterCard   ☐ DISCOVER

CCOUNT #: _____

KPIRATION DATE: ___ _____

GNATURE: _____

Mail this page along with $2.00 shipping and handling to:
Love Spell Book Club
PO Box 6640
Wayne, PA 19087
Or fax (must include credit card information) to:
610-995-9274

ou can also sign up online at **www.dorchesterpub.com**.

*lus $2.00 for shipping. Offer open to residents of the U.S. and Canada only. Canadian
residents please call 1-800-481-9191 for pricing information.
f under 18, a parent or guardian must sign. Terms, prices and conditions subject to
ange. Subscription subject to acceptance. Dorchester Publishing reserves the right to
reject any order or cancel any subscription.